A TEXT BOOK OF

ENGINEERING CHEMISTRY

FOR

SEMESTER – I

FIRST YEAR DEGREE COURSES IN ENGINEERING

**Strictly According to New Revised Credit System Syllabus
of Savitribai Phule Pune University
(Effective from Academic Year – June 2015)**

COMMON FOR ALL DEGREE ENGINEERING BRANCHES

Dr. MANISHA Y KHALADKAR
M.Sc. (Chemistry) Ph. D
Head, Applied Science Deptt.,
College of Engineering, Pune

Dr. SUNIL D KULKARNI
M.Sc., Ph.D., SET
Asst. Prof., Deptt. of Chemistry
Sir Parashurambhau College, Pune.

Dr. ADITI K DIWAN
M.Sc., Ph.D.
Assistant Professor, Deptt. of Chemistry,
Sinhgad College of Engineering,
Vadgaon (Bk), Pune

Dr. DEEPAK V NIGOT
M.Sc, B.Ed., Ph. D
Associate Professor, Deptt. of Chemistry,
AISSM's College of Engineering,
Pune

NIRALI
PRAKASHAN
ADVANCEMENT OF KNOWLEDGE

N2753

ENGINEERING CHEMISTRY (FE)   **ISBN 978-93-82448-12-9**

| Third Edition | : | June 2017 |
| © | : | Authors |

Published By :   Polyplate
NIRALI PRAKASHAN
Abhyudaya Pragati, 1312, Shivaji Nagar,
Off J.M. Road, Pune – 411005
Tel - (020) 25512336/37/39, Fax - (020) 25511379
Email : niralipune@pragationline.com

☞ **DISTRIBUTION CENTRES**

PUNE

Nirali Prakashan   : 119, Budhwar Peth, Jogeshwari Mandir Lane, Pune 411002, Maharashtra
Tel : (020) 2445 2044, 66022708, Fax : (020) 2445 1538
Email : bookorder@pragationline.com, niralilocal@pragationline.com

Nirali Prakashan   : S. No. 28/27, Dhyari, Near Pari Company, Pune 411041
Tel : (020) 24690204 Fax : (020) 24690316
Email : dhyari@pragationline.com, bookorder@pragationline.com

MUMBAI

Nirali Prakashan   : 385, S.V.P. Road, Rasdhara Co-op. Hsg. Society Ltd.,
Girgaum, Mumbai 400004, Maharashtra
Tel : (022) 2385 6339 / 2386 9976, Fax : (022) 2386 9976
Email : niralimumbai@pragationline.com

☞ **DISTRIBUTION BRANCHES**

JALGAON

Nirali Prakashan   : 34, V. V. Golani Market, Navi Peth, Jalgaon 425001,
Maharashtra, Tel : (0257) 222 0395, Mob : 94234 91860

KOLHAPUR

Nirali Prakashan   : New Mahadvar Road, Kedar Plaza, 1st Floor Opp. IDBI Bank
Kolhapur 416 012, Maharashtra. Mob : 9850046155

NAGPUR

Pratibha Book Distributors   : Above Maratha Mandir, Shop No. 3, First Floor,
Rani Jhanshi Square, Sitabuldi, Nagpur 440012, Maharashtra
Tel : (0712) 254 7129

DELHI

Nirali Prakashan   : 4593/21, Basement, Aggarwal Lane 15, Ansari Road, Daryaganj
Near Times of India Building, New Delhi 110002
Mob : 08505972553

BENGALURU

Pragati Book House   : House No. 1, Sanjeevappa Lane, Avenue Road Cross,
Opp. Rice Church, Bengaluru – 560002.
Tel : (080) 64513344, 64513355,Mob : 9880582331, 9845021552
Email:bharatsavla@yahoo.com

CHENNAI

Pragati Books   : 9/1, Montieth Road, Behind Taas Mahal, Egmore,
Chennai 600008 Tamil Nadu, Tel : (044) 6518 3535,
Mob : 94440 01782 / 98450 21552 / 98805 82331,
Email : bharatsavla@yahoo.com

niralipune@pragationline.com | www.pragationline.com
Also find us on   ⨍ www.facebook.com/niralibooks

PREFACE TO THE THIRD EDITION

We are glad and excited to announce that the Second Edition of this book received an overwhelming response from the engineering student community, compelling us to release its **Third Edition** within a very short period of time.

This thoroughly revised **Third Edition** has been **updated** with **additional matter**, many solved problems, including **all University Examination Papers** and Numerous Exercises for practice.

Special care has been taken to maintain high degree of accuracy in the theory and numericals throughout the book.

We take this opportunity to express our sincere thanks to Dineshbhai Furia of Nirali Prakashan, a reputed and pioneer in the field of publication. Our special thanks to Jignesh Furia for their effective cooperation and great care in bringing out this revised edition. We also appreciate the efforts of M. P. Munde and the entire staff of Engineering Books Deptt. of Nirali Prakashan namely Mrs. Deepali Lachake (Co-ordinator) and Mrs. Shilpa Kale for bringing this book to the students in a timely manner.

We sincerely hope that this "**Third Edition**" will also be warmly received by all concerned as in the past.

Valuable suggestions from our esteemed readers to improve the book are most welcome and highly appreciated.

Pune   **–Authors**

PREFACE TO THE FIRST EDITION

It gives us great pleasure in publishing this text book on **"Engineering Chemistry"** for the Students of First Year Degree Course in Engineering. This book is strictly written According to New Revised Credit System Syllabus of Savitribai Phule Pune University (2015 Pattern).

As per the policy of the University, Engineering Syllabi is revised every five years. Last revision was in the year 2012. New revision is coming little earlier, as university has introduced **Online** system of examination from year 2012.

In New Credit System, there will be two online examinations conducted at the end of first and second month in every semester. The first online (Phase I – 25 Marks) examination will be based on units I and II and the second online (Phase II – 25 Marks) examination will be based on units III and IV. Both the online examinations will be based on Multiple Choice Questions. End Semester Examination (Theory - 50 Marks) will be based on all six units and will be descriptive type and theory course will have 4 credits.

We have given Free Separate book of Multiple Choice Questions (MCQ's) which will be very useful to the students, especially for Online Examinations.

The subject matter is presented in a lucid, fluent and comprehensive manner. All efforts have been taken to present the text matter in Simple & Lucid Language, Illustrative Figures, University Question Papers and Solved Problems with Answers have been added. Also, University Question Papers (New Pattern) have given (Dec. 12 to Nov. 16) at the end of the Book, and it will help student to understand nature of questions that could be asked in the final examination.

We take this opportunity to express our sincere thanks to Shri. Dineshbhai Furia, Shri. Jignesh Furia, Mrs. Nirali Verma and Shri. M. P. Munde and entire team of Nirali Prakashan namely Mrs. Deepali Lachake (Co-ordinator) who really have taken keen interest and untiring efforts in publishing this text.

Finally, we express our gratitude to our family members for their continuous support and encouragement, thanks to all.

We have no doubt that like our earlier texts, student's community will respond favourably to this new venture.

The advice and suggestions of our esteemed readers to improve the text are most welcomed, and will be highly appreciated.

July 2016   **Authors**
Pune.

SYLLABUS

Unit I : Water Technology and Green Chemistry   (8 Hrs.)

Water Technology : Impurities in water. Hardness of water and its determination by EDTA method, Alkalinity of water and its determination. Numericals Ill effects of hard water in boilers. Boiler feed water treatment :   (1) Internal treatment - Calgon, Colloidal and Phosphate conditioning, (2) External treatment - (a) Zeolite process and its numericals, (b) Ion exchange method. Desalination of brackish water / Purification of water by Reverse osmosis and Electrodialysis. **Green Chemistry :** Definition, Goals of Green Chemistry, Efficiency parameters, Need of Green Chemistry, Major uses - Traditional and Green pathways of synthesis of Adipic acid, Polycarbonate, Indigo dye.

Unit II : Electro Analytical Techniques   (8 Hrs.)

Introduction : Types of reference electrode (Calomel electrode), Indicator electrode (Glass electrode), Ion selective electrode, Half cell reaction and complete cell reaction. **Conductometry :** Introduction, Kohlrausch's law, Conductivity cell, Measurement of conductance, Applications - Conductometric titrations, Acid-base titrations, Precipitation titrations. **pH Metry :** Preparation of Buffers, Standardization of pH metry, Mixture of acids versus strong base titration, Differential plots. **Potentiometry :** Introduction, Potentiometric titrations - Differential plots, Applications - Redox titrations Fe/Ce titration. **UV/Visible spectroscopy :** Interaction of radiation with matter, Beer Lambert's law, Chromophore and Auxochrome, Types of electronic transitions. Instrumentation and Principle - Block diagram of Single and Double Beam Spectrophotometer. Applications of UV-Visible spectroscopy.

Unit III : Synthetic Organic Polymers   (8 Hrs.)

Introduction, Functionality of Monomer, Polymerization-Free radical mechanism and Step growth polymerization. Concept and significance of - Average molecular weight, Crystallinity in polymers, T_m and T_g. Thermoplastic and Thermosetting polymers. Compounding of plastics. Techniques of polymerization. Preparation, Properties and Engineering applications of : Polyethylene (LDPE and HDPE) and Epoxy resin, Elastomers - Natural rubber - Processing and Vulcanization by Sulphur. Synthetic rubbers - SBR. **Speciality polymers :** Engineering thermoplastics - Polycarbonate, Biodegradable polymers – Poly (hydroxybutyrate-hydroxyvalarate), Conducting polymers - Polyacetylene, Electroluminescent polymers - Polyphenylene vinylene, Liquid crystalline polymers - Kevlar, Polymer composites - Fibre Reinforced Plastic (FRP).

Unit IV : Fuels and Combustion   (8 Hrs.)

Fossil fuels : Definition, Calorific values, Determination - Bomb calorimeter, Boy's gas calorimeter, Numericals. **Solids fuel :** Coal - Proximate and Ultimate analysis. Numericals. **Liquid fuels :** Petroleum - Composition and refining. Octane number of petrol, Cetane number of Diesel, Power alcohol, Biodiesel. **Gaseous fuel :** Composition, Properties and Applications of NG, CNG, LPG. **Combustion :** Chemical reactions, Calculations for air required. Numericals. **Fuel cells :** Definition, Advantages and limitations, Phosphoric acid fuel cell, Polymer electrolyte membrane fuel cell.

Unit V : Chemistry of Hydrogen and Carbon   (8 Hrs.)

Chemistry of Hydrogen : The elements - isotopes-importance. Methods of preparation : (1) Laboratory-from aqueous acid and alkali. (2) Industrial-steam reforming of methane and coke, Electrolysis of water. (3) From solar energy (water splitting). Storage-chemical (sodium alanates), Physical (carbon materials), Difficulties in storage and transportation. Compounds of hydrogen, Methods of preparation and applications : (a) Molecular hydrides - Hydrocarbons, Silane, Germane, Ammonia. (b) Saline hydrides - LiH, NaH. Applications of hydrogen, Hydrogen as a future fuel. **Chemistry of Carbon :** Position in the periodic table, Occurrence, Isotopes. Allotropes (crystalline and amorphous) - Occurrence, Structure based on bonding and applications in detail.

Unit VI : Corrosion Science   (8 Hrs.)

Introduction. Types of corrosion - Dry corrosion - Mechanism, Pilling-Bedworth rule. Wet corrosion - Mechanism. Factors influencing corrosion - Nature of metal, Nature of environment. Methods of corrosion control : Pourbaix diagram, Cathodic and anodic protection, Use of inhibitors, Protective coatings : Surface preparation : (a) Metallic coatings : Types of coatings, Methods of applications (hot dipping, cladding, electroplating and cementation), Electro less coatings, (b) Non-metallic coatings : Chemical conversion coatings, Powder coatings.

CONTENTS

✠ ✠ ✠

WATER TECHNOLOGY AND GREEN CHEMISTRY

WATER TECHNOLOGY

1.1 INTRODUCTION

Water is essential for survival of life on the earth. Life has originated and evolved in water. Water acts as a solvent and medium for all living body reactions. Water is also essential for development of human civilization. All the ancient civilizations developed on the banks of rivers.

The industrial revolution in Europe started with the invention of the steam engine by James Watt. The steam is generated from water. Water is an important component of the infrastructure essential for industrial development. Water plays a significant role in industries such as textile, paper, food processing, etc. in addition to that of agriculture.

Although water is abundant on the earth's surface, only a very small quantity (4-5%) of water is useful. The significant portion of water ($\approx$ 96%) is present in the seas and oceans which is salty and hence cannot be used directly either for drinking or for industrial purpose. The remaining small quantity which is present in the lakes, rivers and as underground water.

The focus in the present chapter will be on chemical analysis of water, its requirement in the industry, hardness of water and water softening methods.

1.2 STRUCTURE OF WATER

- Water is a covalent compound represented by H_2O or H–O–H. It contains two O–H bonds. The structure of water can be explained on the basis of hybridization of atomic orbitals of oxygen.

- The atomic number of oxygen is 8 and the electronic configuration can be written as $1s^2$, $2s^2$, $2p_x^2$, $2p_y^1$, $2p_z^1$. The outermost 2s and 2p orbitals undergo sp^3 hybridization. The partially vacant $2p_y$ and $2p_z$ orbitals overlap with partially filled 1s orbitals of hydrogen. For these two orbitals, two hydrogen atoms are required and hence H_2O is formed.

- The structure of water molecule can be drawn as

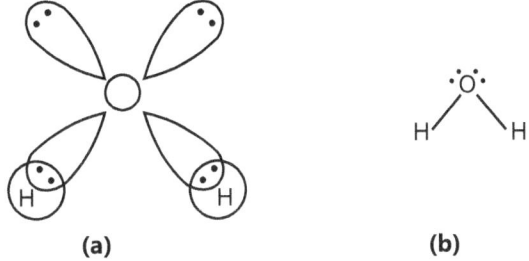

(a)   (b)

Fig. 1.1: Structure of sp^3 hybridized H_2O molecule

- The bond angle H–O–H is found to be 104.5°. It is 'V' shaped molecule. The shape is due to the repulsion between two lone pairs of electrons (present in 2s and $2p_x$) and the hydrogen bonded electrons.

- Another important aspect of O–H bond in water molecule is its polar nature. It is known that, the electronegativity of oxygen is more than that of hydrogen. Due to this, oxygen atom attracts (pulls) bonded electrons towards itself and hence electron cloud is oriented on oxygen resulting in the partial negative charge on oxygen and partial positive charge on the hydrogen as shown in Fig. 1.2.

- Due to this, there is a charge separation. This is as if a dipole is formed. Hence, water molecule can be regarded as a combination of two dipoles. This dipole formation gives dipole moment to water.

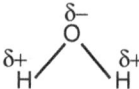

Fig. 1.2: Partially polarized O–H bonds in water

- The polar nature of O–H bonds in H_2O has imparted many unique properties to water.

1.3 PHYSICAL PROPERTIES OF WATER

Due to the structure and polar nature, water has the following physical properties:

- Bond length (O–H)   =   98 pm
- Bond energy   =   0.47 MJ/mole
- Latent heat   =   2.4 kJ/mole
- Bond angle   =   104.5°
- Dielectric constant   =   78.6 at 25°C
- Dipole moment   =   1.8 Debye

1.3.1 Dielectric Constant of Water

- The dielectric constant gives an idea about the ease with which water can separate the anions and cations in ionic compounds when dissolved.

i.e.   D.C. $= \dfrac{W_m}{W_v}$

where,   D.C. = Dielectric constant

W_v = Work required to separate the charges in vacuum

W_m = Work required to separate the charges in medium

- Experimentally, the dielectric constant of water is found to be 78.6 at room temperature.

- This means that if the ionic compounds (in which the charges i.e. ions are well separated) are dissolved in water, then the ions will be separated 78.6 times faster than that of in vacuum or, in other words, it can be stated that the amount of work required for water to separate ionic charges is 78.6 times less than that required by vacuum at the given temperature.

- Hence because of the high dielectric constant of water, the ionic substances are easily soluble in water.

1.3.2 Hydrogen Bonding in Water

- Hydrogen bonding is generally observed in the compounds which contain atoms with difference in the electronegativities. Water contains hydrogen and oxygen with significant differences in electronegativities, hence hydrogen bonding is observed in water.

- In water, there is a intermolecular hydrogen bonding i.e. hydrogen atoms in one molecule form a weak hydrogen bond with oxygen atom of other molecules resulting in the cluster of water molecules as shown in Fig. 1.3.

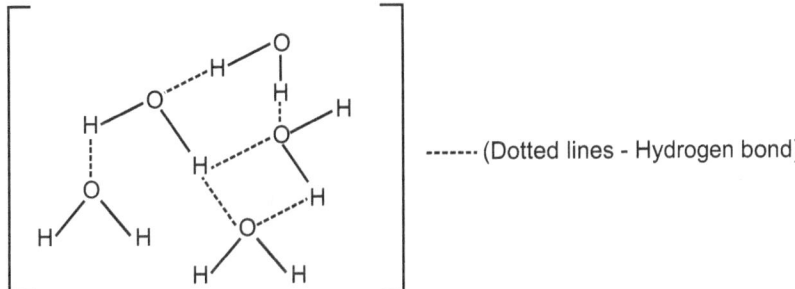

------- (Dotted lines - Hydrogen bond)

Fig. 1.3: Hydrogen bonding in water molecules

- In the case of ice, each H_2O molecule is hydrogen bonded with four other H_2O molecules resulting in the rigid tetrahedral structure.

Due to structure, polar nature, hydrogen bonding, water has unique properties. The important one is the physical state, it is a stable solvent in the common temperature range (0 – 100°C) i.e. liquid, it is solid below 0°C and can be used as solid coolent and it is a steam (gaseous state) above 100°C which can be used for many industrial applications involving steam engines and boilers.

1.4 IMPURITIES IN WATER   [May 09, Dec. 10]

- Water condensed from the steam or rain water does not contain any impurity, hence can be regarded as the purest form of water. For industrial applications, this form of water is not available readily. The water available for industrial applications always contains some impurities.

- Pure water is colourless, odourless and tasteless but because of the presence of impurities, colour, odour and taste are imparted to water. The impurities present impart hardness to water. The commonly occurring impurities due to which water becomes hard are discussed in the following sections.

1.4.1 Suspended Matter

- When water is flowing in the river or present in the lake, then it appears turbid due to the presence of fine impurities visible to eyes. Such suspended impurities in water are called as suspended matter. Such suspended matter can be removed from water by simple filtration using suitable assembly.

- The commonly occurring suspended impurities are clay particles, precipitates of iron hydroxides, calcium carbonates, bicarbonates and silicates. These impurities are of inorganic type.

- In addition to this, water may contain organic impurities such as from decay of living matter (animals and plants), pesticides, etc.

- Underground water contains almost negligible suspended matter impurities due to the filtering action of soil and rocks during the time it reaches the underground level.

- When suspended matter particle size exceeds 1 μm, then they are called colloidal impurities.

1.4.2 Biological Impurities

- When water is flowing in the rivers or dammed in lakes and dams, then the biological impurities, which include many micro-organisms, fungi grow in the water because of dissolved oxygen. Commonly occurring biological impurities are bacteria (aerobic and anaerobic), fungi, viruses, many pathogens, parasites, water hyacinth etc. Under favourable conditions, these impurities grow in concentration with time.

1.4.3 Dissloved Impurities

- Rain drops while coming down to the earth's surface, get impure due to dissolution of the gases such as O_2, SO_2, NH_3, H_2S, CO_2 etc. present in the atmosphere.

- If water from these sources is directly used for industrial applications, then there is a possibility that it will cause many problems to the materials (storage tanks, boilers etc.) that it is in contact with.

- Underground and surface water when they come in contact with soil, rocks, asbestos then inorganic cations such as Ca^{++}, Mg^{++}, Fe^{++}, Mn^{++}, Al^{3+}, Na^+, K^+ and anions such as Cl^-, NO_3^-, HCO_3^-, SO_4^{--} are present in the water.

- In speciality industries such as sugar and fermentation, pesticides, agrochemicals, fertilizers the effluent water contains dissolved organic compounds such as sugars, alcohols, carboxylic acids, aldehydes and ketones.

- Hence dissolved gaseous, inorganic and organic impurities are present in water and in order to remove these impurities, various physical and chemical methods such as filtration, boiling, chemical treatment, oxidation have to be employed.

1.5 NEED FOR CHEMICAL ANALYSIS OF WATER

- Water which contains excessive impurities cannot be used either for drinking or for industrial applications.
- At the same time water in its purest form is not available readily and economically.
- The acceptable levels of impurities in drinking water are fixed by international standardizing agencies such as World Health Organization (WHO), Indian Council of Medical Research (ICMR) etc.
- If the concentrations of impurities present in the water are above the level stated by these agencies, then the water cannot be used for drinking purpose.
- Similarly, acceptable impurity levels in the water that can be used for industrial purpose are also fixed and water sample that contains more impurities than the acceptable level cannot be used.
- In order to determine the suitability of water for drinking or industrial purpose, the given water sample has to be analysed for its impurity levels. Hence, chemical analysis of water is an essential parameter in water resource management.
- Once using chemical analysis, if type and the concentration of impurity in the given water sample is determined then the method that can be used to remove the impurities can be selected.

1.6 CHEMICAL ANALYSIS OF WATER   [Dec. 07, 08]

- Chemical analysis of water is qualitative and quantitative determination of impurities present in water.
- The impurities present in water with higher concentrations are generally carbonate and bicarbonate salts of monovalent and divalent cations such as K^+, Na^+, Ca^{2+}, Mg^{2+} etc. in the dissolved form in addition to that of chloride.
- In chemical analysis of water, the important parameters are:
  - ➢ Hardness of water.
  - ➢ Chloride content in water.
  - ➢ Alkalinity.
- These parameters will be studied in the following section.

1.6.1 Hardness of Water

- When soap is dissolved in distilled water or rain water that does not contain any impurities, then lather (foam) is formed. This water is called as **soft water**.
- If water contains certain impurities and if soap is dissolved in such water, then lather is not formed instead scum (curd like insoluble impurities) is formed. This type of water is called as **hard water**.

- The soluble salt impurities present in water impart hardness to water.
- If carbonate, bicarbonate, sulphate, nitrate and chloride salts of bivalent cations such as Mg^{++}, Fe^{2+}, Mn^{2+}, Ca^{2+} are present in water, then the hardness of water is high as compared to that due to presence of salts of monovalent cations such as K^+ and Na^+.
- Hard water is not suitable for industrial applications.
- The hardness of water is of two types:

(a) Temporary Hardness/Carbonate Hardness:

- Temporary hardness is also called as **carbonate hardness**. If hardness of water is due to presence of carbonate and bicarbonate salts such as $CaCO_3$, $MgCO_3$, $Ca(HCO_3)_2$, $Mg(HCO_3)_2$, etc., then it is called temporary or carbonate hardness.
- This type of hardness can be removed easily by simply boiling the water. During boiling the carbonates and bicarbonates are converted into the form (generally hydroxide) that is insoluble in water.
- The insoluble precipitate formed can be removed by simple filtration method.

$$Mg(HCO_3) \xrightarrow[100°C]{\Delta} Mg(OH)_2 \downarrow + 2\ CO_2 \uparrow$$

$$MgCO_3 + H_2O \xrightarrow[100°C]{\Delta} Mg(OH)_2 \downarrow + CO_2 \uparrow$$

$$Ca(HCO_3) \xrightarrow[100°C]{\Delta} CaCO_3 \downarrow + H_2O + CO_2 \uparrow$$

- Since the hardness can be removed by simply boiling and filtering the water, it is called as **temporary hardness**.

(b) Permanent Hardness:

- Permanent hardness to water is caused by presence of dissolved salts of metals other than carbonates or bicarbonates.
- These salts are generally chlorides, sulphates and nitrates.
- The commonly occurring salts that cause the permanent hardness to water are $CaCl_2$, $MgCl_2$, $CaSO_4$, $MgSO_4$, $Ca(NO_3)_2$, $Mg(NO_3)_2$, $FeCl_2$, $CuCl_2$, etc.
- This type of hardness cannot be removed simply by boiling but needs special chemical treatments.
- Total hardness of water is due to temporary as well as permanent hardness and hence can be calculated by adding them.

i.e. | **Total hardness = Temporary hardness + Permanent hardness** |

1.6.2 Experimental Method to Determine Total Hardness of Water

- The most commonly used experimental method to determine the total hardness of water is the complexometry using ethylene diamine tetra acetic acid (EDTA) as a complexing agent.

- This is a volumetric method of analysis using Eriochrome black-T (EBT) dye as an indicator. Sometimes chalcones can also be used as indicators under suitable conditions.

- The commercially available form of EDTA is its disodium salt and its structure is as:

Disodium salt of EDTA

- It is well known that EDTA forms a stoichiometric 1: 1 complex with monovalent and divalent cations. Hence, if suitable reaction conditions are maintained, this complexometric reaction can be used to determine the metal ion concentration in water responsible for causing hardness.

- This complexometric reaction takes place at pH = 10, hence suitable basic buffer solution (NH_4OH + NH_4Cl) must be used to maintain constant pH throughout the reaction/titration.

- Initially during the titration, the indicator (EBT) is added to water sample whose hardness is to be determined along with the buffer solution. The indicator reacts with metal ions in water to give wine red complex. This reaction can be written as:

$$M^{2+} + EBT \xrightarrow{pH = 10} M - EBT$$

Metal ions in water   Wine red

- Then this wine red solution is titrated with standardized EDTA. This leads to formation of M-EDTA (metal-EDTA) complex because M-EDTA complex is more stable than M-EBT complex i.e. EBT in the complex is displaced by EDTA.

- Once M-EDTA complex is formed, then the reaction mixture contains EBT (displaced) which gives blue colour to the solution. This reaction can be written   as:

$$M\text{-}EBT + EDTA \xrightarrow{pH = 10} M\text{-}EDTA + EBT$$

Wine red   Colourless   Blue

- A sharp colour change from wine red to blue can be taken as the end point of the reaction and using the concentration and volume of EDTA required to achieve the end point, the concentration of metal ions causing hardness to water can be calculated.

- The structure of M-EDTA complex can be written as:

Experimental Procedure:

- The experiment can be performed in two parts:

Part I: Standardization of EDTA:

- Prepare accurately 0.01 M $ZnCl_2$ solution and approximate 0.01 M EDTA solution.
- Fill the burette upto the mark with EDTA solution.
- In a conical flask, pipette out 25 ml of $ZnCl_2$ solution. Add 10 ml of pH = 10 buffer and 2 ml of EBT indicator. The colour of reaction mixture becomes wine red.
- Titrate this reaction mixture with EDTA solution from burette till colour changes to blue.
- Record the burette reading at the end point.
- Calculate concentration of EDTA using following equality.

> 1 M 1000 ml $ZnCl_2$ $\equiv$ 1 M EDTA

Alternatively, the standardization of EDTA can also be done using standard hard water.

Part II: Total Hardness of Water:

- Fill the burette with standardized EDTA.
- Pipette out 25 ml of the given water sample in a conical flask and repeat the procedure as mentioned above to get the constant burette reading at the end point.
- Calculate the hardness of water using following equality:

> 1 M 1000 ml EDTA $\equiv$ 1 M $CaCO_3$ eq. hardness
>
> i.e.   1 M 1000 ml EDTA $\equiv$ 100 g $CaCO_3$ eq. hardness

(Molecular weight of $CaCO_3$ = 100)

- Express the obtained hardness in terms of parts per million (ppm).
- If the water sample is taken without boiling and then filtered then the hardness obtained by EDTA method is total hardness.

- Then take the same sample, boil and filter and then if again EDTA method is performed on this sample, then the permanent hardness is obtained.

- Then using total and permanent hardness, the temporary hardness can be calculated.

SOLVED PROBLEMS

Example 1.1: *It was found that, 50 ml of a water sample requires 12.7 ml of 0.02 M EDTA during titration. Calculate hardness of water.*   **(4 M) (Dec. 11)**

(**Note:** Hardness is always calculated as $CaCO_3$ equivalents, molecular weight of $CaCO_3$ = 100, equivalent weight = 50).

Given: Volume of EDTA required   = 12.7 ml

Concentration of EDTA = 0.02 M

Volume of water = 50 ml

Solution: Water ≡ EDTA

$$M_1V_1 = M_2V_2$$

$$M_1 \times 50 = 0.02 \times 12.7$$

$$M_1 = \frac{0.02 \times 12.7}{50}$$

$$M_1 = 0.00508 \text{ M}$$

∴   Concentration of hardness causing substances is 0.00508 M.

$$\text{Hardness (CaCO}_3 \text{ eq)} = \text{Concentration} \times 100 \text{ g/L}$$

$$= 0.508 \text{ g/L}$$

$$= 508 \text{ mg/L}$$

$$\text{Hardness} = 508 \text{ ppm } CaCO_3 \text{ eq.}$$

OR

$$\text{Total hardness} = \frac{V_1}{V} \times M \times 10^5 \text{ ppm } CaCO_3 \text{ eq.}$$

where, V_1 = Volume of EDTA required to achieve end point

V = Volume of water sample taken for analysis

M = Molarity of EDTA

∴ $$\text{Total hardness} = \frac{12.7 \times 0.02}{50} \times 10^5 \text{ ppm } CaCO_3 \text{ eq.}$$

$$= 5.08 \times 10^{-3} \times 10^5 \text{ ppm } CaCO_3 \text{ eq.}$$

$$= \boxed{508 \text{ ppm } CaCO_3 \text{ eq.}}$$

Example 1.2: *50 ml of a water sample consumed 15 ml of 0.01 M Na$_2$-EDTA before boiling and 5 ml of same EDTA after boiling. Calculate total, permanent and temporary hardness.* **(3 M) (Dec. 12)**

Solution: Given:

$$\text{Volume of water sample} = 50 \text{ ml}$$
$$\text{Volume of EDTA before boiling} = 15 \text{ ml}$$
$$\text{Volume of EDTA after boiling} = 5 \text{ ml}$$
$$\text{Concentration of EDTA} = 0.01 \text{ M}$$
$$\text{Hardness} = ?$$

Part-1: Total Hardness (Before Boiling)

$$\text{EDTA} \equiv \text{Water}$$
$$M_1V_1 = M_2V_2$$
$$0.01 \times 15 = M_2 \times 50$$
$$M_2 = \frac{0.01 \times 15}{50}$$
$$= 3 \times 10^{-3} \text{ M}$$
$$\text{Total hardness} = \text{Concentration} \times \text{Molecular weight of CaCO}_3$$
$$= 3 \times 10^{-3} \times 100 \text{ g/L}$$
$$= 0.3 \text{ g/L}$$

$\therefore$ 　　　　　　$\boxed{\text{Total hardness} = 300 \text{ ppm CaCO}_3 \text{ eq.}}$

Part-2: Permanent Hardness (After Boiling and Filtering)

$$\text{EDTA} \equiv \text{Water}$$
$$M_3V_3 = M_4V_4$$
$$5 \times 0.01 = M_4 \times 50$$
$$M_4 = \frac{5 \times 0.01}{50} = 1 \times 10^{-3} \text{ M}$$
$$\text{Permanent hardness} = 1 \times 10^{-3} \times 100$$
$$= \boxed{100 \text{ ppm CaCO}_3 \text{ eq.}}$$

Part-3: Temporary Hardness:

$$\text{Temporary hardness} = \text{Total hardness} - \text{Permanent hardness}$$
$$= 300 - 100 \text{ CaCO}_3 \text{ eq.}$$

$\boxed{\text{Temporary hardness} = 200 \text{ ppm CaCO}_3 \text{ eq.}}$

Example 1.3: *0.5 g of $CaCO_3$ was dissolved in dil. HCl and the volume is made upto 500 ml with distilled water. 50 ml of the solution required 48 ml of EDTA solution in titration. 25 ml of hard water required 7.5 ml of EDTA and after boiling and filtering 5 ml of EDTA. Calculate hardness of given water sample.*

Solution: Part-1: Standardization of EDTA:

Given: Weight of $CaCO_3$ taken = 0.5 g, Volume of standard hard water = 500 ml

Volume of SHE taken for titration = 50 ml, Volume of EDTA = 48 ml.

$$\text{Concentration of } CaCO_3 = \frac{\text{Weight}}{\text{Molecular weight} \times \text{Volume}}$$

$$= \frac{0.5}{100 \times 0.5} = 0.01 \text{ M } CaCO_3$$

$$SHE \equiv EDTA$$

$$M_1V_1 = M_2V_2$$

$$0.01 \times 50 = M_2 \times 48$$

$$M_2 = \frac{0.01 \times 50}{48} = 0.0104 \text{ M}$$

i.e. $\boxed{\text{Concentration of EDTA} = 0.0104 \text{ M}}$

Part-2: Hardness Calculations:

(a) Total Hardness (Before Boiling):

Given: Volume of EDTA = 7.5 ml

Volume of water = 25 ml

Concentration of EDTA = 0.0104 M

$$\text{Total hardness} = \frac{V_1}{V} \times M \times 10^5 \text{ ppm } CaCO_3 \text{ eq.}$$

$$= \frac{7.5}{25} \times 0.0104 \times 10^5 \text{ ppm } CaCO_3 \text{ eq.}$$

$$= \boxed{312.5 \text{ ppm } CaCO_3 \text{ eq.}}$$

(b) Permanent Hardness (Non-Carbonate Hardness) after Boiling:

Given: Volume of EDTA = 5 ml

Volume of water = 25 ml

Concentration of EDTA = 0.0104 M

$$\text{Permanent hardness} = \frac{V_1}{V} \times M \times 10^5 \text{ ppm CaCO}_3 \text{ eq.}$$

$$= \frac{5}{25} \times 0.0104 \times 10^5 \text{ ppm CaCO}_3 \text{ eq.}$$

$$= \boxed{208 \text{ ppm CaCO}_3}$$

(c) Temporary Hardness (Carbonate Hardness):

$$\text{Temporary hardness} = \text{Total hardness} - \text{Permanent hardness}$$

$$= 312.5 - 208 \text{ ppm CaCO}_3 \text{ eq.}$$

$$= \boxed{104.5 \text{ ppm CaCO}_3 \text{ eq.}}$$

Example 1.4: *Calculate total hardness of water containing 16.8 mg/L Mg(HCO₃)₂, 19 mg/L MgCl₂, 24 mg/L MgSO₄ and 22.2 mg/L CaCl₂.*

Solution: Hardness is expressed in $CaCO_3$ equivalents.

Since hardness due to 1 M of salt $\equiv$ 1 M $CaCO_3$.

(i) Due to $Mg(HCO_3)_2$ i.e. 146 ppm hardness due to $Mg(HCO_3)_2 \equiv 100$ ppm $CaCO_3$

$$16.8 \text{ mg/L or ppm} \equiv ?$$

$$= \frac{16.8 \times 100}{146}$$

$$\boxed{\text{Hardness} = 11.5 \text{ ppm CaCO}_3 \text{ eq.}}$$

(ii) Due to $MgCl_2$, $\text{Hardness} = \dfrac{19 \times 100}{95} = \boxed{20 \text{ pm CaCO}_3 \text{ eq.}}$

(iii) Due to $MgSO_4$, $\text{Hardness} = \dfrac{24 \times 100}{120} = \boxed{20 \text{ ppm CaCO}_3 \text{ eq.}}$

(iv) Due to $CaCl_2$, $\text{Hardness} = \dfrac{22.2 \times 100}{111} = \boxed{20 \text{ ppm CaCO}_3 \text{ eq.}}$

$$\text{Total hardness} = 11.5 + 20 + 20 + 20 \text{ ppm}$$

$$\boxed{\text{Total hardness} = 71.5 \text{ ppm CaCO}_3 \text{ eq.}}$$

Example 1.5: *0.8 g of ZnSO₄ is dissolved in water and diluted to 250 ml. 25 ml of this ZnSO₄ solution is titrated with Na₂-EDTA solution from burette to obtain end point 14.3 ml. This standardized EDTA solution was titrated with 50 ml of water sample to obtain 8.6 ml burette reading. Calculate hardness of water.*

Solution: Part-1: Standardization of EDTA:

Given: Weight of $ZnSO_4$ = 0.8 g, Volume of $ZnSO_4$ = 0.25 L

Molecular weight of $ZnSO_4$ = 161.4.

$$\text{Molarity of } ZnSO_4 = \frac{\text{Weight}}{\text{Molecular weight} \times \text{Volume}}$$

$$= \frac{0.8}{161.4 \times 0.25} = 0.0198 \text{ M}$$

$$ZnSO_4 \equiv EDTA$$

$$M_1V_1 = M_2V_2$$

$$0.0198 \times 25 = M_2 \times 14.3$$

$$M_2 = \frac{0.0198 \times 25}{14.3} = 0.0347 \text{ M}$$

$\therefore$ Concentration of EDTA = 0.0347 M

Part-2: Determination of Hardness:

$$\text{Total hardness} = \frac{V_1}{V} \times M \times 10^5 \text{ ppm } CaCO_3$$

$$= \frac{8.6}{50} \times 0.0347 \times 10^5 \text{ ppm } CaCO_3 \text{ eq.}$$

$$= \boxed{596 \text{ ppm } CaCO_3 \text{ eq.}}$$

Example 1.6: *How many litres of hard water of hardness 340 ppm $CaCO_3$ eq. can be softened by a zeolite which requires 8 L of 12% NaCl for regeneration ?*

Solution: Volume of hard water = ?

Hardness of water = 340 ppm

Volume of NaCl solution for regeneration = 8 L

[NaCl] = 12%

Step 1: Calculation of 'mg' of NaCl required for regeneration

100 ml or 0.1 L $\equiv$ 12 g × 1000 mg

8 L $\equiv$?

$$= \frac{12 \times 1000 \times 8}{0.1} = 9.6 \times 10^5 \text{ mg NaCl}$$

Step 2: $CaCO_3$ eq. for above calculated NaCl

58.5 mg NaCl $\equiv$ 50 mg $CaCO_3$

9.6×10^5 mg NaCl $\equiv$?

$$= \frac{9.6 \times 10^5 \times 50}{58.5}$$

$$= 8.205 \times 10^5 \text{ mg } CaCO_3$$

Step 3:

$$\text{Hardness} = \frac{\text{mg } CaCO_3 \text{ eq.}}{\text{Volume of hard water}}$$

$\therefore$

$$\text{Volume of hard water} = \frac{8.205 \times 10^5}{340}$$

| Volume of hard water = 2413.3 L of water |

Example 1.7: *How many litres of 8% NaCl solution will be required to regenerate a zeolite bed which has the capacity of softening 2500 L of hard water of hardness 400 mg CaCO₃ eq. per litre ?*

Solution: Given:

Volume of NaCl = ?, Suppose it be 'x'

[NaCl] = 8%

Volume of hard water = 2500 L

Hardness of water = 400 ppm

Step 1: Calculation of 'mg' of NaCl eq.

$$0.1 \text{ L} \equiv 8 \times 1000 \text{ eq.}$$

$$x \text{ L} = ?$$

$$= \frac{8000 \times x}{0.1} = 8 \times 10^4 \times x \text{ 'mg'}$$

Step 2: Calculation of $CaCO_3$ eq.

$$58.5 \text{ mg NaCl} \equiv 50 \text{ mg } CaCO_3 \text{ eq.}$$

$$8 \times 10^4 \times x \text{ mg NaCl} = ?$$

$$= \frac{8 \times 10^4 \times x \times 50}{58.5}$$

Step 3:

$$\text{Hardness} = \frac{CaCO_3 \text{ eq.}}{\text{Volume of hard water}}$$

$$400 = \frac{8 \times 10^4 \times x \times 50}{58.5 \times 2500}$$

$\therefore$

$$x = \frac{400 \times 58.5 \times 2500}{8 \times 10^4 \times 50} = \boxed{14.625 \text{ L}}$$

$\therefore$ Volume of NaCl required for regeneration = 14.625 L

1.7 ALKALINITY OF WATER   [Dec. 08, 11, May 10]

- Pure water is neutral and its pH should be 7. But generally water present in the lakes, rivers and underground is slightly alkaline or basic.

- The basic nature of water may be due to hydrolysis of the salts that are present in the dissolved state or due to presence of alkaline substances.

- The commonly occurring alkaline substances in water are hydroxides such as $Ca(OH)_2$, $Mg(OH)_2$ and NH_4OH, bicarbonates such as $Ca(HCO_3)_2$, $Mg(HCO_3)_2$, $NaHCO_3$ and carbonates such as $MgCO_3$, Na_2CO_3, $CaCO_3$.

- It is known that hydroxides and carbonates are stronger bases than bicarbonates and all these substances are present in the form of a mixture in the water sample.

- The concentration (amount) of these substances in water is referred to as alkalinity. Depending on the presence of these anions in water, the alkalinity is called as carbonate and bicarbonate alkalinity.

- The alkalinity of water sample can be simply determined by volumetric analysis wherein the alkaline water sample is titrated with standard strong acids using phenolphthalein and methyl orange as indicators.

- Initially, a fixed volume of water sample is titrated with a standard strong acid (e.g. HCl). Hydroxide ions (OH^-) present in water will be neutralized and carbonate ions (CO_3^{2-}) will be half neutralized to bicarbonate ions (HCO_3^-). The reactions can be written as:

$$OH^- + H^+ \rightarrow H_2O$$
$$CO_3^{2-} + H^+ \rightarrow HCO_3^-$$

- As OH^- and CO_3^{2-} are strong bases, the end point is in the basic region and hence phenolphthalein [pH range 8-11, pK_{in} = 9.6] can be used as an indicator.

- The alkalinity due to OH^- and CO_3^{2-}, whose neutralization can be indicated by phenolphthalein is called **'phenolphthalein alkalinity'** and is denoted by **'P'**.

- After phenolphthalein end point, only bicarbonate ions are present in water which are weak bases. If this sample is further titrated with standardized acid using methyl orange (pH range 3-5, pK_{in} = 3.7), after complete neutralization of bicarbonate, then alkalinity obtained is called as **'methyl orange alkalinity'**. It is denoted by **'M'**.

The reaction can be written as:

$$HCO_3^- + H^+ \rightarrow H_2CO_3 \rightarrow CO_2 \uparrow + H_2O$$

- In short, during phenolphthalein titration, only OH^- and CO_3^- are neutralized and during methyl orange titration, all the alkaline anions present in the water sample are neutralized i.e. total alkalinity.

Alkalinities due to
$$\left.\begin{array}{l} OH^- \\ CO_3^{2-} \\ HCO_3 \end{array}\right\} \begin{array}{l} \text{P} \\ \\ \end{array} \left.\begin{array}{l} \\ \\ \end{array}\right\} M$$

Experimental Procedure:

- Fill the burette with standard strong acid with concentration Z.
- Pipette out fixed volume of water (V) in a conical flask and check its pH with the help of a pH-meter or a pH paper. If initial pH of the sample is greater than 8 then add few drops of the phenolphthalein. Water sample must turn pink.
- Titrate this sample with acid in the burette. Record the end point when pink colour has disappeared completely. Let this burette reading be V_1.
- Add 2-3 drops of methyl orange indicator to the *same* water sample. The water sample will be colourless (or yellowish) and *continue* the titration with strong acid from burette till pink colour appears. Record the burette reading and let it be denoted by V_2.
- Phenolphthalein alkalinity (P) can be calculated as:

$$\text{Water} \equiv \text{Acid}$$
$$N_W \times V = Z \cdot V_1$$
$$N_W = \frac{Z \cdot V_1}{V}$$

Phenolphthalein alkalinity (P) = Concentration × Eq. Wt. of $CaCO_3$
$$P = N_W \times 50 \ CaCO_3 \text{ eq. g/L}$$
$$= N_W \times 50 \times 1000 \ CaCO_3 \text{ eq. mg/L}$$
$$P = \frac{Z \cdot V_1}{V} \times 50 \times 1000 \text{ ppm } CaCO_3 \text{ eq.}$$

- Similarly, methyl orange alkalinity can be calculated by using the formula
$$M = \frac{Z \cdot V_2}{V} \times 50 \times 1000 \text{ ppm } CaCO_3 \text{ eq.}$$

(Equivalent weight of $CaCO_3$ = 50)

Once P and M are determined experimentally, then the amounts of individual ions present in the water sample also called as types of alkalinities can be calculated using Table 1.1.

Table 1.1: Concentrations of Alkalinity Causing Ions from P and M Values

Volume of Acid	Alkalinity (ppm)	[OH⁻] (ppm)	[CO₃] (ppm)	[HCO₃] (ppm)
$V_1 = 0$	P = 0	0	0	M
$V_1 = V_2$	P = M	M	0	0
$V_1 = 1/2 V_2$	P = 1/2 M	0	2P	0
$V_1 > 1/2 V_2$	P > 1/2 M	2P – M	2 (M – P)	0
$V_1 < 1/2 V_2$	P < 1/2 M	0	2P	M – 2P

SOLVED PROBLEMS

Example 1.8: *100 ml of water sample on titration with N/50 HCl requires 8.0 ml upto phenolphthalein indicator end point and 9.0 ml of acid to methyl orange indicator end point. Calculate types and extent of alkalinities in the water sample.*

Solution: Given: Volume of water = 100 ml

Concentration of HCl = N/50 = 0.02 N

Volume upto phenolphthalein end point = 8.0 ml

Volume upto methyl orange end point = 9 ml.

Part-1: Calculation of P:

$$HCl \equiv Water$$

$$N_1V_1 = N_2V_2$$

$$0.02 \times 8 = N_2 \times 100$$

$$N_2 = \frac{0.02 \times 8}{100} = 1.6 \times 10^{-3} \, N$$

$$\text{Phenolphthalein alkalinity (P)} = 1.6 \times 10^{-3} \times 50 \, CaCO_3 \, eq.$$

$$= 0.08 \, g/L \, CaCO_3 \, eq.$$

$$= \boxed{80 \, ppm \, CaCO_3 \, eq.}$$

Part-2: Calculation of M:

$$HCl \equiv Water$$

$$N_3V_3 = N_4V_4$$

$$0.02 \times 9 = N_4 \times 100$$

$$N_4 = 1.8 \times 10^{-3} \, N$$

$$\text{Methyl orange alkalinity (M)} = 1.8 \times 10^{-3} \times 50 \times 1000 \, CaCO_3 \, eq.$$

$$\boxed{M = 90 \, ppm \, CaCO_3 \, eq.}$$

Part-3: From P and M then

$$P > \frac{1}{2}M - \text{See Table 1.1}$$

(i)

$$[OH^-] = 2P - M$$

$$= 2 \times 80 - 90$$

$$= 160 - 90$$

$$= \boxed{70 \, ppm \, CaCO_3 \, eq.}$$

(ii)
$$[CO_3^-] = 2(M - P)$$
$$= 2(90 - 80)$$

$$\boxed{[CO_3^-] = 20 \text{ ppm CaCO}_3 \text{ eq.}}$$

(iii)
$$\boxed{[HCO_3^-] = 0 \text{ ppm}}$$

Example 1.9: *100 ml of water sample required 4 ml of N/20 H_2SO_4 for neutralization to phenolphthalein end point. Another 16 ml of the same acid was needed to methyl orange end point. Determine the types and amounts of alkalinities.*

Solution: Given: Volume of water = 100 ml

$$[H_2SO_4] = N/20 = 0.05 \text{ N}$$

Volume of H_2SO_4 upto P = 4 ml

Volume of H_2SO_4 upto M = 4 + 16 = 20 ml

Part-1: Calculation of P: Water ≡ H_2SO_4

$$N_1V_1 = N_2V_2$$

$$N_1 \times 100 = 0.05 \times 4$$

$$N_1 = \frac{0.05 \times 4}{100}$$

$$N_1 = 2 \times 10^{-3} \text{ N}$$

Phenolphthalein alkalinity (P) = $2 \times 10^{-3} \times 50 \times 1000$ ppm $CaCO_3$ eq.

$$\boxed{P = 100 \text{ ppm CaCO}_3 \text{ eq.}}$$

Part-2: Calculation of M:

$$\text{Water} \equiv H_2SO_4$$

$$N_3V_3 = N_4V_4$$

$$N_3 \times 100 = 0.05 \times 20$$

$$N_3 = 0.01 \text{ N}$$

$$M = 0.01 \times 50 \times 1000 \text{ ppm CaCO}_3 \text{ eq.}$$

$$\boxed{M = 500 \text{ ppm CaCO}_3 \text{ eq.}}$$

Part-3: Amounts of Alkalinities:

From values of P and M, P < $\frac{1}{2}$ M, then

$$[CO_3^{2-}] = 2P$$

$$= 2 \times 100 = \boxed{200 \text{ ppm } CaCO_3 \text{ eq.}}$$

$$[HCO_3^-] = M - 2P$$

$$= 500 - 2\,(100)$$

$$= \boxed{300 \text{ ppm}}$$

1.8 WATER FOR INDUSTRY

- As mentioned earlier, water is one of the most important components of infrastructure. Almost every industrial establishment needs water directly or indirectly.

- Water finds applications in the chemical industry, where it can be used as a solvent, reaction medium or coolent where it can be used to absorb the heat produced during exothermic reactions.

- Water is an inseparable part of power generation industry where water is converted to steam and steam can be tapped to produce electricity.

- Water is an inherent part of the automobile industry where steam engines utilize water. In fact the industrial revolution in the 17th century started in the United Kingdom with the invention of the steam engine by James Watt.

- Realty industry cannot be imagined without water. Water is used in concrete for solid, firm, strong foundations and buildings.

- Although water has innumerable uses and immense importance in all types of industries, the water should qualify for a certain criteria to be used for industrial applications. These are:

  ➤ It should not be a hard water (~ 25 ppm $CaCO_3$ eq.).
  ➤ It should not contain biological impurities.
  ➤ It should not be too alkaline or
  ➤ Dissolved solid content should be within a permissible level.

1.9 BOILER FEED WATER

- The most important use of water as an engineering material is in steam generation. Our focus in the present section will be on water for steam generation. Water is converted into steam using boilers and the steam is converted into a usable form using heat exchangers.

- Modern and advanced boilers and heat exchangers need water with very particular specifications of purity to work at the optimum efficiency.

- If these specifications are not met by water (i.e. if water is impure) then it hampers the performance of boiler, the heat exchanger and the related accessories.

- Impurity levels permitted in boiler feed water depend on the pressure at which the boiler assembly converts water into steam.

- If impurity levels in water are higher than that of the requirement of boiler operation, then water has to be treated (mechanically or chemically) to remove the impurities. These methods are called as water softening methods.

- Major boiler problems due to the use of impure (unsuitable) water are

  (A) Priming and foaming (carry over).

  (B) Scale and sludge formation.

  (C) Corrosion.

  (D) Caustic embrittlement.

1.10 PRIMING AND FOAMING   [Dec. 09, May 12]

1.10.1 Priming

During the steam production in boilers at a rapid rate, it may happen that, small droplets of hot water are carried along with steam. The presence of droplets of water in the steam is called as priming and the steam is called as 'wet steam'. These small droplets of water are carried to all parts of the boiler along with steam. This is called as carry over.

- **Reasons for Priming:**
  - Presence of large amounts of dissolved solids (> 50 ppm).
  - High transfer rate of steam in boiler compartments.
  - Rapid cycles of boiling and cooling during steam production.
  - Faulty boiler design.
  - Rapid increase in steam production rate.

- **Preventive Actions against Priming:**
  - Soft water should be used with less dissolved solids.
  - Maintaining low levels of water in boilers.
  - Avoiding rapid cycles of boiling and cooling.
  - Proper boiler design.

1.10.2 Foaming

During the production of steam, it is possible that there is continuous formation of bubbles. If the formation of bubbles is persistent, then that leads to formation of foam. Such foam formation hampers the efficiency of boiler.

- **Reasons for Foaming:**
  - Presence of oil like substances in water as suspended matter.
  - Rapid flow of water inside the boilers and heat exchangers.
- **Preventive Actions against Foaming:**
  - Maintaining smooth flow of water inside the boiler.
  - Addition of antifoaming agents like castor oil.
  - Removing of high molecular weight fatty acids (oils) from boiler using the coagulants such as sodium aluminates.
  - By using mechanical purifiers.
  - By properly maintaining the routine of blow down operation.
- **Priming and Foaming Occurs together and is Not Good for Boiler Because:**
  - Dissolved salts present in droplets in priming are carried to super heaters, turbine blades, etc. When the droplets evaporate, the dissolved solids get deposited on the machinery parts and may cause adverse effects.
  - Due to priming and foaming, the water level present in the boiler cannot be judged properly and this situation may cause a lot of difficulties in the operation of pressure boilers.
  - This will increase the maintenance cost of boiler.

1.11 SLUDGE AND SCALE FORMATION   [Dec. 03, 04, 05, 08, Nov. 13]

- This is one of the most serious problems that hampers the boiler operation critically and decreases its efficiency.

1.11.1 Sludges

- If the quantity of dissolved solids in the boiler feed water is high then due to continuous steam formation, these solids form a saturated solution and after that a loose, slimy mass of precipitates is formed (mud like precipitate of salts). This loose, slimy mass of impurities is called as sludge.
- Most commonly the sludges are formed at cooler part of the boiler and they get deposited on edges, bends, valves etc.

Disadvantages of Sludges:

- Sludges are bad conductors of heat and hence waste some part of heat that can be used for steam formation.
- If sludge continuously remains in the boiler, then it gets converted to scale and then it is very difficult to remove from the boiler.
- Sludge can disturb the boiler operation by choking the water flow.

Preventive Actions against Sludges:

- Sludge formation can be prevented by using soft water for boilers.
- By frequent blow down operation (boiler shut down), the sludge formation can be prevented.

- If sludge is formed in the boiler, then during blow down operation it can be removed by using brush as it is loose and slimy.

1.11.2 Scales

- If the boiler feed water contains dissolved salts such as carbonates and bicarbonates, then during steam generation, they form a hard, tough, thick layer (coat) at the inner surface (lining) of the boiler. This hard and tough coating of salts that cannot be removed easily is called as **scale**.
- Scales are formed due to:

(i) Presence of Bicarbonates:

- Generally water contains bicarbonates of Ca and Mg. At high boiler temperature, they undergo following reactions:

$$Ca(HCO_3)_2 \xrightarrow{\text{High temperature}} CaCO_3 \downarrow + H_2O + CO_2 \uparrow$$

$$Mg(HCO_3)_2 \xrightarrow{\text{High temperature}} MgCO_3 \downarrow + H_2O + CO_2 \uparrow$$

The carbonates formed in the reaction get deposited at the inner surface of boilers as scales.

(ii) Presence of Magnesium Salts:

- If magnesium salts of strong acid are present, then they undergo hydrolysis at high temperature and pressure conditions in boiler.

$$MgCl_2 + H_2O \xrightarrow{\text{High temperature}} Mg(OH)_2 \downarrow + 2\,HCl$$

The magnesium hydroxide precipitate formed is converted to scales.

(iii) Presence of Silica (SiO$_2$):

- If sand or silica is present in water even at a very small concentration, it forms a strongly adhered coating at the inner surface of boiler that is very difficult to remove and finally leads to scale formation.

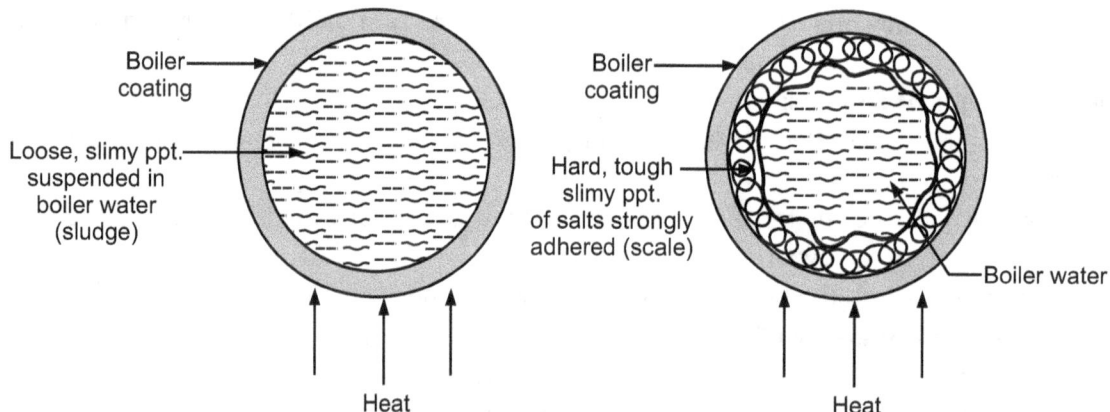

Fig. 1.4: Cross-sectional view of boiler pipe showing scale and sludge formation

Disadvantages of Scale Formation:

- **Wastage of Fuel:** The scales are bad conductors of heat. If the scales are present in the boiler, then more heat is needed to keep the steam pressure constant. More fuel is required for this additional generation of steam. It is observed that if scale layer of thickness just 2.5 mm is present then about 80% of more fuel is required. This obviously increases the production cost of steam.

- **Boiler Safety:** Due to scale formation, if more heat is required for steam generation, then there is concern over boiler safety. The boiler metal/alloy becomes soft and weak leading to decrease in its life. Hence, it has to be replaced frequently. This increases the maintenance cost of the boiler.

- **Danger of Explosion:** It can be seen from Fig. 1.4 that the scale layer formed is not even inside the boiler i.e. in different parts of boiler, the thickness of scale is different. Boiler water will experience more heat where thickness is less as compared to water where scale thickness is more. This will give rise to uneven pressures inside the boiler and may lead to the explosion. This is not only bad for the boiler but also dangerous as the far as safety of personnel working in the vicinity.

Preventive Actions against Scale Formation:

- Hardness causing suspended, colloidal and dissolved impurities should be removed from the water to be used as boiler feed water.

- Boiler feed water should be made free from silica.

- Frequent blow down operations should be carried out. During blow down operation, water saturated with impurities should be removed and the boiler should be filled with fresh softened water.

- Scales should be removed during blow down operation with the help of hammer and chisel, scrappers, knives or blades etc.

- To prevent the formation of scales and sludges, the water should be treated (conditioned) using suitable chemical agents so that impurities are removed completely.

1.12 CORROSION   [May, 06, 13, Dec. 06, 07, 09, 11]

- Corrosion is the most serious problem world wide. Billions of dollars are wasted either due to direct corrosion of materials or on the prevention of corrosion.

- Corrosion of boiler is a phenomenon in which surface of boiler is attacked by dissolved gases, dissolved impurities leading to the complete destruction of metal.

- Predominantly, corrosion takes place due to:

  ➢ Dissolved oxygen.

  ➢ Dissolved carbon dioxide.

  ➢ Hydrolysis of salts of magnesium with strong acid.

1.12.1 Corrosion due to Dissolved Oxygen

- If oxygen is present in water, then at boiler temperature and pressure, it attacks the boiler material. Most commonly used boiler metal is iron or alloy of iron.

$$4\ Fe + 4\ H_2O + 2\ O_2 \xrightarrow{\Delta} 4\ Fe(OH)_2 \downarrow$$

$$4\ Fe(OH)_2 + O_2 \longrightarrow 2\ [Fe_2O_3 \cdot 2\ H_2O] \downarrow$$

$$\text{Rust}$$

- The corrosion takes place via chemical attack of oxygen on boiler metal (Fe) in presence of water at higher temperature leading to the formation of ferrous hydroxide ($Fe(OH)_2$), which further reacts with dissolved oxygen leading to the formation of ferric oxide i.e. rust. Hence, the boiler material gets corroded.

- **Preventive Actions against Corrosion due to Dissolved Oxygen:**

  The best way to stop the corrosion due to dissolved oxygen is the removal of oxygen from boiler free water. This can be done with:

  (a) Mechanical Deaeration Method: The boiler feed water is introduced in a tower consisting of large number of perforated plates. The tower is heated from the sides with a suitable pressure provided by vacuum. Due to large surface area of plates, the oxygen is removed from the water. This deaerated water is fed to the boiler.

  (b) Chemical Method: Oxygen can be removed from water by chemical treatment. Calculated amount of sodium sulphite (Na_2SO_3) or hydrazine ($NH_2 - NH_2$) is added to water to remove the dissolved oxygen.

$$Na_2SO_3 + \frac{1}{2}O_2 \longrightarrow Na_2SO_4$$

Sodium sulphite   Sodium sulphate

$$NH_2 - NH_2 + O_2 \longrightarrow N_2 + 2\ H_2O$$

Hydrazine

1.12.2 Corrosion due to Dissolved CO_2

- If boiler feed water contains dissolved CO_2, then corrosion takes place slowly by the formation of carbonic acid.

$$CO_2 + H_2O \longrightarrow H_2CO_3$$

Carbonic acid is a weak acid and it is well known that metal undergoes corrosion under acidic medium.

- The dissolved CO_2 can be removed from water by adding small but calculated amounts of ammonia.

$$CO_2 + 2\ NH_3 + H_2O \longrightarrow (NH_4)_2CO_3 + H_2O$$

$$\text{Ammonium carbonate}$$

- CO_2 can also be removed by mechanical deaeration method.

1.12.3 Hydrolysis of Salts of Magnesium with Strong Acid

- If boiler feed water contains salts of magnesium such as $MgCl_2$ (salt of weak base and strong acid), then these salts undergo hydrolysis at boiler temperature and pressure. This reaction can be written as

$$MgCl_2 + H_2O \longrightarrow Mg(OH)_2 + 2\,HCl$$

- There are two disadvantages of such hydrolysis reaction inside the boiler:
  (i) $Mg(OH)_2$ leads to formation of scales and sludges and
  (ii) HCl – (strong acid) formed directly attacks the boiler metal.

$$Fe + 2\,HCl \longrightarrow FeCl_2 + H_2$$

Ferrous chloride formed will undergo further hydrolysis leading to formation of rust as:

$$FeCl_2 + 2\,H_2O \longrightarrow Fe(OH)_2 \downarrow + 2\,HCl$$
$$4\,Fe(OH)_2 + O_2 \longrightarrow \underbrace{Fe_2O_3 \cdot 2\,H_2O}_{Rust}$$

Hence, boiler water should be free from salts of weak base and strong acid because they undergo hydrolysis.

- The only preventive action in this case is removal of these salts before the water is fed to the boiler.
- Sometimes the water is made slightly alkaline to neutralize the acid formed during hydrolysis of the salts.

1.13 CAUSTIC EMBRITTLEMENT   [Dec. 06, 07, 09, 10, May 12, 13, 14]

- If boiler feed water is alkaline (basic) in nature, then the problem of caustic embrittlement occurs. One of the commonly used water softening method is addition of sodium carbonate (Na_2CO_3). This carbonate enters the boiler and at high temperature it gets hydrolysed to form hydroxide.

$$Na_2CO_3 + H_2O \xrightarrow{\Delta} 2\,NaOH + CO_2 \uparrow$$

- The caustic embrittlement is observed predominantly at the bends, valves and edges i.e. at the stressed parts in the boiler.

The hydroxide thus formed comes in contact with boiler metal through cracks or through grain boundaries in the boiler alloy.

$$Fe + NaOH + O_2 \longrightarrow NaFeO_2 + H_2$$
$$\text{Sodium ferrite}$$

- Sodium ferrite formed is *brittle* in nature. If attack of NaOH is continuous, then whole boiler becomes brittle and it cannot be used further and has to be replaced time to time. This process is called as caustic embrittlement.
- This increases the running and maintenance cost of boiler.

Preventive Actions against Caustic Embrittlement:

- Phosphate conditioning can be used for water softening instead of soda lime (Na_2CO_3) method.
- The cracks in the boiler surface and grain boundaries in the boiler alloys can be covered with tannins, lignins so that sodium hydroxide cannot attack the metal.
- Proper adjustment of pH of boiler feed water can also prevent the caustic embrittlement.

1.14 TREATMENT OF BOILER FEED WATER   [May 4, 8, Dec. 09, 12]

- It was discussed in the above section that, the presence of impurities in the boiler feed water causes many problems such as boiler corrosion, formation of sludge and scale, caustic embrittlement, etc.
- In order to remove the unwanted substances in water, it should be chemically treated. There are two types of methods available: (i) External treatment and (ii) Internal treatment.
- The chemicals required to remove the impurities are added to the water and this water is fed to the boiler. During steam generation, these chemicals act on the water and water is purified. Such methods are called as *internal treatment methods*. Following Table 1.2 enlists the various methods in internal and external treatment.
- *In external treatment*, the impurities are removed with the help of a few chemicals and this pure water is then fed to the boilers for steam production. Since treatment on water is done before feeding the water to the boiler (i.e. outside the boiler), these methods are called external treatment.

Table 1.2: Various Internal and External Treatment Methods

Internal Treatment	External Treatment
(i) Carbonate conditioning	(i) Zeolite treatment
(ii) Phosphate conditioning	(ii) Ion-exchange method
(iii) Calgon conditioning	
(iv) Aluminate conditioning	
(v) EDTA conditioning	

1.15 INTERNAL TREATMENTS OF BOILER FEED WATER

(i) Carbonate Conditioning (Soda-Lime Treatment):

- This is an internal treatment of boiler feed water in which the dissolved salts of Ca and Mg are removed. The water is added with calculated amounts of lime [$Ca(OH)_2$] or soda (Na_2CO_3). The impurities are then precipitated which can be filtered off as scales or sludges during blow down operation.

$$Na_2CO_3 + Ca^{++} \longrightarrow CaCO_3 \downarrow + 2\,Na^+$$
$$\text{Precipitate of } CaCO_3$$

(ii) Phosphate Conditioning:

- Soda lime method has one disadvantage i.e. Na_2CO_3 added to water forms sodium hydroxide and that leads to caustic embrittlement of boiler metal.

- Hence sometimes phosphate conditioning methods are preferred. The various phosphate salts of sodium are added to boiler water. These phosphate salts react with the dissolved calcium and magnesium impurities in water leading to corresponding phosphate precipitate. This precipitate accumulates in boiler as sludge that can be easily removed during blow down operation.

- The phosphates that are commonly used are NaH_2PO_4, Na_2HPO_4 and Na_3PO_4. The choice of the phosphate depends on the pH conditions of boiler water. If pH is in the acidic region NaH_2PO_4 can be used, if water is neutral, then Na_2HPO_4 can be used and in the case of alkaline water, Na_3PO_4 can be used.

- The phosphate conditioning reactions can be written as

$$3\ CaCO_3 + 2\ Na_3PO_4 \longrightarrow Ca_3(PO_4)_2 + 3\ Na_2CO_3$$

$$3\ CaSO_4 + 2\ NaH_2PO_4 \longrightarrow Ca_3(PO_4)_2 + Na_2SO_4 + 2\ SO_3 + 2\ H_2O$$

$$3\ Mg(OH)_2 + 2\ Na_2HPO_4 \longrightarrow Mg_3(PO_4)_2 + 4\ NaOH + 2H_2O$$

(III) EDTA Conditioning:

- It is known that, EDTA forms stable, water soluble complexes with most of the divalent and monovalent metal ions. Such water soluble complexes do not disturb the steam generation in boilers.

$$M^{++} + EDTA \rightarrow M\text{-EDTA (water soluble complex)}$$

1. Aluminate Conditioning:

- This conditioning method is used to remove the finely divided silica or small oil droplets present in colloidal from the boiler water. When sodium aluminate is added to water, it forms a gelatinuous precipitate of aluminium hydroxide.

$$NaAlO_2 + 2\ H_2O \longrightarrow Al(OH)_3 \downarrow + NaOH$$

- Both the products formed in this reaction after addition of sodium aluminate are useful in the internal treatment of boiler feed water.

- The precipitates of aluminium and magnesium hydroxide have a tendency to trap finely divided silica particles or adsorb oil droplets. This can form a sludge and can easily be removed from boiler during blow down operation.

- Sodium hydroxide formed may further react with the dissolved magnesium salts leading to the formation of magnesium hydroxide.

$$2\ NaOH + Mg^{++} \longrightarrow Mg(OH)_2 \downarrow + 2\ Na^+$$

2. **Calgon Conditioning:**

- Scale forming salts like $CaSO_4$, $Mg(HCO_3)_2$ etc. in the boiler water can be converted into highly **soluble complexes** by addition of small amount (0.5 – 5.0 ppm) of calgon in boiler water.

- Calgon is sodium hexametaphosphate $(NaPO_3)_6$ or $Na_2[Na_4 P_6 O_{18}]$. This substance forms highly soluble co-ordination complexes with Ca^{++}, Mg^{++}, Fe^{++} and thus scale formation is prevented. Calgon can attack on the scale to dissolve it.

- The optimum pH required for complexe formation is 9.0 to 10.5.

$$(NaPO_3)_6 \text{ or } Na_2[Na_4 P_6 O_{18}] \rightleftharpoons 2Na^+ + [Na_4 P_6 O_{18}]^{-2}$$

$$Ca^{++} + [Na_4 P_6 O_{18}]^{-2} \xrightarrow{\text{pH 9 to 10.5}} 2Na^+ + [CaNa_2 P_6 O_{18}]^{-2}$$

$$\text{(Soluble complex)}$$

1.16 EXTERNAL TREATMENT METHODS OR WATER SOFTENING METHODS   [May 14, 16]

1.16.1 Zeolite Method (Permutit Process)

- Zeolites are naturally occurring honey comb like compounds with a complicated cage like structure. They contain fused sodium aluminates and silicates. The general formula for zeolite is $Na_2OAl_2O_3 \cdot x \, SiO_2 \cdot x \, H_2O$. For convenience this complex structure is represented as **Na_2Ze**.

- Zeolite contains loosely bound Na^+ ions. If hard water contains divalent cations (Ca^{++}, Mg^{++}), then these ions get exchanged with Na^+ i.e. two sodium ions in zeolite are replaced by one Ca^{++} or Mg^{++} ion.

- After this water that comes out is free from Ca^{++} and Mg^{++}, it becomes soft water and can be used as boiler feed water.

Softening Process:

A schematic diagram of water softening method using zeolites is shown in Fig. 1.5.

- The apparatus consists of a vertical column with a zeolite bed of fixed width. The hard water enters the column from the inlet provided at the upper region. An inlet for NaCl solution is also provided at the top for regeneration of exhausted zeolite. The soft water is collected from the lower part of column as shown in Fig. 1.5.

Water Softening Process:

- When hard water enters the column, the hardness causing ions (Ca^{++}, Mg^{++}) are trapped and replaced to loosely bound Na^+ ions in zeolite. The exchange can be written as:

$$Ca^{++} + Na_2Ze \rightleftharpoons CaZe + 2 Na^+$$
$$Mg^{++} + Na_2Ze \rightleftharpoons MgZe + 2 Na^+$$

$\left.\right\}$ Removal of hardness causing ions

Once all the Ca^{++} and Mg^{++} present in water are trapped in the zeolite cage, the water that comes out through pores is free from those ions and hence hardness causing ions are removed.

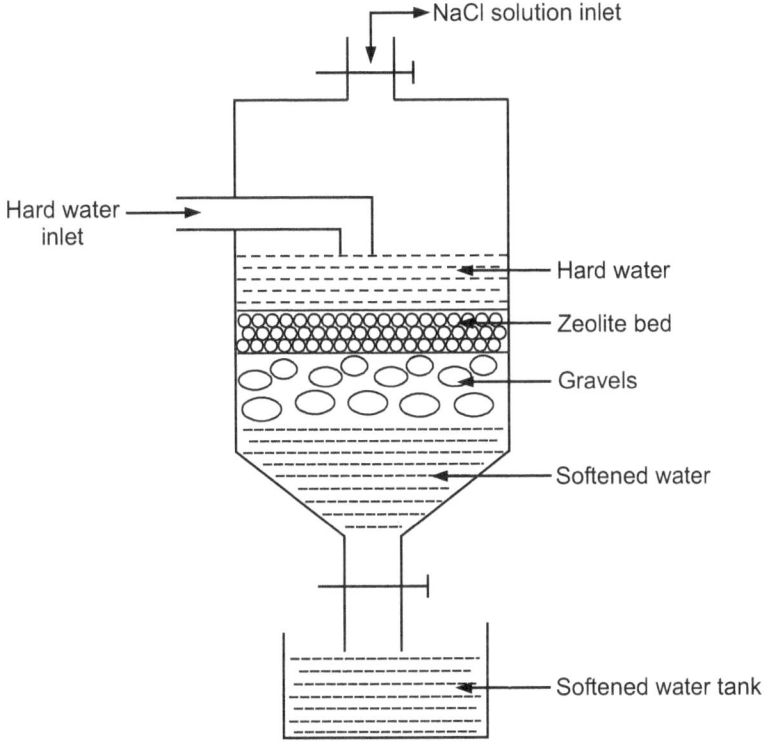

Fig. 1.5: Zeolite filtration method for water softening

- In order to improve the purification efficiency, the hard water is passed at a specific rate (volume of water/hr) through zeolite bed.

- If purification continues, it happens that all the exchange sites (or Na^+) in zeolite bed are replaced by Ca^{++} and Mg^{++} and the capacity to exchange cations becomes zero. Hence, the zeolite cannot trap the impurity cations any more. Such zeolite is called as an *exhausted zeolite*.

- The process of obtaining original zeolite from exhausted one is called as *regeneration*. Regeneration can be done by simply passing calculated amount of NaCl solution through zeolite. This NaCl solution is called as brine. During this process, sodium replaces the trapped cation as the exchange process is reversible.

- The regenerated zeolite bed can be reused for further water softening.

$$CaZe \text{ (or } MgZe) + 2\,NaCl \rightleftharpoons Na_2Ze \qquad + \quad CaCl_2 \text{ (or } MgCl_2)$$

Exhausted zeolite　Brine　　Regenerated zeolite　　Wash　　　　　Regeneration of zeolite bed

Advantages of Zeolite Method:

- The hardness of water obtained after zeolite filtration is < 10 ppm i.e. almost purest form of water is obtained.
- Running cost of softening is very less < 1 Rs./lit.
- If used as boiler feed water, the boiler will be free from problems such as corrosion, caustic embrittlement and formation of sludges and scales thereby increasing its efficiency of steam generation.

Disadvantages:

- Water turbidity cannot be removed using zeolite treatment.
- If Fe^{2+}, Mn^{3+} (heavy metal ions) are present, they cause problems during regeneration.
- Although running cost is low, installation cost is high.
- Cannot remove the dissolved gases such as O_2, CO_2 etc.
- Only *cations* can be removed from water whereas *anion* impurities remain in softened water.
- Natural zeolites are rare and synthesis of zeolite is difficult.

1.16.2 Ion-Exchange Method for Water Softening Or Demineralization Or Deionization

- In ion-exchange water softening method, cation as well as anion impurities can be removed from water. Ion exchangers have polymer base and exchange sites. These polymers are called as ion-exchange resins. These are of two types:

(1) Cation Exchange Resins:

- The cation exchange resins exchange sodium ion or proton to remove Ca^{2+} or Mg^{2+} in hard water.

These are mainly styrene-divinyl benzene copolymers, which on sulphonation or carboxylation become capable to exchange their proton or sodium ions with cations in water. For simplicity, it can be written as $R^- - H^+$.

OR

$$R^- H^+ \qquad\qquad R^- Na^+$$

Sulphonated styrene-vinyl benzyl copolymer (A proton exchanger)   Sodium salt of sulphonated styrene-vinyl benzyl copolymer (A Na^+ exchanger)

(2) Anion Exchange Resins:

- These resins retain anion impurities present in hard water with OH^- which is loosely bound to resins. These are styrene-divinyl benzene copolymers containing quaternary ammonium hydroxide group For simplicity, it can be written as $R^+ - OH^-$.

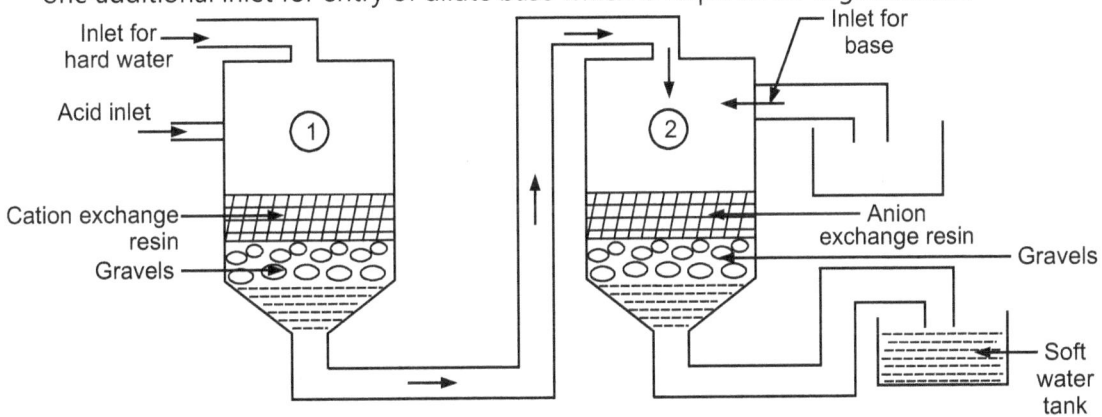

$$R^+ - OH^-$$

Process of Softening using Ion-Exchange Resins:

The schematic diagram for demineralization using ion-exchange resins is shown in Fig. 1.6.

- The demineralization can be done with the help of two columns as shown in Fig. 1.6. First column is fitted with cation exchange resin (denoted by R^-H^+) and second column is fitted with anion exchange resin bed (denoted by R^+OH^-). First column is provided with two inlets, one for entry of hard water and second for entry of dilute acid required for regeneration.

- The outlet of first column is inlet of second column. This column is also provided with one additional inlet for entry of dilute base which is required for regeneration.

Inlet for hard water

Acid inlet

Cation exchange resin

Gravels

Inlet for base

Anion exchange resin

Gravels

Soft water tank

Fig. 1.6: Demineralization using ion-exchange resins

Exchange at Column 1:

- When hard water enters this column, the cation impurities are trapped in the resin as it is a cation exchanger. The exchange reaction is:

$$2\,R^- \cdot H^+ \quad + \quad Ca^{++} \text{ or } Mg^{++} \quad \rightleftharpoons \quad MgR_2 \text{ or } CaR_2 + 2\,H^+$$

Original resin   Impurities in water   Impurities exch.

When all exchange sites are blocked by Ca^{++} and Mg^{++}, then no more exchange takes place and resin is said to be exhausted.

Regeneration of Cation Exchange Resin:

*   The exhausted resin can be regenerated by passing dilute mineral acids such as HCl or H_2SO_4. The regeneration reaction is

$$MgR_2 \text{ or } CaR_2 \quad + \quad 2\,H^+ \quad \rightleftharpoons \quad 2R^-H^+ + Ca^{++} \text{ or } Mg^{++}$$

Exhausted resin   Dil. acids   Regenerated resin

Exchange at Column 2:

*   Water that comes out of column 1 is free from cation impurities but contains anion impurities. This water is fed to column 2 which contains an anion exchange resin. The impurity anions are exchanged as:

$$R^+OH^- \quad + \quad Cl^- \quad \longrightarrow \quad R^+Cl^- \quad + \quad OH^-$$

Anion exchanger   Impurity   Impurities exchanged

$$\text{or } 2R^+OH^- + SO_4^{2-} \longrightarrow R_2^{++}SO_4^{--} + 2\,OH^-$$

Regeneration of Anion Exchange Resin:

*   When all exchange sites are blocked by anions, then resin cannot purify water further and regeneration is required. Regeneration can be done by passing dilute alkali solution as

$$R^+Cl^- \text{ or } R_2^{++}SO_4^{--} + OH^- \text{ or } 2OH \longrightarrow R^+OH^- \text{ or } 2R^+OH^-$$

Exhausted resin   Regenerated resin

*   It can be seen that protons come out of cation exchangers and hydroxide ions come out of anion exchangers. They react among themselves to form water as:

$$H^+ + OH^- \longrightarrow H_2O$$

*   Water that comes out of both the columns is free from cation as well as anion impurities and hence soft water can be obtained that can be directly used as a boiler feed water.

Advantages:

*   Hardness of water obtained after ion exchange is < 10 ppm i.e. very pure water is obtained that can be used for boilers operating at high pressures.
*   Acidic and alkaline water can also be treated.

Disadvantages:

*   Operation cost and installation cost of purification plant is high.
*   Cannot remove turbidity of water in fact turbidity has to be removed then only water can be purified using this method.

1.17 DESALINATION OF BRAKISH WATER

1.17.1 Reverse Osmosis

Definition: It is the process of forcing a solvent from a region of high solute concentration through a semipermeable membrane to a region of low solute concentration by applying a pressure in excess of the osmotic pressure as shown in Fig. 1.7.

In a similar set up of two compartments like osmotic pressure is applied to a compartment of high concentration. Thus there are two forces influencing the movement of water: externally applied pressure on one side and osmotic pressure on another side caused by the difference in solute concentration between the two compartments.

Semipermeable Membrane:

The membrane used for reverse osmosis have a dense barrier layer in the polymer matrix where separation occurs. The membrane is designed to pass through this dense layer while preventing the passage of solute. The size of membrane is 5×10^{-4} to 2×10^{-7} micron.

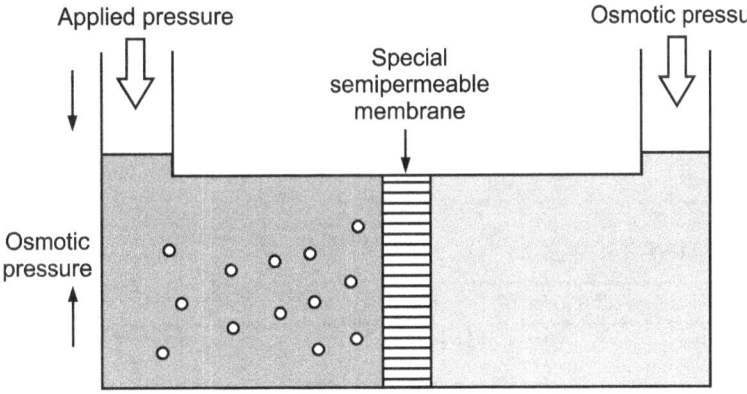

Fig. 1.7: Reverse osmosis

Pressure Requirement:

Reverse osmosis process requires a high pressure exerted on high concentration side of the membrane. (i) for fresh and brakish (salty) water: 30 to   250 psi or 2.17 bar. (ii) sea water: 600 – 1000 psi or 40-70 bar. The osmotic pressure of sea water is 250 psi or 24 bar.

RO System: The system for desalination by reverse osmosis of sea water consists of following components:

*   **Intake:** The sea water is passed through cock in the system.
*   **Pretreatment:** Pretreatment is necessary when working with single pass RO system and nanofiltration membrane due to spiral wound design. This design does not allow for back pulsing with water and removes solids and highly susceptible to fouling.
*   Solids within water must be removed. Also 1-5 μm sized particles should be removed using string wound polypropylene filters. The deactivation of chlorine is necessary which

can destroy thin film composite membrane. If the feed water has a scaling tendency the pH of the solution is adjusted by acid dosing to maintain carbonates in their carbonic acid form. Antiscalants may also be used.

- **High Pressure Arrangement:** The pump is used to supply the pressure needed to push water through a semipermeable special membrane. For brackish water: 15-26 bar or 225-375 psi and for sea water 55-82 bar or 800 to 1180 psi.

- **Membrane Assembly:** It consists of a pressure vessel with membrane that allows feed water to be pressed against it. The membrane should be strong enough to withstand the pressure applied against it. The spiral wound and hollow-fiber configurations are generally used.

- **Remineralisation and pH Adjustment Assembly:** The desalined water coming out from the RO system is corrosive. It is stabilized by adding lime or caustic to adjust the pH at 6.8 to 8.1 to meet the potable water specification, corrosive control to prevent corrosion of concrete lined surfaces.

- **Disinfection Arrangement:** The water coming after pH adjustment is free from pathogenic organisms but not bacteria protozoa and virus. Therefore disinfection is done by treatment of water by means of UV radiation from UV lamp or chlorination process.

Impure Water Containing Ions:

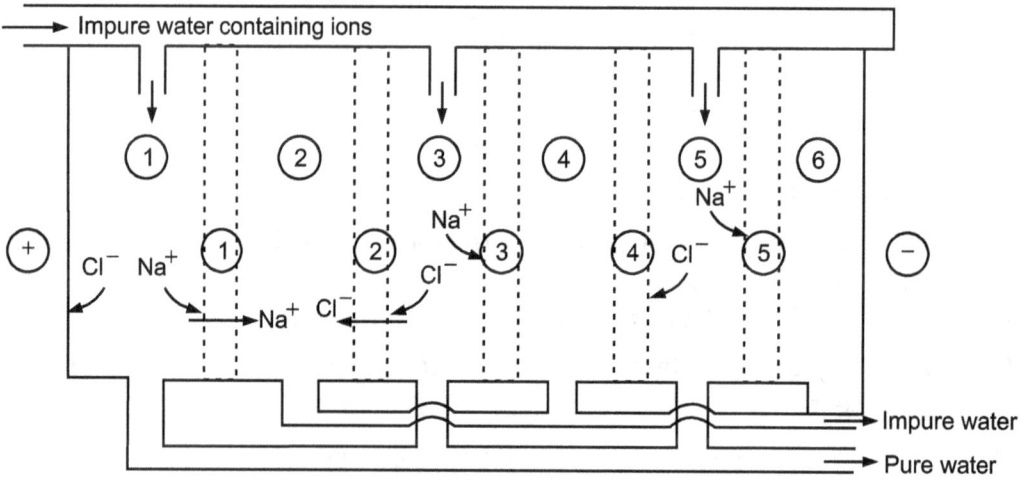

1, 3, 5 – Cation exchanger membrane

4, 2 – Anion exchanger membrane

Fig. 1.8: Impure water containing ions

1.17.2 Electrodialysis

- Electrodialysis is a membrane-based water purification technique. The technique is very helpful if water contains large concentration of salt. Therefore this technique can be used to purify sea water.

- **Principle:** Ions are separated using ion-exchange membrane by application of suitable potential difference.

- A schematic of separating ions using electrodialysis is shown in Fig. 1.8.

- In a container, two electrodes are fitted and are well separated from each other.

- Cation exchanger and anion exchanger membranes are fitted alternately at fixed distance in between these two electrodes.

- Sea water or impure water containing salts is present in the odd number compartments.

- When sufficient potential difference is applied, anions get attracted towards positive electrode and cations pass through cation exchange membrane and enter compartment 2.

- Same process takes place at compartments 3 and 5.

- In compartments 2, 4 ..., the concentration of ions increases and this water can be separated.

- In odd number compartment, pure water is obtained.

SOLVED PROBLEMS

Example 1.10: *25 ml of water sample containing Cl⁻ was titrated with N/40 standard AgNO₃ solution in the Mohr's method. The end point was observed at 3.4 ml of AgNO₃. Calculate Cl⁻ content in water in ppm.*

Solution: Given:

$$\text{Volume of water} = 25 \text{ ml}$$
$$[AgNO_3] = N/40 = 0.025 \text{ N}$$
$$\text{Volume of } AgNO_3 = 3.4 \text{ ml}$$
$$AgNO_3 \equiv \text{Water } (Cl^-)$$
$$N_1V_1 = N_2V_2$$
$$0.025 \times 3.4 = N_2 \times 25$$
$$N_2 = 3.4 \times 10^{-3} \text{ N}$$
$$[Cl^-] = 3.4 \times 10^{-3} \times 35.5 \times 1000 \text{ ppm}$$

$$\boxed{[Cl^-] = 120.7 \text{ ppm } Cl^-}$$

Zeolite Method:

While solving problems on zeolite, please remember

(1) Basically, zeolite is a cation exchanger containing Na^+ as a replaceable ion.

(2) Zeolite bed can be regenerated by passing NaCl solution.

Step 1: Calculate amount of NaCl required for regeneration in mg from its concentration.

Step 2: Convert these many mg of NaCl into its $CaCO_3$ equivalent as 1 equivalent of NaCl $\equiv$ 1 equivalent of $CaCO_3$.

Step 3: Calculate hardness as

$$\text{Hardness} = \frac{CaCO_3 \text{ eq. of NaCl}}{\text{Volume of water sample}}$$

Example 1.11: *1000 L of hard water was softened by zeolite process. The exhausted zeolite was regenerated by passing 25 L of NaCl solution containing 1800 mg/L. Calculate hardness of water.*

Solution: Given:

$$\text{Volume of hard water} = 1000 \text{ L}$$
$$\text{Volume of NaCl solution} = 25 \text{ L}$$
$$[NaCl] = 1800 \text{ mg/L}$$
$$\text{Hardness} = ?$$

Step 1: Calculate milligrams of NaCl required for regeneration

$$1 \text{ L} \equiv 1800 \text{ mg NaCl}$$
$$\text{For } 25 \text{ L} = ?$$
$$= 1800 \times 25$$
$$= 45000 \text{ mg}$$

Step 2: $CaCO_3$ eq. calculation.

$$58.5 \text{ mg NaCl} \equiv 50 \text{ mg } CaCO_3 \text{ eq.}$$
$$45000 \text{ mg NaCl} = ?$$
$$= \frac{50 \times 45000}{58.5}$$
$$= 38461.5 \text{ mg } CaCO_3 \text{ eq.}$$

Step 3:
$$\text{Hardness} = \frac{CaCO_3 \text{ eq.}}{\text{Volume of water}}$$
$$= \frac{38461.5}{1000} = 38.46 \text{ ppm } CaCO_3 \text{ eq.}$$

$\therefore$ $\boxed{\text{Hardness} = 38.46 \text{ ppm } CaCO_3 \text{ eq.}}$

Example 1.12: *By passing 80 L of NaCl solution, containing 300 g/L of NaCl, an exhausted zeolite softener bed was regenerated. Calculate volume of hard water that has been softened by this zeolite bed whose hardness is 400 ppm CaCO₃ eq.*

Solution: Given:

$$\text{Volume of NaCl} = 80\ \text{L}$$

$$[\text{NaCl}] = 300\ \text{g/L}$$

$$\text{Volume of hard water} = ?$$

$$\text{Hardness of water} = 400\ \text{ppm CaCO}_3\ \text{eq.}$$

Step 1: $\quad 1\ \text{L of NaCl solution} = 300\ \text{NaCl} \times 1000\ \text{mg NaCl}$

$$80\ \text{L NaCl solution} = ?$$

$$= 80 \times 300 \times 1000$$

$$= 24000000\ \text{mg NaCl}$$

Step 2: $\quad \text{CaCO}_3\ \text{eq.} = \dfrac{24000000 \times 50}{58.5}$

$$= 20512820\ \text{mg CaCO}_3\ \text{eq.}$$

Step 3: $\quad \text{Hardness} = \dfrac{\text{mg CaCO}_3\ \text{eq.}}{\text{Volume of water}}$

$$400 = \dfrac{20512820.5}{\text{Volume of water}}$$

∴ $\quad \text{Volume of hard water} = \dfrac{20512820.5}{400}$

$$= \boxed{51282\ \text{L}}$$

∴ 51282 L of hard water has been softened.

Example 1.13: *A zeolite bed gets exhausted on softening 1200 L of hard water with hardness 416.7 ppm CaCO₃ eq. Calculate the strength of NaCl required for the regeneration of bed if 5.87 L of NaCl is required. Nov. 13 3 M*

Solution: Given:

$$\text{Volume of hard water} = 1200\ \text{L}$$

$$\text{Hardness of water} = 416.7\ \text{ppm CaCO}_3\ \text{eq.}$$

$$[\text{NaCl}] = ?$$

$$\text{Volume of NaCl} = 5.87\ \text{L}$$

Step 1: Calculation of 'mg' of NaCl

$$1\ \text{L NaCl solution} \equiv x\ \text{mg NaCl}$$

$$5.87 \text{ L NaCl solution} = x \times 5.87 \text{ mg NaCl}$$

Step 2: Calculation of $CaCO_3$ eq. (ppm)

$$58.5 \text{ mg NaCl} \equiv 50 \text{ mg } CaCO_3$$

$$x \times 5.87 \text{ mg NaCl} \equiv ?$$

$$= \frac{50 \times x \times 5.87}{58.5} \text{ mg } CaCO_3$$

Step 3: $\text{Hardness} = \dfrac{\text{mg } CaCO_3 \text{ eq.}}{\text{Volume of hard water}}$

$$416.7 = \frac{50 \times x \times 5.87}{58.5 \times 1200}$$

$\therefore$ $x = \dfrac{58.5 \times 1200 \times 416.7}{50 \times 5.87} = 99667.2 \text{ mg/L}$

$$= \boxed{99.667 \text{ g/L}}$$

$\therefore$ Strength of NaCl used for regeneration is 99.66 g/L.

Example 1.14: *How many litres of 10% NaCl will be required to regenerate exhausted zeolite due to softening of 15000 L of hard water ? The chemical analysis of water is found to be $CaSO_4$ = 43.52 ppm, $MgCl_2$ = 22.8 ppm, $Ca(HCO_3)_2$ = 40.5 ppm, $MgSO_4$ = 36 ppm.*

Given atomic weights of Ca = 40, S = 32, O = 16, Mg = 24, Cl = 35.5, C = 12, H = 1.

Solution: Step 1: Calculation of Total Hardness in ppm $CaCO_3$ eq.:

(1)   1 eq./L $CaSO_4$ $\equiv$ 1 eq. $CaCO_3$ hardness

i.e.   68 mg $CaSO_4$ $\equiv$ 50 mg $CaCO_3$

then 43.52 mg/L $CaCO_3$ = ?

$$= \frac{50 \times 43.52}{68} = 32 \text{ ppm } CaCO_3 \text{ eq.}$$

(2) Similarly for $MgCl_2$, $\text{Hardness} = \dfrac{50 \times 22.8}{47.5} = 24$

(3) For $Ca(HCO_3)$, $\text{Hardness} = \dfrac{50 \times 40.5}{81} = 25$

(4) For $MgSO_4$, $\text{Hardness} = \dfrac{50 \times 36}{60} = 30$

$\therefore$ Total hardness = 32 + 24 + 25 + 30 = 111 ppm $CaCO_3$ eq.

Step 2: Calculation of milligrams of NaCl

$$0.1 \text{ L NaCl solution} \equiv 10 \text{ g NaCl}$$

then x L NaCl solution $\equiv$?

$$= \frac{x \times 10}{0.1} \times 1000 \text{ mg NaCl}$$

$$= x \times 10^5 \text{ mg NaCl}$$

Step 3: Calculation of $CaCO_3$ equivalents:

$$58.5 \text{ mg NaCl} \equiv 50 \text{ mg CaCO}_3$$

then $x \times 10^6$ mg NaCl $\equiv$?

$$= \frac{50 \times x \times 10^5}{58.5} \text{ mg CaCO}_3$$

Step 4:   Hardness $= \dfrac{CaCO_3 \text{ mg}}{\text{Volume}} = \dfrac{50 \times x \times 10^5}{58.5 \times 15000}$

$\therefore$ $111 = \dfrac{50 \times x \times 10^5}{58.5 \times 15000}$

$\therefore$ $\boxed{x = 19.48 \text{ L NaCl}}$

1.18 GREEN CHEMISTRY   [May 13, Dec. 14]

- As it is known, chemistry has revolutionized the human life. It is playing very important role in every development of human civilization. The medical science has seen tremendous development due to synthetic drugs. Every branch of engineering needs smart materials that are gifts of chemistry. The production of food-grains and other agricultural produce is multiplied many a times due to hybrid varieties, better seeds and use of many agrochemicals such as fertilizers, pesticides and herbicides where chemistry has played an important role. Besides standard of ordinary human life has increased many times because of use of many chemical materials used as dyes, plastics (polymers), cosmetics and many more.

- However, this development resulted into environmental pollution, hazardous chemicals, unsafe drinking water, leading to entry of toxic substances into biosphere and the most importantly in the human food chain. So it is important to sustain the human development with new materials but also there is an urgent need to address the hazardous side effects of the materials.

- This thinking led to the research in chemical science and technology that prevent its dangerous side effects in a scientifically sound and cost effective manner. This is the field where 'Green Chemistry' comes into picture.

- The term 'Green Chemistry' is coined by a scientist Paul T. Anastas who is widely regarded as the father of green chemistry.

- Most recently in 2005 scientists Chaurin, Grubbs and Schrock were awarded the Nobel Prize in chemistry for inventing and developing the catalysts responsible for synthesis of organic compounds in the greener ways.

- Green chemistry can be defined as the use of chemistry for environmental pollution prevention by deliberate designing of chemical products or processes that reduce or eliminate the use or generation of hazardous and toxic chemicals.

- Green chemistry can also be referred as clean chemistry, sustainable chemistry, ecofriendly or environmentally benign chemistry or chemistry with good atom economy.

1.19 NEED FOR GREEN CHEMISTRY

- Although chemistry is responsible for improving human life, but all these developments led to many environmental problems. Many times, these problems are so serious that people may disapprove the usefulness of chemicals or the corresponding chemical processes. Green chemistry can play an important role in minimizing or avoiding the harmful effect of chemicals or chemical processes.

- It can be used for making the chemical products that do not harm either environment or our health directly or indirectly.

- It can also be used for developing industrial process that reduce or eliminate use or production of hazardous chemical substances.

- Green chemistry may lead to design efficient processes that minimize or eliminate waste generation.

- Green chemistry can help preventing pollution rather than cleaning up the environment later on.

- Green pathways can help in minimizing energy requirement for a chemical process.

- Green chemistry can help producing biodegradable materials.

1.20 PRINCIPLES OF GREEN CHEMISTRY   [Dec. 12, May 15, 16]

- Paul T. Anastas enlisted 12 principles of given chemistry. These principles are discussed below:

1. **Prevention:** Green chemistry believes in the principle of prevention is better can cure. It is always better to prevent creation and piling up of hazardous materials than to destroy/clean them later on. This can be done by developing a new process by using ecofriendly inputs for the material, which is otherwise produced by using harmful input parameters.

   For example, adipic acid, which is an important starting material for the production of synthetic fibres can be produced from glucose using green pathways rather than traditionally produced by using benzene.

2. **Atom Economy:** In order to understand 'greenness' of a chemical reaction, the concept of atom economy was introduced by Barry Trost of standard university.

*   This concept considers the extent of starting material incorporated in the desired final product.

*   The objective of atom economy is to create synthesis path of a desired material in such a way that all atoms present in the starting material should be present in the desired product.

*   Lesser is the number of unused atoms in the molecules of starting material, better is the atom economy and greater is the synthetic pathway.

*   Percent atom economy (PAE) can be calculated by using the formula:

$$\text{PAE (Percent atom economy)} = \frac{\text{Formula weight (FW) of atom utilized}}{\text{Formula weight of all the reactants used in the reaction}} \times 100$$

*   Most of the organic reactions are one of the following four types:

(a) Rearrangement reactions.

(b) Addition reactions.

(c) Substitution reactions.

(d) Elimination reactions.

(a) **Rearrangement Reactions:** Let us consider the following reaction.

Such type of reactions are 100% atom economical. The percent atom economy of these reactions can be calculated in the following way:

Reactants		No. of Utilized Atoms	
Formula	F.W. (g/mol)	in the final product	F.W./g/m
$C_9H_{10}O$	134.173	$C_9H_{10}O$	134.173

$$\text{\% Atom economy} = \frac{\text{F.W. of utilized atoms}}{\text{F.W. of all reactants}} \times 100$$

$$= \frac{134.173}{134.173} \times 100$$

$$= 100\%$$

*   This indicates that if number of atoms in all the reactant and the **'desired'** product is same, then the atom economy is **100%**.

(b) Addition Reactions: As all the atoms on the reactant side are present in the desired product in addition reaction, such type of reactions are 100% atom economical. Consider the following addition reaction.

$$CH_3 - CH = CH_2 + H_2 \xrightarrow{\text{Ni}} CH_3 - CH_2 - CH_3$$

propene   propane

No. of Reactant Atoms	F.W. (g/mol)	No. of Utilized Atoms	F.W.	No. of Unutilized Atoms
(i) C_3H_6	42	C_3H_8		–
(ii) H_2	2			
Total C_3H_8	46	C_3H_8	46	–

$$\% \text{ atom economy} = \frac{\text{F.W. of utilized atoms}}{\text{F.W. of reactant}} \times 100$$

$$= \frac{46}{46} \times 100 = 100\%$$

Determine the % atom economy of the following reaction:

$$CH_2{=}CH{-}CH{=}CH_2 \ + \ CH_2{=}CH_2 \longrightarrow$$

Butadine   Ethene   Cyclohexene

(c) Substitution Reactions:

- In these type of reactions, an atom or group of atoms is replaced by another atom or group of atoms. The formula weight of replaced atom is not the same as that of the original atom in the desired product. Hence substitution reactions have low atom economy.

- Consider the following reaction in which N-methyl propamide is the desired product and not ethyl alcohol.

$$CH_3 - CH_2 - \overset{\overset{\textstyle O}{\|}}{C} - OCH_2 - CH_3 + CH_3 - NH_2 \longrightarrow$$

ethyl propionate   methyl amine

$$CH_3 - CH_2 - \overset{\overset{\textstyle O}{\|}}{C} - \underset{\underset{\textstyle H}{|}}{N} - CH_3 + OH - CH_2 - CH_3$$

N-methyl propamide   Ethyl alcohol

No. of Reactant Atoms	F.W. of Reactant Atoms	Utilized Atoms in Desired Products	F.W. of Utilized Atoms
Reaction 1: $C_5H_{10}O_2$	102.132	C_3H_5O	57.057
Reaction 2: CH_5N	31.057	CH_4N	30.049
Total: $C_6H_{15}NO_2$	133.189	C_4H_9NO	87.120

$$\% \text{ Atom economy} = \frac{\text{F.W. of utilized atom}}{\text{F.W. of reactants}} \times 100 = \frac{87.120}{133.189} \times 100$$

$$= 65.41\%$$

- It can be seen from the above substitution reaction, $-OCH_2CH_3$ group in the ethyl propionate is substituted by $-NH-CH_3$ group in methyl amine. The unutilized part in the desired product is $-OCH_2CH_3$ from ethyl propionate and one H atom in the methyl amine. Hence atoms that are utilized are C_2H_6O leading to the formation of a side product ethyl alcohol. The generation of undesired product has taken place which is clearly reflected in the % atom economy which is less than 100%. So substitution reactions are comparatively less greener than the chemical rearrangements and addition reactions. Determine % atom efficiency of the above reaction if the desired product is ethyl alcohol.

(d) Elimination Reactions: Elimination reactions are generally opposite to that of addition reactions. In such type of reactions, an atom or group of atoms is completely removed in the product. So always formula weight of any of the products is less than that of the reactants. Hence atom economy of such reaction is most commonly less than that of any of the above discussed reactions.

- Consider the following reaction:

$$CH_3 - CH - CH_2 - \overset{CH_3}{\overset{|}{\underset{\underset{H}{|}}{N^+}}} - CH_3OH^- \overset{\Delta}{\longrightarrow}$$

Trimethyl propyl ammonium hydroxide

$$CH_3 - CH = CH_2 + \overset{CH_3}{\underset{\underset{CH_3}{|}}{N - CH_3}} + H_2O$$

propene   trimethyl amine   water

- If prepene is the desired product in the above reaction, then only three carbons and five hydrogens are utilized in the reactant to form the desired product.

- The percent economy can be calculate as.
  Determine the atom efficiency of the following rearrangement reaction.

| 3,4-dimethyl | 2, 6 octadiene |
| 1,5 hexadiene | |

3. **Less Hazardous Chemical Syntheses:** Green chemistry believes in designing of the pathway (processes) that uses and produces less hazardous chemicals. Such pathways possess little or no toxicity to either human race or any other element in the biosphere.

4. **Designing Safer Chemicals:** Green chemistry designes and develops chemical products that have maximum desired functionality and minimum toxicity.

5. **Safer Solvents and Auxillaries:** Most of the traditional chemical pathways require large number of solvents and many accessories which may be most of the times are useless once the desired end product is produced. This leads to the generation of undisposable waste that possess harmful effect on the environment. Green chemistry demands of avoiding such pathways and suggests the multiple use of the solvents, separating agents and the corresponding accessories. The process is said to be greener if the solvent used is ordinary water.

6. **Energy Efficiency:** Energy consumption to carry out a simple reaction is one of the biggest problems in the traditional chemistry in the form of heat and electricity. Green chemistry believes in obtaining the desired product by utilizing less energy so that overall thermodynamic efficiency of the process is increased. One of the methods to achieve this is use of microwave energy instead of heat energy.

7. **Renewable Feedstock:** Green chemistry suggests the use of renewable feedstock such as wood (cellulose), animal junk or any other biofeedstock wherever possible as the starting material of any chemical reaction. Such feedstocks are renewable and biodegradable.

8. **Reduce Derivatization:** Green chemistry believes in reduction of derivatization during a chemical reaction. Unnecessary derivatization (use of blocking groups, protection, deprotection, temporary modifications of chemical processes) should be minimized because each step requires additional reagents, additional accessories, additional solvents that may finally lead to unnecessary generation of chemical waste.

9. **Catalysis:** Catalytic reagents are superior to stoichiometric reagents in many ways because they increase selectivity, yield. Reaction conditions can be favourably managed by the use of catalyst. Use of catalyst reduces the overall input cost of the reaction. The catalytic reagents can be recycled and reused, hence green chemistry suggests the use of catalyst.

10. **Degradation:** Most of the end products such as plastics, fibres generated by using conventional chemical pathways have long life time. Their degradation is difficult and biodegradation most of the times impossible. Green chemistry suggests that the end

products should be degraded into less harmful products after their use. It is better if the end products are biodegradable.

11. **Real Time Analysis for Pollution Prevention:** Analytical procedures should be developed to allow real time, in process monitoring and control to the formation of hazardous chemicals.

12. **Use of Inherently Safer Chemicals:** Green chemistry suggests that substances used in a chemical process should be chosen so as to minimize the occurrence of any accident such as fire, explosion, skin or eye irritation through releases.

1.21 GREEN CHEMISTRY OF ADIPIC ACID   [Nov. 13]

- As mentioned earlier, adipic acid is an important starting material for synthesis of many polymers. It is estimated that about 100 million kilograms of adipic acid is required every year to fulfill the demand of the polymers.
- Traditionally, adipic acid is synthesized using the following pathway.

- As it can be seen from the above traditional pathway of synthesis of adipic acid, benzene is used as a starting material which is reduced under extreme conditions to cyclohexane.
- Benzene itself is carcinogenic and toxic, so its handling is difficult.
- For this reduction process, high pressure has to be created that increases the energy input.
- Second step oxidation of cyclohexane to cyclohexanone and cyclohexanol also requires high pressure.
- So overall, this process of generation of adipic acid from benzene is not ecofriendly and economical.
- Greener pathway for the synthesis

- The starting material for this pathway is glucose which is obtained from biofeedstock. It is also biodegradable, non-toxic, cheap and easily available.
- The reaction is carried out using enzymes in the bacteria, E.coli.
- In the final reduction step, low pressures are required and it is carried out using Ni or Pt. So the reaction is economical.
- It may be argued that the number of steps in traditional pathway are less (two) as compared to green pathway (3). But it should be noted that first two steps in green pathway are carried out using only one type of bacteria, hence these two steps require no extra input chemicals.

1.22 GREEN CHEMISTRY OF POLYCARBONATES

(A) Traditional Pathway for Synthesis of Polycarbonates:

- Phosgene (used as a starting material) is an extremely poisonous gas, hence its use should be avoided.
- The atom economy of the process is poor.
- The solvent used in the process is dichloromethane which is difficult to remove from the reaction mixture once the desired end product is obtained.
- All these unfavourable factors lead to think of a greener synthesis process of polycarbonates.

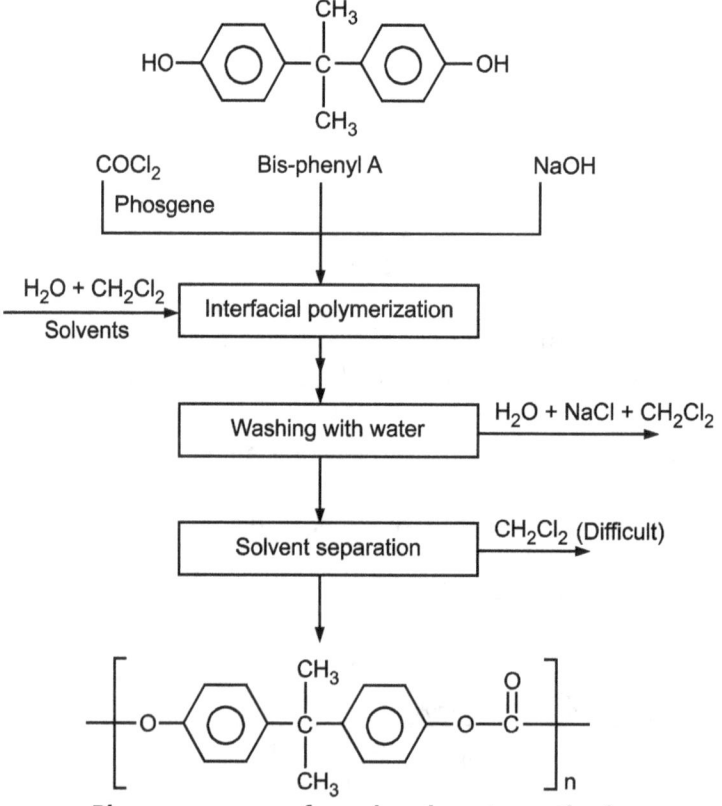

Phosgene process for polycarbonate synthesis

(B) Green Synthetic Pathway (Asahi Solid State Polymerization):

• The most important advantage of this pathway is that, it is a solid state reaction. So no solvent is used. The end product formed is in its crystalline state (pure form).

• Only phenol is obtained as a side product, hence the atom efficiency is superior as compared to the traditional pathway.

• Use of hazardous phosgene gas is eliminated.

• Methyl chloride, a carcinogenic chemical is totally eliminated from the synthesis.

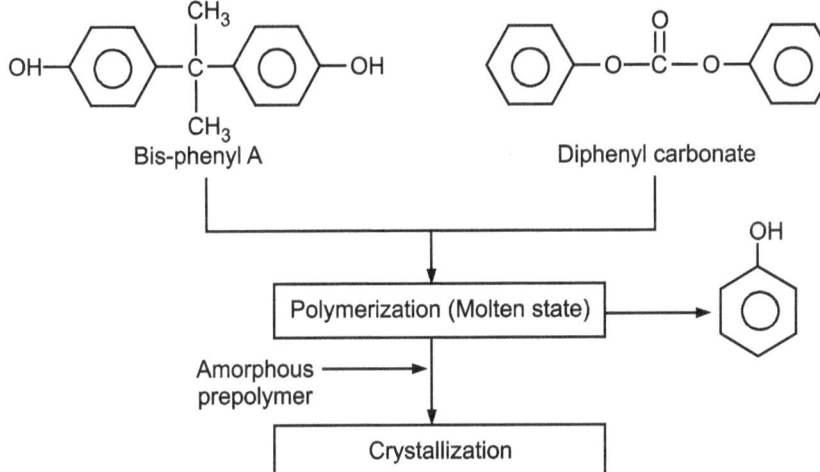

1.23 GREEN CHEMISTRY OF INDIGO DYES   [May 13, Dec. 14]

Green synthesis of indigo dye using enzymes.

Indigo dye used for colouration of jeans fibre can be prepared enzymatically by removal of side chain of tryptophane using enzyme tryptophenase to give indole, which can be further dehydroxylated enzymatically and deoxidized with oxygen to give indigo dye.

D-Glucose (17)   Dihydroquinic acid (18)   Shikimic acid (19)   Anthranilic acid (20)

Indigoglycerol phosphate (21)   Tryptophan (22)

SUMMARY

- Water is essential for the existence and sustenance of life on the earth.

- Water is formed by sp^3 hybridization of oxygen with hydrogens. It has 'V' shaped structure due to presence of lone pair of unpaired electrons on the oxygen atom.

- Water is highly polar solvent with dielectric constant 78.6 D at 25°C.

- Water shows intermolecular hydrogen bonding as hydrogen and oxygen has major differences in the electronegativities.

- Water that is to be used for industrial applications such as steam production generally contains impurities such as suspended matter, biological impurities, the colloidal and dissolved substances.

- Chemical analysis of water to know the levels of impurities present in the water is important as it gives an idea about the suitability of water for industrial applications.

- The important parameters in chemical analysis of water are hardness, chloride content and alkalinity.

- There are two types of hardness: (i) Temporary hardness and (ii) Permanent hardness.

- Temporary hardness of water is due to presence of carbonate and bicarbonate salts of Ca and Mg, hence it is also called as carbonate hardness.

- Temporary or carbonate hardness of water can be simply removed by boiling followed by filtering the water.

- Permanent hardness of water is due to presence of chloride, sulphate and nitrate salts of Ca, Mg, Fe, Cu, Zn etc.

- Permanent hardness can be removed by specific treatment methods such as zeolite method, ion exchange method or chemical treatment methods.

- Total hardness of water is given as:

  Total hardness = Temporary hardness + Permanent hardness.

- Total hardness of water can be determined by complexometric volumetric analysis having EDTA as a ligand, EBT as an indicator at pH = 10 maintained by using $NH_4Cl - NH_4OH$ basic buffer.

- Chloride content in the water can be determined using argentometric precipitation titration method in which water containing Cl^- is titrated with standard $AgNO_3$ using K_2CrO_4 (potassium chromate) as an indicator. The differences in the solubility products of the precipitates of $AgCl$ and Ag_2CrO_4 indicate the end point of the titration.

- Surface water is always slightly alkaline due to presence of hydroxide, carbonate and bicarbonate ions.

- Alkalinity due to hydroxide and carbonate ions is called as phenolphthalein alkalinity as the concentration of these ions in water can be determined by titration with standard strong acid (e.g. HCl, H_2SO_4 etc.) using phenolphthalein as an indicator.

- The alkalinity due to bicarbonate ions is called as methyl orange alkalinity as its concentration can be determined by titration with strong acid using methyl orange indicator.

- Once phenolphthalein and methyl orange alkalinities are evaluated, the concentration of alkalinity causing ions such as OH^-, HCO_3^-, CO_3^{--} can be determined using the end points of the titrations.

- The most important application of water as an engineering material is for steam generation or boiler feed water.

- If impure water is used as a boiler feed water, then commonly occurring boiler problems are (i) priming and foaming, (ii) scale and sludge formation, (iii) boiler corrosion and (iv) caustic embrittlement.

- Scale is tough, hard and strongly adhered layer of impurities present at inner lining of the boiler.

- Sludge is a loose, slimy mass of impurities present in water.

- The boiler metal undergoes corrosion if boiler feed water contains dissolved oxygen, dissolved carbon dioxide, hydrolysis of salts of magnesium etc.

- Caustic embrittlement of boiler metal is due to presence of alkaline impurities in water.

- All problems of boiler can be prevented or cured by using water from which the impurities are removed.

- There are two types of treatments for boiler feed water: (i) internal treatment and (ii) external treatment.

- In internal treatment, certain chemicals (required for purification of water) are added to water which is fed to boiler. During boiler operation, the water undergoes purification inside the boiler.

- External treatment methods are those methods in which water is purified first and then fed to boiler.

- The internal treatment methods include carbonate conditioning, phosphate conditioning, aluminate conditioning and EDTA conditioning, etc.

- External treatment methods include zeolite method and ion exchange method.

- Zeolites are naturally occurring honey comb like compounds with complicated cage like structure containing loosely bound Na^+, while water is treated with zeolite, then hardness causing ions such as Cu^{++}, Mg^{++} etc. are replaced with Na^+.

- In ion exchange methods, anion and cation exchange synthetic resins are used. The mechanism of exchange is same as that of zeolite.

UNSOLVED PROBLEMS

1. 100 ml of water sample requires 14.6 ml of 0.01 M EDTA in titration. 100 ml of same water sample when titrated after boiling and filtration required 9.9 ml of EDTA. Calculate carbonate and bicarbonate hardness of water sample.

    (**Ans.** pH = 146 ppm $CaCO_3$ eq., pH = 99 ppm $CaCO_3$,

    Temperature, H = 47 ppm $CaCO_3$)

2. 30 ml of standard hard water (containing 1.2 g $CaCO_3$/L) requires 26.5 ml of a EDTA solution. 100 ml of the water sample takes 12.8 ml of EDTA solution. Calculate hardness of water. (**Ans.** 173.9 ppm $CaCO_3$ eq.)

3. Calculate hardness of water if 50 ml of it requires 8.5 ml of 0.025 M EDTA in titration at pH 10.   (**Ans.** 425 ppm $CaCO_3$ eq.)

4. 20 ml of standard hard water (containing 15 g $CaCO_3$/L) required 25 ml EDTA solution for end point. 100 ml of water sample required 18 ml EDTA solution, while same water after boiling required 12 ml EDTA solution. Calculate carbonate and non-carbonate hardness of water.

    (**Ans.** Non-carbonate hardness = 1440 ppm $CaCO_3$ eq.

    Carbonate hardness = 720 ppm $CaCO_3$ eq.)

5. 50 ml of a standard hard water containing 1 mg of pure $CaCO_3$/ml consumed 20 ml EDTA. 50 ml of a water sample consumed 25 ml of same EDTA solution, using eriochrome black-T indicator. Calculate total hardness of water sample in ppm $CaCO_3$ eq.   (**Ans.** 1250 ppm $CaCO_3$ eq.)

6. A water sample was alkaline to both phenolphthalein and methyl orange. 50 ml of this water sample required 15 ml of N/50 H_2SO_4 for phenolphthalein end point and additional 10 ml for complete neutralization. Calculate types and amounts of alkalinities in ppm.   (**Ans.** $[CO_3^{2-}]$ = 400 ppm, $[OH^-]$ = 100 ppm $CaCO_3$ eq.)

7. A water sample is not alkaline to phenolphthalein. However, 100 ml of the same sample on titration with N/50 HCl required 16.9 ml to obtain end point using methyl orange indicator. What are types and amounts of alkalinities present in water ?   (**Ans.** $[HCO_3^-]$ = 169 ppm $CaCO_3$ eq.)

8. 100 ml of the water sample required 20 ml of N/50 H_2SO_4 for neutralization to phenolphthalein end point. After methyl orange was added to it 2.5 ml of acid required further. Calculate alkalinities in water in terms of $CaCO_3$ eq. ppm.

9. 50 ml of the water sample required 3.7 ml of 0.025 N H_2SO_4 upto phenolphthalein end point during titration. Calculate types and amounts of alkalinities in water.

10. 50 ml of water sample required 9.2 ml of N/50 HCl upto phenolphthalein end point and total of 13.1 ml for complete neutralization. Find types and amounts of alkalinities in water.

11. An exhausted zeolite softener was regenerated using 150 litres of NaCl solution having strength 150 gm/L of NaCl. How many litres of hard water sample having hardness 400 ppm can be softened by using this softener ?

12. A zeolite bed gets exhausted on softening 1200 L of a water sample. The exhausted bed requires 5.85 L of 10% NaCl solution for regeneration. Calculate the hardness of the water sample.

13. A zeolite bed gets exhausted on softening 2500 L of a water sample and requires 10 litres of 10% NaCl for regeneration. Find the hardness of the water sample.

14. A zeolite softener was completely exhausted and was regenerated by passing 100 litres of sodium chloride solution, containing 120 g/L of NaCl. How many litres of a sample of water of hardness 500 ppm can be softened by this softener ?

15. The total hardness of 1,000 litres of water was completely removed by a zeolite. Softener required 30 litres of sodium chloride solution containing 15 g/lit of NaCl for regeneration. Calculate the hardness of water.

16. A zeolite softener was 90% exhausted, when 10,000 L of hard water were passed through it. The softener required 200 L of NaCl solution of strength 50 g NaCl/L of solution. What is the hardness of water ?

17. An exhausted zeolite softener was regenerated by passing 150 litres of NaCl solution having a strength of 150 g/L of NaCl. If the hardness of water is 600 ppm, calculate the total volume of water that is softened by this softener ?

18. An exhausted zeolite was regenerated by 150 litres of NaCl having strength 150 gm/lit. How many litres of a hard water having hardness 400 ppm as $CaCO_3$ can be softened by this softener ?

UNIVERSITY QUESTIONS

DECEMBER 2012

1. Explain the method of internal treatment of Boiler Feed water.   **(6 Marks)**

   Ans. Refer to Article 1.15 on Page No. 1.26.

2. Explain any six principles of Green Chemistry.   **(6 Marks)**

   Ans. Refer to Article 1.20 on Page No. 1.40.

MAY 2013

1. Explain boiler corrosion and caustic embrittlement as ill effects of using hard water in boilers. State their causes and preventive measures.   **(6 Marks)**

   Ans. Refer to Article 1.12.1, 1.12.2, 1.12.3 and 1.13 on Page Nos. 1.24 to 1.26.

2. 50 ml std. hard water containing 1.2 gm $CaCO_3$ per lit. required 15 ml EDTA solution for the end point. Where as 50 ml sample water required 19 ml of EDTA solution and 50 ml boiled sample water required 11 ml of EDTA solution for the end point. Calculate, total, temporary and permanent hardness of sample water in ppm. **(3 Marks)**

   Ans. Refer to Example No 1.2 on Page No. 1.10 [Problem is same only values are different.]

3. What are the drawbacks of traditional synthesis of Indigo dye? Which is the starting substance in its green route synthesis? What are the advantages of green route synthesis over traditional?   **(3 Marks)**

   Ans. Refer to Article 1.23 on Page No. 1.47 and Article 1.19 on Page No. 1.40.

NOVEMBER 2013

1. Explain formation of scales in boiler, give their disadvantages and methods of removal. **(6 Marks)**

   Ans. Refer to Article 1.11.2 on Page No. 1.22.

2. State the problems in traditional synthesis route and advantages of green route in manufacture of adipic acid. **(3 Marks)**

   Ans. Refer to Article 1.21 on Page No. 1.45 and 1.46.

3. A zeolite softner gets exhausted on softening 4000 litres of hard water. Calculate hardness of the water if the exhausted zeolite requires 10 litres of 10% NaCl solution for regeneration. **(3 Marks)**

   Ans. Refer to Example type 1.13 on Page No. 1.40.

MAY 2014

1. Describe Ion exchange method for softening of hard water. **(6 Marks)**

   Ans. Refer to Article 1.16.2 on Page No. 1.30.

2. Define caustic embrittlement. Give causes and prevention of caustic embrittlement in boiler. **(3 Marks)**

   Ans. Refer to Article 1.13 on Page No. 1.25.

DECEMBER 2014

1. Define scale and sludge. Give the causes, disadvantages and removal of scale and sludge formation in boiler. **(6 Marks)**

   Ans. Refer to Article 1.11.1 on Page No. 1.21.

2. What are the merits of green synthesis and demerits of traditional synthesis of indigo dye ? **(3 Marks)**

   Ans. Refer to Article 1.23 on Page No. 1.47.

3. A water sample is non alkaline to phenolphthalein indicator. However, 100 ml of the same sample on titration with 0.02 N H_2SO_4 requires 14.5 ml of acid to obtain end point using methyl orange indicator. Identify type of alkalinity and determine its extent. **(3 Marks)**

   Ans. Similar to Example 1.9 on Page No. 1.18.

MAY 2015

1. What are 'zeolites' ? Explain zeolite process of softening of water. Give regeneration reactions, advantages and disadvantages of the process. **(6 Marks)**

   Ans. Refer to Article 1.16.1 on Page No. 1.28.

2. Explain any three principles of Green Chemistry. **(3 Marks)**

   Ans. Refer to Article 1.20 on Page No. 1.40.

3. 50 ml of water sample requires 18 ml of 0.5 MEDTA during titration. Whereas 50 ml of boiled water sample requires 12.5 ml of same EDTA in the titration. Calculate total, temporary and permanent hardness of water sample. **(3 Marks)**

   Ans. Refer to Example 1.2 on Page No. 1.10. (Problem is same only values are different).

NOVEMBER 2015

1. Discuss the Ion-Exchange method for softening of hard water with the help of reactions involved in removal of ions and regeneration of the exchangers. Draw a neat labelled diagram and give limitations of the process. **(6 Marks)**

   Ans. Refer to Article 1.16.2 on Page No. 1.30.

2. Give the demerits of the traditional route and merits of the green route of synthesis of polycarbonate. **(3 Marks)**

   Ans. Refer to Article 1.22 on Page No. 1.46.

3. 50 ml of water sample required 12.1 ml of N/50 HCl to reach the phenolphthalein end-point and 18.5 ml of the same acid for the methyl orange end-point. Calculate types and amount of alkalinities present. **(3 Marks)**

   Ans. Refer to Example 1.8 on Page No. 1.17 (Same method).

MAY 2016

1. Describe Demineralisation/Deionization method with figure, process, ion exchange and regeneration reactions for softening of hard water. **(6 Marks)**

   Ans. Refer to Article 1.16.2 on Page No. 1.30.

2. Explain any three principles of green chemistry. **(3 Marks)**

   Ans. Refer to Article 1.20 on Page No. 1.40.

✠ ✠ ✠

ELECTRO ANALYTICAL TECHNIQUES

2.1 INTRODUCTION

In our day to day life, we come across large number of materials ranging from toothpaste, brush, food, clothes, vehicles, various instruments etc. All these items are made up of different materials. Material is constituted of atoms of different elements in some fixed proportion. Each type of material shows some characteristic properties e.g. metals have luster and carry electrical current or diamond has sparkle. Whenever we come across any material, we wonder (i) why the material looks, the way it looks ? (ii) why it behaves, the way it behaves ? (iii) where it can be used and how it can be used ? Answers to most of such questions lie in finding out the chemical constitution of the substance.

There are two aspects of chemical analysis (i) Qualitative and (ii) Quantitative.

•   Qualitative analysis stops at the stage of identification of the elements, ions, i.e. constituents and confirmation of their existence e.g. In 12th standard chemistry practicals viz. qualitative analysis of inorganic powder, one stops after identifying and confirming the acidic and basic radicals.

•   Quantitative analysis goes further and gives its complete chemical constitution in the form of concentration or percentage of each individual constituent e.g. coal sample contains - 80 % carbon, 14 % hydrogen, 2 % oxygen, 0.5 % sulphur, 3.5 % nitrogen.

•   It is easy to see that quantitative analysis gives more substantial information about the chemical constitution of substance under study. To generate such type of information, some analysis should be carried out on the sample.

•   Till the beginning of 20th century, chemical analysis was carried out by separation, purification and identification of chemical constituents. The methods known till that time were distillation, gravimetry and volumetry. These methods are called as classical methods of analysis. The classical methods require simple instruments like burner, filtration pumps, measuring cylinder, burette, pipette, separating funnel, volumetric flask, etc.

In the mid 1930's, chemists began to look for some advance techniques for chemical analysis. This was a result of pain taking efforts of number of scientists working in various branches of physics, chemistry, engineering etc. Scientists working on various forms of energy like light, electricity, magnetism, thermodynamics were responsible for preparing the background work for development of large number of instrumental methods of chemical analysis.

- To illustrate this let us take an example of Swedish Physicist Anderson Joan Angstrom, (1814-1874). He studied the solar spectrum and established that the solar radiation comprises of several regions of different wavelengths ranging from radiowaves with $\lambda - 10^3$ cm to Gamma rays with $\lambda - 10^{-11}$ cm. He studied the solar spectrum and developed valuable technique of spectroscopy. His work fetched him Noble prize and in his honour the unit of wavelength is called as Angstrom unit A° (1 A° = 10^{-8} cm).

- With advancement in electronics, computer, nuclear physics, it is now possible to carry out qualitative as well as quantitative analysis with high speed and accuracy.

- Analytical chemistry has been important since the early days of chemistry, providing methods for determining which elements and chemicals are present in the world around us. During this period significant analytical contributions to chemistry include the development of systematic elemental analysis by Justus von Liebig and systematized organic analysis based on the specific reactions of functional groups.

- The first instrumental analysis was flame emissive spectrometry developed by Robert Bunsen and Gustav Kirchhoff who discovered rubidium (Rb) and caesium (Cs) in 1860. Most of the major developments in analytical chemistry take place after 1900. During this period, instrumental analysis becomes progressively dominant in the field. In particular many of the basic spectroscopic and spectrometric techniques were discovered in the early 20th century and refined in the late 20th century.

- The separation sciences follow a similar time line of development and also become increasingly transformed into high performance instruments. In 1970s many of these techniques began to be used together to achieve a complete characterization of samples.

- Starting in approximately the 1970s into the present day analytical chemistry has progressively become more inclusive of biological questions (bioanalytical chemistry), whereas, it had previously been largely focused on inorganic or small organic molecules. Lasers have been increasingly used in chemistry as probes and even to start and influence a wide variety of reactions. The late 20th century also saw an expansion of the application of analytical chemistry from somewhat academic chemical questions to forensic, environmental, industrial and medical questions, such as in histology.

- Modern analytical chemistry is dominated by instrumental analysis. Many analytical chemists focus on a single type of instrument. Academics tend to either focus on new applications and discoveries or on new methods of analysis. The discovery of a chemical present in blood that increases the risk of cancer would be a discovery that an analytical chemist might be involved in. An effort to develop a new method might involve the use of a tunable laser to increase the specificity and sensitivity of a spectrometric method. Many methods, once developed, are kept purposely static so that data can be compared over long periods of time. This is particularly true in industrial quality assurance (QA), forensic and environmental applications. Analytical chemistry plays an increasingly important role in the pharmaceutical industry where, aside from Quality Assurance, it is used in discovery of new drug candidates and in clinical applications where understanding the interactions between the drug and the patient are critical.

2.1.1 Classical Methods

Although modern analytical chemistry is dominated by sophisticated instrumentation, the roots of analytical chemistry and some of the principles used in modern instruments are from traditional techniques many of which are still used today.

- **Qualitative Analysis**

  A qualitative analysis determines the presence or absence of a particular compound, but not the mass or concentration i.e. it is not related to quantity.

- **Gravimetric Analysis**

  Gravimetric analysis involves determining the amount of material present by weighing the sample before and/or after some transformation. A common example used in undergraduate education is the determination of the amount of water in a hydrate by heating the sample to remove the water such that the difference in weight is due to the loss of water.

- **Volumetric Analysis**

  Titration involves the addition of a reactant to a solution being analyzed until some equivalence point is reached. Often the amount of material in the solution being analyzed may be determined. Most familiar to those who have taken college chemistry is the acid-base titration involving a colour changing indicator. There are many other types of titrations, for example potentiometric titrations. These titrations may use different types of indicators to reach some equivalence point.

2.1.2 Instrumental Methods

Analytical chemistry courses usually emphasize equilibrium, spectroscopic and electrochemical analysis, separations and statistics.

Methods of Detecting Analytes used in Instrumental Methods:

- Physical means
  - mass
  - colour
  - refractive index
  - thermal conductivity
- With electromagnetic radiation (spectroscopy)
  - absorption
  - emission
  - scattering
- By an electric change
  - electrochemistry
  - mass spectrometry

2.2 INSTRUMENTAL METHODS OF ANALYSIS

Due to its chemical constitution a material has peculiar physical, optical, electrical, magnetic and mechanical properties. Investigation of one or more of these properties can give idea about the chemical constitution of the material. This is the general philosophy of instrumental methods of analysis. Interaction of a material with any form of energy can be used for identifying the material. The span of instrumental method has broadened sufficiently and now it has become a very important branch of analytical chemistry. Various techniques used currently are listed in Table 2.1.

Table 2.1: Various Instrumental Methods of Chemical Analysis

Sr. No.	Analyte Property under Study	Instrumental Methods used for Analysis
1.	Absorption of radiation	x-ray, ultraviolet, visible, infrared - spectrophotometry, nuclear magnetic resonance, electron spin resonance spectroscopy.
2.	Emission of radiation	x-ray, UV, visible, IR spectroscopy, fluorescence, phosphorescence
3.	Scattering of radiation	Raman spectroscopy, Turbidimetry, Nephelometry
4.	Diffraction of radiation	x-ray, electron and neutron diffraction analysis.
5.	Rotation of radiation	Polarimetry, circular dichroism
6.	Electrical potential	Potentiometry, chromopotentiometry
7.	Electrical charge	Coulometry, dielectric measurements
8.	Electric current/resistance	Polarography, amperometry, conductometry, volume resistivity
9.	Mass to charge ratio	Mass spectroscopy
10.	Rate of reaction	Chemical kinetics
11.	Thermal properties	Thermogravimetry (TG), Differential thermal analysis (DTA), differential scanning calorimetry (DSC), thermodilatometry, Thermal conductivity measurement
12.	Radioactivity	Neutron activation analysis (NAA), dosimetry
13.	Adsorption of sample on stationary phase and desorption	Gas chromatography (GC)
14.	Partition or distribution of sample in various solvents	Liquid Chromatography (LC), High Performance Liquid Chromatography (HPLC)
15.	Surface analysis	Ion Scattering Spectrometry (ISS), Secondary Ion Mass Spectroscopy (SIMS), Auger Emission Spectroscopy (AES), Electron Spectroscopy for Chemical Analysis (ESCA)
16.	Hydrogen ion concentration	pH metry.

2.3 ADVANTAGES AND LIMITATIONS OF INSTRUMENTAL METHODS

Before going into the details of various methods of analysis, it is relevant to know what are advantages and limitations of instrumental methods.

Advantages:

- Instruments have high sensitivity and very low level sample concentrations. Ingredients can be estimated. e.g. volumetric methods can give sample concentrations upto 10^{-3} N, whereas using atomic absorption spectroscopy concentrations of ppm (parts per million) or ppb (parts per billion) levels can be estimated with high accuracy.

- The results obtained are more accurate and reproducible.

- The reliability of the results is high.

- Large number of samples can be analysed with equal sensitivity and high accuracy.

- Estimations can be carried out on molecular, atomic or even subatomic levels.

- Poisonous, carcinogenic and explosive samples can be handled safely.

- Samples which are costly, scarce or which have historic importance can be estimated using non-destructive testing methods like neutron activation analysis or x-ray powder diffraction methods. After the analysis is complete, sample remains unaffected.

- Instrumental methods are fast as compared to classical methods like gravimetry, hence the results are obtained in less time which is necessary in quality control laboratories.

- These methods require very low amount of sample e.g. in gas chromatography about 10 μl of sample is needed.

- Classical methods require large number of reagents and involve frequent weighing, drying, filtering type of operations whereas instrumental methods require very less number of reagents and very little or no sample preparation is required.

- Instrumental methods can be fully automatic and hence require less human attention due to which personal errors are reduced to a large extent.

- Very slow, very fast reactions or radioactive decay which may require very less or more time (half life period of radioactive isotopes range from few milliseconds to thousands of years) can be studied using instrumental methods.

Limitations:

- Frequent calibration and standardization is necessary.

- Cost of some instruments are high.

- Specialized training is required for handling sophisticated instruments.
- Some instruments occupy large space.
- For most of the instruments, undisturbed power supply is essential.

There are two categories of electrochemical processes that are applied to quantitative measurements:

1. Potentiometry - measurement of a potential (voltage)
2. Amperometry - measurement involving a current

2.4 INTRODUCTION TO ELECTROANALYTICAL METHODS OF ANALYSIS

- Analytical techniques based on electrochemical principles make up one of the three major divisions of instrumental analytical chemistry. Each basic electrical measurement of current, resistance, and voltage has been used alone or in combination for analytical purposes. If these electrical properties are measured as a function of time, many additional electroanalytical methods of analysis are possible. A summary of electroanalytical methods is shown in Table 2.2.

- The individual techniques are best recognized by their excitation-response characteristics. Less confusion arises when each technique is described by an operational nomenclature that consists of an independent-variable part followed by a dependent-variable part. An example is voltammetry. The name is often preceded by system-specific modifiers such as cyclic voltammetry or square-wave voltammetry. There are highly refined ways of making reliable electrical measurements in the submicroampere and microvolt range. Reliable analyses at the picogram range are possible. By contrast, selectivity is one of the weakest aspects of electrochemical methods due to poor resolution. However, the combination of electroanalytical methods with chromatography is a powerful tool for both qualitative and quantitative work. Chromatography provides the selectivity and electroanalytical methods provide the sensitivity.

- Electroanalytical methods are conveniently divided into two categories: steady state and transient. The steady-state or static methods, such as potentiometry are firmly rooted in the basic concepts of equilibrium and mass action, and the rigor of their presentation in introductory analytical and physical chemistry courses is considered adequate. Steady-state methods entail measurements of the potential difference at zero current. The system defined by the solid-solution interface is not disturbed and equilibrium is maintained. Time is effectively eliminated as a variable, and equilibrium is assured by vigorously stirring the solution with the indicator electrode held stationary or vice versa. Any concentration gradients at the solution-electrode interface are completely or nearly completely eliminated. In such cases, the indicator electrode potential is related to bulk and surface concentration.

Table 2.2: Selected Electroanalytical Methods

Quantity Measured	Variable Controlled	Name of Method
E	$i = 0$	1. Ion selective potentiometry 2. Null-point potentiometry
E versus volume of titrant	$i = 0$	Potentiometric titrations
Weight of separated phase	E	Controlled potential electrodeposition
i versus E	Concentration	Voltammetry
	t	Linear potential sweep stripping chronoamperometry
	t	Linear potential sweep voltammetry
i versus volume of titrant	E	Amperometric titrations
Coulombs (current × time)	E	Coulometry
1/R (conductance)	Concentration	Conductance measurements
1/R versus volume of titrant		Conductometric titrations

- Voltammetry is concerned with the current-potential relationship in an electrochemical cell and, in particular, with the current-time response of an electrode at a controlled potential. In a typical voltammetric experiment the amount of material actually removed or converted to another form is quite small. Polarography is the name applied to dc voltammetry at the dropping mercury electrode. Although the term polarography is acceptable in, this context, its more general usage is undesirable.

- The integrated current (current multiplied by time), or charge (coulombs), is a measure of the total amount of material converted to another form. In controlled-potential coulometry and in controlled-potential electroanalysis, this corresponds to the total removal of the reactant solute species. There is yet another group of methods in which electron-transfer reactions and diffusional transport are unimportant. Charge transport by migration forms the basis for conductometry and conductometric titrations.

2.4.1 Criteria for Selection of a Method

As seen from Table 2.2 there are large number of instrumental methods available. When any sample comes to a chemist, selection of proper method of analysis is very important step. Number of factors should be considered for deciding the most appropriate method of analysis. Some important factors are listed on next page.

- Quantity of sample available and cost of the sample.
- Permissible cost of analysis.
- Time available for analysis.

- Level of accuracy which is desired for the result.
- Availability of the instruments and expertise of the analyst.
- Number of samples to be analysed.
- Types of impurities present in the sample and their effect on the analytical results of the sample.

2.5 ELECTROCHEMICAL CELLS

- Electrode potentials are the electromotive force (emf) of electrochemical cells formed by the combination of an individual half-cell with a standard hydrogen electrode, with any liquid-junction potential that arises being set at zero. Thus, when the emf of each half-cell is mentioned, what is actually implied is the emf of the cell:

  Pt, H_2 (1 atm) $|H^+$ (M = 1.228) $\| M^{n+}$ (a = 1) $M°$ ... (2.1)

  Standard hydrogen electrode Individual half-cell liquid junction

- In this notation, a vertical line represents a phase boundary and a comma separates two components in the same phase. A double vertical line represents a phase boundary, which may have an associated liquid-junction potential.

- The overall chemical reaction that takes place in the cell is made up of two independent half-reactions, which describe the real chemical changes. All electro analytical techniques are based on formation of different types of electrochemical cells.

2.6 CONDUCTOMETRY   [Dec. 14, May 14, 15]

Terms Involved:

1. **Electrolytic Conductance:**

The conductance is the property of the conductor (metallic as well as electrolytic) which facilitates the flow of electricity through it. It is equal to the reciprocal of resistance i.e.,

$$\text{Conductance} = \frac{1}{\text{Resistance}} = \frac{1}{R} \qquad \text{... (i)}$$

It is expressed in the unit called reciprocal ohm (ohm^{-1} or mho) or siemens.

2. **Specific Conductance or Conductivity:**

- The resistance of any conductor varies directly as its length (l) and inversely as its cross-sectional area (a), i.e.,

$$R \propto \frac{1}{a} \text{ or } R = \rho \frac{1}{a} \qquad \text{... (ii)}$$

where ρ is called the specific resistance.

If $l = 1$ cm and a = 1 cm^2, then

$$R = \rho \qquad \text{... (iii)}$$

- The specific resistance is, thus defined as the resistance of one centimeter cube of a conductor.

- The reciprocal of specific resistance is termed as the specific conductance or it is the conductance of one centimeter cube of a conductor.

  It is denoted by the symbol ρ. Thus,

$$K = \frac{1}{\rho}, \text{ where } K = \text{Kappa – the specific conductance} \quad \ldots \text{(iv)}$$

- Specific conductance is also called conductivity.

  From equation (ii), we have

$$\rho = \frac{a}{1/R} \quad \text{or} \quad \frac{1}{\rho} = \frac{1}{a} \cdot \frac{1}{R}$$

$$K = 1/a \times C \ (1/z = \text{cell constant}$$

  or   Specific conductance = Conductance × Cell constant

- In the case of electrolytic solutions, the specific conductance is defined as the conductance of a solution of definite dilution enclosed in a cell having two electrodes of unit area separated by one centimeter apart as shown in Fig. 2.1.

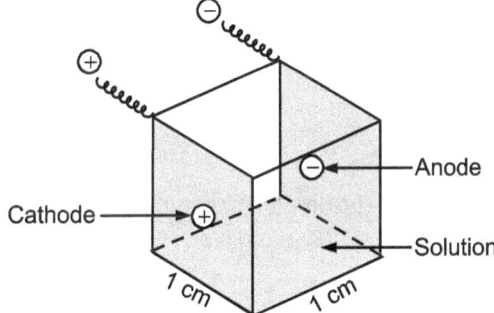

Fig. 2.1: Representation of specific conductance

- The unit of specific conductance is $ohm^{-1} cm^{-1}$.

3. Kohlrausch Law:

- Friedrich Wilhelm Georg Kohlrausch (October 14, 1840 – January 17, 1910) was a German physicist who investigated the conductive properties of electrolytes and contributed to the knowledge of their behaviour. In 1874 he demonstrated that an electrolyte has a definite and constant amount of electrical resistance. By observing the dependence of conductivity upon dilution, he could determine the transfer velocities of the ions (charged atoms or molecules) in solution. He used alternating current to prevent the deposition of electrolysis products; this enabled him to obtain very precise results.

- From 1875 to 1879, he examined numerous salt solutions, acids and solutions of other materials. His efforts resulted in the law of independent migration of ions, that is, each type of migrating ion has a specific electrical resistance no matter what its original molecular combination may have been, and therefore that a solution's electrical resistance was due only to the migrating ions of a given substances. Kohlrausch showed for weak (incompletely dissociated) electrolytes that the more dilute a solution, the greater its molar conductivity due to increased ionic dissociation.

- "At infinite dilution, when dissociation is complete, each ion makes a definite contribution towards equivalent conductance of the electrolyte irrespective of the nature of the ion with which it is associated and the value of equivalent conductance at infinite dilution for any electrolyte is the sum of contribution of its constituent ions", i.e., anions and cations. Thus,

$$\Lambda_\infty = \lambda_a + \lambda_c$$

- The λ_a and λ_c are called the ionic conductance of cation and anion at infinite dilution respectively. The ionic conductances are proportional to their ionic mobilities. Thus, at infinite dilution,

$$\lambda_c = ku_c$$
and
$$\lambda_a = ku_a$$

- where u_c and u_a are ionic mobilities of cation and anion respectively at infinite dilution. The value of k is equal to 96500 C, i.e., one Faraday.

- Thus, assuming that increase in equivalent conductance with dilution is due to increase in degree of dissociation of the electrolyte, it is evident that the electrolyte achieves the degree of dissociation as unity when it is completely ionized at infinite dilution. Therefore, at any other dilution, the equivalent conductance is proportional to the degree of dissociation. Thus,

Degree of dissociation $\quad a = \dfrac{\Lambda}{\Lambda_\infty}$

$$= \frac{\text{(Equivalent conductance at a given concentration)}}{\text{(Equivalent conductance at infinite dilution)}}$$

- Calculation of Absolute Ionic Mobilities:

It has been experimentally found that ionic conductance is directly proportional to ionic mobilities.

$$\lambda_+ \propto u_+$$
$$\lambda_- \propto u_-$$

where u_+ and u_- are ionic mobilities of cations and anions.

$$\lambda_+ = Fu_+$$
$$\lambda_- = Fu_-$$

where,
$$F = \text{Faraday}$$
$$= 96500 \text{ coulomb}$$

$$\text{Ionic mobility} = \frac{\text{Ionic velocity}}{\text{Potential gradient}}$$

$$= \text{Ionic velocity (cm/sec))/Potential gradient (volt)/electrode separation}$$

2.6.1 Conductometric Titrations

- Acid-base titrations (redox titrations) are known to us in which commonly indicators are used to locate the end point e.g. methyl orange, phenolphthalene for acid-base titrations and starch solutions for iodometry type redox process.

- However, electrical conductance measurement can be used as a tool to locate the end point. e.g. HCl versus NaOH. Consider a solution of a strong acid, hydrochloric acid, HCl for instance, to which a solution of a strong base, sodium hydroxide NaOH, is added. The reaction occurs. For each amount of NaOH added equivalent amount of hydrogen ions is removed. Effectively, the faster moving H^+ cation is replaced by the slower moving Na^+ ion, and the conductivity of the titrated solution as well as the measured conductance of the cell fall. This continues until the equivalence point is reached, at which we have a solution of sodium chloride, NaCl.

- If more base is added an increase in conductivity or conductance is observed, since more ions are being added and the neutralization reaction no longer removes an appreciable number any of them. Consequently, in the titration of a strong acid with a strong base, the conductance has a minimum at the equivalence point.

- This minimum can be used instead of an indicator dye to determine the end point of the titration. Conductometric titration curve is a plot of the measured conductance or conductivity values against the number of millilitres of NaOH solution. Fig. 2.2 shows typical conductometric titration curves.

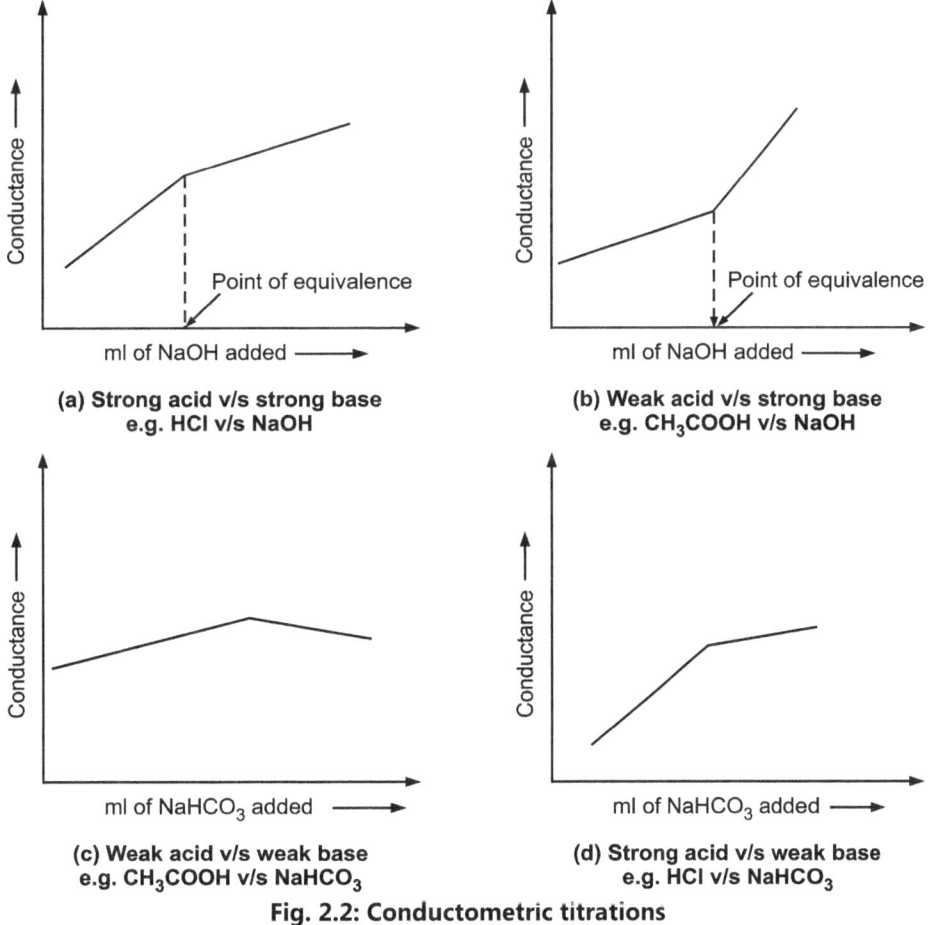

Fig. 2.2: Conductometric titrations

2.7 POTENTIOMETRY

- Potentiometry is the field of electroanalytical chemistry in which potential is measured under the conditions of no current flow. The measured potential may then be used to determine the analytical quantity of interest, generally the concentration of some component of the analyte solution. The potential that develops in the electrochemical cell is the result of the free energy change that would occur if the chemical phenomena were to proceed until the equilibrium condition has been satisfied.

$$\Delta G_{r \times n} = -nFE_{r \times n}$$

- This concept is typically introduced in quantitative analysis courses in relation to electrochemical cells that contain an anode and a cathode. For these electrochemical cells, the potential difference between the cathode electrode potential and the anode electrode potential is the potential of the electrochemical cell.

$$E_{cell} = E_{cathode} - E_{anode}$$

- If the reaction is conducted under standard state conditions, this equation allows the calculation of the standard cell potential. When the reaction conditions are not standard state, however, one must utilize the Nernst equation to determine the cell potential.

$$E_{cell} = E^{\circ} - \frac{RT}{nF} \ln (K_{eq})$$

- Physical phenomena which do not involve explicit redox reactions, but whose initial conditions have a non-zero free energy, also will generate a potential. An example of this would be ion concentration gradients across a semi-permeable membrane. This can also be a potentiometric phenomena, and is the basis of measurements that use *ion-selective electrodes*.

$$E_{mem} = (constant) - \frac{RT}{z_i F} \ln (a_i)$$

- Potentiometric methods embrace two major types of analyses. One involves the direct measurement of an electrode potential from which the activity (or concentration) of an active ion may be derived. The other type involves measuring the changes in the electromotive force (emf) brought about by the addition of a titrant to the sample.

2.7.1 Ion-Selective Electrode (ISE)

- An Ion-Selective Electrode (ISE) produces a potential that is related to the concentration of an analyte. Making measurements with an ISE is therefore a form of *potentiometry*. The most common ISE is the pH electrode, which contains a thin glass membrane that responds to the H^+ concentration in a solution.

- ISEs for other ions must have an appropriate membrane that is sensitive to the ion of interest but not sensitive to interfering ions. For example, a LaF_3 crystal can function as an electrode membrane for fluoride ions. Many of the commercial ISEs use a polymer membrane to embed ion-sensitive species that are sensitive to Ca^{2+}, NO_3^-, NH_4^+ or other common ions.

Theory:

- The potential difference across an ion-sensitive membrane is:

$$E = K + (2.303\ RT/nF)\ \log\ (a)$$

where K is a constant to account for all other potentials, R is the gas constant, T is temperature, n is the charge of the ion (including the sign), F is Faraday's constant, and a is the activity of the analyte ion.

- A plot of measured potential versus log (a) will therefore give a straight line. ISEs are susceptible to several interferences. Samples and standards are therefore diluted 1:1 with total ionic strength adjuster and buffer (TISAB). The TISAB consists of 1 M NaCl to adjust the ionic strength, acetic acid/acetate buffer to control pH, and a metal complexing agent.

Instrumentation

- ISEs consist of the ion-selective membrane, an internal reference electrode, an external reference electrode, and a voltmeter. A typical meter is shown in the document on the pH meter. Schematic of an ISE measurement.

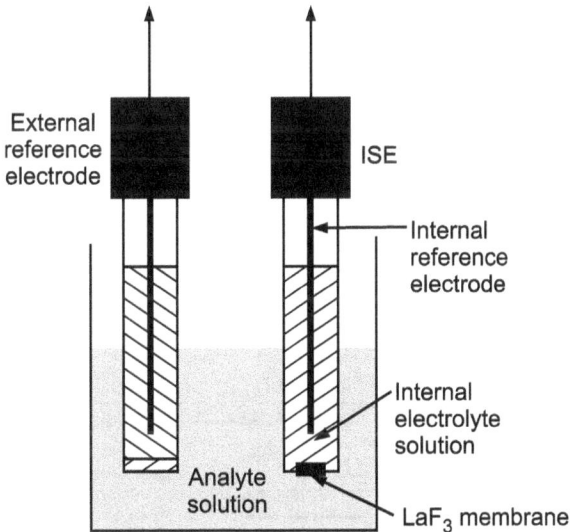

Fig. 2.3: Ion-selective electrode

- Commercial ISEs often combine the two electrodes into one unit that are then attached to a pH meter.

2.7.2 Potentiometric Titrations

- Less rigorous measurement techniques are involved when following the changes in the cell emf brought about by the addition of a titrant of precisely known concentration to the test solution. The equipment needed to carry out a classical potentiometric titration is illustrated in Fig. 2.4.

- The method can be applied to any titrimetric reaction for which an indicator electrode is available to follow the activity of at least one of the substances involved. A reproducible equilibrium is of little concern. Requirements for reference electrodes are greatly relaxed.

- In contrast to direct potentiometric measurements, potentiometric titrations generally offer increased accuracy and precision. Accuracy is increased because measured potentials are used to detect rapid changes in activity that occur at the equivalence point of the titration.

- This rate of emf change is usually considerably greater than the response slope, which limits precision in direct potentiometry. Furthermore, it is the change in emf versus titration volume rather than the absolute value of the emf that is of interest. Thus, the influence of liquid-junction potentials and activity coefficients is minimized.

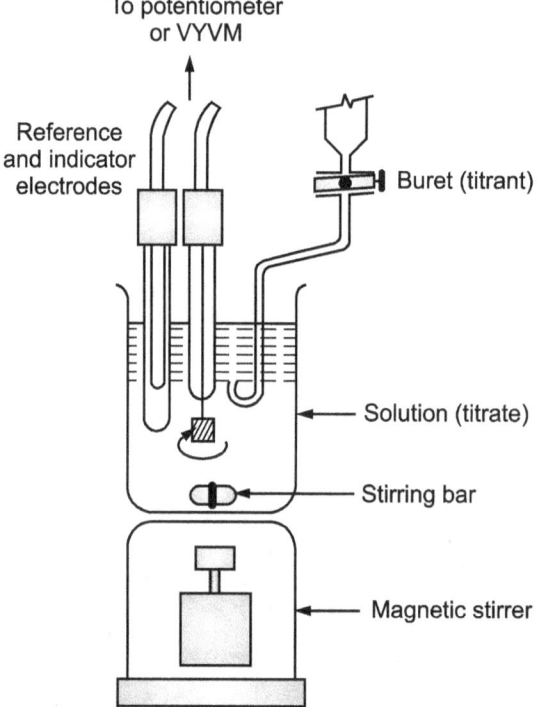

Fig. 2.4: Equipments for potentiometric titrations

2.7.3 Location of the Equivalence Point

- The critical problem in a titration is the recognition of the point at which the quantities of reacting species are present in equivalent amounts - the equivalence point. The titration curve can be followed point by point, plotting as the ordinate successive values of the cell emf versus the corresponding volume of titrant added as the abscissa.

- Additions of titrant should be the smallest accurately measurable increments that provide an adequate density of points, particularly in the vicinity of the equivalence point. Over most of the titration range the cell emf varies gradually, but near the end point the cell emf changes very abruptly. The resulting titration curve resembles Fig. 2.5 (a).

- The problem in general is to detect this sharp change in cell emf that occurs in the vicinity of the equivalence point. The equivalence point may be calculated, as outlined in textbooks on analytical chemistry.

- Usually the analyst must be content with finding a reproducible point, as close as possible to the equivalence point, at which the titration can be considered complete - the end point. By inspection the end point can be located from the inflection point of the titration curve. This is the point that corresponds to the maximum rate of change of cell emf per unit volume of titrant added (usually 0.05 or 0.1 mL). The distinctness of the end point increases as the reaction involved becomes more nearly quantitative.

- Once the cell emf has been established for a given titration, it can be used to indicate subsequent end points for the same chemical reaction. In the immediate vicinity of the equivalence point the concentration of the original reactant becomes very small, and it usually becomes impossible for the ion or ions to control the indicator electrode potential. The cell emf becomes unstable and indefinite because the indicating electrode is no longer bathed with sufficient quantities of each spectroactive species of the desired oxidation/reduction couple.

- Usually a drop or two of the titrant will suffice to carry the titration through the equivalence point and into the region stabilized by the electroactive species of the titrant. However, solutions, more dilute than 10^{-3} M generally do not give satisfactory end points. This is a limitation of potentiometric titrations.

- The end point can be more precisely located from the first or second derivative curves. Although either of these methods of selecting the end point is too laborious to do manually for each titration, the determination of derivatives, inflection points, and equivalence points becomes feasible with appropriate software algorithms.

2.7.4 Potentiometric Titration Fe^{2+}/Ce^{4+}

- It is a redox titration where oxidation of Fe^{2+} takes place, simultaneous reduction of Ce^{4+} takes place to Ce^{3+}, the entire process is involved with one electron transfer. The reaction can be monitored by plotting a potential developed as a function of ml of amount of $CeCl_4$ added.

- The titration uses calomel as a reference electrode. The cell reaction is as given below:

    $Pt \mid Fe^{2+}, Fe^{3+} \parallel Cl^- \mid Hg_2Cl_2, Hg$ Oxidation

and $Pt \mid Ce^{4+}, Ce^{3+} \parallel Cl^- \mid Hg_2Cl_2, Hg$ Reduction

- The experimentation involves use of Ce^{4+} solution in burette and Fe^{2+} in a beaker. The reactions which take place are:

(1) $Fe^{2+} \rightarrow Fe^{3+} + 1e^- \ (\Delta E_1^o = 0.785 \ V)$

(2) $Ce^{4+} + e^- \rightarrow Ce^{3+} \ (\Delta E_2^o = 1.45 \ V)$

Overall reaction: $Fe^{2+} + Ce^{4+} \rightarrow Fe^{3+} + Ce^{3+}$ ($E_{eq\ pt} = 1.1175 \ V$)

- Equilibrium constant of the reaction is 7×10^{11} indicates that reaction will to go quantitative completion.

  (i) The electrode potential at equivalence point is calculated as

  $$E_1 = E_1^o + \frac{0.0591}{n} \log \frac{[Fe^{3+}]}{[Fe^{2+}]} \quad \text{where } n = 1.$$

  (ii) At equivalence point the electrode potential is given by

  $$E_{eq.} = \frac{E_1^o + E_2^o}{2} = \frac{0.785 + 1.45}{2} = 1.1175 \ V$$

  (iii) After the equivalence point the electrode potential is given by

  $$E_2 = E_2^o + \frac{0.0591}{n} \log \frac{Ce^{4+}}{Ce^{3+}}$$

The plot of potentiometric titration will appear as given below.

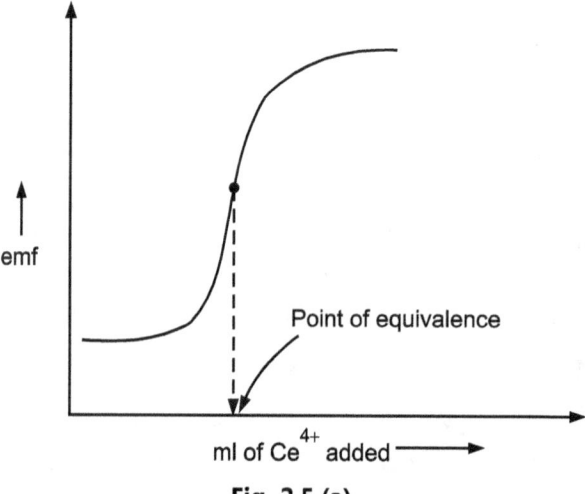

Fig. 2.5 (a)

- It is slightly ambiguous to find out the equivalence point using this plot, hence a derivative plot is advisable. It is obtained by calculating the change in e.m.f. between two consecutive observations as a function of ml of Ce^{4+} added. It is essential to have equal amount of titrant added between every two readings. In the initial part of titration the rate of rise in potential is nearly same towards the end point the rate of change of potential is high.

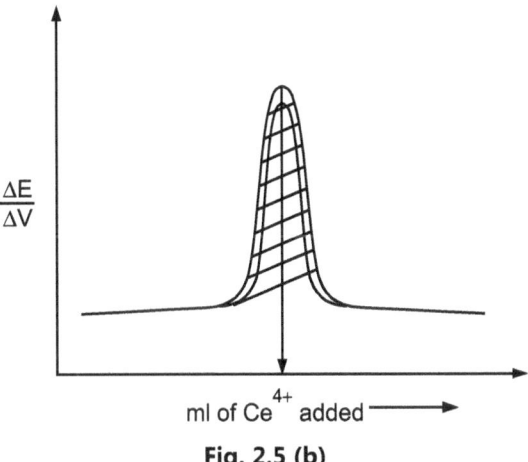

$$\frac{\Delta E}{\Delta V}$$

ml of Ce^{4+} added ⟶

Fig. 2.5 (b)

Second Order Derivative:

If you observe the above plot the peak is not very sharp and the accuracy of the measurement can be further improved further by plotting the second order derivative plot.

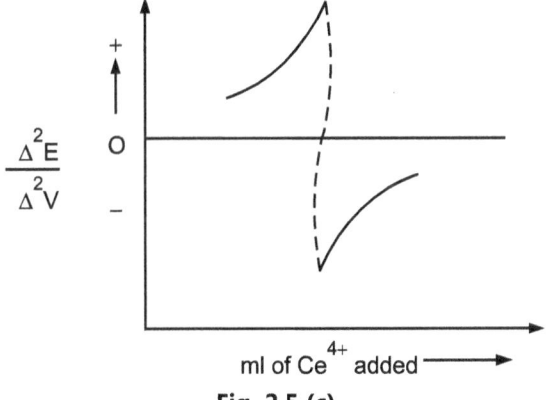

$$\frac{\Delta^2 E}{\Delta^2 V}$$

ml of Ce^{4+} added ⟶

Fig. 2.5 (c)

Here one can easily see that at the equivalence point change in nature of the curve take place removing all ambiguity and accurate measurement of equivalence point occurs.

2.8 ELECTROCHEMICAL CELLS

• In a potentiometric type of sensor, a membrane or sensing surface acts as a half-cell, generating a potential proportional to the logarithm of the analyte activity (concentration). This potential is measured relative to an inert reference electrode that is also in contact with the sample. Potentiometric measurements. Are made under conditions of essentially zero current flow so as not to disturb the equilibrium at the sample-membrane interface.

• For a complete electrochemical cell from which negligible current is drawn, the emf is given by

$$E_{cell} = E_{ind} - E_{ref} + E_j \qquad \qquad ...(2.1)$$

where E_{ind}, E_{ref} and E_j are the potentials of the indicator electrode, the reference electrode, and the liquid-junction potential, respectively. For conditions in which a current is drawn from the cell, the term for the iR drop (the potential gradient across the solution due to the product of the current flowing and the resistance of the solution) must be included in equation (2.1).

- The indicator electrode senses the presence of the analyte in the sample solution, the reference electrode is independent of the sample solution composition, and the liquid (or fluid) junction is an interface between dissimilar solutions.

- In a properly designed system, E_{ref} is a constant and E_j is either constant or negligible. When these conditions are realized, the indicator, electrode can supply information about ion activities.

2.8.1 Reference Electrodes

- A reference electrode is an oxidation/reduction half-cell of known and constant . potential at a particular temperature. Three main requirements for a satisfactory reference electrode systems are reversibility, reproducibility, and stability, which are interrelated. Its potential must not depart from its equilibrium value when current demands are made upon it, such as the passage of a small current through the cell.

- This may become important for miniature electrodes and at low concentrations of the potential-determining ion. The problem can be minimized by selecting a reference electrode with large concentrations of the potential-determining ions with a fairly large active electrode area and a not too small volume of solution.

- Reproducibility involves two aspects. One is the ability of a particular reference electrode to respond according to the Nernst equation without temperature (or concentration) change hysteresis. The other is the feasibility of establishing an easy and standard method of electrode preparation and assembly that will produce electrodes that exhibit a constant potential within an acceptable standard deviation. The third requirement, stability, refers to the useful life of a reference electrode.

- A reference electrode consists three principal parts: (1) an internal element; (2) some filling solution, which constitutes the salt-bridge electrolyte and (3) an area in the tip of the electrode that permits a slow, controlled flow of filling solution to escape the electrode (called the fluid junction) into the sample under a head of a few inches and where an electrical connection is made with the other components of the electrochemical cell.

Internal Elements:

The choice of a reference electrode for most applications is between the mercury/mercury(I) chloride (or calomel) half-cell and the silver/silver chloride half-cell as the internal element. Both are electrodes of the second kind - that is, anion reversible.

When the electrode system is immersed in a filling solution that contains a constant amount of the chloride ion, the electrode potential is constant. The non-polarizability of reference electrodes of this type is specifically designed into the electrode. Through the use of massive metal electrodes accompanied by pastes or coatings of the oxidation product of the half-cell reaction, the internal element offers so large an area that polarization is precluded even at currents considerably larger than those typically drawn by high-input impedance operational amplifiers.

2.8.2 Calomel Electrodes

- Calomel electrodes comprise an inert or unattackable metal, such as platinum, in contact with mercury and paste of mercury chloride, mercury, and potassium chloride, moistened with the filling solution.

- It is enclosed in an inner glass tube and makes contact through a porous plug (e.g. glass wool) with a filling solution of potassium chloride of known concentration (usually 0.1 M, 1.0 M or saturated, 4.2 M) and saturated with mercury(I) chloride.

- The saturated calomel electrode (SCE) is often used because it is easy to prepare and maintain. For accurate work other concentrations of KCl are preferred because they reach their equilibrium potentials more quickly and their potential depends less on temperature.

- The saturated calomel electrode exhibits a perceptible hysteresis following temperature changes, due in part to the time required for a solubility equilibrium to be reestablished. At temperatures higher than 80°C, all calomel electrodes are subject to problems arising from the accelerated disproportionation of mercury(I) to the metal and mercury(II) ions.

2.8.3 Silver/Silver Chloride Electrodes

- The silver/silver chloride electrode is made in wire form and cartridge form. In the former, a silver wire is coated with silver chloride by electrolysis or by dipping into the molten salt. The wire is immersed in a filling solution of potassium chloride of known concentration, usually 1.0 M, and saturated with silver chloride.

- In the cartridge form, the metal is in contact with a paste of the salt moistened with electrolyte, and all is enclosed in an inner glass tube. Contact with the filling solution in the salt bridge is made through a small aperture.

- All silver/silver chloride systems demonstrate excellent electrical and chemical stability. The silver/silver chloride electrode should not be used in solutions that contain proteins, sulfide, bromide, iodide, or any other materials that would precipitate (or complex) with the silver found in the filling solution. Strong reducing agents also should be avoided because they can reduce the silver ions to silver metal at the liquid junction.

2.8.4 Ion-Selective Electrodes

- A number of ion-selective electrodes have taken their place beside the historical pH glass electrode discussed in the preceding section. From the analytical viewpoint, ion-selective electrodes are nearly ideal measurement tools because of their ability to monitor selectively the activity of certain ions in solution both continuously and nondestructively. No oxidation/reduction reactions are involved, in contrast to the direct indicating electrodes used in classical potentiometry.

- All seem to involve an ion-exchange process or a related phenomenon, such as complexation or precipitation, with the active sites on the surface or in the hydrated layer of the electrode membrane.

- The potential of an ion-selective electrode is actually composed of two or more discrete contributions arising from the various processes at the interfaces and in the bulk of the active membrane material. If a charge separation occurs between ions at an interface, a potential difference is generated across that interface. The problem is to find an interface whose composition will selectively favor one type of ion over all others.

- Ion-selective electrodes measure ion activities, the thermodynamically effective free ion concentration.

- In dilute solutions, ion activity usually approaches the ion concentration. Activity measurements are valuable because the activities of ions determine rates of reactions and chemical equilibria. For example, ion activities are important parameters in predicting corrosion rates, extent of precipitation, formation of complexes, solution conductivities, effectiveness of metal pickling baths and electroplating bath solutions and physiological effects of ions in biological fluids.

2.8.5 Glass Membrane Electrodes

- The various types of ion-selective glass electrodes are all members of a continuum of glass electrodes that belong to the "fixed-site" category of ion-exchange membrane electrodes.

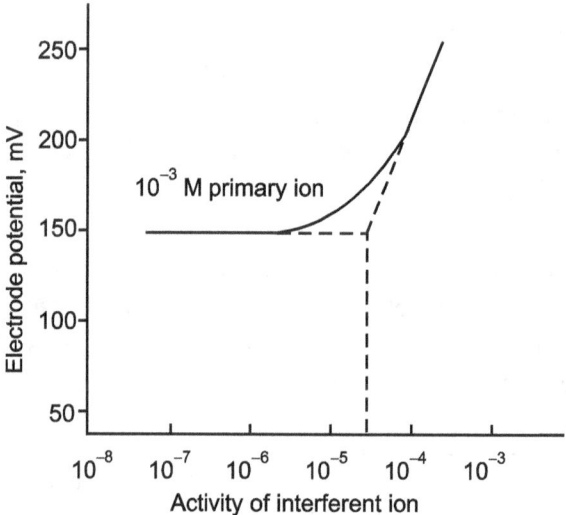

Fig. 2.6: Selective ion electrode response in a solution of the primary ion at varying activities of an interference

- This simply means that the active sites on the surface or in the hydrated layer of the glass are not free to move about during the time scale of the measurement. The electrode potential arises from a combination of cation exchange and cation mobility factors that lead to an accumulation of charge at the glass-solution interface.
- The observed selectivity ratio of these electrodes is the product of the ion-exchange equilibrium constant between the sites and the solution and the mobility ratio of the exchanging ions in the hydrated layer of the glass. Thus, the selectivity properties of a desired electrode can be produced by appropriate adjustment of these parameters by altering the glass composition.

For example, thiocyanate ion can interfere with bromide ion measurements if the reaction

$$SCN^- + AgBr(s) \rightarrow AgSCN(s) + Br^-$$

takes place, which will begin if the ratio of thiocyanate ion activity to bromide ion activity exceeds the value given by the ratio of the solubility products of silver thiocyanate to silver bromide or

$$\frac{1}{k_i} = \frac{a_{SCN}}{a_{Br}} = \frac{1.00 \times 10^{-12}}{5.0 \times 10^{-13}} = 2.0 \qquad \dots (2.2)$$

Failure to give an expected response (slope) also occurs when the concentration of a dilute test solution approximates the solubility of the membrane material.

2.9 PH METRY   [Dec. 12, 14, May 15]

Introduction:

The pH meter measures the pH of a solution using an *ion-selective electrode (ISE)* that responds to the H^+ concentration of the solution. The pH electrode produces a voltage that is proportional to the concentration of H^+ concentration, and making measurements with a pH meter is therefore a form of *potentiometry*. The pH electrode is attached to control electronics which convert the voltage to a pH reading and displays it on a meter.

Instrumentation:

A pH meter consists of a H^+-selective membrane, an internal reference electrode, an .external reference electrode, and a meter with control electronics and display.

2.9.1 The Measurement of pH

- The pH scale is a series of numbers that express the degree of acidity of a solution, as contrasted with the total quantity of acid (or base) in some material as found by an alkalimetric (or acidimetric) titration. Sorensen proposed the term pH and defined it as the negative logarithm of the hydrogen ion concentration, expressed in molarity:

$$pH = -\log [H^+] \qquad \dots (2.3)$$

- The term pH is simply a mathematical symbol of convenience, widely accepted and firmly established, but devoid of exact thermodynamic validity. It is the activity of the hydrogen ion that is formally consistent with the thermodynamics of the pH electromotive cell. The activity definition is

$$paH = \log a_{H^+} \qquad \dots (2.4)$$

- The activity is the product of concentration and an activity coefficient; that is $a_H^+ = f_+[H^+]$. However, single ionic activity coefficients cannot be measured directly, only the mean ionic activity coefficient is available. Now $[H^+]$ and $f_\pm[H^+]$ are often the most useful units for expressing the acidity of aqueous solutions, where $f_\pm$ is the mean ionic activity coefficient. Unfortunately, the established experimental pH method cannot furnish either of these quantities.

Operational Definition of pH:

- The relation by which the emf of a suitable pH measuring electrode is related to the hydrogen ion concentration was developed by Nernst:

$$E = E^\circ - \left(\frac{RT}{nF}\right) \log [H^+]$$

- where E° is a potential dependent on the electrode system used, R is the gas constant, T the absolute temperature, F (the Faraday) is 96,485 coulombs/mole and n is the number of electrons involved in the equilibrium. For $n = 1$, the factor $RT/nF = 0.591$ (at 25°C). Using the Sorenson expression (equation 2.2) for pH,

$$E = E^\circ + 0.0591 \text{ pH} \qquad \qquad \text{... (2.5)}$$

- Equation (2.5) establishes well-known relationship of 59.1 mV per pH unit (at 25°C) for any electrode system that follows the Nernst equation. Strictly, ion-selective electrodes (which include pH-responsive glass electrodes) do not obey the Nernst equation, although, the appropriate equation has a very similar form. The Nernst equation applies to a redox reaction, whereas the equation for ion-selective electrodes applies to an accumulation of charge at an interface without electron transfer.

- Since the glass electrode is widely accepted detector for pH measurements, it is the only pH-responsive element that will be considered in this text. The National Bureau of Standards (USA) pH scale has been established by assigning pH values to certain standard solutions, with the values chosen to give the maximum possible consistency between precise thermodynamic information, such as dissociation constants of weak acids and equation (2.4). In so doing, the pH scale is defined in an operational manner, convenient and easily reproducible but not exact thermodynamically:

$$\text{pH} = \text{pH}_s + \frac{E - E_s}{2.302 \ RT/F} \qquad \qquad \text{... (2.6)}$$

- In this definition, E and E_s are respectively, the emf of an electrochemical cell of the usual design that contains either the unknown solution or a standard reference material of known pH-namely pH_s:

| electrode reversible to hydrogen ions | unknown or standard buffer solution | salt bridge | reference electrode |

- The pH_s reference materials were assigned values from measurements of the emf of cells that contained hydrogen gas and silver/silver chloride electrodes - that is, cells without a liquid junction:

    Pt | H_2 (1 atm), H^+Cl^- (plus K^+Cl^-), AgCl(s) | Ag

    by the equation $E = E° - 0.000198\ T \log f_{H^+}\ f_{Cl^-}\ m_{H^+}\ m_{Cl^-}$ ... (2.7)

- where E° is the standard potential of the cell. By rearranging equation (2.7) in terms of the acidity function, $p(a_{H^+}\ f_{Cl^-})$, one gets

$$p(a_{H^+}\ f_{Cl^-}) = -\log f_{H^+}\ f_{Cl^-}\ m_{H^+} = \frac{E - E°}{0.000198T} + \log m_{Cl^-} \qquad ... (2.8)$$

The pH_s of the chloride-free buffer solution is computed from the equation

$$pH_s = p(a_{H^+}\ f_{Cl^-})° + \log f_{Cl^-}^{\,o} \qquad ... (2.9)$$

- where $p(a_{H^+}\ f_{Cl^-})°$ is the value obtained by evaluating $p(a_{H^+}\ f_{Cl^-})$ at several concentrations of chloride and extrapolation to zero chloride concentration. The activity coefficient of the chloride ion can be estimated for ionic strengths less than 0.1 by the equation

$$-\log f_{Cl^-}^{\,o} = \frac{A\sqrt{\mu}}{1 + 1.5\sqrt{\mu}} \qquad ... (2.10)$$

- where A is a parameter of the Debye-Huckel theory that has a different value at each temperature. The total uncertainty in pH_s, exclusive of any liquid-junction potentials introduced during the calibration of pH equipment, is estimated as 0.005 pH unit (0 to 60°C) and 0.008 pH unit (60 to 95°C). The operational definition of pH is valid for only dilute solutions and for the pH range 2-12 because it is only under these conditions that the liquid-junction potential remains constant between the test solution and the electrolyte in the reference electrode required for the measurement. To detect any serious impairment of the response of a measuring device and electrode assembly outside the pH range 2-12, two secondary standards are included among the pH reference materials. These are potassium tetroxalate and calcium hydroxide solutions.

- For accuracy of ±0.01 pH unit, the temperature should be known to ± 2°C. Not only does the proportionality factor between the cell emf and pH vary with temperature, but dissociation equilibria and junction potentials also have significant temperature coefficients.

- The necessity for estimating the individual activity coefficients of the chloride ion in each reference solution deprives the pH_s value of exact fundamental meaning. Nevertheless, the operational definition of pH, chosen in part for its reasonableness but largely for its utility, agrees as closely as possible with the mathematical concepts evolved from the present state of solution theory. Fortunately, a highly precise knowledge of the solution pH is seldom required. Neither is it necessary to know exactly what a particular pH value means. Often in an industrial process it is sufficient to know that at a certain state a particular pH value is maintained.

2.9.2 pH or pION Measurement System

- The measurement of pH (or pION, or simply pI) is one of the most common analytical techniques used in chemistry laboratories. A pH or pI measurement system always consists of four parts: a sensing electrode, a pH (or ion) meter that contains a high-input-impedance operational amplifier to measure and display the cell potential, a reference electrode and the sample being measured.

- To achieve a reproducibility of ±0.005 pH unit, an amplifier is needed that is reproducible to at least 0.2 mV. The high electrical resistance (5-500 MΩ) of the glass membrane necessitates measuring circuits with a high input-impedance voltmeter. Negligible current must be drawn during the measurement if changes in the ion concentration at the electrode surface are to be avoided and no error is to arise from the voltage drop across the inherent resistance of the electrochemical cell. With glass electrodes the current drawn should be 10^{-12} A or less. pH measurements often suffer from the effects of incorrect materials or incorrect maintenance. Certain protocols should be followed for pH measurements and for properly maintaining a pH meter.

- The pH meter is a voltmeter but with several critical additional functions. Not only does it measure the potential across the pH-sensing and reference electrode system, but it also converts the potential difference measurement at a given temperature into pH terms and it provides mechanisms to correct for the nonideal behaviour of the electrode system.

- The schematic circuit diagram of a potentiometric type of pH or ion meter that is based on an operational amplifier is shown in Fig. 2.7. The operational amplifier not only serves as a high-impedance voltmeter, but also provides stability and automatic operation through the use of the feedback loop. The relationship for the emf of a pH assembly is

$$E = k - KT \, (pH) \qquad\qquad\qquad \text{... (2.11)}$$

Equation (2.11) is the equation of a straight line with slope $-$ KT and a zero-intercept of k.

- The pH-sensing electrode and its reference electrode must have an isopotential point at 0 V. The isopotential point expresses the zero shift in pH terms and is identified with the pH of a solution in which the emf of the pH assembly does not vary with temperature. This is accomplished by using as the internal solution in the pH-sensing electrode a buffer whose pH change with temperature exactly compensates the temperature changes of the internal and external reference electrodes.

- The proper emf/pH slope involves adjusting the KT factor (actually 2.3026 RT/F) to 59.16 mV per pH unit at 25°C by means of a slope control to rotate the emf/pH slope about the isopotential point (usually pH 7.00). The temperature compensator, which is reserved to correct the slope for the actual temperature of the sample, varies the instrument definition of a pH unit from 54.20 mV at 0°C to 66.10 mV at 60°C and 74.04 mV at 100°C. Many pH meters are equipped to accept an automatic temperature compensator probe, which automatically measures the sample temperature and adjusts the meter sensitivity for the correct temperature.

- A single point standardization involves immersing the pH assembly into a standard. reference pH buffer whose value lies near the pH expected for the sample. The meter reading is brought into juxtaposition with the pH_s value by adjusting the intercept (standardization, zero, asymmetry) control.

- This control shifts the response curve laterally until it passes through the isopotential point (Fig. 2.7). The procedure entails adding or subtracting a dc voltage to correct for the offset voltage (from the isopotential point). Once done, the standardization control must remain undisturbed unless the entire standardization step is repeated. Because both the K and T terms affect the slope of the pH response, standardization and calibration are both carried out at the anticipated temperature of the sample.

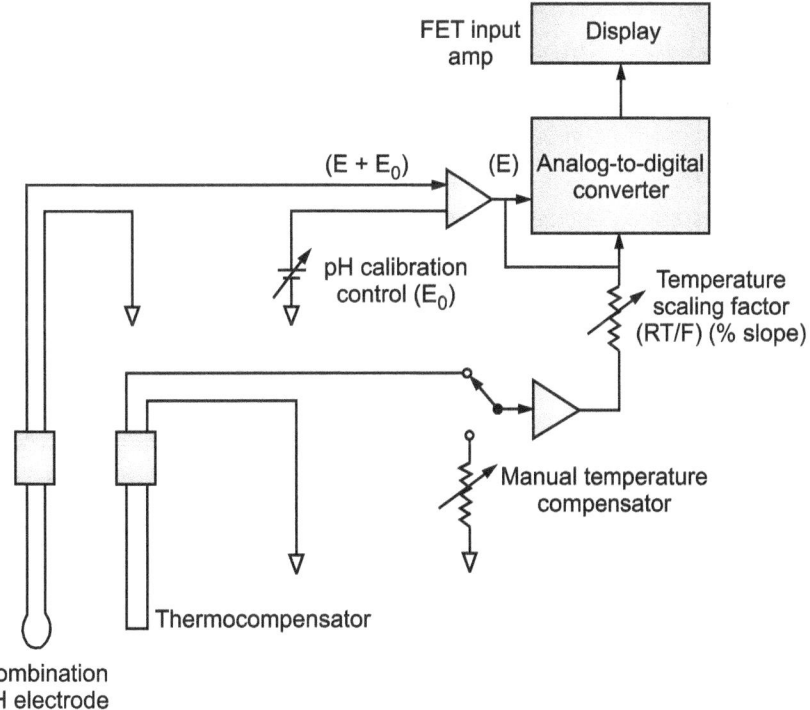

Fig. 2.7: Schematic diagram of a pH meter

- Standardization at only one pH value does not assure the validity of readings at other pH values considerably removed from the value of the standard reference buffer. On pH meters that allow two calibration points, a second step involves the calibration of the pH meter with a second standard reference buffer.

- After the calibration described in the preceding paragraph, the electrode assembly is transferred to either an acidic or basic standard reference buffer so that the two reference buffers bracket the expected pH of the sample. The pH value of the second buffer is set on the meter by adjusting the slope (gain, calibrate) control. What transpires is an adjustment of the amplifier gain to correct for any non-Nernstian behaviour of the indicator electrode. This amounts to adjusting the K term in equation (2.10).

- The preceding discussion concerns traditional pH meters in which an amplifier circuit is used to adjust the signal of the electrode so that it can be read directly in pH units.

- Microcomputer-based pH meters measure the output of the electrode assembly and subject it to appropriate algorithms based on equation (2.11). The algorithms perform compensatory calculations equivalent to standardization and calibration. Most pH meters of this type permit standardization and calibration in any order. However, if steps are taken out of order or steps are introduced in the middle of a prescribed operating protocol, the pH meter may not function properly.

- There is no isopotential point in the meter, the microcomputer typically assumes the isothermal point of the electrode to be pH 7 or 0.0 mV.

2.9.3 Glass-Indicating Electrodes

- The classic electrode assembly consists of a glass pH-indicating electrode and a reference electrode. Typical pH-sensitive glass membranes are either sodium/calcium silicate (Corning 015 glass) or lithium silicates with lanthanum and barium ions added. These added ions act as lattice "tighteners" to retard silicate hydrolysis and lessen alkali ion, chiefly sodium ion, mobility.

- Sodium or lithium ions are the bulk mobile charge carriers under an applied electric field. Upon immersion of the membrane in water, the surface layer becomes involved in an ion-exchange process between the hydrogen ions in the external solution and the sodium or lithium ions of the membrane. The content of H^+ decreases in a complex way with increasing distance into the membrane, whereas Li^+ or Na^+ content increases in such a way that the sum of positive ions, charge carriers, and other cations balances the presumed uniform fixed-site concentration of anions.

- The activity of water in the solution appears to play an important role in the development of the pH response of the glass membrane. If the ionic strength of the solution is extremely high, or if a nonaqueous solvent is present, the measured emf deviates from the expected value. All glass electrodes must be conditioned for a time by soaking in water or in a dilute buffer solution, even though they may be used subsequently in media that are only partly aqueous.

- The conventional pH electrode has an internal reference electrode (silver/silver chloride or calomel) immersed in a chloride salt buffer (usually a phosphate buffet at pH 7) solution, with the glass membrane separating it from the test solution (Fig. 2.8). The body of the glass electrode is a nonconducting glass tube. This is sealed to a bulb made of special conductive glass, which is the pH-sensing membrane.

- The body is filled with a buffered electrolyte with fixed pH value and ionic concentration. A phosphate buffer is used in most electrodes. An external reference electrode completes the assembly. This design assures that constant potentials are developed on the inner surface of the glass membrane and on the internal reference, element.

- When the electrode assembly is immersed in a solution of pH 7, the sum of these fixed voltages approximately balances the voltage developed on the outer surface of the glass membrane and the external reference electrode. The combination electrode contains both the pH-sensing and reference electrodes, combined in a single probe body (Fig. 2.9). With glass pH-responsive electrodes, chemical durability and electrical resistance are linked together. So called universal glass electrodes have an electrical resistance of approximately 100 MΩ at 25°C, permitting their use at temperatures down to at least 0°C where resistance increases to about 1000 MΩ.

- The thick, rugged membrane withstands even rough handling as might be encountered in industrial applications. They exhibit a fast response over the entire 0-14 pH range, the temperature range is from –5 to 110°C. However, they are not recommended for constant use in solutions with very low or very high pH because electrode life is shortened.

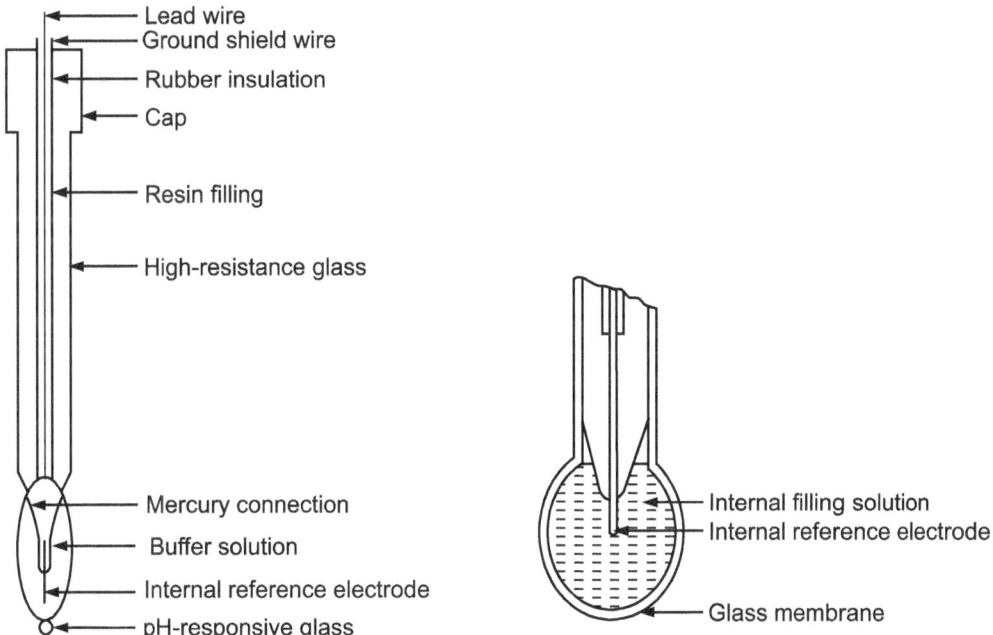

Fig. 2.8: Construction of a glass pH-responsive electrode

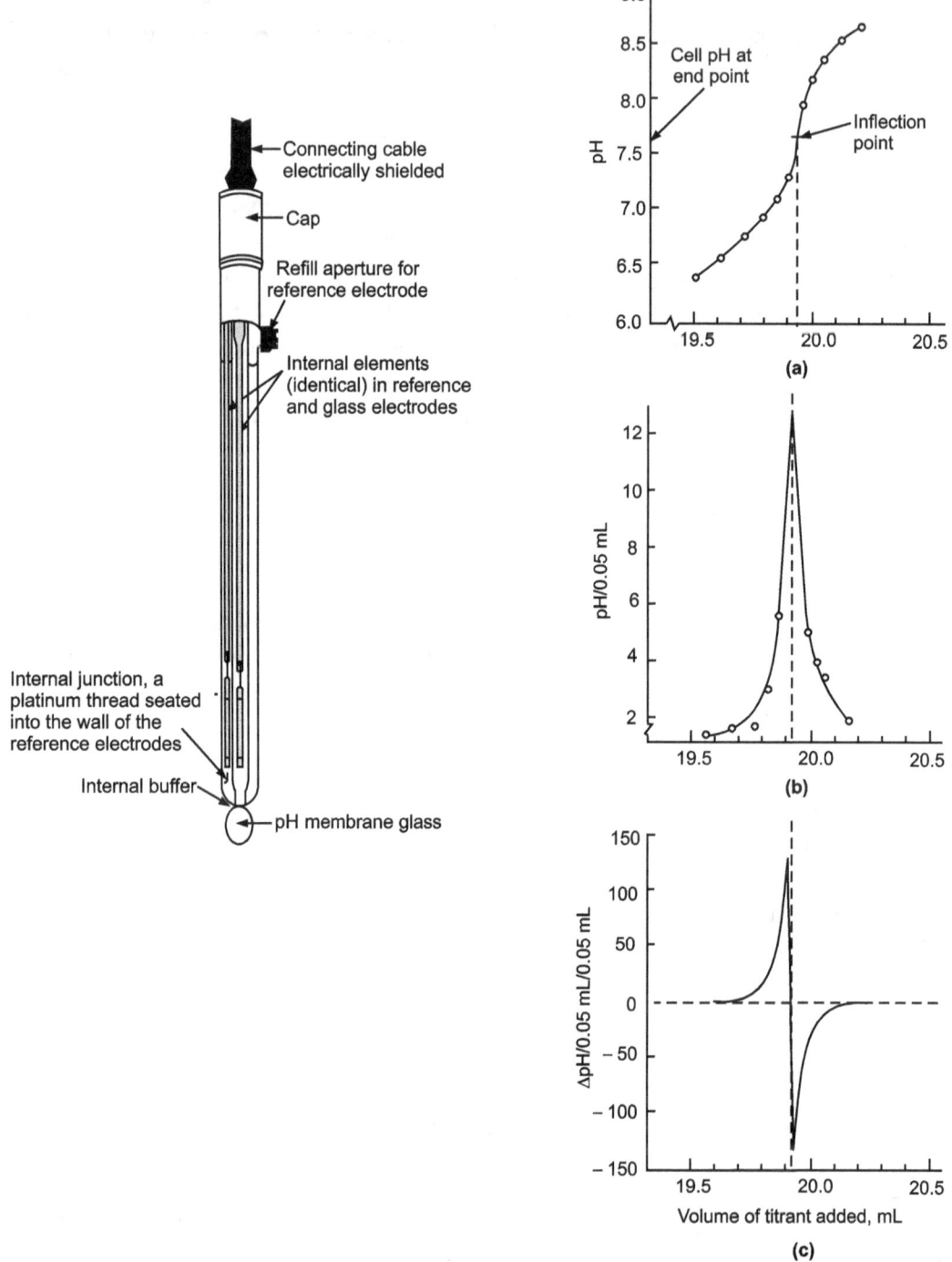

Fig. 2.9: Combination pH/reference electrode

Fig. 2.10: pH titration curves: (a) experimental titration curve, (b) first derivative curve and (c) second derivative curve

- For long-term measurements at extreme pH values, a full-range, high-pH glass electrode should be used. This type of electrode has superior chemical durability, though at the cost of a fourfold increase in electrical resistance and a corresponding elevation of the lower temperature limit of use to 10°C. This is the glass membrane of choice for measurements in solutions with high alkali metal content and high pH values.

- A glass electrode exhibits a reasonably rapid response to rapid and wide changes of pH in buffered solutions. However, valid readings are obtained more slowly in poorly buffered or unbuffered solutions, particularly when changing to these from buffered solutions, as after standardization and calibration.

- The electrode should be thoroughly washed with distilled water after each measurement and then rinsed with several portions of the next test solution before making the final reading. Poorly buffered solutions should be vigorously stirred during measurement, otherwise, the stagnant layer of solution at the glass-solution interface tends towards the composition of the particular kind of pH-responsive glass. Suspensions and colloidal material should be wiped from the glass surface with a soft tissue.

- Commercial glass electrodes are fabricated in a wide variety of sizes and shapes and for many special applications. Syringe and capillary electrodes require only one or two drops of solution or even, less in ultramicro work whereas others penetrate soft solids (such as leather) or pastes. The normal-size electrode operates with a volume of solution of 1-5 mL.

2.10 ABSORPTION SPECTROSCOPY   [Dec. 13, May 15]

- Spectroscopy involves measurement and interpretation of electromagnetic radiation, absorbed or emitted or scattered when atoms, or molecules, or ions of a sample move from one allowed energy state to another. In short, it deals with the consequence of absorption or emission of electromagnetic radiation by a sample. Every atom, ion, molecule responds to electromagnetic radiation in a unique way. Hence by studying these interactions, one can identify the atoms, ions or molecules present in the sample.

- In order to avoid repetition, we will call atoms, ions or molecules as sample collectively. In this chapter, we will study the consequence of absorption of part radiation (UV, visible and IR) by the sample.

2.10.1 The Electromagnetic Radiation

- Electromagnetic radiation is a type of energy that is transmitted through space at enormous velocity. We receive electromagnetic radiation mainly from sun, the contribution of moon and other stars is minor but by no means insignificant. The most easily recognizable forms are heat and light.

- Electromagnetic spectrum encompasses wide range of wavelengths and frequencies. The range is so wide that for representing entire range, one has to use logarithmic scale.

The complete range of spectral regions is shown in Fig. 2.11. In this part we will study the consequence of absorption of radiation by the sample in UV, visible and IR range.

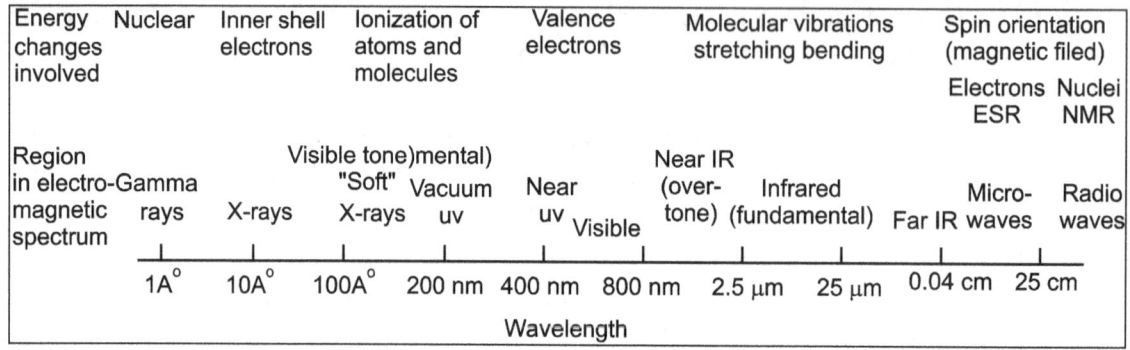

Fig. 2.11: The solar spectrum

2.10.2 Ultraviolet – Visible (UV – Visible) Spectroscopy

The radiations with wavelength 10 - 400 nm are called as ultraviolet (UV) radiation or UV region. It is subdivided as (i) 10 to 200 nm region is called as vacuum UV and (ii) 200 to 400 nm region is called as near UV. For chemical analysis, near UV radiation is used.

Principle:

- When a sample interacts with energy in ultraviolet or visible region, the sample absorbs some incident energy. Due to absorption of this energy, there is displacement of valence electron in a molecule. The absorption spectrum which is generated as a consequence is a function of whole structure of the molecule.

- No unique electronic spectrum is generated which can be used as fingerprint identification for the sample when it is subjected to UV-visible radiation. Hence the information obtained by UV-visible absorption spectrum should be supported by previous history of the compound, synthesis, auxiliary chemical tests.

How UV-Visible Spectroscopy can Generate Structural Information:

- First important condition is the molecule under study must be capable of absorbing radiation with wavelength range 185 – 800 nm. Only covalent compounds absorb in UV range and inorganic coloured compounds absorb in visible range.

- In organic saturated compounds with heteroatoms (other than C and H) like S, N O, P, halides there are unpaired p electrons in addition to σ electrons. Due to absorption of UV radiation, these unpaired p electrons are promoted to antibonding σ orbital. This transition is indicated by n → σ*, due to this transition one can see a gap or absence of radiation with wavelength ranging from 185 to 208.

- In unsaturated (organic compounds with double or triple bond) compounds, absorption of UV radiation results in displacement of π electrons i.e. π → π* or π → σ* transitions, the absorption is observed in the wavelength range of 190 – 300. The molecule as a whole does not absorb energy but a part of it is responsible for absorption. This part is called as chromophore (chromo-color therefore part which is responsible for absorption of color is chromophore). The absorption of light depends upon concentration of the sample and length of absorption, as given by Beer-Lambert's law.

Beer and Lambert's Laws

(A) Lambert's Law:

Lambert (1760) investigated the relation between I_o and I_t. The law states that "when a beam of monochromatic light passes through a homogeneous absorbing medium, the rate of decrease of intensity of light with the thickness of the medium is proportional to the intensity of light.

The law can be stated mathematically, as follows:

$$-\frac{dI}{dt} = KI \qquad\qquad ... (2.12)$$

where 'I' is the intensity of light after passing through the thickness 't', dI is infinitesimally small decrease in the intensity of light after passing through infinitesimally small thickness 'dt' of the medium. In other words, $-\dfrac{dI}{dt}$ gives the rate of decrease of intensity of light with thickness of the absorbing medium. The proportionality constant is called the *absorption coefficient*; the value of which depends upon the absorbing medium.

If I_O is the intensity of light before entering the absorbing medium when t = 0, then the intensity of light I_t after passing through any finite thickness 't' of the medium can be obtained by integrating equation (2.12) within limits t = 0 to t and I_o to I_t.

$$\int_{I_o}^{I_t} \frac{dI}{I} = -K \int_{t=0}^{t=t} dt$$

$$\log_e \left(\frac{I_t}{I_o}\right) = -Kt \quad \text{or} \quad \log_e \left(\frac{I_o}{I_t}\right) = Kt \qquad\qquad ... (2.13)$$

The exponential form of this equation is

$$\frac{I_t}{I_o} = e^{-Kt} \quad \text{or} \quad I_t = I_o \cdot e^{-Kt} \qquad\qquad ... (2.14)$$

But

$$I_a = I_o - I_t$$

$$\therefore \qquad I_a = I_o - I_o \cdot e^{-Kt}$$

$$\therefore \qquad I_a = I_o (1 - e^{-Kt}) \qquad\qquad ... (2.15)$$

By changing the $\log_e$ to the base 10 of equation (2.14),

$$I_t = I_o \cdot 10^{-0.4343\, Kt}$$

$$\therefore \qquad I_t = I_o \cdot 10^{-at} \qquad\qquad ... (2.16)$$

where 'a' is *extinction coefficient* of the absorbing medium and is related to absorption coefficient K by the equation

$$a = \frac{K}{2.303} \qquad \qquad ...(2.17)$$

The *extinction coefficient* can be defined as "*the reciprocal of thickness required to reduce the light to $\frac{1}{10}$th of its intensity*".

Thus from equation (2.16), we can write

$$\frac{I_t}{I_o} = 10^{-at} \qquad \qquad ...(2.18)$$

$$= 0.1 \text{ (if at = 1 and hence a = 1/t)}$$

The ratio I_t/I_o is the fraction of the incident light that is transmitted and is called as *transmission* or *transmittance* 'T'.

The reciprocal of transmittance I_o/I_t or $1/T$ is called as *optical density* or *opacity* 'D' or *extinction* 'E' or *absorbance* 'A' and is given by

$$D = E = A = \log(I_o/I_t) = \log(1/T) \qquad \qquad ...(2.19)$$

(B) Beer's Law or Beer-Lambert's Law (1852):

"When a beam of monochromatic light passes through a solution of an absorbing substance, the rate of decrease of intensity of light with thickness of the absorbing solution is proportional to the intensity of incident light as well as to the concentration of the solution".

$$-\frac{dI}{dt} = K' \, IC \qquad \qquad ...(2.20)$$

where, C = concentration of solution in gm moles per litre

and   K' = molar absorption coefficient.

Integrating the above equation, we get,

$$\int_{I_o}^{I_t} \frac{dI}{I} = -K' \cdot C \int_{t=0}^{t=t} dt$$

$$\therefore \qquad \log_e\left(\frac{I_t}{I_o}\right) = -K' \cdot C \cdot t$$

$$\text{Or} \qquad \log_e\left(\frac{I_o}{I_t}\right) = K' \cdot C \cdot t \qquad \qquad ...(2.21)$$

$$\frac{I_t}{I_o} = e^{-K' \cdot C \cdot t}$$

Or $$I_t = I_o \cdot e^{-K' \cdot C \cdot t} \qquad \text{... Beer-Lambert's law ... (2.22)}$$

Changing $\log_e$ to $\log_{10}$, we get,

$$I_t = I_o \cdot 10^{-\epsilon \cdot C \cdot t}$$

OR

$$\log \left(\frac{I_o}{I_t} \right) = \epsilon \, C \, t \qquad \text{... Beer-Lambert's law ... (2.23)}$$

where $\epsilon = \dfrac{K'}{2.303}$ and is called molar extinction coefficient of the absorbing solution. ϵ depends upon the wavelength of incident light, temperature and solvent used.

$$\text{Optical density,} \quad D = \log \left(\frac{I_o}{I_t} \right) \qquad \text{... from equation (2.19)}$$

Substituting D in equation (2.23), we get,

$$D = \epsilon \, C \, t$$

When $C = 1 \, M$ and $t = 1 \, cm$ then

$$D = \epsilon$$

Thus molar extinction coefficient (ϵ) is the optical density when thickness of the solution is 1 cm and concentration is 1 M.

Deviations from Beer's Law:

According to Beer's law, a straight line passing through the origin should be obtained, when a graph is plotted between absorbance A and concentration. But there is always a deviation from the linear relationship between absorbance and concentration and infact the shape of an absorption curve usually changes with changes in concentration of the solution and, unless precautions are observed, apparent failure of Beer's law will result. Deviations from the law may be positive or negative, according to whether the resulting curve is concave upwards or concave downwards, as shown in the Fig. 2.12.

The deviations from the Beer's law may be due to interaction of the solute molecules with each other or with the solvent or may be due to instrumental factors.

Some of the deviations are briefly given below.

- It is generally found that at high concentrations, the substance absorbs more readily than the equation requires.

- The law also fails when coloured substances ionise, dissociate or associate in solution. For example, benzyl alcohol in chloroform exists in a polymeric equilibrium.

$$4C_6H_5CH_2OH \rightleftharpoons (C_6H_5CH_2OH)_4$$

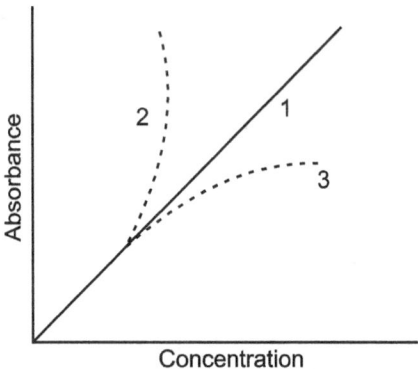

Fig. 2.12: Beer's law (1) Obeyed, (2) Positive deviation, (3) Negative deviation

The dissociation of the polymeric alcohol, however, increases as the solution is diluted. The monomer absorbs at 2.750 to 2.765 μ and the polymer absorbs at 3.000 μ. Hence the absorption at 2.750 μ indicates negative absorption or deviation, while absorption at 3.000 μ shows positive deviation from the Beer's law.

- Another most important chemical deviation from the absorption law is the change of colour of, say dichromate ion on dilution with water. The effect can be represented by the equilibrium:

$$Cr_2O_7^{--} + H_2O = 2HCrO_4^- \rightarrow 2H^+ + 2CrO_4^{--}$$

Orange   Yellow

As a solution of dichromate is progressively converted to chromate upon dilution with water, the maximum at 450 mμ decreases more slowly, so that the deviation at 450 mμ is positive and at 350 mμ negative. The negative deviation can be encountered as a result of the use of polychromatic radiation.

- Negative deviation can always be expected when the illumination is not monochromatic. For example, when a series of solutions of potassium chromate at some constant high pH are examined, all colours are transmitted equally at zero concentration.

At high concentration, nearly all the blue light will be absorbed, and light of wavelength above 500 nm will be transmitted as freely as before. At one half of this concentration, a large fraction of blue light will come through, along with all the higher wavelengths. A moment's thought will indicate that the total absorbance over all visible wavelengths can not be linear with concentration.

- The presence of impurities that fluoresce or absorb at the required absorption wavelength, may also cause deviation from the Beer's law.

- If the width of the slit is not proper, deviations are expected to occur, because improper slit width may allow undesirable radiations to fall on the detector. These undesirable radiations might be absorbed by the impurities present in the solution of the sample and would cause an apparent change in the absorbance of the sample. This deviation becomes quite appreciable if the concentration of the sample is high.

- Deviation from Beer's law also arise, because it depends upon the refractive index of the solution. Thus, if concentration change causes significant alternations in the refractive index n of a solution, deviation from Beer's law is observed.

- Beer's law is not applicable in case of suspension. The latter can be estimated colorimetrically after preparing a reference curve with known concentration.

Reasons for Deviation from Beer's Law:

The most important reasons that cause deviation are:

- Environment, such as temperature, pressure and solvent.

- Instrumental errors, such as stray radiation, stability of radiation source, wavelength selector, slit control, electronics and reliability of the optical parts.

- Chemical deviations, such as changes in chemical equilibrium and pH, presence of complexing agents, competitive metal ion reactions, and concentration dependence.

- Refractive index of the sample.

- Non-monochromaticity of radiation.

Table 2.3: Electronic Absorption Bands for Representative Chromophores

Chromophore	System	λ_{max}	ϵ_{max}	λ_{max}	ϵ_{max}	λ_{max}	ϵ_{max}
Ether	$-O-$	185	1000				
Thioether	$-S-$	194	4600	215	1600		
Amine	$-NH_2$	195	2800				
Thiol	$-SH$	195	1400				
Disulfide	$-S-S-$	194	5500	255	400		
Bromide	$-Br$	208	300				
Iodide	$-I$	260	400				
Nitrile	$-C \equiv N$	160					
Acetylide	$-C \equiv C-$	175 - 180	6000				
Sulfone	$-SO_2-$	180					
Oxime	$-NOH$	190	5000				
Azido	$>C = N-$	190	5000				
Ethylene	$-C = C-$	190	8000				
Ketone	$> C = O$	195	1000	270 - 285	18 - 30		

Chromophore	System	λ_{max}	$\in_{max}$	λ_{max}	$\in_{max}$	λ_{max}	$\in_{max}$
Thioketone	$> C = S$	205	strong				
Esters	$- COOR$	205	50				
Aldehyde	$- CHO$	210	strong	280 - 300	11 - 18		
Carboxyl	$- COOH$	200 - 210	50 - 70				
Sulfoxide	$> S \rightarrow O$	210	1500				
Nitro	$- NO_2$	210	strong				
Nitrite	$- ONO$	220 - 230	1000 - 2000	300 - 4000	10		
Azo	$- N = N -$	285 - 400	3 - 25				
Nitroso	$- N = O$	302	100				
Nitrate	$- ONO_2$	270 (shoulder)	12				
	$- (C = C)_2 -$ (acyclic)	210 - 230	21,000				
	$- (C = C)_3 -$	260	35,000				
	$- (C = C)_4 -$	300	52,000				
	$- (C = C)_5 -$	330	118,000				
	$- (C = C)_2 -$ (alicyclic)	230 - 260	3000 - 8000				
	$C = C - C \equiv C$	219	6500				
	$C = C - C = N$	220	23,000				
	$C = C - C = O$	210-250	10000 - 20000			300 - 350	weak
	$C = C - NO_2$	229	9500				
Benzene		184	46700	202	6900	255	170
Diphenyl				246	20000		
Naphthalene		220	112000	275	5600	312	175
Anthracene		252	199000	375	7900		
Pyridine		174	80000	195	6000	251	1700
Quinoline		227	37000	270	3600	314	2750
Isoquinoline		218	80,000	266	4000	317	3500

Instrumentation:

The instrument that can find out absorbed radiation in UV-visible range is called as spectrophotometer. The instrument used in the wavelength range 400 - 800 nm (visible region) is called as colorimeter. Fig. 2.13 shows schematic diagram of a double-beam spectrophotometer (varian 634).

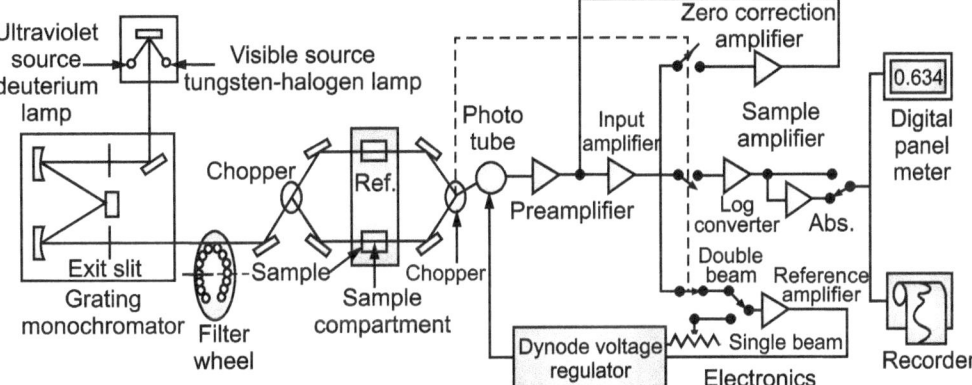

Fig. 2.13: Schematic diagram of a double-beam spectrophotometer (varian 634) with dual-source, single grating, Czerny-Turner monochromator

Spectrophotometers have developed to current stage through (i) colour comparator, (ii) colorimeter with specific colour filters (5 to 8 filters with various wavelengths and a band of 30 - 40 nm for each filter), (iii) colorimeter with continuous wavelengths through which any wavelength with a band of 2 - 5 nm can be selected, (iv) single beam instruments and (v) double beam spectrophotometer which is shown in Fig. 2.13..

The instrument consists of following parts:

Source: It produces light in the desired wavelength range (200-800 nm). The main conditions/requisites of source are (i) it should be a continuous source with constant and sufficient intensity, (ii) it should give out sufficient radiant energy in the entire wavelength range (200 - 800 nm).

Hydrogen or deuterium discharge lamp is used as a source between 160-360 nm, hence it is a useful source for UV radiation.

Incandescent filament lamps like tungsten lamp, tungsten-halogen lamp are useful in UV as well as visible region. Tungsten lamp is useful in near IR range upto 1000 nm.

Filters: For spectrophotometric analysis require isolation of discrete bandwidths of radiation. If a small bandwidth falls on sample at a time accurate measurement of the absorbed radiation can be carried out.

Various types of filters are available but their primary function is to allow a small portion (fixed wavelength about 0.2 nm to 20 nm) of radiation to pass through and effectively cut off all other radiations.

Various types of filters used in different UV-visible spectrophotometers are –

- **Interference Filters:** It is also called as Fabry-Perot filter. It uses a dielectric spacer film sandwiched between two parallel metal plates which are partially reflecting.

  Wedge type filter, multilayer, long-wave pass filters are some other examples.

  Monochromators are also used as filters, they are used in good quality spectrophotometer. Their bandpass is very small ~1 nm or below. It consists of (i) an entrance slit through which small portion of radiation enters, (ii) a collimator that restricts spreading or scattering of incoming light, (iii) a grating or prism to disperse the incident radiation, (iv) a collimator to reform images of the entrance slit and (v) an exit slit to isolate the desired spectral band.

Chopper: When a double beam instrument is used, this part is essential. The radiation which comes out of filter or monochromator falls on chopper which divides the light in two identical sources i.e. change an incoming single beam into two identical outgoing beams.

Chopper is a system consisting of rotating sector mirrors and corner mirrors. The open sector passes the beam to one channel and reflects it to the second channel.

Sample Compartment: In a single beam spectrophotometer there is only one slot for holding sample. In case of double beam instrument there are two slots; one for sample and other for reference material. Reference slot contains the solvent in which sample is prepared.

The sample and reference solutions are kept in transparent holders, like test tubes which are called as cuvettes. In UV region, quartz cuvettes are used and in visible region ordinary glass cuvettes are adequate.

Chopper: In a double beam instrument after sample compartment there is again a chopper situated. When radiation falls on sample material, sample absorbs a large portion of incident radiation and only a small portion is transmitted. When radiation falls on reference only a very small part of radiation is absorbed and most of the radiation is transmitted. So there are two transmitted radiations. A chopper cuts off one transmitted signal at a time and allows passage of the other. The chopper consists of rotating sector mirrors as described earlier.

Signal Amplifiers: The chopper gives out transmitted radiation by sample and reference material which should be enhanced in order to make it recognisable by the read out device. Amplifiers are used to enhance the transmitted signal. They are also called as detectors. Various types of signal amplifiers are available. Single element detectors such as photovoltaic cells, solid-state photodiodes, photoemissive tube, photomultiplier tube. Multiple-element detectors such as solid-state array detectors.

Function of amplifier or detector is to convert electromagnetic radiation into electrons and flow of electrons will generate current which will flow into read out device.

Read out Device: The amplified signal is then passed into a dynode voltage regulator. The dynode voltage is varied to maintain a constant reference signal. The signal of sample amplifier and reference amplifier is compared and output is given in the form of percentage transmittance. The recorder and read out device (which is a pannel meter or digital indicator) give out the transmitted radiation.

Applications:

- Structures of organic compounds which are colourless or pale yellow or greenish in colour can be determined using UV spectrophotometry.

- Transition metal salts which are coloured e.g. $CuSO_4$ - blue, $KMnO_4$ - purple, $FeSO_4$ - blue-green can be estimated qualitatively as well as quantitatively by visible spectrophotometry or colourimetry.

- Differentiate between para substituted isomers from ortho or meta-substituted isomers.

- For predicting the wavelength of maximum absorption.

- Differentiate between cis and trans isomers.

- Predict presence or absence of particular functional groups. e.g. organic nitro compounds show strong absorption at 210 nm, hence the sample if shows strong absorption at this range may contain - NO_2 group which can be further confirmed if it shows absorption corresponding to $C - N$ group.

- Determination of unknown concentration of a substance by plotting standardisation curve using four to five known concentrations of the same substance.

- Carry out analysis of mixtures which absorb in two well separated regions.

UNIVERSITY QUESTIONS

DECEMBER 2012

1. Explain different types of electronic transitions that occur in an organic molecule after absorbing UV radiations. **(6 Marks)**

   Ans. Refer to Articles 2.10, 2.10.1 and 2.10.2 on Page No. 2.29 and 2.30.

2. Explain the pH metric titration of mixture of weak acid-strong acid against standard alkali, giving chemical reactions, procedure, titration curve and calculations. **(6 Marks)**

   Ans. Refer to Articles 2.9, 2.9.1, 2.9.2 and 2.9.3 on Page Nos. 2.21 to 2.29.

MAY 2013

1. Which are possible transitions, that occur when molecule absorbs uv-visible radiation? which type of electronic transitions will be possible in following molecules. **(3 Marks)**

i) $CH_2 = CH - CH_2 - CH_3$ ii) $CH_3 - CH_2 - OH$

iii) $CH_3 - \overset{\overset{\displaystyle O}{\|}}{C} - CH_3$ iv) $CH_3 - CH_2 - CH_2 - CH_2 - CH_3$

Ans. Refer to Article 2.10.2 on Page Nos. 2.30 and 2.31.

2. State the reference electrode and standard electrode used in pH metery, potentiometry and conductometry. **(3 Marks)**

   Ans. Refer to Article 2.9.3 on Page No. 2.26.

3. Explain effect of dilution on specific conductance and equivalent conductance. **(3 Marks)**

   Ans. Refer to Article 2.6 on Page No. 2.8 and Kohrowche's Law on Page No. 2.9.

4. Explain the titration curve for conduct metric titration in case of strong acid weak base titration. **(3 Marks)**

   Ans. Refer to Article 2.6.1 on Page No. 2.10 and 2.11.

NOVEMBER 2013

1. Calculate potential or redox electrode dipped in titration mixture, when 20 m l of 0.1 N Ce^{4+} soluition from the burette is added in 100 ml 0.1 N Fe^{2+} solution. Standard reduction potentials for $Fe^{3+} \rightarrow Fe^{2+}$ and $Ce^{4+} \rightarrow Ce^{3+}$ are 0.75 V and 1.45 respectively. **(3 Marks)**

   Ans. Refer to Article 2.7.4 on Page No. 2.15 and 2.16.

2. Explain the conductometric titration of KCl against $AgNO_3$ solution from burette. **(3 Marks)**

   Ans. Refer to Article 2.6.1 on Page No. 2.10 and 2.11.

3. Explain the principle, instrumentation and applications of UV-visible spectrophotometer. **(6 Marks)**

   Ans. Refer to Instrumentation on Page No. 2.30 and 2.31.

MAY 2014

1. What is reference electrode? Draw neat labeled diagram of Glass electrode and give its representation. **(3 Marks)**

   Ans. Refer to Article 2.8.1., Fig. 2.18 Page No. 2.18 and 2.27.

2. Explain condutometric titration curve for reaction between weak acid and strong base. **(3 Marks)**

   Ans. Refer to Article 2.6.1 Fig 2.2 (b) on Page No. 2.11.

3. Explain different types of electronic transitions occurring in organic molecules on absorption of UV-visible radiations. **(6 Marks)**

   Ans. Refer to Article 2.10.2 p.g. 2.30. How Uv-vis sp. can generate st-info.

DECEMBER 2014

1. State and derive Beer Lamberts law.   **(3 Marks)**

   Ans. Refer to Article 2.10.2 (B) on Page No. 2.32.

2. Define specific conductance, equivalent conductance and molar conductance.   **(3 Marks)**

   Ans. Refer to Article 2.6 on Page No. 2.8.

3. Explain the pH metric titration of – mixture of weak acid – strong acid against std. Alkali giving chemical reaction procedure with titration curve.   **(6 Marks)**

   Ans. Refer to Article 2.9.2 on Page No. 2.24.

MAY 2015

1. Explain titration curve of conductometric titration in case of strong acid and weak base.   **(3 Marks)**

   Ans. Refer to Article 2.6.1 on Page No. 2.11.

2. Explain the following terms with suitable example: **(3 Marks)**

   (i)   Chromophore   (ii)   Auxochrome.

   Ans. Refer to Article 2.10.2 on Page No. 2.30.

3. Explain the pH metric titration of mixture of H_3PO_4 (phosphoric acid) and HCl (hydrochloric acid) against std. NaOH, giving chemical reactions, procedure, titration curve and calculations.   **(6 Marks)**

   Ans. Refer to Article 2.9.2 on Page No. 2.24.

NOVEMBER 2015

1. Define the following terms: **(3 Marks)**

   (i)   Bathochromic shift   (ii) Hypochromic shift

   (ii) Chromophore.

   Ans. Refer to Article 2.10.2 on Page No. 2.30.

2. Explain the conductometric titration curve for the reaction between KCl and $AgNO_3$.   **(3 Marks)**

   Ans. Refer to Article 2.6.1 on Page No. 2.11.

3. Explain the potentiometric titration of Fe^{2+} against Ce^{4+} giving reactions. Draw the titration curve and give the formulae for calculating emf of the cell at various stages of the titration.   **(6 Marks)**

   Ans. Refer to Article 2.7.4 on Page No. 2.15.

4. Define glass transition temperature. Give its significance and discuss any four factors affecting it. **(6 Marks)**

   Ans. Refer to Article 2.10.2 on Page No. 2.30.

MAY 2016

1. What is reference electrode ? Draw neat labelled diagram of glass electrode and give its representation. **(3 Marks)**

   Ans. Refer to Article 2.8.1 & 2.8.5 on Page Nos. 2.18 and 2.20.

2. Explain principle, instrumentation and applications of UV visible spectrophotometer. **(6 Marks)**

   Ans. Refer to Article 2.10.2 on Page No. 2.30.

✠ ✠ ✠

SYNTHETIC ORGANIC POLYMERS

3.1 INTRODUCTION

Some billions of years ago, free atoms of elements such as C, H, O, N, S were present on the earth. Under favourable climatic conditions like temperature, pressure and composition, they combine together in a specific way to form numerous compounds. These elements combined together in more specific and complex way to form biopolymers such as proteins, carbohydrates, starch, DNA, RNA, etc. These are called macromolecules or biomolecules because they are the building blocks of all living organisms. In short, life on the earth originated and evolved due to these biopolymers.

About hundred years ago, with improved human understanding of materials, many synthetic polymers such as polyester, polystyrene, polyethene were synthesized and commercialized. These synthetic polymers have occupied the human life to such an extent, that now a comfortable living cannot be imagined without using polymers, such as plastics and rubbers.

- The polymers are also important engineering materials. They are important in electrical and electronic industry. As they are very good insulating materials, they can also be used for making wires, ducts and various pannels.

- Recently, new type of polymers called conducting polymers are synthesized whose conductivity can be tailored and they have found many applications in microelectronics and smart devices.

- Some polymers because of their mechanical strength, have found applications in mechanical engineering such as body of automobiles, heavy machines, lubricants, etc.

- In civil engineering polymers are commonly used as flooring materials, tiles, plastic wall paper covers, water-proofing materials, etc.

- In addition to this, almost every article which we use in our day-to-day life such as clothes (nylon), brushes and brooms, baggage, furniture, adhesive is either made up of polymers or polymer composites.

- Because of its importance in all walks of life and their extensive applications, it is important to study the Polymer chemistry as a branch of science and technology.

3.2 HISTORICAL DEVELOPMENTS IN POLYMER SCIENCE

It has taken centuries of human understanding to realize the importance of polymers and for converting polymers into smart materials. But most of the developments in synthesis and commercialization of polymers took place in the 20th century. Hence, sometimes 20th century is called as 'century of polymers'.

The chronological sequence of developments in the polymer science is given below:

Development of Polymers:

15th Century AD: Christopher Columbus noticed native South Americans playing a bouncing game with a solid ball made from dried sap of 'weeping wood', which is now known as natural rubber.

17th Century: Joseph Priestley showed that the solid ball can rub off marks of pencil and called the material rubber.

19th Century: Vulcanization of rubber was achieved by sulphur dust as a cross-linking agent by Charles Goodyear.

Later 19th Century: Christian Schonbein discovered nitro-cellulose, which later on gave first plastic-cellulose nitrate.

20th Century: 1907 discovery of phenol formaldehyde resin by Leo Baekeland who named the plastic as Bakelite.

Between 1907 and 1950 many commercial plastics were manufactured for the first time.

- Polyvinyl chloride.
- Discovery of nylon or celluloid.
- Melamine, polyester, butyl rubber, polyethylene.
- Fluorocarbons, SBR, polyurethanes. (Styrene butadiene rubber)
- Epoxy, ABS (Acrylonitrile styrene butadiene)

1950: PP, polycarbonate, polysulfones (Polypropylene)

1975: Liquid crystalline polymers.

1990: Conducting polymers, polypyrrole, polyanilines, PPV.

2000: Light emitting polymers, use of liquid crystals for TV, Computer screens.

3.3 DEFINITIONS AND IMPORTANT TERMINOLOGY

The word 'polymer' is made from two Greek words: 'poly' meaning 'many' and 'mer' meaning units. Hence the literature meaning of the word polymers is 'something which is made up of or composed of many units.'

(a) Functionality of Monomers:

The small, individual molecules having low molecular weight with at least two reactive sites combining together in a specific way to form a large molecule (polymer) is called monomer.

e.g. Ethylene ($CH_2 = CH_2$), butadine ($CH_2 = CH - CH = CH_2$), styrene $CH_2 = CH - C_6H_5$, acetylene $CH_3 - C \equiv CH$, etc.

The molecular weight of a monomer is known exactly.

An ideal monomer should have at least two reactive positions so that it can react with other monomer unit to form a long chain. The number of reactive sites present in a monomer unit is called its **'functionality'**. In the case of most of the organic monomers functional groups such as $-OH$, $-COOH$, $-NH_2$, $-COOR$ in addition to the $C = C$ are the reactive groups or sites.

Examples:

Ethylene Glycol (Bifunctional monomer)

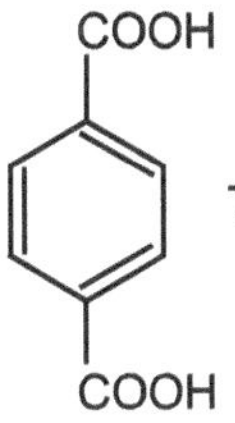

Terephthalic acid (Bifunctional monomer)

(b) Polymers:

Same or different types of monomers combined together repetitively in a specific manner to form a large molecule with very high molecular weight are called as polymers.

Sr. No.	Polymer	Monomer	Structure
1.	Polyethane	Ethylene	$CH_2 = CH_2$
2.	Nylon-6	Caprolactum, adipic acid	
3.	DNA/RNA	Amino acids	
4.	Starch	Glucose, fructose	

(c) Polymerization:

A chemical reaction / process in which large number of monomer molecules combine together under specific conditions to form polymer is called polymerization.

$$\text{e.g. } n\,CH_2 = CH_2 \xrightarrow[\text{Specific reaction conditions}]{\text{Polymerization}} -\left[CH_2 - CH_2\right]_n -$$

Monomer   Polymer

(Ethylene)   (Polyethene)

(d) Degree of Polymerization (D_p):

During the process of polymerization, the number of monomer units that come together to form a polymer is called as degree of polymerization. It is denoted by D_p.

e.g. Let us consider that during a polymerization process, 100 ethylene molecules form polyethene.

$$100\ CH_2 = CH_2 \xrightarrow{\text{Polymerization}} -\left[CH_2 - CH_2\right]_{100} -$$

Since 100 ethylene molecules form the polymer, D_p = 100. If 1000 ethylene molecules undergo polymerization, then D_p = 1000 and so on.

If degree of polymerization (D_p) for a polymerization process is exactly known, then the molecular weight of the polymer formed in the process can be calculated exactly as

$$M_W = m \times D_p$$

where M_W = Molecular weight of the polymer formed

m = Molecular weight of the monomer

D_p = Degree of polymerization

For above reaction, where D_p = 100, the M_W is

$$M_W = 28 \times 100 \quad \text{(since molecular weight of ethylene = 28)}$$

$$= 2800$$

If D_p = 1000, $\quad M_W = 28 \times 1000 = 28000$ and so on.

3.4 MECHANISM OF POLYMERIZATION

Presence of C = C is a prime requirement for addition polymerization reactions. These reactions are fast and exothermic. The molecular weight of polymer formed is an exact integral multiple of the molecular weight of monomer units. No byproducts are formed in addition reactions. A catalyst or an initiator is required to start the polymerization. Depending on the nature of catalyst used, the addition polymerization has three different mechanisms, they are:

(a) Free Radical Mechanism:

In free radical polymerization, free radicals (chemical species formed by homolytic fission, has an unpaired electron, are highly reactive) are catalysts. Catalysts used are H_2O_2, benzoyl peroxide, lauryl peroxide, etc.

Initially free radicals are produced by catalysis either by irradiation with light or heat.

Ex. 1. $H - O - O - H \xrightarrow{h\upsilon / \Delta} 2\ OH$

Hydrogen peroxide   Hydroxyl radicals

Ex. 2.

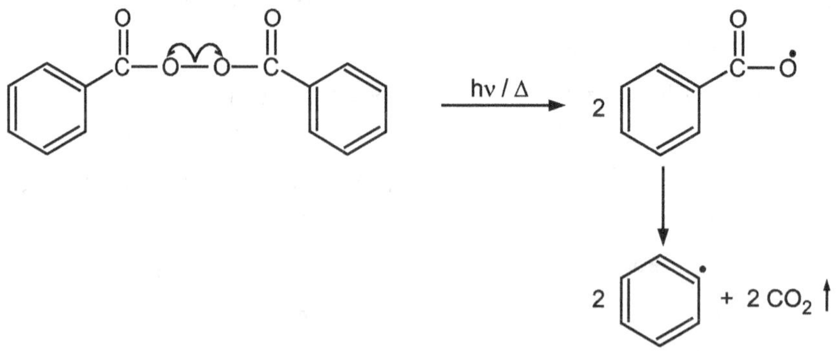

After formation of free radicals, the polymerization proceeds via three steps:

(1) Initiation, (2) Propagation, (3) Termination.

1. Initiation:

In this step, the polymerization starts by attack of free radical on the monomer units. For example, let us consider polymerization of propylene.

$$\overset{\bullet}{O}H \; + \; CH_2 \!=\! CH \;|\; CH_3 \longrightarrow OH\!-\!CH_2\!-\!\overset{\bullet}{C}H \;|\; CH_3$$

It is clear from above equation that, one new free radical is formed at the end of initiation. It should also be noted that, the unpaired electron is present on the terminal carbon atom through which it can undergo further reaction.

2. Propagation:

During propagation, this newly formed radical attacks on other monomer units and chain length of the polymer starts increasing.

$$OH\!-\!CH_2\!-\!\overset{\bullet}{C}H \;|\; CH_3 \; + \; CH_2\!=\!CH \;|\; CH_3 \longrightarrow OH\!-\!CH_2\!-\!CH\!-\!CH_2\!-\!CH \;|\; CH_3 \quad|\; CH_3$$

$$OH\!\!-\!\!\left[CH_2\!-\!CH \;|\; CH_3\right]_2\!\!-\!CH_2\!-\!\overset{\bullet}{C}H \;|\; CH_3 \longleftarrow \; + \; CH_2\!=\!CH \;|\; CH_3$$

If n number of monomer units are combined then,

$$OH\!\!-\!\!\left[CH_2\!-\!CH \;|\; CH_3\right]_n\!\!-\!CH_2\!-\!\overset{\bullet}{C}H \;|\; CH_3$$

Propagation in the chain length of the polymer

3. Termination:

After propagation, the polymerization can be stopped either by disproportion or by addition of suitable chain terminator.

(i) Disproportions:

$$OH\!\!-\!\!\left[CH_2\!-\!CH \;|\; CH_3\right]_n\!\!-\!\overset{H}{\underset{H}{C}}\!-\!CH \;|\; CH_3 \; + \; \overset{\bullet}{C}H\!-\!CH_2 \;|\; CH_3 \!\!-\!\!\left[CH\!-\!CH_2 \;|\; CH_3\right]_n\!\!-\!OH \longrightarrow$$

$$OH\!\!-\!\!\left[CH_2\!-\!CH \;|\; CH_3\right]_n\!\!-\!CH\!=\!CH \;|\; CH_3 \; + \; CH_2\!-\!CH_2 \;|\; CH_3 \!\!-\!\!\left[CH\!-\!CH_2 \;|\; CH_3\right]_n\!\!-\!OH$$

(ii) Addition of chain terminator:

$$OH - \left[- CH_2 - CH - \right]_n - CH_2 - \overset{\bullet}{CH} + HR \longrightarrow OH - \left[- CH_2 - CH - \right]_n - CH_2 - CH_2 + \overset{\bullet}{R}$$
$$\qquad\qquad\quad CH_3 \qquad\quad CH_3 \qquad\qquad\qquad\qquad\qquad CH_3 \qquad\qquad CH_3$$

(b) Cationic Chain Polymerization Mechanism:

Catalysts used are H_2SO_4, HBF_4, etc.

$$H_2SO_4 \longrightarrow H^+ + HSO_4^-$$

$$HBF_4 \longrightarrow H^+ + BF_4^-$$

Consider polymerization of a typical vinylic monomer.

1. Initiation:

$$H^{\oplus} + CH_2 = CH \longrightarrow CH_3 - \overset{\oplus}{CH} \quad \Big\} \text{ Initiation}$$
$$\qquad\qquad\quad R \qquad\qquad\qquad\quad R$$

2. Propagation:

$$CH_3 - \overset{\oplus}{CH} + CH_2 = CH \longrightarrow CH_3 - CH - CH_2 - \overset{\oplus}{CH} + CH_2 = CH$$
$$\qquad R \qquad\qquad R \qquad\qquad\qquad R \qquad\qquad R \qquad\qquad\qquad R$$

$$CH_3 - CH - CH_2 - CH - CH_2 - \overset{\oplus}{CH}$$
$$\qquad\quad R \qquad\qquad R \qquad\qquad R$$

If there are 'n' number of monomers, the polymer cation can be

$$CH_3 \left[CH - CH_2 \right]_n CH_2 - \overset{\oplus}{CH}$$
$$\qquad\quad R \qquad\qquad\qquad R$$

3. Termination:

$$CH_3 \left[CH - CH_2 \right]_n CH_2 - \overset{\oplus}{CH} + HSO_4^- \longrightarrow CH_3 \left[CH - CH_2 \right]_n CH_2 - CH_2 + SO_2{\uparrow} + O_2{\uparrow}$$
$$\qquad\quad R \qquad\qquad\qquad\quad R \qquad\qquad\qquad\qquad\quad R \qquad\qquad\qquad\qquad R$$

OR

$$CH_3 \left[CH - CH_2 \right]_n CH_2 - \overset{\oplus}{CH} + BF_4^- \longrightarrow CH_3 \left[CH - CH_2 \right]_n CH_2 - CH - F + BF_3$$
$$\qquad\quad R \qquad\qquad\qquad\quad R \qquad\qquad\qquad\qquad\quad R \qquad\qquad\qquad\qquad R$$

(c) Anionic Chain Polymerization Mechanism:

Catalysts are $\overset{+}{Li} - \overset{-}{R}$, $\overset{+}{Na} - \overset{\ominus}{NH_2}$, etc.

1. Initiation:

$$\overset{\ominus}{R} + CH_2 = \underset{\underset{X}{|}}{CH} \longrightarrow R - CH_2 - \underset{\underset{X}{|}}{\overset{\ominus}{CH}}$$

2. Propagation:

$$R - CH_2 - \underset{\underset{X}{|}}{\overset{\ominus}{CH}} + CH_2 = \underset{\underset{X}{|}}{CH} \longrightarrow R - CH_2 - \underset{\underset{X}{|}}{CH} - CH_2 - \underset{\underset{X}{|}}{\overset{\ominus}{CH}} + CH_2 = \underset{\underset{X}{|}}{CH}$$

$$\longrightarrow R - CH_2 - \underset{\underset{X}{|}}{CH} - CH_2 - \underset{\underset{X}{|}}{CH} - CH_2 - \underset{\underset{X}{|}}{\overset{\ominus}{CH}} \text{ and so on.}$$

3. Termination: Strong cation is added to stop the reaction.

$$R\left[CH_2 - \underset{\underset{X}{|}}{CH}\right]_n CH_2 - \overset{\ominus}{CH} + H^+ \longrightarrow R\left[CH_2 - \underset{\underset{X}{|}}{CH}\right]_n CH_2 - \underset{\underset{X}{|}}{CH_2}$$

Step Growth Polymerization:

This polymerization takes place via stepwise addition of monomers through functional groups. For such reactions catalyst may or may not be required. Simple molecules such as H_2O, NaCl, R–OH, etc. are formed as byproducts in the reaction. Such reactions are slow and endothermic. The substituent groups present at the end of the polymer chain are alive i.e. they can further undergo polymerization depending on availability of monomer units. The mechanism involves condensation between functional groups of the monomer molecules. Let us consider synthesis of Nylon-6 by condensation mechanism from ω-amino caproic acid.

$$NH_2 - (CH_2)_5 - \overset{\overset{O}{\|}}{C} - OH + H - NH - (CH_2)_5 - \overset{\overset{O}{\|}}{C} - OH$$

$$\xrightarrow[- H_2O]{\Delta} NH_2 - (CH_2)_5 - \overset{\overset{O}{\|}}{C} - NH - (CH_2)_5 - \overset{\overset{O}{\|}}{C} - OH + n\ H_2O \text{ and so on.}$$

Then general structure of nylon-6 is

$$H - \left[- NH - (CH_2)_5 - \overset{\overset{O}{\|}}{C} - \right]_n - OH$$

3.5 IMPORTANT CONCEPTS AND SIGNIFICANCE: MOLECULAR WEIGHT   [Dec. 08, May 10]

- When a polymerization reaction starts, many polymer chains start growing simultaneously and instantaneously. So when polymerization reaction is stopped, the reaction mixture contains large number of polymer chains. In each polymer chain, different number of monomers may be present i.e. each chain has different degree of polymerization with different molecular weights.

- So finally the polymer becomes a complex mixture of large number of polymer chains all with different molecular weights. Hence the exact molecular weight of the polymer sample cannot be determined as exact degree of polymerization is not known for each polymer chain. It should be noted that, although synthesizing a polymer with an exact molecular weight is not possible, molecular weight during synthesis can be controlled by just changing the polymerization reaction conditions such as concentration of monomer, temperature, pressure and time required for the process.

- So one can determine only average molecular weight of a polymer sample experimentally that contains many polymer chains of same chemical nature but different molecular weight. In this situation, the molecular weight of the polymer sample can be expressed as average of molecular weights contributed by individual polymer chain that make the entire sample.

The most common methods to determine the average molecular weight of a polymer are -

➢ Number average molecular weight ($\bar{M}_n$) and

➢ Weight average molecular weight ($\bar{M}_w$).

3.5.1 Number Average Molecular Weight $\bar{M}n$

Let us consider a polymer sample which contains 'n' number of polymer chains (or molecules). As stated earlier, all 'n' molecules in the polymer sample do not have same molecular weight. Let us assume that out of these 'n' number of molecules, 'n_1' molecules in the sample have 'm_1' molecular weight. Similarly, 'n_2' number of molecules have 'm_2' molecular weight and so on. This can be illustrated by Fig. 3.1.

Now, total number of molecules in the given polymer sample are

$$n = n_1 + n_2 + n_3 + \ldots\ldots + n_i$$

$$n = \sum_{i=1}^{i=i} n_i$$

The contribution of fraction n_1 to total sample i.e. number fraction

$$= \frac{n_1}{n} = \frac{n_1}{\sum_{i=1}^{i=i} n_i}$$

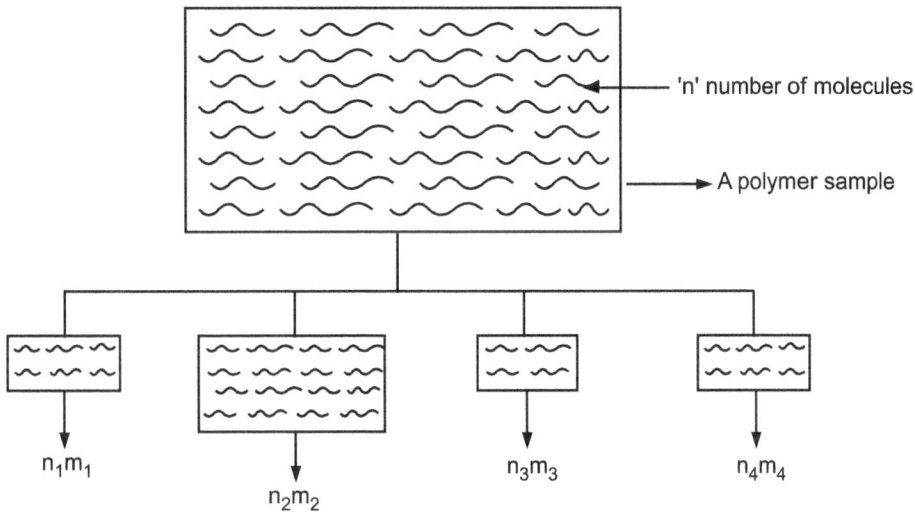

Fig. 3.1

Then contribution of fraction n_1 to total molecular weight of the sample

$$= \frac{n_1\, m_1}{\sum\limits_{i=1}^{i=i} n_i}$$

Similarly, the contribution from other fractions is given by

$$\frac{n_2\, m_2}{\sum\limits_{i=1}^{i=i} n_i}, \quad \frac{n_3\, m_3}{\sum\limits_{i=1}^{i=i} n_i} \quad \text{and so on.}$$

Then, the number average molecular weight is the addition of all these contributions by all fractions.

$$\overline{M}_n = \frac{n_1\, m_1}{\sum\limits_{i=1}^{i=i} n_i} + \frac{n_2\, m_2}{\sum\limits_{i=1}^{i=i} n_i} + \frac{n_3\, m_3}{\sum\limits_{i=1}^{i=i} n_i} + \ldots\ldots\ldots$$

$$\therefore \quad \overline{M}_n = \frac{\sum\limits_{i=1}^{i=i} n_i\, m_i}{\sum\limits_{i=1}^{i=i} n_i}$$

All experimental methods involving the colligative properties such as cryoscopy, ebulliometry and osmometry can be used to determine the number average molecular weights of the polymers.

3.5.2 Weight Average Molecular Weight ($\bar{M}w$)

Let us consider that the total weight of a given sample is 'W'. Similarly, let us assume that in the polymer sample there are n_1 number of polymer chains with molecular weight m_1 (fraction-1), n_2 number of polymer chains with molecular weight m_2 (fraction-2) and so on.

The weight of fraction 1 with n_1 polymer chains and m_1 molecular weight is

$$w_1 \;=\; n_1 \times m_1$$

Similarly, contribution from fraction-2 is

$$w_2 \;=\; n_2\, m_2$$

and so on.

Then weight fraction of fraction-1 $= \dfrac{n_1\, m_1}{W}$

Similarly, the weight fraction of fraction-2 $= \dfrac{n_2\, m_2}{W}$

and so on.

The contribution of weight fraction of fraction-1 to the molecular weight of polymer

$$= \text{Weight fraction} \times \text{Molecular weight}$$

$$= \frac{n_1\, m_1}{W} \times m_1 = \frac{n_1\, m_1^{2}}{W}$$

Similarly, for fraction-2, $= \dfrac{n_2\, m_2^{2}}{W}$

Then weight average molecular weight is

$$\bar{M}_w \;=\; \frac{n_1\, m_1^{2}}{W_1} + \frac{n_1\, m_1^{2}}{W_2} + \ldots\ldots\ldots + \frac{n_i\, m_i^{2}}{W_i}$$

$$\therefore \qquad \bar{M}_w \;=\; \frac{\displaystyle\sum_{i=1}^{i=i} n_i\, m_i^{2}}{\displaystyle\sum_{i=1}^{i=i} n_i\, m_i}$$

All experimental methods involving the weight of molecules such as scattering of light, ultracentrifugation can be used to determine the weight average molecular weights of the polymers.

Properties of Polymer Based on Molecular Weight

Molecular weight of a polymer is an important quantity. Many properties of polymer depend on the molecular weight. Some of the important properties are discussed here.

- Glass transition temperature and melting temperature: Higher is the molecular weight of a polymer, higher is its glass transition temperature and melting temperature.

- Flexibility and softness: Polymers with low molecular weight are flexible and soft.

- High molecular weight polymers are generally highly cross-linked and coiled whereas low molecular weight polymers are straight chain polymers.

- Many physical properties of polymers such as melt viscosity, impact strength, tensile strength also depend on the molecular weight of polymers.

3.6 CRYSTALLINITY IN POLYMERS

- Among various differences in polymers and other non-polymeric materials, crystallinity is a very significant one. The class of solid materials is divided into crystalline and amorphous materials. The number of crystalline materials is very large as compared to amorphous ones. In non-polymeric solids, a crystalline material shows same periodicity, geometry throughout the structure and that gives structural stability, rigidity, hardness to the material. An amorphous material does not possess long range order, specific geometry through the structure, hence such materials possess less strength lower hardness and lack in rigidity.

- In polymers however there is absence of complete order and periodicity in the material but within the solid there are regions of higher and lower degree of regularity. This leads to a unique property of percentage crystallinity which is not observed in other solids. Elasticity, flexibility, heat absorption can be related to percentage crystallinity in polymers.

- Crystallinity of a plastic can be externally controlled or tailored by addition of appropriate compounding agents like plasticizers. But such addition are known to reduce tensile strength and chemical resistance of compounded plastic. The degree to which molecules of a polymer are arranged in orderly pattern with respect to each other, is a measure of crystallinity of the polymer. Linear, straight chain polymers like nylon, polyester fibers have a better chance to have parallel orientation.

- Many polymers specially fibers are partially crystalline. Observation of X-ray diffraction pattern of such polymers show both sharp features associated with where there is 3-D order as well as more diffused or greasy pattern associated with molecularly disordered structure like liquid or glass. An additional proof of partial crystallinity comes from measurement of density it is always intermediate between completely crystalline and amorphous form of polymer. Fully extended chains are found in PE, PVA, PVC and polyamides.

- There has been evidence that single crystal of polymer can be produced. All structures of polymer signal crystal appear similar they are composed of flat platelets with thickness ~ 100 A° and area of several micrometers, helical, double helical, spherulite are other more complicated structures pressed by polymers.

- One can say that above Tg amorphous or low crystallinity polymers have rubbery state, moderately crystalline polymers appear tough and leathery and highly crystalline polymer appear stiff, hard and brittle. Below their Tg same polymers will appear glassy brittle, hornlike and tough and stiff, hard and brittle respectively.

3.7 PHASE TRANSITIONS IN POLYMERS T_M AND T_G

[Mar. 10, May 11, 12]

- If polymers are heated above certain temperature, the polymer chains in the sample try to go apart from each other after absorbing heat. This may lead to the state in which the polymer becomes a thick, highly viscous liquid. If the polymer is further heated, it becomes less viscous and slowly starts flowing.

- Viscous polymers are generally elastic in nature. This state of the polymer is called 'visco-elastic state'. The temperature above which the visco-elastic state of polymer is achieved is called melting temperature, it is denoted by T_m.

- If polymers are cooled below certain temperature, the polymer chain gets entangled in each other and it is very difficult to separate them. Under such conditions, the polymer becomes hard and brittle and behaves like a glass. This hard and brittle state of the polymer is called as 'glassy state'.

- The temperature below which the glassy state of the polymer is achieved is called as glass transition temperature. It is denoted by T_g.

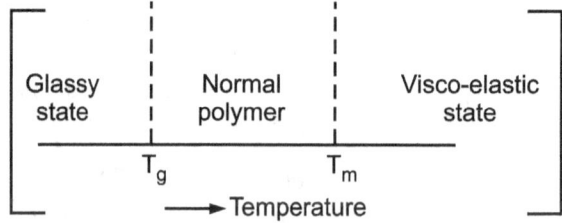

Definition of Glass Transition Temperature:

It is a temperature below which polymers are hard and brittle and above they become soft and flexible is called as glass transition temperature.

Following Table 3.1 shows T_g of commonly used polymers.

Table 3.1: Few Examples of Polymer with Melt Temperature and Glass Transition Temperature

Sr. No.	Polymer	T_g /°C	T_m / °C
1.	Polystyrene	100	250
2.	Polyvinyl chloride	80	310
3.	Polypropylene	− 18	208
4.	Polyacrylonitrile	97	341

Factors Affecting Glass Transition Temperature:

Molecular Weight:

If molecular weight of a polymer is high, then its density increases, hence high temperatures are required to convert the polymers to their visco-elastic state and they possess high glass transition temperature value.

Cross-Linking and Coiling:

If polymer chains are highly cross-linked or coiled in a polymer sample, then glass transition temperature for the polymers is high.

Intermolecular Forces of Attraction between Polymer Chains:

If a polymer contains a functional group such that the intermolecular forces of attraction between the chains are higher, then glass transition temperature of such polymers is higher.

Flexibility of Polymer Chains:

If polymer chains in a polymer sample are flexible such as simple straight chain hydrocarbon polymers (polyethene, polypropylene, etc.) then the glass transition temperature of such polymers is lower.

Addition of Plasticizers:

If plasticizers are added to polymers for a special purpose, they increase the flexibility, hence polymers become soft and glass transition temperature for such polymer decreases.

3.8 THERMOPLASTIC AND THERMOSETTING POLYMERS
[Dec. 08, 09, 14, May 08]

Polymers are classified into two classes depending on their reaction to heat/or temperature. These are:

- Thermosoftening or thermoplastic polymers.
- Thermosetting polymers.

- **Thermosoftening or Thermoplastic Polymers:**

The polymers which become soft, weak and flexible on heating and become hard and brittle on cooling are called thermosoftening or thermoplastic polymers.

The process of heating and cooling can be done reversibly then also these polymers do not loose their original properties, hence these polymers can be recycled easily.

- **Thermosetting Polymers:**

These polymers do not show the properties of thermosoftening polymers due to heating or cooling. If they are heated to higher temperature, they deform permanently and hence they cannot be recycled.

The differences between thermosoftening and thermosetting polymers are shown in the following table 3.2.

Table 3.2

Thermoplastic/Thermosoftening Polymers	Thermosetting Polymers
1. Thermoplastic polymers are generally formed by monomers containing C = C by addition reaction.	1. These polymers are generally formed by the monomers having functional groups such as $- NH_2$, $- COOH$, $- COOR$, etc. by condensation reaction.
2. They contain linear chain with negligible cross linking.	2. They are three dimensional, since they are highly cross-linked.
3. They are reversible to action of heat. i.e. they become soft on heating and hard on cooling repeatedly.	3. They do not become soft on heating, but if they are heated excessively, they decompose or burn or turn to ash.
4. The molecular weights of thermoplastic polymers are relatively lower.	4. The molecular weights of thermosetting polymers range from moderate to higher.
5. They are soluble in some of the organic solvents.	5. Almost all thermosetting polymers are insoluble due to higher degree of cross-linkage.
6. They can be recycled.	6. They cannot be recycled.
7. Shape and size can be changed number of times.	7. Shape and size of the thermosetting polymers is permanent and can be changed once they are moulded.
8. They are soft, weak and less brittle.	8. They are hard, strong and brittle.
9. Polyethylene (PE), polystyrene (PS), polyvinylchloride (PVC), etc.	9. Phenol-formaldehyde, urea-formaldehyde, silicones, etc.

3.9 COMPOUNDING OF PLASTICS   [Dec. 09, 11, May 09]

- The term compounding is applied to both selection of additives to modify the properties of polymers. It is the process that converts powdery, gummy or deliquescent polymer into soft homogeneous and mouldable mixture.

- The traditional compounding device is a two-roll mill which looks like a sugarcane juice miller. By proper selection of temperature, speed of rotation, the plastic is mode to adhere to the front roll. The compounding ingredients called as additives are added to the plastic mass. In many cases, the roll mill is supplemented by a mixer or extruder. Other compounding devices in common use are internal mixers such as kneaders, masticators and paddle blenders, tumblers and blenders.

- Pure polymers obtained from manufacturing plant cannot be directly used. Mostly they are amorphous, mechanically weak, colourless and hence need further processing.

- Conversion of this raw polymers/plastics into more usable form can be done by adding many external agents such as plasticizers, vulcanizing agents, stabilizers, fillers, colouring agents, flame retardants and lubricants is called as 'compounding of plastics.'

- These agents convert the raw plastic into the usable form. The functions of these adhesives are discussed here.

1. **Plasticizers:** Some polymers have horny texture and cannot be moulded easily. Plasticizers are added to such plastics and they are converted to soft and remouldable form. The function of plasticizers is to convert hard and tough polymers into soft one. e.g. for polyvinyl chloride, dibutyl pthalate, dioctyl sebacate are used as plasticizers.

2. **Vulcanizing Agents:** Linear and natural rubber is converted into highly cross-linked and usable rubber by adding vulcanizing agent by a process called vulcanization. Vulcanized rubber is strong and durable. e.g. Sulphur is a vulcanizing agent for natural rubber.

3. **Stabilizers:** It is known that polymers are not thermally stable at high temperature, also with passage of time decolouration takes place. In order to make them thermally stable and to avoid wear and tear due to time, stabilizers are added to plastic. e.g. Alkaline earth metals, salts, organometallic salts, epoxy compounds are added to PVC to make it a stable polymer.

4. **Fillers:** The polymers in their pure form are not mechanically strong. Fillers are added to polymers during processing in order to make them mechanically strong. e.g. Carbon black, $CaCO_3$, sand, etc. are added to natural rubber for mechanical strength.

5. **Colouring Agents:** Polymers in their pure form are generally colourless. In order to impart beautiful colours to plastic articles, colouring agents are added during processing. e.g. Paints and salts of transition metals.

6. **Lubricants:** Lubricants like wax, metal stearates, oleates, soaps, etc. are added to the plastic material, to release the finished article from the mould with ease and to impart a glossy finish to the product.

7. **Accelerators:** They are catalysts added to thermoset resins to speed up curing reactions. The common accelerators used in the manufacture of plastics are zinc oxide, calcium oxide, oxalic acid, etc.

8. **Anti-oxidants:** They prevent either slow oxidative degradation in service or rapid oxidative degradation at high temperatures. Plastics being organic, compounds are prone to oxidative degradation.

3.10 TECHNIQUES OF POLYMERIZATION   [Dec. 12, May 15]

On commercial scale, polymers are manufactured by four basic processes. viz bulk polymerization, solution polymerization, suspension and emulsion polymerization.

Bulk Polymerization: Generally used for reactions which are slow, less exothermic and involving condensation or step growth unit processes involved are mixing the reactants, agitation, material transfer, separation of byproduct and recycling of unreacted monomer. In continuous process, better control over heat of reaction can be achieved due to less amount of reactants per pass, this ensures lesser/smaller molecular weight distribution in the product. But in bulk polymerization, fast reactions like chain growth or highly exothermic reactions as there is a risk of hot spot formation or reaction may go out of control. Polymethyl methacrylate is manufactured by bulk polymerization.

Solution Polymerization: Homopolymerization reactions like polyvinyl acetate to be converted to polyvinyl alcohol are carried by solution polymerization. The choice of the solvent is most critical in this case; as the solvent is also used as heat transfer medium and the product formed should be used in partially wet form as it is very difficult to remove all the solvent. The above two methods are used in case of homogeneous system.

Suspension Polymerization: This process is heterogeneous polymerization. Name given to the process is suspension because the monomer is taken in solution phase and the product is formed as dispersed solid phase. In typical suspension polymerization, the initiator is dissolved in the monomer phase and the kinetics is same as that of bulk polymerization.

Polymerization of PMMA (polymethyl methacrylate) and polyvinyl chloride is done by this method. The limitation of the process is agglomeration which may happen if polymerization advances to a point where the polymer beads become sticky. At the completion of polymerization, the product is separated from the stabilizer by washing and dried. The products can be used as it is or can be compacted if required.

Emulsion Polymerization: An emulsion is a mixture of aqueous and non-aqueous solutions. The initiator is added in the aqueous phase and the monomer – polymer particles are quite small, of the size 0.1 µm in diameter. The soap plays an important role in emulsion polymerization. At the beginning of the reaction, the polymer is formed in soap micelles, these represent a favourable environment for the free radical generated in aqueous phase. The monomer droplets are unstable at this stage, if stirring is stopped, they coalesce into continuous oil phase containing no polymer. The rate of polymerization increases with increase in soap concentration.

3.11 PREPARATION, PROPERTIES AND APPLICATIONS OF COMMERCIAL PLASTICS   [Dec. 10, May 09, 11, 14]

3.11.1 Polyethene (PE)

Polyethene has huge commercial value because of its applications in everyday life. This is a simple hydrocarbon polymer and ethylene ($CH_2 = CH_2$) is used as a monomer.

Depending on commercial method of synthesis, there are two types of polyethene: **LDPE and HDPE.**

(i) Low Density Polyethene (LDPE):

  Synthesis:

$$n\ CH_2 = CH_2 \xrightarrow[\text{180 - 250°C / 1500 atm}]{\text{Initiators (0.1\%)}} -[-CH_2 - CH_2 -]-_n$$

  Ethylene   Polyethylene (LDPE)

The low density polyethene is produced at high pressures ($\approx$ 1500 atm) and small quantity of initiators ($\approx$ 0.1%) are sufficient to start the polymerization reactions.

The most commonly used initiators are oxygen, peroxides, hydroperoxides and azo group containing compounds.

The reactions take place at elevated temperatures of around 180 - 250°C.

Properties:

● The density of polyethene is low i.e. 0.91 to 0.92 g/cc. During the polymerization process, because of high temperature and pressure, 'chain transfer reactions' take place that lead to branching of the main polymer chain. These branches cannot be accommodated in small space i.e. the polymer does not remain compact, hence its density decreases.

- The LDPE has low crystallinity because of branching (40%).

- The melting temperature range for LDPE is 110 - 125°C.

- Practically it is insoluble in most of the solvents at room temperature, but it is observed that, it is soluble in many solvents such as CCl_4, $C_6H_5 - CH_3$ (Toluene), xylene, decaline and trichloroethylene at high temperatures.

- It is soft, weak, waxy and electrical insulator.

Uses:

- Packaging of articles, tools, textiles. Used as carry bags.
- Squeeze bottles and attractive containers.
- Water pipes for agricultural, irrigation and domestic water connection.
- Insulating material to electrical cables.

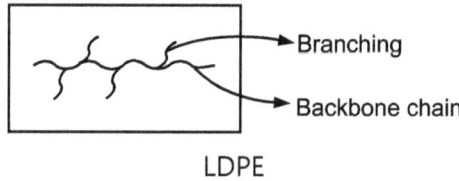

LDPE

(ii) High Density Polyethene (HDPE):

Synthesis:

(i)　$n\ CH_2 = CH_2$　$\xrightarrow[\text{10 - 20 atm / 60 - 100°C}]{\text{AlR}_3 + \text{TiCl}_3}$　$-[- CH_2 - CH_2 -]-_n$

　　　Ethylene　　　　　　　　　　　　　　Polyethene (HDPE)

(ii)　$n\ CH_2 = CH_2$　$\xrightarrow[\text{10 - 20 atm / 60 - 100°C}]{\text{CrO}_3 \text{ or MoO}_3}$　$-[- CH_2 - CH_2 -]-_n$

There are two methods to synthesize HDPE. In the first method, ethylene is polymerized to polyethene in the presence of Zieglar-Natta catalyst ($AlR_3 + TiCl_3$) at comparatively low temperatures (60 - 100°C) and low pressure (10 - 20 atm). In the second process, the polymerization is carried out in the presence of transition metal oxides such as chromium oxide or molybdenum oxide at 60 - 100°C and 10 - 20 atm.

Properties:

- The density is comparatively higher (0.945 - 0.965 g/cc) because, there is no branching in the polymer chains. So the chains arrange themselves compactly in a small space.

- The crystallinity of HDPE is higher ($\approx 90\%$) as the polymer chains are perfectly arranged.

- The melting temperature range of HDPE is 145 - 150°C.

- It shows the similar solubility properties as that of LDPE.
- It is stiff, strong and has high tensile strength and hardness.
- It is an electrical insulator.

Applications:

- Manufacture of toys and other household appliances where polyethene with high stiffness is required.
- It is used as lining for chemical reactors.

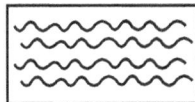

HDPE

Table 3.3: Differences between LDPE and HDPE

Characteristics	LDPE	HDPE
• Structure	Branched	Linear
• Density	Low (0.91 – 0.925 g/cm^3)	High (0.95 – 0.97 g/cm^3)
• Crystallinity	Low (~ 55 %)	High (80 – 90 %)
• Mechanical properties	Tough and flexible	Stiff and hard
• Water and gas permeability	High	Low
• Softening temperature	Low (115°C)	High (135°C)
• Applications	• Toys	• Crates
Mouldings	• Squeeze bottles for detergents	• Milk bottles
	• Mugs	• Food tubs,
		• Industrial containers
	• Carrier bags	• Overhead tanks
Films	• General packaging	• Films for wrapping food products

3.11.2 Epoxy Resins

These resins derived their name from the fact that monomer and the polymer (before cross-linking) contains epoxide groups. In fact, chemically they are polyethers.

Preparation:

They are prepared by condensation of bis phenol A and excess of epichlorohydrin so that each end of low molecular weight polymer has presence of epoxy group. This helps in cross-linking of polymer during thermosetting of the resin. The reaction is given below.

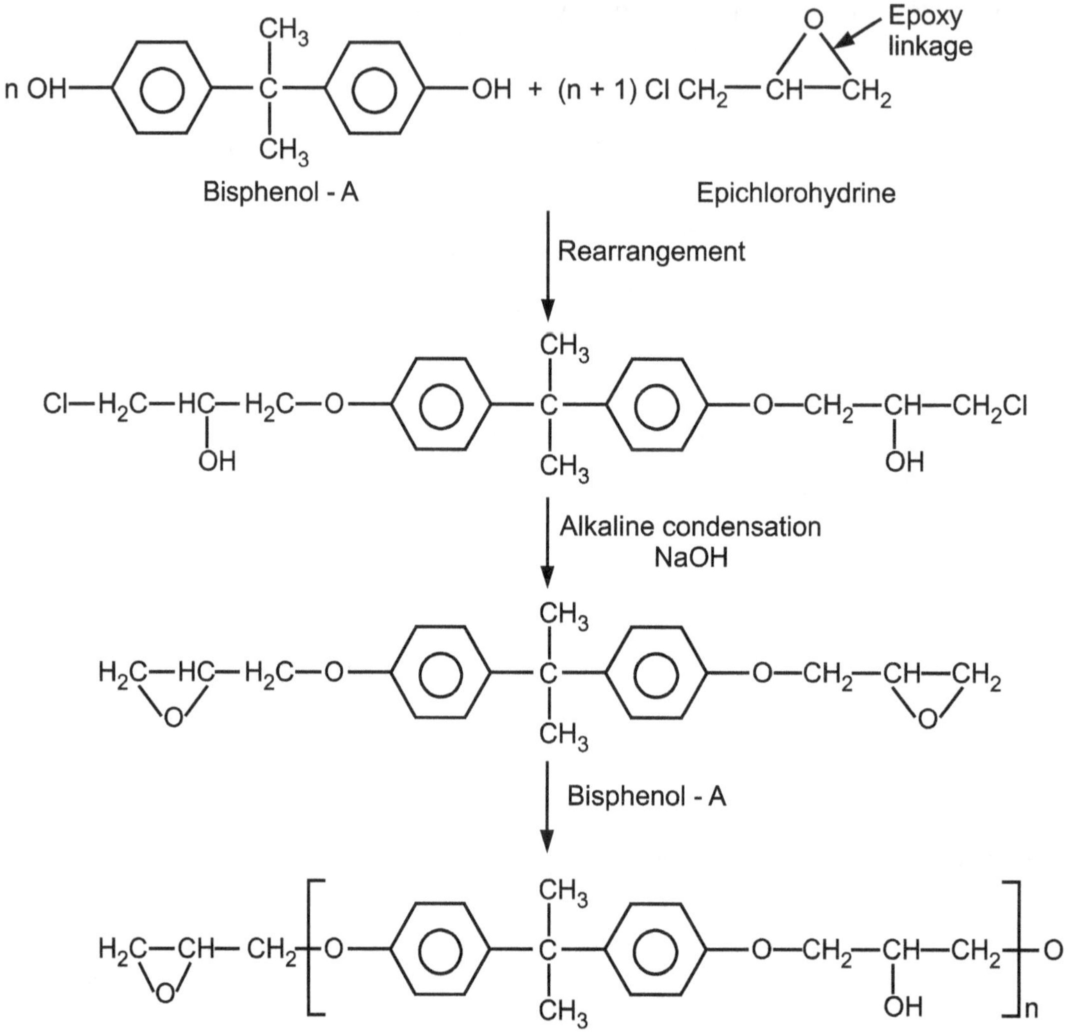

Bisphenol - A   Epichlorohydrine

Rearrangement

Alkaline condensation
NaOH

Bisphenol - A

Epoxy resin (Araldite)

The epoxy resin formed contains an epoxy group $\left[\begin{array}{c} CH_2 - CH \\ \diagdown O \diagup \end{array} \right]$ at one end. This group can

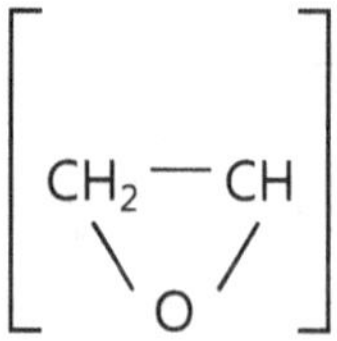

be used for making a cross-linked polymer. The process of preparing cross-linked polymer from linear polymer is called as **'curing'**. The commonly used cross-linking agents are amines, polysulphides and polyamides.

The cross-linked polymer gets formed by following reaction:

Epoxy resin

Cross-linked epoxy resin at epoxy group

Properties and Applications:

- Epoxy resins have excellent resistance to wear, they are also tough and heat resistant. Hence, they are used for surface coatings particularly for making skid-resistant surfaces for highways, road junctions and round about.

- Being polar, they have excellent adhesive characteristics and are used as adhesives for glass, metals etc. and are popularly known as araldite.

- Low water absorption tendency, dimensional stability, good heat and electrical resistance make them very good material for electronic applications particularly in mouldings containing inserts and encapsulation.

Major application of epoxy resins is in adhesives. Adhesives are compounds which can firmly hold or join two or more materials such as metal to metal, glass to metal, glass to glass, papers, plastics, etc.

Epoxy Resins Act as Adhesives with Following Advantages:

- Adhesion is carried out quickly.
- It is economic as compared to welding, screwing, rivetting, etc.
- The surfaces which are joined together are free from corrosion.
- Heterogeneous materials can be joined together.

Adhesives fall in two categories:

(i) Natural adhesives e.g. gum, glue, starch, caesin. They have lower strength and cannot bond different types of materials.

(ii) Synthetic adhesives e.g. epoxy resins (araldite), urea formaldehyde, phenol formaldehyde, silicones. They become hard on curing. These adhesives have high strength, more durability and better holding capacity for heterogeneous materials.

3.12 ELASTOMERS   [Dec. 08, 09, May 09, 11, 12, 13, 15]

- Rubbers are polymers with high molecular weight. They occur naturally and further processed, so that it can be used freely. They can also be synthesized in the laboratory using butadine or substituted butadine as monomers.

- Rubbers are also called as elastomers because they possess elasticity. i.e. if a stretching force is applied, they get elongated and if removed, they return back to the original length.

- The elasticity of rubbers is due to spring like (coiled) structure of polymeric chains in the whole sample. The coiled structure is due to presence of butadine and substituted butadine monomers. There are two types of rubbers: (i) Natural rubbers, (ii) Synthetic rubbers.

3.12.1 Natural Rubbers

(a) Isolation, Extraction and Preparation:

The chemical name of natural rubber is cis-1,4, polyisoprene. Isoprene is a methyl substituted butadine. Its structure is $CH_2 = C - CH = CH_2$.

$$| \\ CH_3$$

The natural rubber is obtained from 'Latex' extracted from rubber tree (Botanical name: Hevea brasiliensis). A 'T' shaped cut is made on the trunk of rubber tree. A white emulsion that comes out of the cut is collected. This white emulsion is called as latex.

The chemical composition of latex is

Isoprene: 30 - 60%

Plant proteins: 1 - 1.5%

Ash and sugars: 2%

and remaining water: 25 - 55%

Once the latex is obtained from tree, it is thoroughly washed with water to remove soluble impurities and filtered to remove solid impurities.

Then it is added to 1% acetic acid or formic acid.

Under these mild acidic conditions, cis-isoprene present in the emulsion undergoes polymerization to form a natural rubber.

cis - isoprene   cis - polyisoprene (natural rubber)

The natural rubber is present in a coagulated form. The coagulated solid rubber is removed from the bath and it is washed thoroughly.

(b) Processing of Natural Rubber:

Once the coagulated natural rubber is obtained, it is sent through rollers with gap of around 3 mm so that it is converted to thin sheets.

These thin sheets of rubber are exposed to smoke of tar oil so as to convert into the smoked rubber. The purpose of smoking is to avoid / resist the attack of micro-organisms and further degradation.

The smoked sheets of rubber are further compounded and hence converted to more useful form.

(c) Structure of Natural Rubber:

Natural rubber is cis-isomer of polyisoprene ($-CH_2$ groups are on the same side). Because of double bonding, the polymer chains get coiled as shown in the following figure with CH_3 groups pointing out of the spring. It is observed that the distance between the successive CH_3 groups is 8.1 A°.

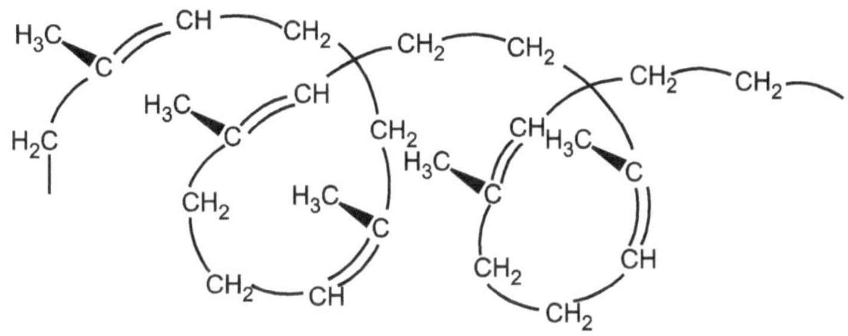

Coiled structure of cis - polyisoprene

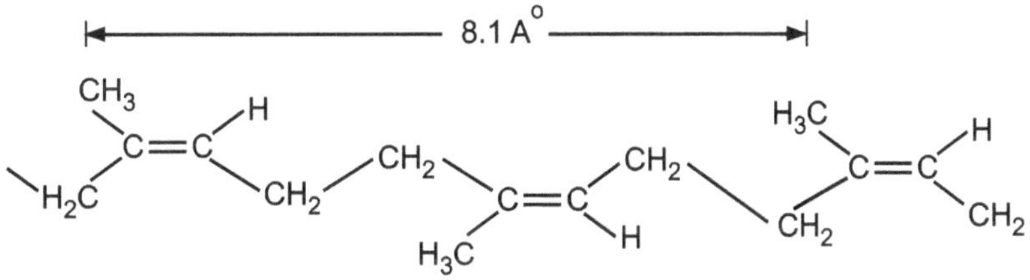

(d) Properties and Drawbacks of Natural Rubber:

● Raw or crude rubber becomes soft and sticky in hot summer, while in cold weather it becomes hard and brittle.

● It has low tensile strength (200 kg/cm²), so it is weak.

● It is attacked by oxidizing agents like HNO_3, conc. H_2SO_4, etc.

● It undergoes swelling and gradual disintegration in organic solvents.

● It possesses tackiness, which means that under pressure two fresh raw rubber surfaces coalesce together to form a single piece.

● When stretched to a great extent, some molecular chains undergo sliding or slippage over each other which results in permanent deformation.

- It is not durable as it undergoes oxidation in air.

To improve the properties of rubber, the process of vulcanization is done.

3.12.2 Processing and Vulcanization by Sulphur

Vulcanization is done on natural rubber to remove the drawbacks and on synthetic rubber to improve its useful properties.

Definition:

Vulcanization is the process during which natural or synthetic rubber is converted to its highly cross-linked form by heating the rubber at 110 - 150°C in the presence of suitable vulcanizing agents.

Sulphur and sulphur related compounds (S_2Cl_2, thioacids), zinc oxide (ZnO), benzoyl peroxide (Bz_2O_2) are most commonly used vulcanizing agents.

During vulcanization, structural changes take place in rubber so that, it is converted to mechanically strong and chemically resistant form.

(a) Vulcanization of Rubber by Sulphur:

Vulcanization of rubber is carried out by using sulphur as a vulcanizing agent or cross-linking agent.

Natural rubber is heated at 110 - 150°C to carry out the process of vulcanization.

The structural changes that take place during vulcanization are shown by following reaction.

$$
\begin{array}{c}
\quad\quad CH_3 \quad\quad\quad\quad\quad\quad CH_3 \\
\quad\quad | \quad\quad\quad\quad\quad\quad\quad\quad | \\
-CH_2-C=CH-CH_2-CH_2-C=CH-CH_2- \\
\\
-CH_2-C=CH-CH_2-CH_2-C=CH-CH_2- \\
\quad\quad | \quad\quad\quad\quad\quad\quad\quad\quad | \\
\quad\quad CH_3 \quad\quad\quad\quad\quad\quad CH_3
\end{array}
\quad + S_8
$$

$$\downarrow \;\; \Delta / 110 - 150°C$$

$$
\begin{array}{c}
CH_3\; H \quad\quad\quad\quad\quad CH_3\; S \\
| \quad\; | \quad\quad\quad\quad\quad\quad | \quad\; | \\
-CH_2-C-C-CH_2-CH_2-C-CH-CH_2- \\
| \quad\; | \quad\quad\quad\quad\quad\quad | \\
S \quad S \quad\quad\quad\quad\quad\quad S \\
| \quad\; | \quad\quad\quad\quad\quad\quad | \\
S \quad S \quad\quad\quad\quad\quad\quad S \\
| \quad\; | \quad\quad\quad\quad\quad\quad | \\
-CH_2-C-C-CH_2-CH_2-C-CH-CH_2- \\
| \quad\; | \quad\quad\quad\quad\quad\quad | \quad\; | \\
CH_3\; H \quad\quad\quad\quad\quad CH_3\; S \\
\quad\quad\quad\quad\quad\quad\quad\quad\quad\quad |
\end{array}
$$

The stiffness and hardness of the vulcanized rubber depend on the extent of vulcanization or amount of vulcanizing agent added during the process.

The comparison between vulcanized and unvulcanized rubber (raw or natural rubber are given below).

Table 3.4: Comparison between Vulcanized and Unvulcanized Rubber

Vulcanized Rubber	Raw/Natural or Unvulcanized Rubber
1. Since they are saturated (do not contain double or triple bond), they are strong mechanically and chemically.	1. They are comparatively weak since they contain unsaturated sites.
2. Mechanically strong and hard.	2. They are soft and weak.
3. High tensile strength > 2000 kg/cm^2.	3. Tensile strength is in the order of 100-200 kg/cm^2.
4. They have high molecular weight and are insoluble in common solvents.	4. Comparatively low molecular weight and are soluble in common organic solvents.
5. They can be used in wide temperature range of – 50 to 150°C.	5. They can be used only in 10 to 60°C.
6. They show no tackiness, do not absorb water, good abrasion resistant and do not show elongation.	6. They show tackiness, absorb water, poor abrasion resistant, high elongation property.

3.12.3 Synthetic Rubber-Styrene-Butadine Rubber (SBR)

Styrene-butadine rubber (SBR) is the first commercially made available synthetic rubber. It is a copolymer made up of two monomers i.e. styrene and butadine by free radical mechanism.

Synthesis:

Styrene - butadine rubber

Properties:

- It has high resistance to heat and ageing.
- Since double bonds are present in the rubber, it gets attacked by air, oxygen and ozone i.e. it gets oxidized easily.
- It has high load bearing capacity and endurance.
- It has low tensile strength, but it can be increased by vulcanization (vulcanization is possible since double bond is present) and addition of fillers such as carbon black.
- It has high abrasion resistance, but it swells in oils and many organic solvents.

Applications:

- Used for making tyres for motors and light vehicles.
- In footware industry, it can be used for making soles of shoes and other footware components.
- It can be used making floor tiles, lining of water tanks and reactors.
- Manufacture of pressure gaskets and adhesives, etc.

3.13 SPECIALITY POLYMERS

The specific applications like aerospace composites, membranes for gas liquid separation, fabric for fire fighting, flame retardants, racing suits, sutures and surgical implants, artificial heart valves, conducting polymers, liquid crystalline polymers, biopolymers, smart gels, etc. need polymers with special properties. Such polymers are called speciality polymers.

These polymers are developed for specific special applications which are not served by common plastics. Their properties can be modified by

- Selection of appropriate monomer.
- Selection of special additives.
- Use of controlled temperature, pressure, catalyst, stirring speed during polymerization.

The commonly used speciality polymer classes are:

- Conductive/Conducting polymers
- Liquid crystalline polymers (LCP)
- Thermally stable polymers
- Biodegradable polymers and
- Polymer composites

Polymers have some inherent limitations like

- Electrical insulators.
- Materials with low structural strength.
- Non-biodegradable.
- Low thermal stability.

But by proper choice of monomers and additives, one or more of above limitations can be overcome as what results is a speciality polymer. Such polymers are developed for certain specific applications. For example,

- For high impact strength and high heat resistance – polycarbonate, kevlar.

- For better electrical conduction and electroluminescence–polyacetylene, polypyrrole, polyphenylene vinylene.

- Biodegradable, biocompatible – polyhydroxy butyrate. Some of these members are discussed below.

The theory and reasons of above properties like theory of conductivity, luminescence is beyond the scope of the book, hence these materials are discussed on the basis of preparation, properties and uses.

3.13.1 Engineering Thermoplastics

Polycarbonate like inorganic carbonate plastic polycarbonate contains – CC OO – repeating units.

Polycarbonate can be prepared by the reaction between phosgene and bisphenol-A or by ester exchange between bisphenol A and diphenyl carbonate.

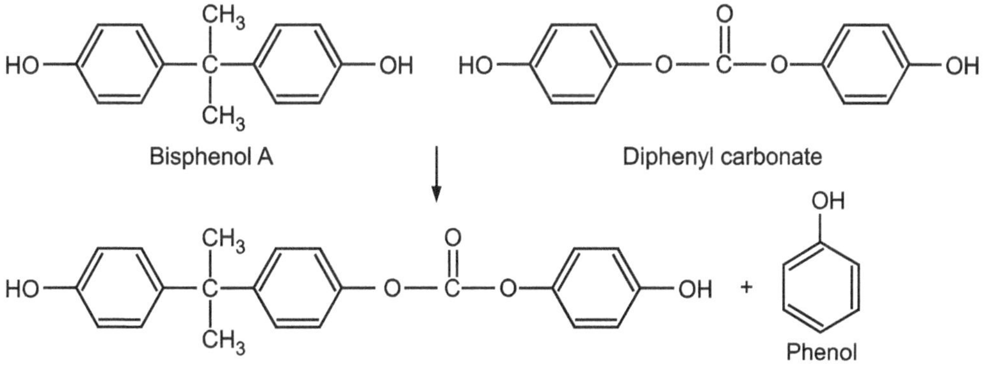

Bisphenol A   Diphenyl carbonate

                                        Phenol

It is commercially manufactured by injection moulding.

Properties:

- It is crystalline thermoplastic.

- It shows very good mechanical properties like high impact strength, even at low temperature.

- It has low moisture absorption.

- High heat resistance (140°C).

- High thermal and oxidation stability in molten state.

- It is transparent and self extinguishing.

Applications:

- All types of housing or casing for electrical appliances, home appliances, computer peripherals.

- Automobile head and tail light casing and lenses.

- Telephone and cell phone casings.

- Unbreakable crockery and glazing glass substitutes.

3.13.2 Conducting/Conductive Polymers

Most of the polymers do not conduct electricity, infact they are excellent electrical insulators. With developments in the technology of experimental methods in 1990s, few polymers are prepared that can conduct electricity to certain extent. It is observed that the conductivity of these specially prepared polymers lies between semiconductors and good conductors.

Table 3.5

Sr. No.	Nature of the Substance	Conductivity (mho/cm^2)	Example
1	Insulators	10^{-18} to 10^{-8}	PE, PP, Nylon, Glass
2	Semiconductors	10^{-5} to 10^2	Si, Ge, etc.
3	Conductive polymers	10^2 to 10^5	Polyacetylene, polyphenylene, polypyrrol, polythiophene
4	Metals/Good conductors	$> 10^5$	Iron, copper, graphite, etc.

Mechanism of Conductivity:

Some polymers are inherently conductive i.e. they conduct electricity on their own. Such conducting polymers are called as intrinsic conductors.

Some polymers are made (externally) conducting by addition of suitable substance to the polymer. The process of adding foreign substance to polymer and to make them conducting is called as doping. Such doped conducting polymers are called as extrinsic conductors.

Intrinsic Conductors:

If alternate double bonds are present in the polymer chain then the polymer conducts electricity on its own. Such a system is called as conjugated system. (It should be noted that out of these two bonds, one is a strong σ bond and the other is a weak π bond.)

In these systems (polymers) there is overlapping of conjugated π bonds over the entire polymer chain. This leads to formation of conduction bond (CB) and valence bond (VB). If the excitation of π electrons present in the VB is done by either supplying heat or exposing to light, then the polymer conducts electricity.

Examples:

1. **Conjugated Trans-Polyacetylene:**

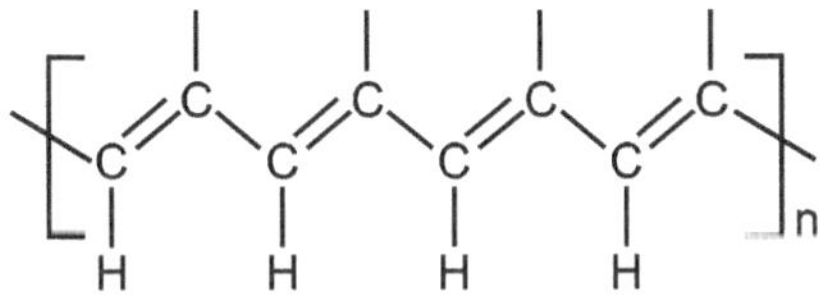

2. **Polyparaphenylene:**

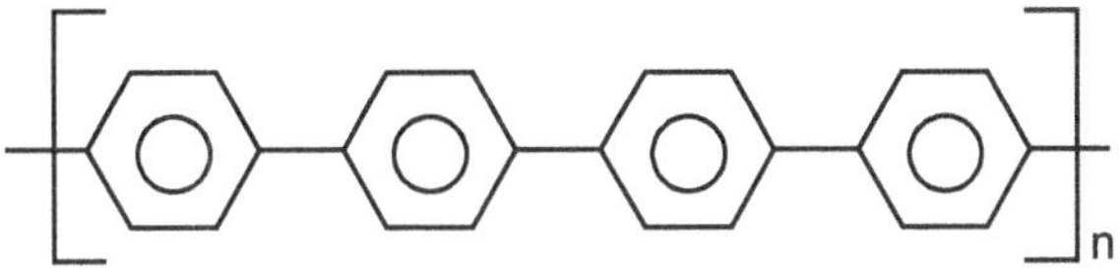

3. **Polypyrrole:**

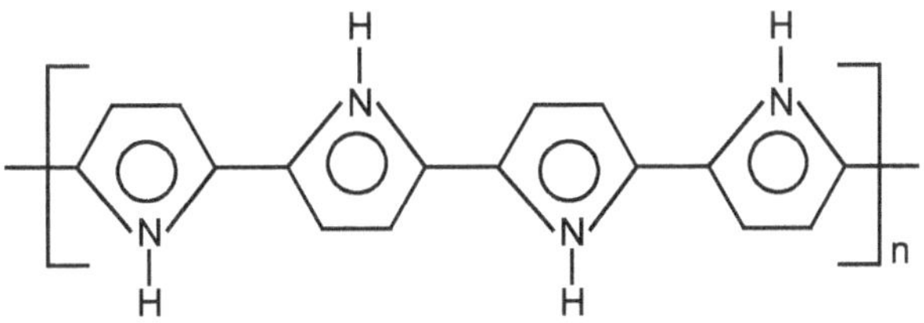

4. **Polyaniline:**

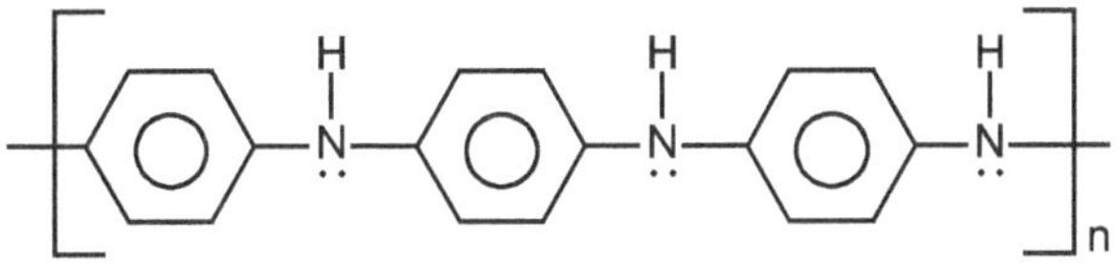

5. **Polythiophene:**

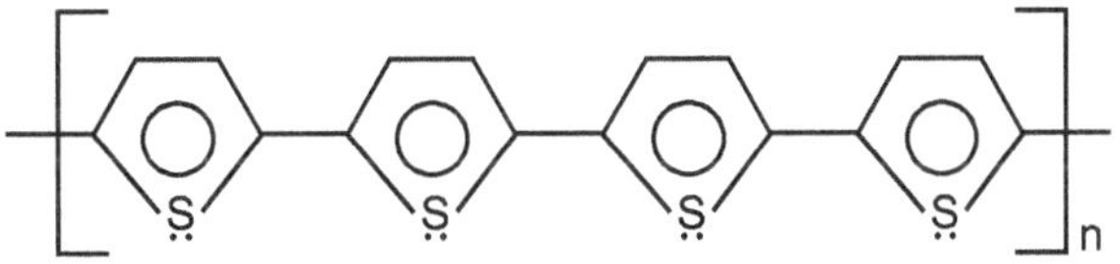

Extrinsic Conductors:

If the polymers are made conducting by doping, it is called extrinsic conductor. There are two types of doping.

(a) P-type Doping or Oxidative Doping:

A suitable oxidizing agent (e.g. halogen molecules) are added to conjugated polymer chains. The oxidizing agent extracts a pair of π electrons from chain and makes it a positively charged cation.

Delocalization of positive charge (hole) takes place over the whole polymer chain and it becomes conducting. e.g. polyacetylene + I_2.

$$\sim CH=CH-CH=CH-CH=CH-CH=CH-\sim + I_2$$

$$\sim CH = CH - CH = CH - CH = CH - \overset{\oplus}{CH} - CH \cdot I_2^-$$

(Delocalization of π electrons to fill the 'hole')

(P-type doping or Oxidative doping)

This is called as oxidative doping because the polymer chain has actually lost the π electrons to halogen molecule.

(b) N-type Doping or Reductive Doping:

A suitable reducing agent (e.g. Alkali metal atoms like Na, K, Li) are added to conjugated polymer chain which donate a pair of electrons to polymer chain. This makes the polymer chain a negatively charged anion (i.e. electron rich) and it becomes conducting.

e.g. Polyacetylene + Na

$$\sim CH=CH-CH=CH-CH=CH-CH=CH-CH\sim + \overset{..}{\underset{..}{Na}}$$

$$\sim CH = CH - CH = CH - CH = CH - CH - CH - \overset{\ominus}{CH} \sim \cdot \overset{+}{Na}$$

(Delocalization of π electrons to accommodate extra electrons)

(N-type doping or Reductive doping)

This is called as reductive doping because polymer chain has accepted electrons (hence gets reduced) from the metal atom.

3.13.3 Liquid Crystal Polymers (LCP)

- Liquid crystal is the term applied to any compound or polymer that shows the structural properties of liquids and pure crystals. Generally polymers are amorphous in nature with polymer chain entangled in each other and are highly disorganized.

- In order to make the polymer chains organized (i.e. to convert them to crystalline form), they have to be crystallized. The crystallization of a polymer can be done either by slowly cooling the melt of the polymers or slowly evaporating the solvent if they are present in the form of solution.

- Liquid crystal polymers are those polymers which have tendency to align the polymer chains over long distance before crystallization from their melts or solution.

- This means that in liquid crystal polymers, the polymer chains are present in the organized manner even when the polymer is not physically crystallized.

- This intermediate phase is also termed as mesophase and individual polymer chains are called as mesogens.

There are two types of liquid crystal polymers.

(A) Lyotropic Liquid Crystal Polymers:

The polymers which have tendency to align their polymer chains (mesogens) over a long distance before their crystallization from the solution is called as lyotropic liquid crystal polymers.

(B) Thermotropic Liquid Crystal Polymers:

The polymers which have tendency to align their polymer chains (mesogens) over a long distance before their crystallization from the melt is called as thermotropic liquid crystal polymers.

Further depending on alignment of the polymer chains (mesogens) in a liquid crystal along with an imaginary axis (called director), the liquid crystalline polymers are classified into three categories.

(a) Nematic Liquid Crystal Polymers:

The polymer chains (mesogens) are arranged in parallel or nearly parallel arrangement to each other along with the 'director'. The mesogens can rotate freely about the director.

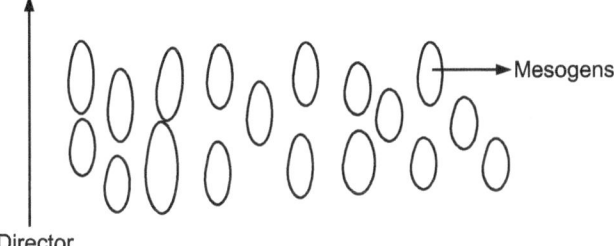

Fig. 3.2: Nematic liquid crystal polymers

It should be noted that, although the mesogens are parallel to each other, they are not present in one plane.

(b) Smectic Liquid Crystal Polymers:

The polymer chains (mesogens) are arranged in a parallel fashion as well as a group of mesogens is present in one plane.

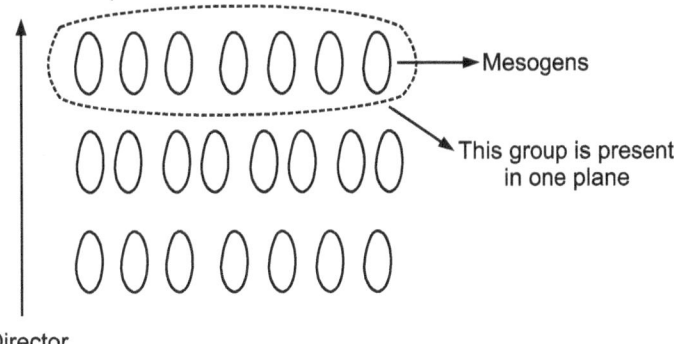

Fig. 3.3: Smectic liquid crystal polymers

These are highly ordered liquid crystal polymers.

(c) Cholesteric Liquid Crystal Polymers:

This is a modified nematic phase. In this type of LCP, the groups of mesogens in the nematic orientation come together in such a way that they form a disc like structure present over one another. Many directors are possible.

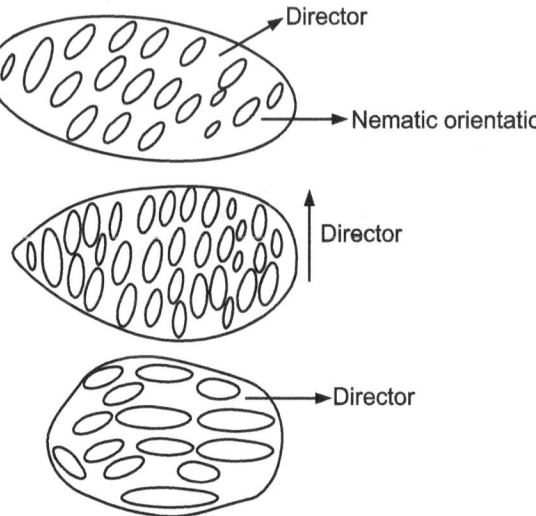

Fig. 3.4: Cholesteric liquid crystal polymers

The combination of all the discs is a cholesteric phase.

Examples of Liquid Crystal Polymers:

1. **Kevlar (Aramid):**

2. **Polyethylene terephthalate copolymer with p-hydroxy benzoic acid:**

Properties of Liquid Crystal Polymers:

- Liquid crystal polymers have high crystallinity (due to long range alignment of the polymer chains).

- The fibrous structure imparts thermal stability and mechanical strength.

- Because of high crystallinity, they have high melting temperature (T_m) and high glass transition temperature.

- Because of proper alignment of the polymer chains, if the light enters the polymer, it undergoes multiple reflections. i.e. they can behave like an optical fiber.

- Although they have high T_m and T_g, they are easy to process from melt solution.

Applications of Liquid Crystal Polymers:

- They can be used as optical fibers in digital telecommunications.
- They can be used as sensors for light in aerospace technology and day-to-day functioning of airports.
- Strategic applications: Military communications, automobiles and transport.
- Consumer appliances, etc.
- Liquid crystal displays.

3.13.4 Biodegradable Polymers

- The synthetic polymers do not undergo degradations easily. The life period of polymers range from few hundred years to millions of years.
- Polymers can be degraded by thermal, mechanical, ultrasonic waves, photo degradation, high energy radiations and oxidation. But most of the times, these processes produce by-products or degradation products that are harmful to environment. Also these methods are not commonly available.
- In order to overcome these drawbacks, biodegradation has become an attractive option. In biodegradation, polymers are converted to simple low molecular weight compounds such as CO_2, H_2O, NH_3, CH_4, etc.
- This degradation is generally carried out by the microorganisms, enzymes, environment and sometimes the nature of polymer itself is responsible for biodegradation.

(a) Degradation by Micro-Organisms:

Commonly occurring bacteria in the nature such as pseudomonas, bacilli, protozoa, many types of fungi act on the polymer and break the C – C bond slowly. In this process, the polymers are degraded slowly.

(b) Degradation by Enzymes:

Enzymes are the natural catalysts that speed up the process of degradation of polymers. e.g. α-amylose converts the natural polymer starch into simple sugars such as maltose.

(c) Degradation by Environmental Factors:

The constituents of atmosphere such as moisture, oxygen, ozone act on the σ bonds in the polymer chain and are responsible for breaking the long polymer chain into smaller chains that finally get converted to low molecular weight constituents such as N_2, NH_3, CO_2, CO, CH_4 and finally one can say that the polymer is degraded although the process is very slow.

(d) Nature of the Polymers:

All condensation polymers contain some functional group. If the functional groups present in the polymer chains are alike $-NH_2$ or carboxylic then such polymers undergo degradation easily as these groups have tendency to absorb water/moisture and swell and finally decompose.

Applications of Biodegradable Polymers:

- **Medical / Medicines:** Biodegradable polymers can be used for organ transplant and organ regeneration. They can also be used for making artificial organs. The biodegradable polymers find important applications in targeted drug delivery. The drug molecule is encompassed in the polymer and directed towards the site of pain. Here the drug molecule is released and polymer capsule cover undergoes biodegradation in the body itself.

- **Medical Surgicals:** The surgical apparatus such as gloves, syringes, etc. are now-a-days made from the biodegradable polymers.

- **Packaging Industry:** Biodegradable polymers are extensively being used in the packaging industry because conventional polymers are difficult to recycle.

Examples of Biodegradable Polymers: Poly lactic acid, poly glycolic acids, poly dioxane, copolymer of 3-hydroxy butyrate and 3-hydroxy valerate, etc.

For example, polyhydroxy butyrate (PHB). This polymer has ester functional group as repeating unit. In nature, under the conditions of physiological stress micro-organisms like Ralstonia eutrophus and Bacillus megaterium produce this polymer. It is a primary product of carbon assimilation, it is produced as an energy storage molecule when other commonly available forms like sugars or carbohydrates are not available it can be used as an energy source.

Preparation: Microbial biosynthesis of PHB starts with the condensation of two molecules of acetyl-COA to give acetoacetyl-COA which is subsequently reduced to hydroxy butyryl COA (carboxy alkanoate). This compound is then used as a monomer to polymerize PHB.

Polyhydroxy alkanoate

Other biodegradable polymers of the class which are also produced by variety of organisms are poly 4-hydroxy butyrate (P_4HB), polyhydroxy valerate (PHV), polyhydroxy hexanoate (PHH) and their copolymers.

3.13.5 Polymer Composites

For enhancing the properties of polymers such as mechanical strength or dimensional stability, some materials are added to the polymer matrix.

The addition of external materials to the polymer matrix is called as reinforcement and the polymers formed after reinforcement are called as polymer composites.

The polymer is called as substrate or matrix whereas the reinforced material is called as 'dispersed phase'.

Depending on the nature of reinforced materials, there are two types of polymer composites:

(a) Particle Reinforced Polymer Composites:

The materials having particle nature such as metal oxides, powders, nanoparticles, dust, various salts are added to polymer matrix as a dispersed phase.

(b) Fiber Reinforced Polymer Composites:

The materials having fibrous nature such as glass wool, carbon fibers, cellulose are added to the polymer matrix as a dispersed medium.

Change in Properties of polymers due to reinforcement OR Properties of polymer composites:

- **Decrease in Flexibility:** Due to reinforcement, the flexibility of the polymer decreases as compared to the original polymer matrix.
- The polymer composites are mechanically stronger than original polymers as well as reinforcement increases the dimensional stability of polymers.
- If metal oxides or metal particles are added to polymer matrix, then its conductivity (thermal as well as electrical) increases.
- The glass transition temperature (T_g) and the melting temperature (T_m) of the polymer composites is higher than that of the original polymer matrix.
- Due to reinforcement of cheaper substances, the cost of composites is lower as compared to the matrix.

Applications of Polymer Composites:

- Automobile engineering: Most of the automobile components such as main body, chassis, etc. need mechanically strong polymers. Polymer composites are excellent for such uses.
- They can be used for making boat parts, aircraft shafts and other aircraft components.
- High speed machinery parts, PCB, refrigerator components, coolers, cabins, etc.

3.13.6 Environmental Considerations and their Impact

Plastics and synthetic polymers are produced from hydrocarbons which do not decompose and they have to be stored, burnt or recycled at the end of their use. This is very detrimental impact on environment and it is known to increase green house gas emission and result into IR absorption etc. As PHB and other members of the class are compostable/ biodegradable, the number of environmental issues get taken care of. Fermentation can also be used to produce alcohol which can be used for plastic production.

Metabolix a U.S. company manufactured PHB in 2001 and received Presidential Green Chemistry Challenge Award for their cost effective manufacture of PHB in 2005.

Biopol (commercial name for PHB) is being used for internal suture as it is non-toxic, biodegradable and need not be removed after recovery.

Properties:

- Water insoluble, moisture resistant.
- Biodegradable.
- Good oxygen permeability.
- Good UV-resistance.
- Poor resistance to acids and bases.
- Soluble in chlorinated hydrocarbons.
- T_g - 2°C, T_m - 175°C.
- Non-toxic, denser than water.

SUMMARY

- Polymers are the substances formed by joining small molecules called as monomers.
- Number of functional groups or reactive sites on the monomer is called as functionality of monomer.
- The total number of monomer units combined together to form a polymer is called as degree of polymerization.
- Since exact number of monomer units in a polymer molecule cannot be known exactly, molecular weight of polymer cannot be calculated exactly.
- There are two methods to calculate average molecular weight of polymers: (i) weight average molecular weight, (ii) number average molecular weight.
- The temperature below which the polymers become brittle and behave like glass is called glass transition temperature.
- Polymers are classified based on number of monomer units, structure, tacticity, thermal behaviour, constitution, type of polymerization reaction etc.
- The polymerization reaction mechanisms are step growth polymerization and chain polymerization.
- Elastomers are molecules showing very high elasticity e.g. natural rubber, synthetic rubber, polyurethanes etc.
- Drawbacks of natural rubber can be removed by vulcanization.
- Important inorganic polymers are silicon base polymers, they show better thermal stability at high temperature than organic polymers. There biocompatibility is better than organic polymers, hence used in heart implant, artificial marrow.
- Specialty polymers are developed for specification applications like electronic display light emitting diode etc.
- Degradation of polymer can be brought by photo degradation or biodegradation.

UNIVERSITY QUESTIONS

DECEMBER 2012

1. Explain bulk and emulsion polymerization techniques.   **(6 Marks)**

2. Explain Kevlar and FRP with respect to their properties and applications.   **(6 Marks)**

MAY 2013

1. Define vulcanization. Explain vulcanization of natural rubber along with Chemical reaction involved. Compare natural rubber with vulcanized rubber w.r.t their properties.   **(6 Marks)**

2. Explain free-radical reaction mechanism for addition polymerization w.r.t monomer as vinyl chloride and initiator as acetyl peroxide.   **(3 Marks)**

3. What are intrinsic and extrinsic polymers? Explain with their examples.   **(3 Marks)**

NOVEMBER 2013

1. Give structural change on vulcanization of natural rubber molecules with sulphur. How does it affect the strength?   **(3 Marks)**

2. State the purpose of compounding polymers with plasticizers and filters.   **(3 Marks)**

3. Define biodegradation of polymers. State favourable structure of polymer for biodegradation. Write structure of biopol (PHBV).   **(3 Marks)**

4. Give any six differences in thermosoftening and thermosetting polymers.   **(3 Marks)**

MAY 2014

1. Define addition polymerization. Explain free radical reaction mechanism with suitable example.   **(6 Marks)**

2. Distinguish between LDPE and HDPE (any four Points).   **(3 Marks)**

3. Give preparation reaction, properties and uses of SBR.   **(3 Marks)**

DECEMBER 2014

1. Give preparation reaction, properties and uses of following polymers.   **(3 Marks)**

    (a) LDPE   (b) Styrene-butadiene rubber

2. Distinguish thermoplastic and thermosetting, polymer with suitable example.

3. What is biodegradable polymer ? Give the structure of PHBV and its applications ?

MAY 2015

1. What is vulcanization of rubber ? Explain chemical reaction involved in vulcanization process. Compare natural rubber with vulcanized rubber.   **(3 Marks)**

2. Explain with suitable diagram bulk polymerization technique to bring about addition polymerization. **(3 Marks)**

3. Give structure, properties and applications of polyphenylenevinylene (PPV). **(3 Marks)**

NOVEMBER 2015

1. Give the purpose and examples of the following constituents used during the compounding of plastics: **(3 Marks)**

    (i)   Fillers   (ii) Lubricants   (iii) Plasticizers.

2. Explain solution polymerization technique. Draw the figure and state the disadvantages of this technique. **(3 Marks)**

MAY 2016

1. Give preparation, reaction, properties and applications of following: **(6 Marks)**

    (i) Styrene-butadiene rubber   (ii)   HDPE.

2. Explain bulk polymerisation technique. Draw the figure and state its disadvantages. **(3 Marks)**

3. Distinguish between thermosoftening and thermosetting polymer with example. **(3 Marks)**

✠ ✠ ✠

FUELS AND COMBUSTION

4.1 FOSSIL FUELS

Energy has been the basic requirement of everyday life. Due to changing life styles and developments in the science and technology the human dependence on energy and the materials producing energy has increased by many folds. Energy is essential for transportation, manufacturing, electricity generation as well as for domestic consumption including cooking food, home lighting etc. Even for breathing, humans need energy. In fact it is known that standard of living of a population depends on per capita consumption of electricity (i.e. energy).

- Wood, coal and petroleum-based solid, liquid and gaseous fuels are the ultimate choice for energy generation because of low cost, ease of operation and easy availability. But overconsumption of these fuels is leading to their depletion. So newer sources of energy are being explored such as solar, nuclear energy, hydroelectricity, wind power, hydrogen as energy source. But as on today, these newer sources have only partially replaced the conventional fossil fuels.

- Nuclear fuels are superior of the conventional fuels because the amount of energy generated by nuclear fuels is much higher as compared to the conventional fuel. Consider the following nuclear reaction (fission).

$$_{92}^{235}U + _{0}^{1}n \longrightarrow _{56}^{144}Ba + _{36}^{90}Kr + 3\,_{0}^{1}n + \sim 200 \text{ MeV/atom}$$

- It is clear that if one atom of ^{235}U undergoes fission then the amount of energy generated is ~ 200 MeV.

Since 335 g $^{235}U \equiv 1$ mole of $^{235}U \equiv 6.023 \times 10^{23}$ atoms.

Fission of 1 atom gives 200 MeV then 1 mole of ^{235}U gives

$$6.023 \times 10^{23} \text{ atoms give } = 200 \times 6.023 \times 10^{23} \text{ MeV}$$

$$= 1.20 \times 10^{26} \text{ MeV}$$

We know that, $\qquad\qquad 1 \text{ eV } = 1.6 \times 10^{-19} \text{ J}$

then $\qquad\qquad 1.2 \times 10^{26} \text{ MeV } = ? \text{ J}$

$$= 1.6 \times 10^{-19} \times 1.2 \times 10^{26} \text{ MJ}$$

$$= 1.92 \times 10^{7} \text{ MJ}$$

- It is clear that, 1 mole i.e. 235 g of ^{235}U gives approximately 2×10^7 MJ of energy which is approximately equal to the energy produced by 10 tonnes of the coal. Hence nuclear fuels are concentrated source of energy.

- It should also be noted that, if 10 tonnes of the coal is burnt, then large volume of polluting gases such as CO_2, CO, CO_3 etc. are produced whereas radioactive waste produced by nuclear reactions is comparatively less, hence nuclear fuels are also cleaner sources of energy.

- Our focus in this chapter is on fossil fuels because they are the main sources of energy today and it is very difficult to imagine a better life without them.

4.2 DEFINITION AND CLASSIFICATION

Fuels are the substances which produce large amount of energy (or heat) on burning in presence or absence of oxygen.

4.2.1 Classification of Fuels

1. On the basis of mode of occurrence and preparation, fuels may be classified into two types:

   - Primary or natural fuels

   - Secondary or derived fuels

- **Primary or Natural Fuels:**

  Primary or natural fuels are defined as those fuels which can be used directly as they are obtained from nature to produce heat or energy.

  For example, cow dung, coal, wood etc.

- **Secondary or Derived Fuels:**

  Secondary or derived fuels are obtained by modifications in the primary fuel. These are derived from primary fuels.

  For example, petrol, diesel, naphtha etc.

2. On the basis of physical state of a fuel, fuels may be classified into three types such as:

   - Solid fuels

   - Liquid fuels and

   - Gaseous fuels.

4.2.2 Solid, Liquid and Gaseous Fuels

Solid, liquid and gaseous fuels can be compared on the basis of their characteristic properties as given follow:

Table 4.1: Comparison of Solid, Liquid and Gaseous Fuels

Sr. No.	Characteristic Property	Solid Fuels	Liquid Fuels	Gaseous Fuels
1.	Calorific Value (C.V.)	C.V. is least as compared to liquid and gaseous fuels.	C.V. is higher than solid fuels.	C.V. is the highest.
2.	Thermal Efficiency	Thermal efficiency is the least.	Thermal efficiency is higher than that of solid fuels.	Thermal efficiency is highest.
3.	Ignition Temperature	Highest.	Lower than solid fuels.	Lowest.
4.	Speed and Control of Combustion	Combustion is slow process and its control and stopping is not easy.	Quick combustion takes place. It can be controlled and stopped when needed.	Combustion takes place rapidly and more efficiently. Greater flexibility in usage is obtained available by controlling air supply.
5.	Tendency to form either ash and or Smoke during Combustion	Ash is always produced and its disposal is a problem, smoke is invariably produced.	No ash is produced and burning is clean, but aromatic fuels may produce smoke.	Neither ash nor smoke is produced.
6.	Application in Internal Combustion Engines	They cannot be used in internal combustion engines.	They can be used in internal combustion engines.	They can also be used in internal combustion engines.
7.	Amount of Air Needed for Combustion	They require excess of air for burning.	They burn in slight excess of air.	They also burn in slight excess of air.
8.	Availability and Cost	Easily available and cheap.	More costly than solid fuels.	Except natural gas, other fuels are costly.
9.	Transport, Storage and Handling	Transport, storage and handling is convenient without any risk of spontaneous explosion.	Can easily be transported through pipes, but care must be taken to store them in closed containers only.	Must be stored in leak-proof storage tanks and can be distributed through pipelines.
10.	Examples	Wood, coal.	Petrol, diesel.	CNG, LPG etc.

4.2.3 Criteria for Selection

The following characteristics are taken into consideration for the selection of fuel for various applications.

- The fuel selected should be most suitable for the process i.e. coke obtained from bituminous coal is most suitable for blast furnace, LPG – Domestic cooking, CNG – Light and medium vehicles, gasoline – Light and medium vehicles, diesel – heavy vehicles.

- The calorific value of a fuel should be as high as possible, so that its use becomes economical.

- The fuel should be low cost and readily available.

- The ignition temperature of a fuel should be moderate i.e. it should not be too high or too low.

- The rate of combustion of fuel should be moderate and controllable.

- The products formed during combustion of a fuel should be harmless, non-toxic and non-polluting.

- A fuel should be easy to transport, low cost, require less space for storage.

4.3 CALORIFIC VALUE   [May 09, 13, Dec. 09, 10, 15]

The most important property of a fuel is its calorific value. It is defined as:

"The amount of heat energy liberated when unit mass of a solid or non-volatile liquid fuel or unit volume of the gaseous fuel is completely burnt in the presence of oxygen at STP".

Units of Calorific Value: The units of calorific value in different systems are as follows:

System	Solid Fuel/Liquid Fuel	Gaseous Fuel
CGS	cal/gm	cal/lit
MKS	kcal/kg	$kcal/m^3$
SI	J/kg	J/m^3

The interrelations among different units of calorific value are:

1 cal/gm = 1 kcal/kg = 4.187 kJ/kg.   (for solid and liquid fuels)

$1 \ kcal/m^3 = 4.187 \ kJ/m^3$ (for gaseous fuels at STP)

4.3.1 Types of Calorific Values

- Main chemical composition of fossil fuels is carbon (C), hydrogen (H), oxygen (O), nitrogen (N), sulphur (S) along with a small amount of ash (i.e. inorganic components).

- Carbon is the main constituent responsible for heat generation as its oxidation liberates large amounts of energy i.e. $C + O_2 \rightarrow CO_2$ + Energy.

- When fuel is burnt, CO_2, H_2O, SO_2, SO_3, NO_2, NO_3 etc. gases are produced as byproducts. These are called as combustion products.

- Sometimes if the combustion products are condensed then latent heat of condensation is liberated which is additional to that of heat liberated during actual condensation.

- So depending on whether the combustion products are condensed or not, calorific values of fuels are of two types.

(a) Higher or Gross Calorific Value (GCV):

- "It is the amount of heat liberated when unit mass of a solid or non-volatile liquid fuel or unit volume of gaseous fuels are burnt in the presence of sufficient oxygen or air and the combustion products are allowed to cool at room temperature."

- During the cooling of combustion product, water vapour which is a combustion product gets converted to liquid water and latent heat of condensation is liberated. This is additional to the actual heat generated by combustion of carbon.

$$\therefore \quad \text{Total heat generated} = \begin{bmatrix} \text{Heat generated due} \\ \text{to combustion of fuel} \end{bmatrix} + \begin{bmatrix} \text{Heat liberated due to} \\ \text{condensation of water vapour} \end{bmatrix}$$

$$\therefore \quad \text{Gross calorific value} = \begin{bmatrix} \text{Heat generated} \\ \text{by combustion} \end{bmatrix} + \begin{bmatrix} \text{Heat liberated} \\ \text{by condensation of} \\ \text{water i.e. latent} \\ \text{heat of condensation} \end{bmatrix}$$

- The latent heat of condensation of other combustion products such as CO_2, SO_2, NO_2 is not considered because they cannot be condensed easily.

(b) Lower or Net Calorific Value (NCV):

- "It is the amount of heat liberated when unit mass of a solid or non-volatile liquid fuel or unit volume of gaseous fuel is completely burnt in the presence of sufficient oxygen or air and combustion products are allowed to escape as soon as they are formed".

- Since combustion products are allowed to escape, there is no question of their condensation.

- Latent heat of condensation of combustion products does not contribute to the calorific value measurements.

- Heat liberated is only due to the combustion of the constituents of fuel. Hence, this is also called as lower calorific value.

$$\therefore \qquad \text{GCV} = \text{NCV} + \text{L}$$

where, $\qquad \text{L} = \text{Latent heat of condensation of water}$

$$\text{L} = \frac{9 \times \% \, \text{H} \times 587}{100}$$

or $\qquad \text{L} = 0.09 \times \text{H} \times 587 \text{ cal/g or kcal/kg}$

$\therefore$ $\qquad \text{GCV} = \text{NCV} + 0.09 \times \text{H} \times 587 \text{ cal/g or kcal/kg}$

4.4 DETERMINATION OF CALORIFIC VALUE OF FUELS

- The experimental determination of calorific values is done by using apparatus called as 'calorimeters'.

- As it is known, the rate of ignition, ignition temperature, amount of air/oxygen required for combustion differ for solid, liquid and gaseous fuels.

- So the design of calorimeters is different for different types of fuels.

- For solid fuels (such as coal, starch, wood) and non-volatile or low volatile liquid fuels (alcohols, petrol, diesel), bomb's calorimeter is used.

- For gaseous fuels (LPG, CNG), boy's calorimeter is used.

4.4.1 Bomb's Calorimeter [Calorific values of Solid or Non-volatile Liquid Fuels]

Principle:

- "A known quantity of fuel is combusted in the calorimeter and the heat generated is allowed to absorb by known quantity of water. From rise in temperature of water, the calorific value of the combusted fuel can be determined by using the law of conservation of energy."

- It is difficult to make the design of calorimeter in such a way that the heat liberated is only absorbed by water.

- Some part of generated heat is always absorbed by calorimeter accessories such as bomb pot, stirrer etc.

- In order to account for heat absorbed by these accessories, the water equivalent of the calorimeter should be taken into consideration.

Construction:

- Fig. 4.1 shows the schematic diagram of bomb's calorimeter.

- The bomb's calorimeter contains outermost water jacket to make the system 'isolated' from the surrounding.

- Inside the water jacket, there is a copper calorimeter.

- The copper calorimeter is a removable part in water jacket and screw fitted during the experiment.

- Inside the copper calorimeter, there is most important apparatus called as bomb pot where actually the combustion of the fuel takes place.

- The space between the copper calorimeter and the bomb pot is filled with known quantity of water.

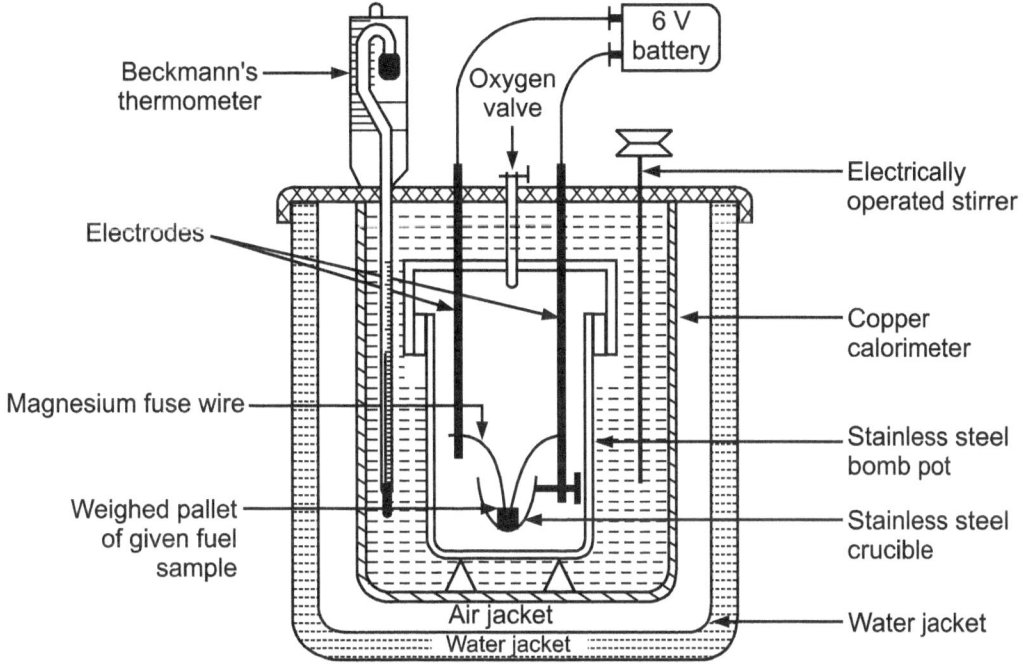

Fig. 4.1: Bomb's calorimeter

- In this space, the calorimeter accessories such as Beckmann's thermometer, stirrer are also fitted.
- Inside the bomb pot, there is a crucible which holds the fuel.
- Two metallic electrodes are inserted inside the bomb pot. The fuel in the crucible is brought in contact with electrodes with the help of magnesium fuse wires.
- These electrodes are attached to 6 V DC battery to start the combustion.
- As combustion takes place in the presence of oxygen/air, there is also an arrangement made so that oxygen can enter the bomb pot through oxygen valve.

Working:

- A known quantity of fuel (x gm) is kept in the crucible and the known quantity of water (W) is filled in the copper calorimeter.
- The calorimeter is fitted into the outer water jacket and screw fitted.
- The electrodes are brought in contact with the fuel with the help of fuse wires.
- The stirring of the water is started and initial temperature (i.e. temperature before combustion of fuel) is recorded with the help of thermometer (T_1).
- The oxygen is pumped into the bomb pot and its pressure is maintained at the pressure of 25 atmospheres.
- The desired current is passed through the battery for 3-4 sec that generates a spark so that the fuse wires are burnt.

- Since fuse wires are in contact with the fuel, the ignition of the fuel starts and the heat is liberated.

- This heat flows out of bomb pot and is absorbed by the water present in the calorimeter.

- The absorption of heat is made uniform by stirring the water continuously.

- The temperature of the water starts rising and the maximum temperature observed is recorded i.e. final temperature (T_2).

- The water equivalent of the calorimeter (w) is determined in a separate experiment using a standard fuel (e.g. Benzoic acid) whose calorific value is already known.

Calculations:

Let x = Mass of fuel burnt (gm)

W = Mass of water in the calorimeter (gm)

w = Water equivalent of calorimeter, stirrer, thermometer and bomb pot assembly (gm)

T_1 = Initial temperature of water before combustion of fuel (°C)

T_2 = Maximum temperature reached by water after combustion (°C)

S = Specific heat of water (cal/g/°C)

GCV = Gross calorific value of fuel (cal/g)

NCV = Net calorific value of the fuel (cal/g)

L = Latent heat of water

From the principle of conservation of energy,

Total heat generated by combustion of fuel = Heat absorbed by water + Heat absorbed by the calorimeter apparatus

$$x \cdot GCV = [S \cdot W (T_2 - T_1) + S \cdot w (T_2 - T_1)]$$

$$\therefore \quad x \cdot GCV = (W + w) \cdot S \cdot (T_2 - T_1)$$

Since S = Specific heat or heat capacity of water at constant pressure is 1 cal/g/°C.

$$\therefore \quad GCV = \frac{(W + w) \cdot (T_2 - T_1)}{x} \text{ (cal/g) } (S = 1 \text{ cal/g/°C})$$

$$\therefore \quad GCV = \frac{(W + w)(T_2 - T_1)}{x} \text{ cal/g}$$

$$\text{or} \quad GCV = \frac{4.184 (W + w)(T_2 - T_1)}{x} \text{ J/g as S = 4.184 J/g/°C} \quad \dots (1)$$

We know that,

$$GCV = NCV + L$$

$$NCV = GCV - L$$

$$NCV = \frac{(W + w)\ (T_2 - T_1)}{x} - \frac{9 \times \% \ H \times 587}{100} \ cal/g$$

In this way, GCV and NCV of a solid or non-volatile liquid fuels are determined using bomb's calorimeter apparatus.

From the bomb's calorimeter experiment, GCV of fuels can be obtained. But this value has to be corrected by applying correction because rise in temperature of the water has other contributions also.

(i) Fuse wire Correction:

The heat liberated, as measured by bomb experiment, includes the heat given out by ignition of the fuse wire. This heat, however small should be **deducted** from the gross heat liberated.

(ii) Acid Correction:

Fuels contain sulphur and nitrogen and produce SO_2 and NO_2. Water present in the calorimeter and formed during combustion dissolves these gases and produce H_2SO_4 and HNO_3.

These reactions are exothermic and produce heat which should be **deducted** from the gross heat liberated.

$$S + O_2 \ \rightarrow SO_2 + \frac{1}{2} O_2 \rightarrow SO_3$$

$$SO_3 + H_2O \ \rightarrow H_2SO_4$$

$$N + O_2 \ \rightarrow NO_2 \ \rightarrow \ NO_2 + 2\ H_2O \ \rightarrow \ 2\ HNO_3 + H_2$$

(iii) Cooling Correction:

Time taken to cool the water in the calorimeter from maximum temperature to room temperature is noted. From the rate of cooling (dt/min) and the time of cooling (t min.), the cooling correction of dt × t is to be added to the rise in temperature.

After applying all the above corrections, the gross calorific value is given by

$$GCV = \frac{(W + w)\ (t_2 - t_1 + cooling\ correction) - (Acid + fuse\ wire\ correction)}{Mass\ of\ fuel}$$

The latent heat of steam is 587 cal/gm or 2.54 J/kg. If 'H' is the percentage of hydrogen in fuel, the net calorific value can be calculated by the following equation.

$$N.C.V. = G.C.V. - \frac{9 \times H \times latent\ heat\ of\ condensation\ of\ water\ vapour}{100}$$

$$= G.C.V. - 0.09 \times H \times 587 \ cal/gm\ (kcal/kg)$$

4.4.2 Boy's Calorimeter [Calorific Values of Gaseous and Volatile Liquid Fuels]

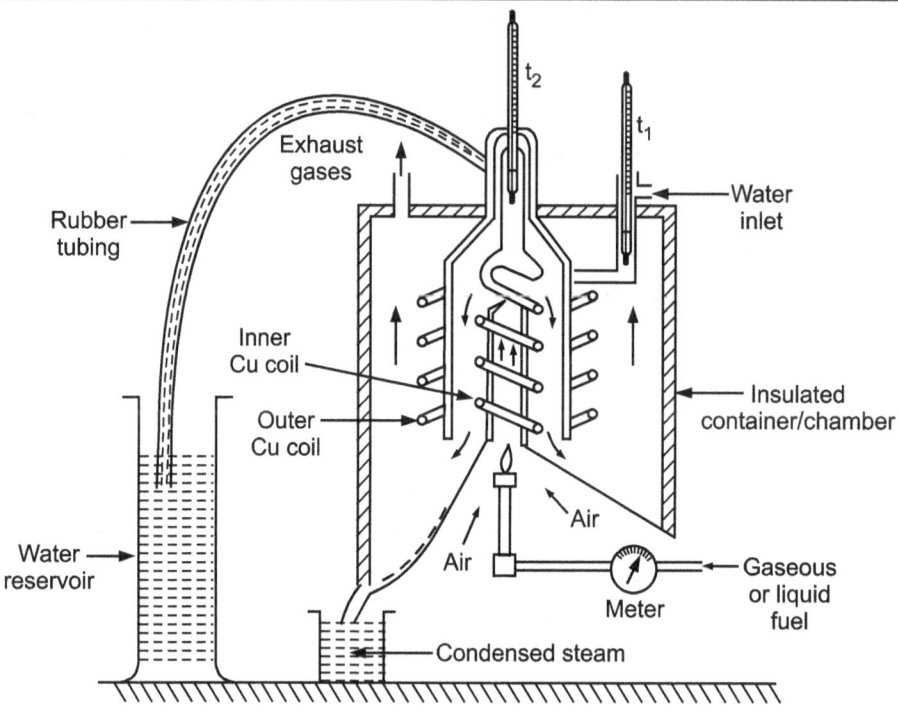

Fig. 4.2: Boy's calorimeter

Principle:

- "The heat liberated by combustion of known volume of fuel is allowed to be absorbed by known quantity of water circulating in the calorimeter. From rise in temperature of water and amount of steam condensate collected, the calorific value of gaseous and volatile liquid fuels can be determined".

Construction: Fig. 4.2 shows the schematic diagram of a boy's calorimeter.

- Boy's calorimeter consists of a gas burner connected to gaseous fuel reservoir and fuel enters the burner at constant pressure.

- The gas burner is surrounded by a hood whose inner surface and outer surface has hollow tube through which known quantity of water can be circulated during the experiment.

- The copper tube winding is done in such a way that the water circulates on the outer surface first, enters the inner surface of the hood from bottom and after circulating in the inner surface of the hood, goes out of the calorimeter as shown in Fig. 4.2.

- Two thermometers T_1 and T_2 are provided at the inlet and outlet of the circulating water to record the initial and final temperatures of water.

- The hood, burner and the circulating water is made an 'isolated' system by fitting them in an insulated container/chamber.
- There is also an arrangement to collect the condensed steam.
- The heated water that comes out of the inner copper tubing is collected in a water reservoir.

Working:

- Initially, water inlet and outlet are opened and the rate of flow of water entering the calorimeter is regulated and maintained at constant rate.
- The temperature of water (before combustion) is recorded as T_1 at inlet.
- Then the gas burner is started and the pressure of the gas entering the burner is maintained at 3-4 L/min.
- The heat generated by burning of the gas is absorbed by circulating water and its temperature rises.
- After sometime of burning of gas, the final temperature of water at the outlet is recorded as T_2.
- During this burning period, the mass of steam condensed is collected and recorded.

Calculation:

$$V = \text{Volume of gas burnt at S.T.P. in time 't'}$$
$$W = \text{Weight of circulating water}$$
$$T_1 = \text{Temperature of water at inlet}$$
$$T_2 = \text{Temperature of water at outlet}$$
$$m = \text{Mass of steam condensate collected}$$
$$L = \text{Gross calorific value}$$

and $\qquad S = \text{Specific heat of water}$

By law of conservation of energy,

Total heat produced by fuel combustion

$$= \text{Heat absorbed by circulating water}$$
$$VL = W(T_2 - T_1) \times S$$

$\therefore \qquad L = \dfrac{W(T_2 - T_1)}{V} \quad$ cal/g as $S = 1$ cal/g/°C

or $\qquad L = \dfrac{4.184 \times W(T_2 - T_1)}{V} \quad$ J/g as $S = 4.184$ J/g/°C

Net calorific value N,

$$N = L - \text{Latent heat of steam generated per cubic metre of fuel burnt}$$

$$N = \left[L - \frac{m \times 587}{V}\right] \text{kcal/m}^3$$

SOLVED EXAMPLES

Example 4.1: *0.72 g of a fuel contains 80% carbon, when burnt in a bomb's calorimeter, increased the temperature of water from 27.3° to 29.1 °C. If the calorimeter contains 250 g of water and its water equivalent is 150 g, calculate GCV of the fuel.* **(2 M) (May 05)**

Solution: Given: Weight of fuel = 0.72 g, T_2 = 29.1°C, T_1 = 27.3°C

$$W = 250 \text{ g, } w = 150 \text{ g}$$

$$GCV = \frac{(W + w)\,(T_2 - T_1)}{\text{Weight of fuel}} = \frac{250 + 150\,(29.1 - 27.3)}{0.72}$$

$$= \boxed{1000 \text{ cal/g or kcal/kg}}$$

Example 4.2: *1.6 g of coal sample in Kjeldahl's experiment liberated ammonia which was absorbed in 50 ml 0.5 N sulphuric acid. The resultant solution required 14 ml of 0.1 N NaOH for complete neutralization of H_2SO_4 in back titration. The reading for blank titration was 25 ml. Find percent of N in coal.* **(3 M) (Dec. 04)**

Solution: Given: Weight of coal = 1.6 g, V_1 = 50 ml, Conc. of H_2SO_4 = 0.5 N

After neutralization,

Volume of NaOH = 14 ml, Conc. of NaOH = 0.1 N

Reading for blank titration = 25 ml. % N in coal.

$$\% \text{ N} = \frac{(\text{Blank} - \text{Back}) \times \text{Conc. of acid} \times 1.4}{\text{Weight of coal}} = \frac{(25 - 14) \times 0.1 \times 1.4}{1.6}$$

$$\boxed{\% \text{ N} = 0.95\%}$$

Example 4.3: *1.2 g of coal sample was heated in silica crucible in an electric oven at 110 °C for 1 hr. The residue weighed 1.16 g.*

The crucible was ignited to a constant weight of 0.09 g. In another experiment, 1.2 g of sample was heated in a silica crucible covered with vented lid at 950 °C for 7 mins. After cooling the residue weighed 0.80 g. Calculate percent fixed carbon and GCV using Goutel formula. (G = 116). **(6 M) (Dec. 04)**

Solution: Given: (i) For % M,

Weight of coal = 1.2 g, Weight of residue after heating = 1.16 g

(ii) For ash content,

Weight of ash = 0.09 g

(iii) For % V_m,

Weight of coal = 1.2 g, Weight of residue = 0.8 g

(iv) Also calculate % FC and GCV.

$$G = 116$$

(i) $\% \text{ M} = \dfrac{\text{Weight of coal} - \text{Weight of residue}}{\text{Weight of coal}} \times 100$

$= \dfrac{1.2 - 1.16}{1.2} \times 100$

$\% \text{ M} = 3.3\%$

(ii) $\% \text{ Ash} = \dfrac{\text{Weight of ash}}{\text{Weight of coal}} \times 100$

$= \dfrac{0.09}{1.2} \times 100$

$\% \text{ Ash} = 7.5\%$

(iii) $\% \text{ V}_m = \dfrac{\text{Weight of coal} - \text{Weight of residue}}{\text{Weight of coal}} \times 100$

$= \dfrac{1.2 - 0.8}{1.2} \times 100$

$\% \text{ V}_m = 33.3\%$

(iv) $\% \text{ FC} = 100 - (\% \text{ M} + \% \text{ V}_m + \% \text{ Ash})$

$= 100 - (3.3 + 33.3 + 7.5)$

$= \boxed{55.9\%}$

Now, using Gothal formula,

(v) $\text{GCV} = 82 \times \% \text{ FC} + \text{G} \times \text{V}_m$

$= 82 \times 55.9 + 116 \times 33.3 \text{ cal/g}$

$= 8446.6 \text{ cal/g}$

$= \boxed{8.446 \text{ kcal/g}}$

4.5 SOLID FUELS

- The important solid fuels are wood, peat, lignite, coal, charcoal and briquetted fuels.
- In addition to these, certain agricultural and industrial wastes such as bagass, rice husk, coconut shells and nutshells are also used as fuels.

Wood:

- Wood is obtained from trees.
- It contains 25 to 50% moisture, which is reduced to 15% on air-drying.
- The calorific value of air-dried wood is about 3500 to 4500 kcal/kg. Wood is used as a domestic fuel.
- The average composition of wood on drying is C = 55%, H = 6%, O = 43%, Ash = 1%.

4.5.1 Coal

* Wood when converted into coal has higher fuel value.
* Coal is the product obtained by the continuous effect of heat, pressure and bacteria on the vegetable matter that got buried and remained underground for years together.
* Such progressive transformation of underground wood and other vegetable matter into coal with time is known as coalification. This process of coalification is associated with:
    1. Decrease in the moisture content.
    2. Decrease in hydrogen, oxygen, nitrogen and sulphur content with the corresponding rise in carbon content.
    3. Decrease in volatile matter content.
    4. Increase in calorific value.
    5. Increase in hardness.
* The various intermediates formed during coalification of wood are,

Wood $\longrightarrow$ Peat coal $\longrightarrow$ Lignite coal $\longrightarrow$ Bituminous coal $\longrightarrow$ Anthracite

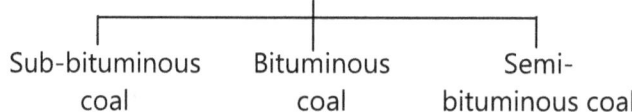

| Sub-bituminous | Bituminous | Semi- |
| coal | coal | bituminous coal |

Fig. 4.3 shows the variation in composition of coal at different stages of coalification with time.

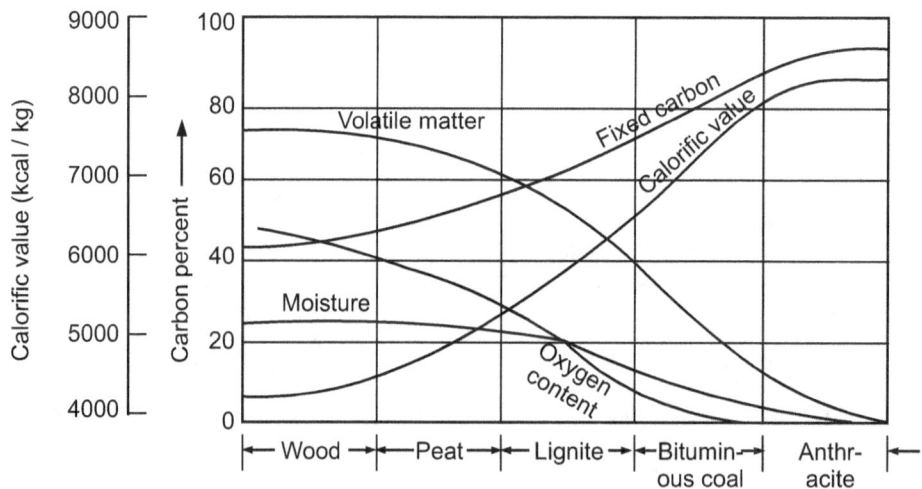

Fig. 4.3: Stages of coalification

Classification of Coal:

The conversion of wood (plant matter) into coal takes place progressively. Depending on extent of transformation, coals are divided into 4 types or grades or ranks.

    (1) Peat   (2) Lignite

    (3) Bituminous   (4) Anthracite.

Table 4.2: Properties and Uses of Different Grades of Coal

Type of Coal	C%	Texture	C.V. cal/gm	Uses
Peat	57	Brown and fibrous	5400	Domestic and industrial fuel, soil conditioning, thermal insulation, packing, gas purification.
Lignite	65	Intermediate between peat and black coal i.e. brownish black and compact.	6700	Power generation, domestic and industrial fuel, making 'producer gas', road and recovering various aromatic chemicals.
Sub-bituminous	75	Harder and denser than lignite, grey black and dull waxy lusture.	7000	Domestic and industrial purpose.
Bituminous	80	Bonded and laminated structure with after bright and dull layers, black, dense and hard.	8000	Making metallurgical coke and coal gas, domestic and industrial fuel, generation of steam and power.
Semi-bituminous	85	Between bituminous and anthracite coal, low volatile matter, coking.	8400	Making of coke, high temperature heating, coal gas and chemicals.
Anthracite	95	Lustrous black, hard, chonchoidal fracture. Burns with non-smoky short blue flame.	8700	Specific industrial purpose, metallurgical fuel, making electrodes, high temperature heating purpose.

4.5.2 Analysis of Coal and its Significance

- The composition of coal varies widely with respect to place and time. It is therefore necessary to analyze the given sample of coal and interpret the results for proper utilization and price fixation.
- Chemical analysis is also useful in grading a coal sample and determination of calorific value.

- The two types of analysis of coal are:
  1. The proximate analysis and
  2. The ultimate analysis.

(A) The Proximate Analysis:

- In proximate analysis, determination of percentage of moisture (% M), percentage of volatile matter (% V_m), percentage of ash (% A) and percentage of fixed carbon (% FC) in coal is done.
- It is a sequential analysis and the contents of coal sample are determined strictly in a particular order.
- Proximate analysis decides the suitability of a coal sample for a particular application.
- These results can be used to determine calorific value of coal sample.

(a) Moisture:

- A known weight of powdered and air-dried coal sample is taken in a crucible and it is placed in hot air oven for 1 hr at 110°C.
- Then the coal sample is cooled in a desiccator and weighed.
- If the initial weight of coal is m gm and final weight m_1 gm, then loss in weight $(m - m_1)$ corresponds to moisture in coal.

$$\text{Moisture \%} = \frac{\text{Loss in weight}}{\text{Weight of coal sample}} \times 100$$

$$\text{\% M} = \frac{m - m_1}{m} \times 100 \qquad \qquad \dots (1)$$

Significance of Moisture:

The percentage of moisture should be very low for a given coal sample, because

- Moisture in the coal evaporates during the burning of coal and it takes some of the heat liberated in the form of latent heat of evaporation, thus it lowers the effective calorific value of coal.
- More moisture causes clinker formation during burning of coal, which is not desirable.
- Moisture increases the weight of coal sample, due to which transportation charges increase as well as coal requires more space for storage.

Hence, lesser the moisture content, better is the quality of coal as a fuel.

(b) Determination of Percentage of Volatile Matter:

- Moisture free coal left in the crucible (m_1) from previous experiment is covered with a lid.
- Then it is heated to **925°C in a muffle furnace for 7 minutes**.

- The crucible is taken out and cooled in a dessicator. Then it is weighed (m_2 gm). The loss in weight ($m_1 - m_2$) is due to loss of volatile matter in the original m gm of the coal sample.

$$\% \, V_m = \frac{\text{Weight of volatile matter}}{\text{Weight of air dried coal}} \times 100 = \frac{m_1 - m_2}{m} \times 100$$

Alternatively, it can also be determined by taking fresh weight of air dried coal but the loss in weight at 925°C will be due to moisture as well as volatile matter.

Then in order to determine the % V_m, the % M should be subtracted.

Let,   w = weight of air dried coal, w_1 = mass of coal left

$$\therefore \quad \% \, V_m = \frac{(w - w_1) \times 100}{w} - \% \, M$$

Significance:

- Volatile matter is nothing but the matter, which escapes unburnt during the combustion of coal.
- Hence, if percentage of volatile matter is high, it lowers the calorific value. Coal with high volatile matter burns with a long flame and high smoke. Therefore, larger furnaces are required.
- Moreover, if the volatile matter consists of gases such as SO_2, CO, H_2S etc. it may affect the health of the operator. Hence, lesser the percentage of volatile matter, higher the overall quality of coal.

(c) Ash %:

- The residual coal in the above experiments is heated and burnt in an open crucible at above **750°C for 1/2 hr**. The combustible material is burnt completely.
- The coal gets burnt. The ash left in crucible is cooled and weighed (m_3). Ash is the non-combustible inorganic matter present in the coal.

$$\% \, Ash = \frac{\text{Weight of ash}}{\text{Weight of coal}} \times 100 = \frac{m_3}{m} \times 100$$

Significance of Ash Determination:

- Ash being the non-combustible matter, lowers the calorific value of coal and its disposal is another problem.
- Hence lower the ash content, better is the quantity of coal.
- The ash consists of silica, alumina, iron oxide and small quantities of magnesia, Na_2O, K_2O also and CaO.
- As coal/coke are used as reducing agents in several metallurgical operations, the composition of ash affects the slag and metal composition, its characteristics and it is the most important factor governing the selection of proper flux.

- Sometimes (depending on the composition) ash results in the formation of clinkers (lumps of ash) which causes uneven burning due to interruption of air supply.

(d) Fixed Carbon:

- The residue left on expulsion of volatile matter from coal contains inorganic matter originally present and fixed carbon.

  The fixed carbon = 100 – (% Moisture + % Volatile matter + % Ash)

- Fixed carbon varies inversely with volatile matter from coal.

- It represents the amount of carbon that will burn in solid state with primary air supply. More the percentage of fixed carbon, higher is the calorific value.

- As stated earlier, if the proximate analysis results are known, then the calorific value of the coal sample can be determined theoretically using following formula called as Gouthel formula:

$$GCV \; = \; 82 \times F.C. \; \% + a \cdot V_m \; \%$$

(B) The Ultimate Analysis:

In ultimate analysis, estimation of percentages of carbon, hydrogen, sulphur, nitrogen and oxygen in a given coal sample is carried out. The ultimate analysis is essential for calculating heat balances in any process for which coal is employed as a fuel.

(i) Determination of Carbon (C) and Hydrogen (H) in Coal.

Principle:

- Known weight of powdered and air dried coal sample is burnt in the presence of pure oxygen in a combustion apparatus.

- The carbon in the coal gets oxidized to CO_2 and hydrogen to water vapours on burning in the presence of pure oxygen.

Construction:

- The carbon and hydrogen composition of a coal sample can be determined using a combustion tube as shown in Fig. 4.4.

- It is a tubular chamber containing a porcelain boat is used to ignite the coal sample.

- A proper arrangement is made for pure oxygen supply.

- Two removable U tubes are attached to combustion tube containing anhydrous $CaCl_2$ (U-tube 1) and KOH solution (U-tube 2).

- It is known that $CaCl_2$ absorbs water vapour and KOH absorbs CO_2.

Working:

- Both the U-tubes are removed, their initial weights are recorded and again attached.

- A known quantity of coal sample is kept in the porcelain boat.

- O_2 is pumped in combustion tube and heated with the help of furnace.

- Combustion of fuel takes place leading to the formation of H_2O and CO_2 as combustion products of H and C respectively.

- Anhydrous $CaCl_2$ absorbs H_2O and KOH absorbs CO_2.

- Both the U-tubes are removed and their final weight is recorded.

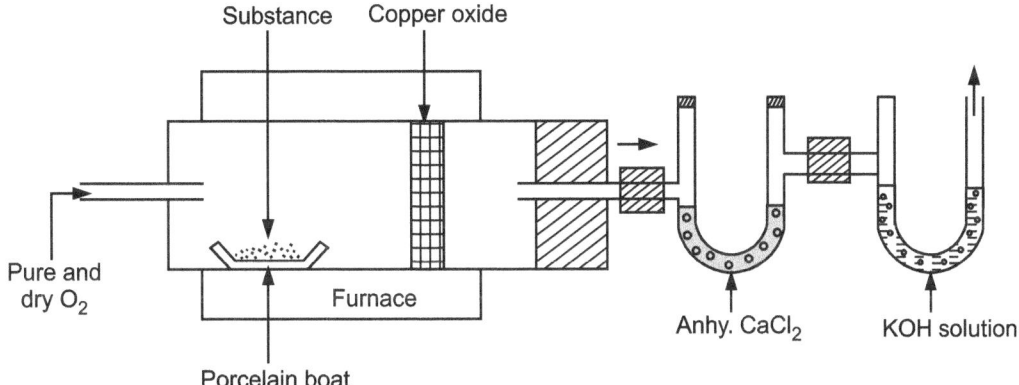

Fig. 4.4: Combustion tube

The increase in weights of U-tubes containing anhydrous $CaCl_2$ and KOH solution corresponds to weights of water formed and CO_2 formed respectively.

Calculations:

$$C + O_2 \;\rightarrow\; CO_2 \qquad\qquad 2\,KOH + CO_2 \rightarrow K_2CO_3 + H_2O$$
$$12 \qquad\qquad 44$$
$$2H + \tfrac{1}{2}\,O_2 \;\rightarrow\; H_2O \qquad\qquad CaCl_2 + H_2O \;\rightarrow\; CaCl_2 \cdot H_2O$$
$$2 \qquad\qquad 18$$

$$C\% \;=\; \frac{\text{Weight of } CO_2 \text{ formed (or increase in weight of KOH U-tube)} \times 12 \times 100}{\text{Weight of coal sample} \times 44}$$

$$H\% \;=\; \frac{\text{Weight of } H_2O \text{ formed (or increase in weight of } CaCl_2 \text{ U-tube)} \times 2 \times 100}{\text{Weight of coal sample} \times 18}$$

(ii) Nitrogen in coal (Kjeldhal's method):

Principle:

- Nitrogen in coal gets converted to ammonium sulphate by the action of hot conc. H_2SO_4 and then on treatment with alkali solution, equivalent amount of NH_3 is liberated.

Procedure:

- A known weight of powdered and air-dried coal is heated with conc. H_2SO_4 along with K_2SO_4 catalyst in a long necked Kjeldhal's flask.

- Formation of clear solution of $(NH_4)_2SO_4$ in the flask indicates complete conversion of nitrogen in the coal to $(NH_4)_2SO_4$.

- Ammonium sulphate thus formed is allowed to react with a strong alkali solution such as NaOH or KOH. This reaction gives out the gaseous ammonia (NH_3).

$$N + H_2SO_4 \xrightarrow[K_2SO_4]{\Delta} (NH_4)_2SO_4 \xrightarrow[\substack{Alkali \\ (KOH \text{ or } NaOH)}]{\Delta} NH_3$$

Standard acid

Volumetry

- The liberated ammonia (weak base) is allowed to react with standard acid.

- From the change in the concentration/volume of acid, the percentage of nitrogen in the coal sample can be calculated as:

$$N\% = \frac{\text{Volume of acid consumed} \times \text{Normality of acid} \times 1.4}{\text{Weight of coal sample}}$$

Or

$$N\% = \frac{\text{Volume of acid} \times \text{Change in normality of acid} \times 1.4}{\text{Weight of coal sample}}$$

(iii) Sulphur in Coal by Gravimetric Analysis:

- The sulphur content of a coal sample can be determined by using a bomb's calorimeter experiment.

- Take about 10 ml of distilled water in the bomb pot.

- Burn the known weight of powdered and air-dried coal sample in the bomb's calorimeter.

- Sulphur in the coal gets oxidised to SO_2 and SO_3 which on reaction with distilled water leads to the formation of H_2SO_4 as

$$S + O_2 \rightarrow SO_2 + \frac{1}{2}O_2 \rightarrow SO_3 + H_2O \rightarrow H_2SO_4$$

- Then collect the washings of the Bomb pot in a beaker and add $BaCl_2$ solution to it. The precipitate of $BaSO_4$ is formed.

$$H_2SO_4 + BaCl_2 \rightarrow BaSO_4 \downarrow + 2\,HCl$$

- It should be noted that the 'S' in $BaSO_4$ comes from the 'S' in the coal sample.

- Filter the precipitate of $BaSO_4$, dry it and weigh the precipitate of $BaSO_4$. From weight of $BaSO_4$ precipitate, sulphur % can be calculated as

$$S\% = \frac{\text{Weight of } BaSO_4 \text{ ppt.} \times 32 \times 100}{\text{Weight of coal sample} \times 233}$$

$$S \xrightarrow{O_2} SO_2 \xrightarrow{\frac{1}{2}O_2} SO_3 \xrightarrow{H_2O} H_2SO_4 \xrightarrow{BaCl_2} BaSO_4 \downarrow + 2HCl$$

(iv) Ash %:

Same as carried out in proximate analysis.

(v) Oxygen in Coal:

It is obtained by difference:

$$O\% = 100 - (C\% + H\% + N\% + ash\% + S\%)$$

Using the ultimate analysis results, the theoretical or gross calorific value can be calculated by using the following formula called as Dulong formula.

$$GCV = \frac{1}{100}[8.08 \times \%C + 34.44\left(\% H - \frac{\%O}{8}\right) + 2.25\% S] \text{ kcal/g}$$

$$GCV = \frac{1}{100}\left[33.8 \times \%C + 144\left(\% H - \frac{\% O}{8}\right)\right] + 9.357 \text{ kJ/g}$$

Significance of Ultimate Analysis:

- Since it is the analysis of chemical components in coal, hence it gives an idea about the combustible components responsible for energy of fuel.

- Calorific value of coal can be determined theoretically using ultimate analysis results.

- Carbon, hydrogen, nitrogen and sulphur when oxidised, liberate energy as these oxidation reactions are exothermic.

SOLVED EXAMPLES

Example 4.4: *A coal sample contains carbon = 4.185 kmole, hydrogen = 1.395 kmole, sulphur = 0.37 kmole and oxygen = 18.04 kmole. Calculate theoretical oxygen requirement per unit weight of coal and theoretical air requirement per unit weight of fuel.*

Solution: Basis: 100 kg coal is received.

1 kmole of carbon contain 12 kg, thus 4.185 kmole will contain 50.22 kg of carbon.

1 kmole of hydrogen contain 2 kg of hydrogen, thus 1.395 kmole will contain 2.79 kg of hydrogen.

1 kmole of sulphur contain 32 kg of sulphur, thus 0.012 kmole of sulphur contain 0.37 kg.

1 kmole of oxygen contain 32 kg of oxygen, thus 0.564 kmole contain 18.04 kg of oxygen.

Total oxygen requirement for 100 kg of coal

$$= \left[\frac{8}{3}C + 8H + S - O\right] kg$$

$$= \left[\frac{8}{3} \times 50.22 + 8 \times 2.79 + 0.37 - 18.04\right]$$

$$= [133.92 + 22.32 + 0.37 - 18.04]$$

$$= 138.57 \text{ kg of } O_2$$

Theoretical oxygen requirement for unit weight of coal

$$= \frac{138.57}{100} = \boxed{1.3857 \text{ kg } O_2/\text{kg coal}}$$

Theoretical air requirement for 100 kg of coal

$$= \frac{100}{23} \left[\left(\frac{8}{3} C + 8 H + S\right) - O\right]$$

$$= \frac{100}{23} \times 138.57$$

$$= \boxed{602.4782 \text{ kg}}$$

Theoretical air requirement for 1 kg of coal

$$= \frac{602.4782}{100} = \boxed{6.02478 \text{ kg/kg coal}}$$

Example 4.5: *The ultimate analysis of residual fuel oil (RFO) sample is given below:*

C = 88.4 %, H = 9.4 % and S = 2.2 %   **(3 M) (May 14)**

(1) Find the theoretical oxygen requirement, (2) Theoretical air requirement in kmoles.

Solution: (1) Basis: 100 kg RFO

Oxygen requirement of RFO $= \left(\frac{8}{3} C + 8 H + S\right)$

$$= \left(\frac{8}{3} \times 88.4 + 8 \times 9.4 + 2.2\right)$$

$$= 313.13 \text{ kg}$$

Theoretical air requirement in kmole

$$= \frac{\text{Theoretical oxygen requirement in kmole}}{0.21}$$

Theoretical oxygen requirement in kmole

$$= \frac{313.13}{32} = 9.785 \text{ kmole} = \frac{9.785}{0.21} = \boxed{46.5967 \text{ kmole}}$$

(2) A fuel has the following composition by mass: C = 86%, H = 11.75%, O = 2.25%. Calculate the theoretical air supply per kg of fuel.

$$\text{Basis} = 1 \text{ kg of fuel}$$
$$C = 86\% = 0.86 \text{ kg}$$
$$H = 11.75\% = 0.1175 \text{ kg}$$
$$O = 2.25\% = 0.0225 \text{ kg}$$

$$\text{Theoretical air supply} = \frac{100}{23}\left[\frac{8}{3}C + 8H + S - O\right]$$

$$= \frac{100}{23}\left[\frac{8}{3} \times 0.86 + 8 \times 0.1175 - 0.0225\right]$$

$$= \boxed{13.96 \text{ kg}}$$

Example 4.6: *The gravimetric analysis of coal gives 80 % C, 8 % H, 4 % moisture, 8 % ash. Actual air supplied is 18 kg/kg of coal. Determine the theoretical amount of air required if 80 % carbon is burnt to CO_2 and remaining to CO.*

Solution: Basis: 1 kg of coal

$$C = 0.8 \text{ kg}, \quad H = 0.08 \text{ kg}, \quad \text{moisture} = 0.04 \text{ kg}, \quad \text{ash} = 0.08 \text{ kg}$$

$$80\% \text{ burns to } CO_2 = 0.64 \text{ g}$$

$$20\% \text{ burns to } CO = 0.16 \text{ g}$$

$$\text{Theoretical oxygen required} = \left(\frac{8}{3} \times 0.64 + \frac{4}{3} \times 0.16 + 0.08 \times 8\right)$$

$$= \boxed{2.56 \text{ kg/kg coal}}$$

$$\text{Theoretical air required} = \frac{100}{23}(2.56) = \boxed{11.13 \text{ kg}}$$

Example 4.7: *A gas has the following composition by volume: H_2 = 20 %, CH_4 = 6 %, CO = 18 %, CO_2 = 8 %, O_2 = 5 %, N_2 = 43 %. If 25 % excess air is used, find the weight of air actually supplied per m^3 of this gas.*

Solution: Basis: 100 moles of gas.

Constituent	% and Moles	Moles of O_2 Required
H_2	20	10
CH_4	6	12
CO	18	9
O_2	5	− 5
N_2	43	−
		26

Air required for 100 moles of the gas

$$= 26 \times \frac{100}{21} = 123.8 \text{ moles.}$$

Air supplied actually (25 % excess) for 100 moles of gas

$$= 123.8 \times \frac{125}{100} = 154.75 \text{ moles}$$

$$\text{Air supplied for 1 mole of gas} = \frac{154.75}{100} = 1.5475 \text{ mole}$$

$$\text{Air supplied for 1 m}^3 \text{ of gas} = 1.5475 \text{ m}^3$$

$$= \frac{1.5475 \times 28.97}{22.4} = \boxed{2 \text{ kg}}$$

(Since 22.4 m³ of air i.e. 1 kg moles at N.T.P. weighs 28.95 kg).

Example 4.8: *1.2 gm of coal sample was heated in a silica crucible in an electric oven at 105-110°C for one hour, the residue weighed 1.16 gm. The residue was ignited at a constant of 0.09 gm. In another experiment, 1.2 gm of sample was heated in silica crucible covered with lid at 950 ± 20°C for 7 min. After cooling the residue weighed 0.8 gm. Calculate percentage of fixed carbon.*   **(4 M) (Nov. 07)**

Given:

(1) Weight of coal = 1.2 g

(2) Weight of coal after removal of moisture = 1.16 g

(3) Weight of ash = 0.09

(4) Weight of coal before experiment =1.2 g

(5) Weight of residue after experiment = 0.8 g

Calculate % of C.

Solution:

(1)   % Moisture (M) $= \dfrac{M - M_1}{M} \times 100$

$$= \frac{1.2 - 1.16}{1.2} \times 100$$

% M = 3.33 %

(2)   % Ash $= \dfrac{\text{Weight of ash}}{\text{Weight of coal}} \times 100$

$$= \frac{0.09}{1.2} \times 100$$

% Ash = 7.5%

(3) $\% \ V_m = \dfrac{M - M_3}{M} \times 100$

$= \dfrac{1.2 - 0.8}{1.2} \times 100$

$\% \ V_m = 33.3\%$

(4) $\% \ F.C. = 100 - (\% \ M + \% \ Ash + \% \ V_m)$

$= 100 - (3.33 + 7.5 + 33.3)$

$\boxed{\% \ F.C. = 55.8}$

Example 4.9: *Compare the proximate analysis results: 1.8 g of coal sample losses 0.270 g weight at 110°C. 1.5 g of the same coal sample loses 0.36 g weight at 925°C and 2.2 g of the coal sample leaves 0.28 g of ash.* **(4 M) (May 07)**

Solution: Given: (i) For moisture content, loss in weight = 0.27 g

(ii) For volatile matter, loss in weight = 0.36 g

(iii)   Weight of the ash = 0.28.

(1) $\% \ M = \dfrac{\text{Loss in weight of 110°C}}{\text{Weight of coal}} \times 100$

$= \dfrac{0.27}{1.8} \times 100 = \boxed{15\%}$

(2) $\% \ V_m = \dfrac{\text{Loss in weight}}{\text{Weight of coal}} \times 100$

$= \dfrac{0.36}{1.5} \times 100$

$\boxed{\% \ V_m = 24\%}$

(3) $\% \ Ash = \dfrac{\text{Weight of ash}}{\text{Weight of coal}} \times 100$

$= \dfrac{0.28}{2.2} \times 100$

$\boxed{\% \ Ash = 12.7\%}$

$\% \ FC = 100 - (\% \ M + \% \ Ash + \% \ V_m)$

$= 100 - (15 + 24 + 12.7)$

$\boxed{\% \ FC = 48.3\%}$

Example 4.10: *A coal sample was subjected to ultimate analysis, following are the results of different analysis:*

   (1) *0.24 g of sample on combustion gave 0.792 g of CO_2 and 0.0216 g of H_2O.*

   (2) *1.4 g of sample in a Kjeldahl's experiment liberated ammonia which was absorbed in 50 ml N/10 H_2SO_4. The resultant solution required 10 ml of N/10 NaOH solution for complete neutralization.*

   (3) *3.2 g of sample was analysed by Eschka method and gave 0.233 g $BaSO_4$.*

   Using Dulong's formula, calculate gross and net calorific value of the coal.

(Dec. 2006) (6 M)

Solution: Given: (1) For CO_2 and H_2O, Weight of coal $= 0.24$

Weight of $CO_2 = 0.792$ g, Weight of $H_2O = 0.216$ g

(2) For nitrogen, Weight of coal $= 1.4$ g, Conc. of $H_2SO_4 = 0.1$ N, $V_1 = 50$ ml,

   $V_2 = 10$ ml.

(3) For sulphur, Weight of coal $= 3.2$ g, Weight of $BaSO_4 = 0.233$ g

(1) $\% \, C = \dfrac{12}{44} \times \dfrac{0.792}{0.24} \times 100 = 90\%$

   $\% \, C = 90\%$

   $\% \, H = \dfrac{2}{18} \times \dfrac{0.0216}{0.24} \times 100 = 1\%$

$\therefore$ $\% \, H = 1.0\%$

(2) $\% \, N = \dfrac{\text{Volume of acid consumed by } NH_3 \times \text{Conc. of } BaSO_4 \times 1.4}{\text{Weight of coal}}$

   $= \dfrac{(50 - 10) \times 0.1 \times 1.4}{1.4} = 4\%$

$\therefore$ $\% \, N = 4.0\%$

(3) $\% \, S = \dfrac{32}{233} \times \dfrac{\text{Weight of } BaSO_4}{\text{Weight of coal}} \times 100$

   $= \dfrac{32}{233} \times \dfrac{0.233}{3.2} \times 100$

   $= 1\%$

$\therefore$ $\% \, S = 1.0\%$

   $\% \, O = 100 - (\% \, C + \% \, H + \% \, N + \% \, S)$

   $= 100 - (90 + 1 + 4 + 1)$

$\therefore$ $\% \, O = 4\%$

Now, using Dulong formula,

$$GCV = \frac{1}{100}\left[8.08 \times \% \, C + 34.44 \left(\% \, H - \frac{\% \, O}{8}\right) + 2.25 \, \% \, S\right]$$

$$= \frac{1}{100}\left[8.08 \times 90 + 34.44 \left(1 - \frac{4}{8}\right) + 2.25 \times 1\right]$$

$$\boxed{GCV = 7.467 \ \text{kcal/g}}$$

$$NCV = GCV - 9 \times \% \, H \times 0.587$$

$$= 7.467 - 9 \times 1 \times 0.587$$

$$\boxed{NCV = 2.184 \ \text{kcal/g}}$$

Example 4.11: *Calculate C, H, N, S % from the following observations for a sample of coal.*

   (1) *2.05 gm of the coal is burnt in combustion tube. The increase in weight of anhydrous 0.55 gm and increase in weight of KOH tube is 5.75 gm.*

   (2) *0.75 gm of the coal in Kjeldahl's experiment released NH_3, which is passed in 50 ml HCl. The HCl requires 4 ml of 0.12 N NaOH to neutralize in back titration.*

   (3) *Washings of the bomb pot when 1.8 gm of the coal sample in bomb calorimeter experimented with $BaCl_2$ solution to give 0.31 gm $BaSO_4$.*   **(6 M) (May 06)**

Solution: (i) For C, H percentage,

Weight of coal = 2.05 g, Increase in weight of $CaCl_2$ = 0.55 g,

Increase in weight of KOH = 5.75 g.

(ii) For % of nitrogen,

   Weight of coal sample = 0.75 g, V_2 = 50, V_1 = 4 ml,

     Conc. of NaOH = Conc. of HCl = 0.12 N

(iii) For % of sulphur, Weight of coal = 1.8 g, Weight of $BaSO_4$ = 0.31 g

(i) % of C,

$$\% \, C = \frac{12}{44} \times \frac{\text{Increase in weight of KOH U-tube}}{\text{Weight of coal}} \times 100$$

$$= \frac{12}{44} \times \frac{5.75}{2.05} \times 100$$

$$\boxed{\% \, C = 76.5 \, \%}$$

(ii) % of H, $\% \, H = \dfrac{2}{18} \times \dfrac{\text{Increase in weight of } CaCl_2 \text{ U-tube}}{\text{Weight of coal}} \times 100$

$$= \frac{2}{18} \times \frac{0.55}{2.05} \times 100$$

$$\boxed{\% \, H = 2.98\%}$$

(iii) % of N, $\%\,N = \dfrac{(V_2 - V_1) \times \text{Conc. of acid} \times 0.4}{\text{Weight of coal}}$

$= \dfrac{(50 - 4) \times 0.14 \times 1.4}{0.75}$

$\therefore$ $\boxed{\%\,N = 10.3\%}$

$\%\,S = \dfrac{32}{233} \times \dfrac{\text{Weight of BaSO}_4 \text{ ppt}}{\text{Weight of coal}} \times 100$

$= \dfrac{32}{233} \times \dfrac{0.31}{1.8} \times 100$

$\boxed{\%\,S = 2.36\%}$

Example 4.12: *2.5 g of air-dried coal sample was taken in a silica crucible after heating it in an electric oven at 105-110 ℃ for 1 hour. The residue weighed 2.395 g. The residue was then ignited at 700-750 ℃ to a constant weight of 0.252 g.*

In an another experiment, 1 g of the same sample was heated in a silica crucible covered with a vented lid at a temperature 950 ± 20 ℃ for exactly 7 minutes. After cooling, weight of residue was found to be 0.635 g. Calculate % of fixed carbon.   **(6 M) (Dec. 05)**

Solution: Given: (i) For moisture content,

Weight of coal = 2.5 g, Weight of residue after heating = 2.395 g,

(ii) Weight of ash = 0.252 g (Heating at 700 – 750°C per one hour)

(iii) For V_m content,   Weight of coal = 1 g, Weight of residue = 0.635 g.

(iv) Also calculate % FC.

(i) $\%\,M = \dfrac{\text{Weight of coal} - \text{Weight of residue}}{\text{Weight of coal}} \times 100$

$= \dfrac{2.5 - 2.395}{2.5} \times 100$

$\%\,M = 4.2\,\%$

(ii) $\%\,Ash = \dfrac{\text{Weight of ash}}{\text{Weight of coal}} \times 100$

$= \dfrac{0.252}{2.5} \times 100$

$\%\,Ash = 10.1\,\%$

(iii) $\%\,V_m = \dfrac{\text{Weight of coal} - \text{Weight of residue}}{\text{Weight of coal}} \times 100$

$$= \frac{1 - 0.635}{1} \times 100$$

$$\% \ V_m \ = \ 36.5 \ \%$$

(iv) $$\% \ FC \ = \ 100 - (\% \ M + \% \ V_m + \% \ Ash)$$

$$= \ 100 - (4.2 + 36.5 + 10.1)$$

$$\boxed{\% \ FC \ = \ 49.2 \ \%}$$

4.6 CARBONIZATION

- Carbonization is the process of heating bituminous coal at a suitable high temperature in **absence of air** (or oxygen) to obtain **coke and byproduct** gas which have superior properties as compared to coal.

- There are two types of carbonization,

  1. low temperature and

  2. high temperature carbonization. Table 4.3 gives the comparison between two types of carbonization processes.

Table 4.3

Sr. No.		Low Temperature Carbonization	High Temperature Carbonization
1.	Heating temperature	500 – 700°C	900 – 1200°C
2.	Coke yield	75 – 80%	65 – 75%
3.	Strength of coke	Lower strength	Higher strength
4.	Use of coke	Domestic, industrial	Metallurgy
5.	Quantity of byproduct gas	130 – 150 m^3/ton	300 – 400 m^3/ton
6.	C.V. of gas	6500 – 9500 kcal/m^3	5000 – 6000 kcal/m^3
7.	Aromatic hydrocarbon percentage	Low	High
8.	Percentage of alkanes in gas	Lower	Higher
9.	Hardness of coke products	Lower	Higher
10.	Smoke on burning coke	Slight smoke produced	No smoke
11.	Use of byproduct gas	As fuel	For tar, NH_3, aromatics etc.

4.7 LIQUID FUELS   [Dec. 08, 09, 10, 11, May 08, 09]

- The liquid fuels and lubricants in use today are obtained from petroleum or crude oil and a very small percentage comes from other natural sources like trees and animal fats also.

- The major source for liquid fuels is crude petroleum. Petra means rock and oleum means oil. It is a dark, greenish brown, viscous oil found deep in earth's crust.

4.7.1 Composition of Petroleum

- The chemical analysis of petroleum shows the presence of hydrocarbons such as paraffin, cycloparaffins or napthenes, olefins and aromatics along with a small percentage of organic compounds containing oxygen, nitrogen and sulphur.

- The approximate elemental composition of crude petroleum is:

$$C = 79.5\% \text{ to } 87.1\%$$
$$H = 11.5\% \text{ to } 14.8\%$$
$$S = 0.1\% \text{ to } 3.5\%$$

N and O together $= 0.1\%$ to 0.5%

4.7.2 Origin of Petroleum

(1) Carbide Theory or Mendeleef's Inorganic Theory:

- This theory postulates that, petroleum formed on the earth is due to inorganic substance (or elements) such as calcium and aluminium.

- This theory believes the formulation of petroleum from carbides of metals.

- Carbides are formed as a result of reaction between metals and carbon at high temperature and high pressure.

- The reaction sequence in formation of hydrocarbons from inorganic substances is

$$Ca + 2C \xrightarrow{\text{High temperature and high pressure}} CaC_2$$

Calcium carbide

$$4\,Al + 3C \xrightarrow{\text{High temperature and high pressure}} Al_4C_3$$

Aluminium carbide

$$CaC_2 + 2\,H_2O \longrightarrow Ca(OH)_2 + C_2H_2$$

Acetylene

$$Al_4C_3 + 12\,H_2O \longrightarrow 4\,Al(OH)_3 + 3\,CH_4$$

Methane

- Further, these lower hydrocarbons undergo hydrogenation, polymerization etc. to give higher hydrocarbons, paraffins, cycloparaffins and aromatic hydrocarbons.

Limitations:

This theory fails to explain the presence of

- Optically active compounds.
- Nitrogen and sulphur compounds and
- Chlorophylls, porphyrin etc. in the petroleum.

(2) Engler's Theory or Organic Theory:

- This theory explains the formation of petroleum from marine animals.
- Petroleum is formed by the partial decomposition of marine animals under high temperature and pressure.
- The aquatic life and vegetative matter like sea weeds get buried during natural calamity. In due course of time they got converted into petroleum under high temperature and high pressure over a period of few thousand years.
- This theory could explain following aspects of petroleum.
  (a) The existence of brine/sodium chloride solution in petroleum also suggests sea as its origin.
  (b) The presence of optically active sulphur and nitrogen compounds in petroleum suggests an organic origin of petroleum.
  (c) Presence of fossils in petroleum also suggests organic origin.

Limitation:

This theory fails to explain the presence of chlorophyll and radioactive compounds in petroleum.

(3) Modern Theory:

- According to this theory, petroleum has resulted from the partial decomposition of marine animals and vegetable matter of prehistoric forests.
- During natural calamities like heavy floods, volcanic eruptions the living matter got buried underground and eventually got converted into petroleum at high temperature and high pressure.
- The conversion of these materials into various hydrocarbons has been thought to be brought on either under the influence of radioactive substances like Uranium and/or by the anaerobic bacterial decomposition and high reducing conditions and under high temperature and high pressure.

4.7.3 Mining of Petroleum

- Crude oil is taken out from the earth's crust by drilling holes into it and inserting pipes in them. Oil usually comes out by itself due to electrostatic pressure of natural gas. It also may be taken out by mechanical pumps like lift or air-lift pumps.

- The air-lift pumps consist of two coaxial pipes lowered into the base oil bed. Compressed air is forced through the outer pipe, whereby oil rushes out through the inner pipe.

- The outcoming oil is sent for refining by a system of pipelines. A schematic diagram of mining of crude oil is given below.

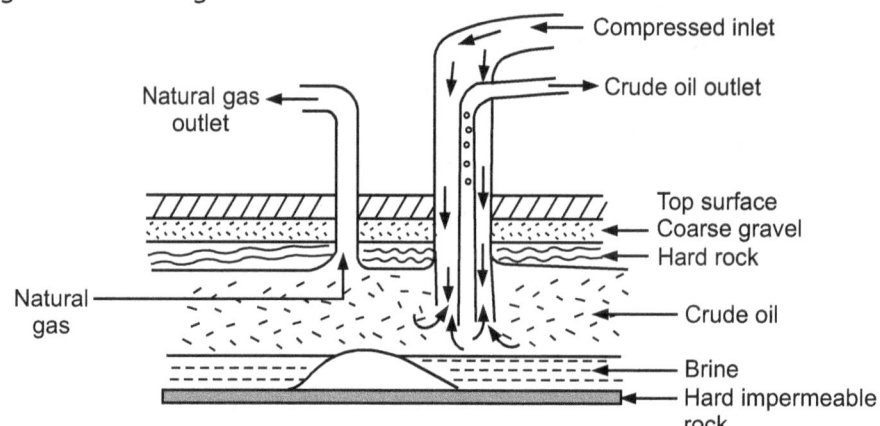

Fig. 4.5: Mining of crude oil and natural gas

4.7.4 Refining of Crude Oil

- The crude oil taken out from the oil wells cannot be directly used as fuel. It is a very thick oil with various impurities. It is separated into various useful fractions by fractional distillation. Unwanted ingredients and impurities are thereby removed and the desired products are obtained as distillations.

- The whole process is called as refining of crude oil. The plant set up for this purpose is called oil refinery.

- The process of refining of crude oil is carried out in the following steps.

Step I: Separation of Water by Cottrell's Process:

- From the oil well, oil is obtained in the form of a stable emulsion of oil and salt water. Hence, it is necessary to separate this emulsion into water and oil.

- It is carried out by allowing the crude oil to flow between the two highly charged electrodes.

- The colloidal water droplets coalesce to form large drops, which separate out from the oil.

Step II: (a) Removal of Harmful Sulphur Compounds:

- It involves treatment of oil with copper oxide. In reaction, copper sulphide precipitate, which is then removed by filtration.

$$2\,CuO + 2\,S \longrightarrow 2\,CuS + O_2$$

Copper sulphide

(b) Removal of NaCl and MgCl$_2$:

* Salts can corrode the refining equipment and cause scale formation in the heating pipes. Hence, modern techniques of electrical desalting and dehydration are developed for this purpose.

Step III: Fractional Distillation:

* **Principle:** *The fractions in the petroleum can be separated by using their boiling points. The fractions with lower B.P. are separated first followed by fractions with higher boiling points.*

* The crude oil is heated upto 400°C in an iron retort in which all volatile constituents except asphalt or coke are evaporated.

* The hot vapours are then passed up in a fractionating column.

* This process is carried out in a tall cylindrical tower containing a number of horizontal stainless steel trays at short distances as shown in Fig. 4.6.

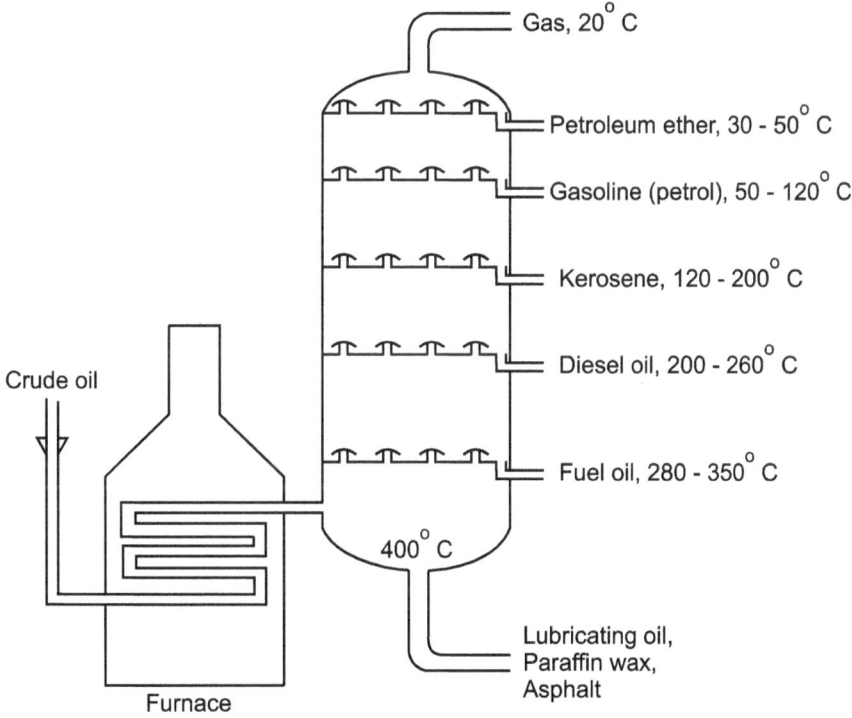

Fig. 4.6: Fractional distillation of crude oil

* Each tray has a small chimney, which is covered with a loose cap. As the vapours go up, they become gradually cooler and get condensed at different levels in the column.

* High boiling fractions (more than 350°C) condense first, while the lower boiling fractions (less than 350°C) condense at higher levels turn by turn.

- Various products obtained during fractional distillation are shown in Table 4.4.

Table 4.4: Fractions Obtained from Crude Oil

Sr. No.	Name of the Fraction	Boiling Range	Approximate Composition in Terms of Hydrocarbons	Use
1.	Uncondensed gases	Below 30°C	C_1 to C_4 such as ethane, propane, isobutene.	As a domestic or industrial fuel under the name L.P.G.
2.	Petroleum ether	30-70°C	$C_5 - C_7$	As a solvent.
3.	Gasoline or petrol or motor spirit	80-120°C	C_5-C_9 (Calorific value = 11,250 kcal/kg)	As a motor fuel, solvent and in dry cleaning.
4.	Naphtha solvent spirit	180-250°C	C_9-C_{10}	As a solvent and in dry cleaning.
5.	Kerosene oil	180-250°C	C_{10}-C_{16} (Calorific value = 11,000 kcal/kg)	As an illuminant, jet engine fuel and for preparing laboratory gas.
6.	Diesel oil or fuel oil or gas oil	250-320°C	C_{15}-C_{18} (Calorific value = 11,000 kcal/kg)	Diesel engine fuel.
7.	Heavy oil fraction	320-400°C	C_{17}-C_{30}	For getting gasoline by cracking process.
	(a) Lubricating oil	–	C_{17}-C_{20}	(a) As a lubricant
	(b) Petroleum jelly	–	C_{20}-C_{22}	(b) As a lubricant, cosmetics and medicines.
	(c) Grease	–	C_{23}-C_{27}	(c) As a lubricant.
	(d) Paraffin wax	–	C_{27}-C_{30}	(d) Candles, boot polishes, wax paper, tarpolin cloth etc.
8.	Residue may be either			
	(a) Asphalt or	Above 400°C	C_{30} and above	Water proofing of roofs and road making.
	(b) Petroleum coke	–	–	As a fuel and in moulding arc light rods.

4.8 KNOCKING   [Dec. 08, 10, May 12, 13, 15]

Definition of Knocking:

- Knocking is the sharp metallic rattling noise, in the internal combustion engine, developed due to the spontaneous ignition of the last unburnt portion of the fuel mixture.

- In an internal combustion engine (Spark ignition type), mixture of petrol vapour and air acts as a fuel and oxidizer respectively.

- In the downward stroke of the piston, a mixture of petrol vapour and air is drawn into the cylinder from the carburetor.

- It is known as the suction stroke. This mixture is compressed by an upward stroke of the piston.

- The ratio of the original volume of the fuel mixture to the fuel mixture to the final volume obtained after compression is called the compression ratio. This compression ratio is the ratio of the cylinder volume at the end of suction stroke to the volume at the end of compression stroke of the piston.

  Hence, compression ratio = $\dfrac{V_2}{V_1}$

- Efficiency of the internal combustion engine depends on this ratio. At the end of compression (upward) stroke, a spark from the ignition system ignites the compressed fuel mixture in the region close to the spark plug.

- The flame travels through the remaining fuel mixture rapidly but at a regular and orderly rate. The flame traverses the charge or the fuel mixture until it is completely consumed at a velocity of about 30 meters per second (Here, the essential chemical reaction is the oxidation of the hydrocarbon molecules in the petrol).

- The expanding gas drives the piston down the cylinder. As a result, the power is produced in the right direction.

- However, when the compression ratio exceeds the limit, the ignition of the charge or the fuel mixture takes place in a disordered manner.

- The first portion of the charge burns in a normal manner, but the last portion burns instantly. This causes a large momentary pressure imbalance in the cylinder.

- This sets in pressure waves or shock waves, because of these shock waves a rattling metallic noise of constant pitch is called 'knock'.

Factors (Reasons) Responsible for Knocking:

Following are the factors responsible for knocking:

- The design of the engine.
- Shape of the cylinder head.

- Location of spark plug and the manner in which it is operated.
- Type of fuel.

Overall knocking of the engine or overall knocking tendency depends mostly on the fuel used.

Effects of Knocking:

- Knocking increases the cylinder head temperature. To control the heating of engine, large amount of coolant is required.

4.8.1 Octane Number of Petrol

Definition of Octane Number:

- Octane number of a fuel is defined as the percentage by volume of iso-octane in an iso-octane and n-heptane mixture which matches the fuel in knocking property as the fuel under test.

- A good fuel should have a minimum knocking tendency. In other words, a good fuel should have the maximum anti-knock property.

- The extent or the degree of anti-knock property of a fuel is expressed in terms of octane number.

- Knocking quality of petrol is measured in terms of octane number which was introduced by Graham Edgar in 1926.

- Octane number is an arbitrary scale which expresses commonly the knocking characteristics of a petrol. A good fuel is that which has the minimum tendency to knock.

- The rating or scale is based upon the anti-knock property of standard mixture of iso-octane and n-heptane.

- It is observed that, the component iso-octane (C_8H_{18}) with the structural formula as shown below has very good combustion properties.

- It shows very high anti-knocking property. It is assigned the octane value 100.

- On the other hand, the straight chain hydrocarbon n-heptane C_7H_{16} with the structure $CH_3-CH_2-CH_2-CH_2-CH_2-CH_2-CH_3$ has the maximum knocking tendency or the minimum anti-knocking property.

- The octane number assigned to n-heptane is zero.

- The various percentage mixtures of these two components make a series of fuels which will have anti-knock property or octane number from 0 to 100.

- These mixtures are standard. The fuel under consideration is compared with these mixtures.

- If the sample of gasoline matches the knocking of the mixture of 85 parts of iso-octane and 15 parts of n heptane, then the octane number given to the gasoline sample is 85.

$$CH_3 — (CH_2)_5 — CH_3$$

n - heptane, octane number = 0

$$CH_3 — \underset{\underset{CH_3}{|}}{\overset{\overset{CH_3}{|}}{C}} — CH_2 — CH_2 — CH_2 — CH_3$$

Iso - octane, octane number = 100

Chemical Structure of Fuel and Knocking:

- Knocking mostly depends upon the fuel used. Tendency of gasoline to undergo knocking depends upon the nature and structure of the hydrocarbons present in the gasoline.

- Petrol containing straight chain paraffin knocks the most and petrol containing aromatics knocks the least.

- Gasoline formed by cracking has higher octane number than the straight run gasoline.

- The tendency of the knocking decreases in the following order:

  Straight chain > Branched chain > Olefins > Cycloparaffins > Aromatics > Paraffins.

Anti-knocking Agents

- The knocking tendency of gasoline is controlled by addition of some chemical reagents like Tetra Ethyl Lead (TEL), Aromatic phosphates like cresyl diphenyl phosphate etc.

4.8.2 Cetane Number of Diesel

Definition of Cetane Number:

- The cetane number of a diesel oil is defined as the percentage by volume of cetane in a mixture of cetane and a methyl naphthalene which exactly matches in its knocking property of the oil under test.

- Cetane number is a measure of knocking characteristics of a Diesel oil.

- In petrol engines, knocking is due to the sudden spontaneous combustion of the last portion of the fuel.

- While in diesel engines, knocking is due to the delay in spontaneous combustion of the first part of the fuel.

- Thus, an oil of high cetane number has a low octane number and vice versa.

- A crude oil sample, which gives petrol of high octane number gives a diesel oil of low cetane number.

- The time interval between the injection and the start of combustion is called ignition delay period or ignition lag period.

- The combustion of a fuel in a diesel engine is not instantaneous and the interval between the injection and the start of ignition is called ignition delay and is an important quality of the diesel fuel.

- Cetane (C_6H_{34}) a saturated hydrocarbon ignites very quickly and thus has a very short ignition lag or delay. Hence, it has been given the cetane number 100 in the rating scale.

- Whereas 2-methyl naphthalene which just matches the knocking characteristics of diesel oil under test.

- The tendency of knocking of hydrocarbons increases in the following order.

  Straight chain hydrocarbon > Cycloparaffins > Alkenes > Branched chain hydrocarbon > Aromatics.

- Least ignition delay (High Cetane No.). Highest ignition delay (Low Cetane No.)

- The Cetane Number of diesel fuel can be increased by addition of certain substances called dopes. Dopes like Ethyl nitrite ($C_2H_5NO_2$), Ethyl nitrate ($C_2H_5NO_3$), Isoamyl nitrate $(CH_3)_2CH - CH_2 - CH_2NO_3$ and acetyl peroxide.

2-methyl naphthalene
(cetane number = 0)

m-hexadecane
(cetane number = 100)

4.9 BIODIESELS   [Dec. 11, 12, 13, 14]

- *"Biodiesels are the mixture of methyl esters of long chain carboxylic fatty acids".*

- These can be manufactured by **trans-esterification** reaction.

- In this reaction, low cost starting materials such as vegetable oils or animal fats can be utilized.

- Methyl alcohol is another starting material used in the reaction and sodium methoxide is added as a catalyst.

- The transesterification reaction used for producing the biodiesel is

Mixture of methyl esters
(Biodiesel)

Glycerol

Industrial Method for the Manufacture of Biodiesel:

- Economical starting materials such as vegetable or fat oils are taken in a large container and about 20% methanol (w/v) is added to the container.

- 2% sodium methoxide which act as a catalyst is added to this bath.

- The bath is heated at 110°C and the mixture of biodiesel and glycerol is produced.

- This reaction mixture is poured in a water bath.

- Being water soluble, glycerol gets dissolved and insoluble layer of biodiesel is separated.

- The separated biodiesel is further processed by adding suitable antioxidants to increase the stability.

Advantages of Biodiesel:

- Biodiesel is produced from cheap starting materials such as vegetable oils, animal fats or waste oils, hence its manufacturing cost is low and hence it is cheaper overall.

- Biodiesel has a high cetane number in the range of 46-54.

- It has a high calorific value of about 35-45 kJ/L.

- It produces less polluting gases after combustion and hence environment friendly and a clean source of energy. Since it is oily in nature, it has got lubricity to a certain extent, hence no need to use extra lubricating material if used in IC engines.

4.10 POWER ALCOHOL

- Ethyl alcohol that is mixed with fuel (petrol) in a proper proportion is called power alcohol.

- In different countries varying percentage of power alcohol is recommended but in India fuel containing alcohol consists of 75% petrol and 15% alcohol. These composite fuels are also called as blended fuels or simply blend.

Manufacturing of Power Alcohol:

- In India, alcohol is manufactured mostly from sugar molasses, a viscous, semi-solid material left after the crystallization of sugar from concentrated sugarcane juice.

- For alcohol manufacture, the molasses are diluted with water to bring its sugar concentration to about 10-12%. To this solution, ammonium sulphate and ammonium phosphate and some sulphuric acid are added to bring its pH value between 4 and 5.

- Proper quantity of yeast is added and temperature is maintained at about 30°C. The ethanol formation takes place as shown in following reaction sequence.

- The invertase of the yeast converts sucrose into glucose and fructose.

$$C_{12}H_{22}O_{11} + H_2O \xrightarrow[\text{Yeast}]{\text{Invertase from}} C_6H_{12}O_6 + C_6H_{12}O_6$$

Sucrose   Glucose   Fructose

- The zymase of yeast then converts glucose and fructose into ethyl alcohol and carbon dioxide.

$$C_6H_{12}O_6 \xrightarrow{\text{Zymase in yeast}} 2\,C_2H_5OH + 2\,CO_2 \uparrow$$

Glucose   Ethyl alcohol

- The total time required for the completion of this process is about 36 to 38 hours.
- The fermented liquid contains about 18-20% alcohol.
- The fermented liquid is fractionally distilled to get rectified spirit, which contains 90-95% alcohol.
- For use in internal combustion engines, 100% alcohol should be prepared.
- For getting 100% alcohol, the rectified spirit is digested with lime for two days then distilled.

Advantages or Merits of using Power Alcohol:

- Alcohol has an octane number 90, while petrol has 60-70. Addition of alcohol to petrol increases its octane number.
- There is no operational difficulty if alcohol along with petrol is used in the working of internal combustion engine.
- Added alcohol absorbs the traces of moisture present in petrol.
- There is no loss in power or increase of fuel consumption.
- Increases the octane value of petrol.
- Reduces atmospheric pollution.
- Reduces need for gasoline which is non-renewable.
- Ethanol is a renewable source.
- Blend does not affect the power output of the fuel.
- Alcohols are excellent solvents for gun formed in engine from petrol.
- Blend decreases wearing of piston rings in engine.

Disadvantages or Demerits:

- Alcohol lowers the calorific value of petrol, because its calorific value is two thirds that of petrol.
- The design of carburettor needs to be modified, because due to high surface tension of alcohol, it is difficult to atomize.
- Alcohol gets oxidized to acids easily, hence causes corrosion if proper material for engine is not selected.
- Dry alcohol is expensive.

- At higher temperature, alcohol gets oxidized to acid which can cause corrosion.

- Due to lower vapour pressure, therefore, at lower temperature, there is starting difficulty.

- Availability should be easy at all the place.

4.11 GASEOUS FUELS

- Gaseous fuels are by far the most efficient fuels among conventional fuels.

- Free from ash, non-combustible matter, moisture and harmful.

- Due to these properties they have become best domestic fuels and even a substitute for gasoline.

- Petroleum is a major source of gaseous fuels like LPG, CNG, LNG etc.

(a) Natural Gas:

- Natural gas which is generally associated with petroleum deposits is obtained from wells dug in the oil bearing regions. Natural gas associated with liquid petroleum oil is called as wet gas.

- Wet gas is treated to remove C_3 and C_4 hydrocarbons, which are later used as LPG.

- Sometimes, if natural gas is not associated with crude oil, it is called as 'dry gas'.

- It is easier and cheaper to purify and separate water, dust, CO_2, N_2 and heavier liquifiable hydrocarbon (propane, butane, butene etc.).

- If H_2S gas is associated with natural gas, it must be separated from natural gas by leaching away H_2S in monoethanol amine $H_2N \cdot CH_2 \cdot CH_2 \cdot OH$.

- The approximate composition of natural gas is:

    (i) CH_4 (methane) = 70 to 90%.

    (ii) C_2H_6 (ethane) = 5-10%.

    (iii) H_2 (hydrogen) = ~ 3%.

    (iv)   Remaining CO + CO_2.

- Depending upon the composition, the calorific value varies from 12,000 – 14000 kcal/m^3.

Uses:

- It is an excellent domestic fuel and can be transported easily over long distances in 'pipelines'.

- It is used as a raw material for the manufacture of carbon black and as a source of H_2 gas.

- Synthetic proteins used in animal feed are manufactured by microbial fermentation of methane.

- Used as a raw material for the manufacture of industrial solvents.

(b) Compressed Natural Gas (CNG):

- It is a natural gas compressed to about 1000 atmospheres.
- A steel cylinder containing 15.4 kg of CNG contains about 2×10^4 L or 20 m^3 of natural gas at 1 atmospheric pressure.
- CNG is used as a substitute for gasoline and diesel fuel.

Advantages of CNG over LPG:

- It is a much safer fuel since the ignition temperature is less than that for gasoline or diesel.
- Conversion of gasoline operated engine to CNG-based engine is cheap and easily available.
- Combustion of CNG leads to much less fuel.
- Its CV is 13,000 cal/L.

Composition of CNG:

After removing CO_2, NH_3 and H_2S from the natural gas, CNG is formed. The main constituents of CNG are:

- CH_4 = 88%
- $C_2 - C_4$ – hydrocarbons = 10%
- CO = 0.5 to 1%

Applications of CNG:

- Excellent domestic fuel.
- It can replace petrol as an automobile fuel.
- It can be used as a raw material for the manufacture of carbon black and hydrogen gas.
- It is an excellent industrial fuel.

(c) Liquified Natural Gas (LNG):

- If natural gas is liquified at cryogenic temperatures (−150 – 170°C) and stored at one atmospheric pressure, then it is called as liquified natural gas (LNG).

Composition:

- The composition of LNG is same as that of the natural gas. The main components are methane, ethane, propane, butane, pentane and small quantities of CO_2 and CO.

Properties of LNG:

- Density of LNG is 0.41 to 0.5 kg/L
- GCV and LCV are 24 MJ/L and 21 MJ/L respectively.

(d) Liquified Petroleum Gas (LPG):

- When propane and butane components in natural gas are separated, stored in tanks and transported for further applications, then it is called as liquified petroleum gas (LPG).

Composition:

- Propane – 60%,
- Butane – 40% +
- Small quantities (traces) of propylene and butylene.

Properties:

- It burns clearly with a blue flame with no soot.
- It does not produce SO_x during combustion.
- It has a high octane number 108.
- It has a high calorific value 41.6 MJ/kg.

Applications:

- It is used as a motor fuel.
- It is used as a refrigerant in gas absorption refrigerators. It can replace CFC in refrigeration.
- It is used as a fuel for cooking food. For domestic purpose, it is supplied in pressure cylinders through pipe lines.

4.12 HYDROGEN GAS AS A FUEL

- Fossil fuels are going to deplete totally one day because of their excessive use.
- So search is on for new fuels with potential to replace existing fossil based fuels.
- Hydrogen gas is a promising fuel as it has high calorific value, is environment friendly and available in plenty.
- It is also an important fuel for rockets, hydrogen fuel cells etc. It is prepared from low cost raw materials such as hydrocarbons, coal etc.
- Methods for H_2 production:
  - ➢ Steam reformation of hydrocarbons.
  - ➢ From coal and steam (coal gasification).
  - ➢ Electrolysis of water.
  - ➢ Thermal decomposition of hydrocarbons.
- The hydrogen is produced by steam reformation method in two steps:
  - (i) Steam reforming and (ii) Shift reaction.

(i) Steam Reforming:

- In this step, steam is reacted with hydrocarbon containing materials such as natural gas, naphtha, petroleum fractions at high temperature in presence of Ni as a catalyst to obtain hydrogen and carbon monoxide.

$$CH_4 + H_2O_{(steam)} \xrightarrow[800°C]{Ni} CO + 3\,H_2$$

(ii) Shift Reaction:

- In this step, the CO formed in the steam reforming process is again reacted with steam at low temperature in the presence of FeO as a catalyst.

- This increases the hydrogen yield through conversion of CO (which is toxic) to CO_2. In this way, the overall process is made more efficient and economical.

$$CO + H_2O_{(steam)} \xrightarrow[350°C]{FeO\ catalyst} CO_2 + H_2$$

- Then mixture of CO_2 and H_2 gas formed at the end of shift reaction is compressed and cooled to get liquid CO_2 and H_2 gas.

- From liquid mixture, CO_2 liquid can be removed by scrubbing with a alkali solution and pure hydrogen gas can be obtained that can be further stored and transported.

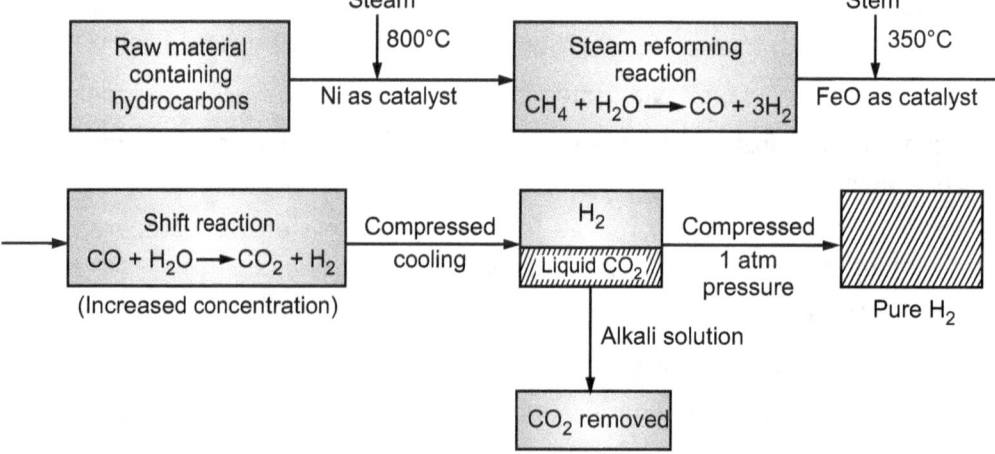

Fig. 4.7: Flow diagram for steam reforming of hydrogen

The overall reaction of H_2 generation by steam reformation method is:

$$CH_{4\,(g)} + 2H_2O_{(steam)} \longrightarrow 4H_2 + CO_2$$

(iii) Electrolysis:

- Hydrogen gas can be generated by electrolysis of water or ammonia. Hydrogen gas is liberated at negatively charged cathode. Hydrogen gas is obtained in its purest form by electrolysis. The reactions for electrolysis are:

$$2\,H_2O \rightarrow 2\,H_2 + O_2$$

$$2\,NH_3 \rightarrow 3\,H_2 + N_2$$

(iv) Thermal Decomposition of Hydrocarbons:

- Thermal decomposition of hydrocarbons also yield hydrogen gas. In this method, natural gas or hydrocarbons of petroleum fraction are subjected to temperatures from 800 to 900°C, which undergo thermal cracking and produce hydrogen gas.

$$C_nH_{2n+2} \rightarrow nC + (2n+2)\,H_2$$

Purification of Hydrogen Gas:

- Gaseous impurities are removed by scrubbing. Further purification of hydrogen gas can be done by (i) liquification process, (ii) diffusion through palladium film of low porosity at 300°C temperature. Purity reaches to 99.9%.

Coal Gasification:

- It is the second most common method used for producing hydrogen gas. It is similar to that of steam reforming of hydrocarbons except the raw material which is coal.

- In steam reforming step, the steam reacts with carbon in coal, thereby forming carbon monoxide and hydrogen $C_{(coal)} + H_2O_{steam} \rightarrow CO + H_2$ while in shift reaction CO reacts with steam and thereby increasing the hydrogen yield.

$$CO + H_2O_{(steam)} \rightarrow CO_2 + H_2$$

Applications of Hydrogen Gas:

- **Rocket Fuel:** Liquid hydrogen is the lightest fuel and also it possesses extremely high calorific value, hence it is the best fuel for rockets and missiles.

- **Fuel Cell:** Hydrogen gas is also the best fuel for fuel cells, which are used as emergency source of electricity for various purposes and also for automobiles.

- **Use in I.C. Engine:** Hydrogen gas now can be used in I.C. engine as fuel, which is more efficient, less polluting and safer than fossil fuel.

- **Fuel for Domestic Purposes:** Hydrogen gas can be used as domestic fuel such as in water heaters.

- **Industrial Uses:** Hydrogen gas has wide applications in industries such as

  ➢ H_2 can be used in fertilizer industries.

  ➢ For softening of food in food industries.

  ➢ For annealing of metals.

➤ For high temperature brazing and welding.

➤ For cutting of metals under water.

➤ Oxy-hydrogen flames are suitable for fabrication of quartz and glass.

➤ Heating of furnaces.

Storage and Transportation:

• Hydrogen is the lightest known element to the humans. It has a very low density and hence large volume.

• Because of this, the storage and transportation of hydrogen gas is difficult. So it is produced and transported locally.

(1) Compressed Gaseous Hydrogen:

• Hydrogen gas is the lightest and hence voluminous.

• Compression is a good method for stationary hydrogen storage installation. But it is not practical to transport the hydrogen gas. As the weight of compressed hydrogen gas is almost 20 times more than gasoline and takes up nearly 15 times the space.

• Very high pressure of compressed hydrogen gas could be dangerous and hydrogen is highly inflammable.

• Under exceptional conditions, the transportation of hydrogen gas is done by high pressure gas cylinder and high pressure cylinder trailers.

(2) Liquid Hydrogen:

• Generally, hydrogen is stored in liquid form which is widely used in space and aircraft as fuel, because of its light weight.

• But liquid hydrogen is more expensive than gaseous hydrogen. Liquid hydrogen is transported in insulated portable containers and in cryogenic tankers.

(3) Metal Hydride:

• The hydrogen gas can also be stored on the powdered metal hydrides.

• These hydrides have an improved weight density as compared to compressed hydrogen gas and volume density similar to liquid hydrogen.

• This method is considered to be the safest method for storing hydrogen.

4.13 ROCKET PROPELLANTS

Definition:

• Rocket propellant is a high oxygen containing fuel or a mixture of a fuel and oxidizer.

• This mixture acts as low explosive and gives a large extent of thrust or push to the rocket.

4.13.1 Characteristics of Good Propellants

- It should have high specific impulse, it is the thrust delivered divided by the rate of propellant burnt.

- It should produce low molecular weight products like H_2, CO, CO_2 and N_2.

- It should burn at a slow and steady rate.

- It should have ignition delay.

- It should possess high density.

- It should be stable over wide temperature range.

- It should be safe to store and handle, should not explode under shock, heat or impact.

- It should ignite at a predictable burning rate.

- It should be non-toxic, non-corrosive, non-hygroscopic, should not leave solid residue on burning.

Classification of Propellants:

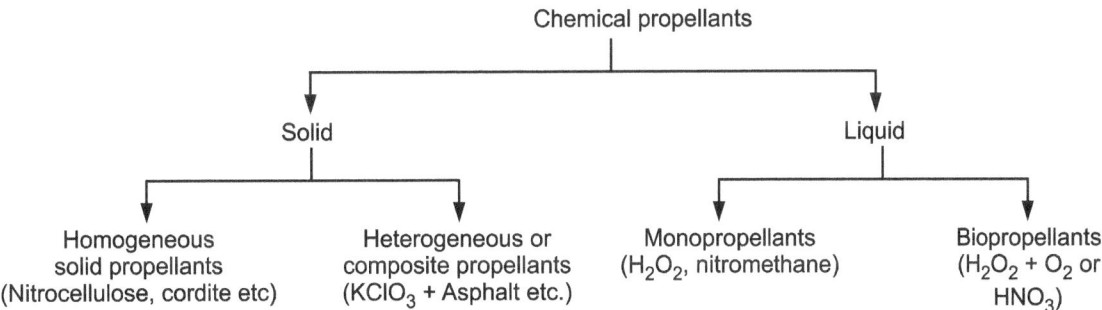

Solid Chemical Propellants:

Homogeneous Rocket Propellants:

- They consist of nitrocellulose and nitroglycerine, plus additives in small quantity.

- There is no separate fuel and oxidizer. The molecules are unstable, and upon ignition break apart and rearrange themselves, liberating large quantities of heat. These propellants are used in smaller rocket motors.

  e.g. Nitrocellulose, nitroglycerine, ballistite, cordite etc.

Composite Solid Rocket Propellants:

- Here, separate fuel and oxidizer chemicals are used, intimately mixed in the solid grain.

- The oxidizer is usually ammonium nitrate, potassium chlorate, or ammonium chlorate, and often comprises as much as four-fifths or more of the whole propellant mix.

- The fuels used are hydrocarbons, such as asphaltic-type compounds, or plastics.

- As the oxidizer has no significant structural strength, the fuel must not only perform well but must also supply the necessary form and rigidity to the grain.

- Much of the research in solid propellants is devoted to improving the physical as well as the chemical properties of the fuel.

Liquid Rocket Propellants:

- The fuel and oxidizer to be used as a propellant are liquid. They have got one advantage over solid propellants as they impart high specific impulse to the rocket but require complex engine design. There are two types of liquid propellants.

  Monopropellants: If a liquid propellant functions as a fuel as well as an oxidizer, then such propellants are called monopropellants.

  e.g. H_2O_2, nitromethane, ethylene oxide, hydrazine etc.

  Tripropellants: If fuel and oxidizers are different chemicals then such propellants are called tripropellants.

  e.g. Kerosene, alcohol, H_2 etc. act as fuel and O_2, HNO_3, H_2O_2 are good oxidizers.

4.14 COMBUSTION

- To perform any kind of work, energy is needed. Fossil fuels have locked energy which becomes available during exothermic combination with oxygen. This exothermic combination or oxidation is called as combustion.

- Combustion is defined as an exothermic chemical reaction, which is accompanied by development of heat and light at a rapid rate, so that there is considerable rise in temperature.

- When a fossil fuel undergoes combustion, following reactions take place.

$$C_{(s)} + O_{2(g)} \rightarrow CO_{2(g)} + 8080 \text{ kcal/kg}$$

$$2\,H_{2(g)} + O_{2(g)} \rightarrow H_2O_{(g)} + 34{,}500 \text{ kcal/kg}$$

$$S_{(s)} + O_{2(g)} \rightarrow SO_{2(g)} + 2{,}240 \text{ kcal/kg}$$

- For proper combustion, the substance must be brought to its kindling or ignition temperature. Ignition temperature is defined as the minimum temperature at which the substance ignites and burns spontaneously.

- A gaseous fuel undergoes combustion on ignition only if it's volume concentration in the fuel-air mixture is in between the lower and upper combustion limits. The range covered by the lower and upper limits, is known as explosive range of fuel.

- If the fuel air composition is outside the explosive range, then the fuel does not burn on combustion. For example, explosive range of hydrogen is 6 to 71 methane 6 to 13, gasoline vapour – 2 to 4.5. The explosive range limits the fuel to air ratio when used for combustion purpose.

Calculations of Air Quantities Required for Complete Combustion of Fuels:

- It is necessary to follow certain elementary principles for calculation of the amount of air required for combustion of a unit amount of fuel. The principles are given below:

  ➢ Substances always combine in definite proportions and these proportions are determined by the molecular masses of the substances involved and the products formed. For example, when carbon combines with oxygen and forms carbon dioxide, the mass proportion

$$C_{(s)} + O_{2(g)} \rightarrow CO_{2(g)}$$
$$12 \quad\quad 32 \quad\quad 44$$

  indicates that the mass proportion of carbon, oxygen and carbon dioxide formed is 12: 32: 44 respectively.

  Similarly, $2\,H_2 + O_2 \rightarrow 2H_2O$
  $$2 \times 2 \quad 32 \quad\quad 18 \times 2$$

  indicates that the mass proportion of hydrogen, oxygen and steam formed are 4: 32: 36 respectively.

  ➢ Molecular mass of air is taken as 28.94 g/mol.

  ➢ Minimum amount of oxygen required for combustion of unit amount of fuel is = Theoretical amount of O_2 required – Amount of O_2 present in the fuel.

  ➢ Minimum amount of O_2 required is calculated on the basis of complete combustion. If the combustion products are CO and O_2, then excess O_2 is to be found out by subtracting the amount of O_2 required to burn CO to CO_2.

  ➢ The mass of dry flue gases formed is calculated by balancing the carbon in the fuel and carbon in the flue gas.

  ➢ The mass of any gas can be converted to its volume at certain temperature and pressure by using the gas equation

$$PV = nRT$$

  where,   T = Temperature in degrees Kelvin

  P = Pressure of gas in atmospheres

  V = Volumes of gas in litres

  n = Number of moles of the gas

SOLVED EXAMPLES

Example 4.13: *A producer gas used as a fuel has the following volumetric composition: H_2 = 28 %, CO = 12 %, CH_4 = 2 %, CO_2 = 16 %, N_2 = 42 %. Find the volume of air required for complete combustion of 1 m³ of the gas. Air contains 21 % by volume of oxygen.*

Solution: Basis: 1 kg of producer gas. H_2 = 0.28 kg, CO = 0.12 kg, CH_4 = 0.02 kg.

Combustion reactions:

(1)
$$H_2 + \frac{1}{2}O_2 \rightarrow H_2O$$

1 mole   0.5 mole   1 mole

Thus, 1 mole H_2 requires 0.5 moles of oxygen.

(2)
$$CO + \frac{1}{2}O_2 \rightarrow CO_2$$

1 mole   0.5 mole   1 mole

Thus, 1 mole of CO requires 0.5 moles of oxygen.

(3)
$$CH_4 + 2O_2 \rightarrow CO_2 + 2H_2O$$

1 mole   2 moles   1 mole   2 moles

1 mole of CH_4 requires 2 moles of O_2.

CO_2 and N_2 do not undergo combustion.

$$\text{Theoretical air required} = \frac{100}{21} [(0.5\ CO + 0.5\ H_2 + 2\ CH_4) - O_2]\ m^3$$

$$= \frac{100}{21} [(0.5 \times 0.12 + 0.5 \times 0.28 + 2 \times 0.02) - O_2]$$

$$= \boxed{1.143\ m^3}$$

Example 4.14: *Find the volume of air required for the complete combustion of 1 m^3 of methane and weight of air necessary for combustion of 1 kg of fuel.*

Solution: Let us write combustion reaction as

$$CH_4 + 2O_2 \rightarrow CO_2 + 2H_2O$$

1 vol.   2 vol.   1 vol.   2 vol.

Oxygen required per m^3 of CH_4 = 2 m^3

$$\text{Air required per } m^3 \text{ of } CH_4 = 2 \times \frac{100}{21} = 9.52\ m^3$$

Further,

1 mole of methane requires 2 moles of oxygen

16 kg of CH_4 requires 64 kg of O_2

[molecular weight of CH_4 = 16 and O_2 = 32]

$$O_2 \text{ to be supplied per kg of fuel} = \boxed{\dfrac{64}{16} \text{ kg}}$$

$$\text{Air to be supplied per kg of } CH_4 = \dfrac{64}{16} \times \dfrac{100}{23} = \boxed{17.39 \text{ kg}}$$

Example 4.15: *0.25 g of a coal sample is burnt in a combustion chamber in a current. Find C, H % in the coal.* **(4 M) (June 08)**

Solution: Given: Weight of coal = 0.25 g

Increase in weight of $CaCl_2$ U-tube = 0.075 g

Increase in weight of KOH U-tube = 0.52 g

(i) Percentage of H

$$\% H = \dfrac{2}{18} \times \dfrac{\text{Increase in weight of } CaCl_2 \text{ U-tube}}{\text{Weight of coal sample}} \times 100$$

∴
$$\% H = \dfrac{2}{18} \times \dfrac{0.075}{0.25} \times 100$$

∴
$$\boxed{\% H = 3.3\%}$$

(ii) Percentage of C

$$\% C = \dfrac{12}{44} \times \dfrac{\text{Increase in weight of KOH U-tube}}{\text{Weight of coal}} \times 100$$

∴
$$\% C = \dfrac{12}{44} \times \dfrac{0.52}{0.25} \times 100$$

$$\boxed{\% C = 56.7\%}$$

4.15 FUEL CELLS [May 15]

- Fuel cell is a device that converts the chemical energy from a substance into electricity through a redox reaction system.
- Fuel cell contains two chemical agents (1) a fuel which undergoes oxidation and (2) an oxidizing agent that undergoes reduction.
- The most commonly used fuel is gaseous hydrogen but hydrocarbons such as natural gas can also be used.
- The most commonly used oxidizing agent is gaseous oxygen or air.
- In addition to these two chemical agents, fuel cell also contains an electrolyte useful for carrying the ions from one side to another.
- The redox reaction is carried out at the surface of electrodes. Positively charged electrode is anode and negatively charged electrode is cathode.

4.15.1 Phosphoric Acid Fuel Cell (PAFC)

- In this type of fuel cell, pure and concentrated phosphoric acid (H_3PO_4) is used as an electrolyte.
- Fig. 4.8 shows the schematic diagram of the phosphoric acid fuel cell.

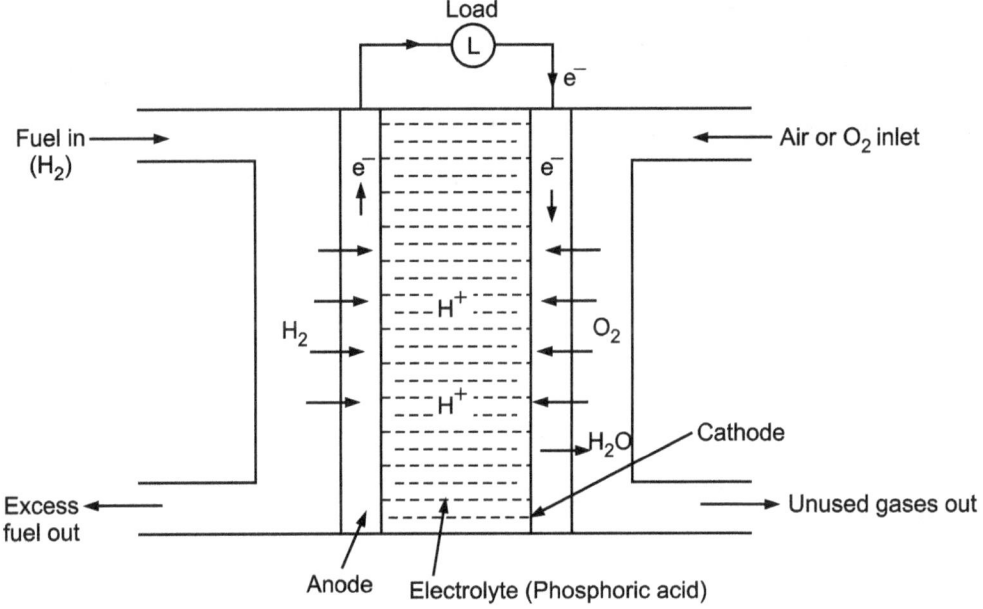

Fig. 4.8: Phosphoric Acid Fuel Cell (PAFC)

Construction and Working of PAFC:

- Oxygen (oxidizing agent) and hydrogen (fuel) enter the fuel cell pot as shown in Fig. 4.8.
- Hydrogen gas adsorbed on the anode which is generally made up of carbon and coated with finely powdered platinum metal.
- The operating temperature of PAFC is in the range of 150°C to 200°C.
- At anode oxidation of hydrogen (or fuel) takes place.

  The anode reaction is

  $$2H_2 \longrightarrow 4H^+ + 4e^-$$

- The hydrogen ions formed in the reaction are discharged in the electrolyte i.e. phosphoric acid whereas the liberated electrons flow the outer circuit through load.
- The electrons reach the cathode which is also made up of carbon and coated with finely divided platinum.
- At cathode, reduction of oxygen takes place due to these externally flown in electrons as:

  Cathode reaction:

  $$O_2 + 4H^+ + 4e^- \longrightarrow 2H_2O$$

- So the overall reaction is $2H_2 + O_2 \longrightarrow 2H_2O$
- As mensioned earlier, the electrolyte is the phosphoric acid.
- In practice, liquid H_3PO_4 is not used but it is mixed thoroughly with the matrix of silicon carbide (SiC) which acts as a electrolyte.

Advantages of PAFC:

- As the operating temperature of this fuel cell is high (150-200°C), water produced as a byproduct gets converted to steam. This steam can be further used to produce power. This increases the efficiency of the fuel cell upto 70%.
- PAFCs are carbon dioxide and carbon monoxide tolerant. So hydrocarbons can be conveniently used as fuels.

Disadvantages of PAFC:

- High operating temperatures are difficult to handle. Phosphoric acid is a poor conductor at low temperatures.
- If liquid hydrocarbons (petrol, diesel etc.) are used as a fuel, then sulphur should be completely removed as SO_2. SO_3 produced may lower the efficiency.
- Platinum coated electro-catalysts sometimes get poisoned by CO.

4.15.2 Polymer Electrolyte Membrane Fuel Cells (PEMFC)

- In this type of fuel cell, a polymer membrane is used as an electrolyte. The chemical composition of these membranes is such that, they permit only protons to pass through it and they block the passage of all other gases present in the fuel cell.
- The construction of PEMFC is shown in Fig. 4.9.

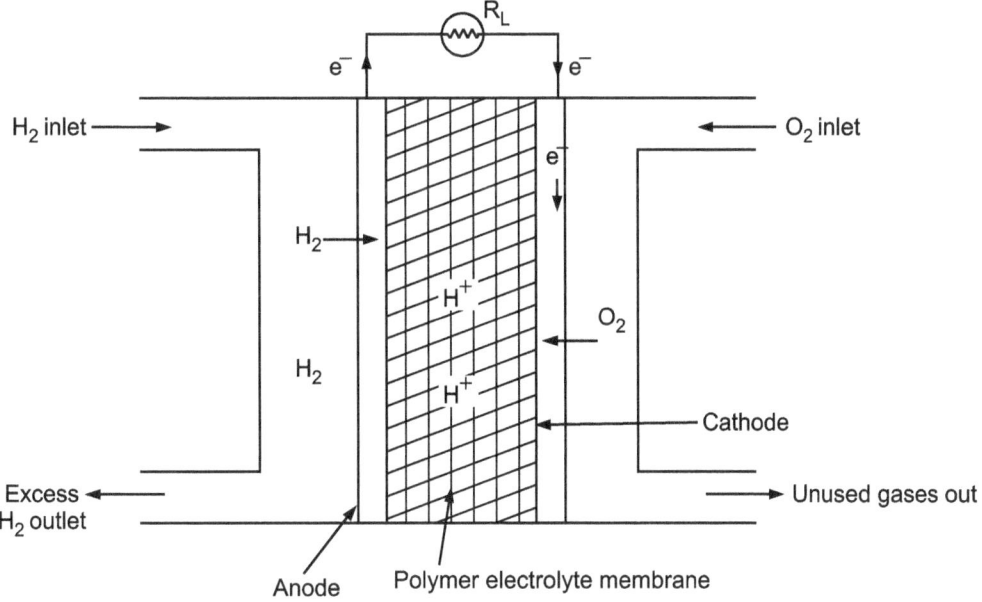

Fig. 4.9: Polymer Electrolyte Membrane Fuel Cells (PEMFC)

- The construction of polymer electrolyte membrane fuel cell is same as that of phosphoric acid fuel cell.
- The difference is that instead of phosphoric acid, the polymer exchanger membrane is used as a electrolyte.
- The working of PEMFC is also same as that of PAFC.

Working:

- A stream of hydrogen is delivered to the anode side of the cell where it splits into protons and electrons, with the help of platinum catalyst at anode, i.e. at anode oxidation of hydrogen takes place as:

  Anode reaction: $H_2 \longrightarrow 2H^+ + 2e^-$

- These protons pass through the polymer membrane towards the cathode side. The electrons flow through outer circuit i.e. through load resistor (R_L) producing voltage.
- At cathode side, oxygen enters the cell assembly through oxygen inlet.
- Oxygen molecules react with protons diffused through membrane and electrons in the outer circuit. The cathode reaction is the reduction of oxygen.

  Cathode reaction: $\frac{1}{2}O_2 + 2H^+ + 2e^- \longrightarrow H_2O$

  The net redox reaction is $H_2 + \frac{1}{2}O_2 \longrightarrow H_2O$

Advantages of PEMFC:

- Operating temperature is low in the range of 50°C to 400°C as membrane can carry protons at low temperature.
- Membranes also block the flow of gases to opposite side.

Limitations:

- Low mechanical efficiency.
- Possibility of electrode poisoning due to hydrocarbon fuels.

SUMMARY

- Fuels are classified as primary and secondary.
- According to physical state, fuels are classified as solid, liquid and gaseous.
- Efficiency of fuels is measured by calculation of calorific value.
- For determination of calorific value, Bomb's calorimeter and Boy's calorimeter are used.
- Coal gradation shows peat as first stage of coalification and anthracite as last stage.
- Bituminous coal is the best variety of commercial coal.
- Estimation of coal is done by proximate analysis and ultimate analysis.

- Most significant source of fossil fuels is crude oil or petroleum.

- Various liquid fuels are separated using fractionating column.

- Gasoline, kerosene and diesel are the most important fractions of crude oil used for transportation.

- Straight chain fractions have high knocking tendency.

- Tetra ethyl lead is used as an antiknocking agent.

- Power alcohol is a blended fuel which is made from 5 – 15% ethanol and 95 – 85% gasoline. It has a low cost as compared to gasoline.

- Gasoline can be obtained by cracking as well as polymerization.

- Synthetic gasoline is made from coal gas by Bergius process and Fischer – Tropsch process.

- Natural gas, LPG, CNG are significant gaseous fuels.

- Due to fast depleting reserves of fossil fuels, alternative fuels should be researched and promoted.

- Cheapest source of energy which has the highest calorific value is hydrogen.

- It is very risky to store, transport and use hydrogen.

- A hydrogen-fuel cell separates hydrogen from water.

- All fossil fuels give out energy by the process of combustion.

- Combustion requires oxygen.

EXERCISE

1. What are chemical fuels ? Give complete classification of chemical fuels with examples.

2. What are the different types of fuels ? What are the characteristics of a good fuel ?

3. Mention a criteria for selecting a good fuel.

4. Distinguish between solid, liquid and gaseous fuel.

5. Distinguish between gross and net calorific values of fuel.

6. What is meant by calorific value of a fuel ?

7. Describe how the calorific value of a solid fuel is determined using Bomb calorimeter.

8. What are the fuels used for the determination of water equivalent of Bomb calorimeter and why ?

9. Explain proximate analysis of coal. How is it carried out ? What is its significance ?

10. Differentiate between proximate and ultimate analysis of coal.

11. Discuss the importance of ultimate analysis of coal.

12. Explain the determination of net calorific value of coal from the data of ultimate analysis.

13. What are the advantages of liquid fuels over solid fuels ?

14. Explain carbonization of coal.

15. Why is coke preferred to coal in metallurgical purposes ?

16. What is crude oil ? Write a short note on refining of crude petroleum. What are the various fractions obtained from petroleum ? Mention the industrial uses to which they are put.

17. Define octane number and cetane number. What are the structural features of hydrocarbons in unlead petrol and diesel ?

18. What is meant by cracking of petroleum ? Explain fluid-bed catalytic method for obtaining gasoline. Give its mechanism.

19. What are the advantages of catalytic cracking process ? Describe with a neat diagram, the fixed-bed catalytic cracking process.

20. Differentiate between thermal and catalytic cracking.

21. What is reforming of petrol ? How does reforming increases octane number ? Give any two reforming reactions.

22. What is meant by knocking ? How is it related to chemical constitution ? Describe the function of TEL. Explain octane number and cetane number.

23. Describe the methods employed for the refining of gasoline.

24. How can power alcohol be helpful in fuel crises ?

25. Describe the manufacture of gasoline by Fischer-Tropsch method.

26. What does the abbreviation CNG stand for ? What is synthetic petrol ?

27. What are propellants ?

28. Give characteristics properties of propellants.

29. Write a complete note on solid, liquid and hydride propellants.

UNSOLVED PROBLEMS

1. LPG has the following composition: propane = 55%, butane = 25%, ethane = 18%, pentane = 2%. Calculate the volume of air for combustion of 1 m^3 of the LPG.

   Ans. 24.59 m^3 air.

2. A coal sample requires 15% excess air for complete combustion. Calculate weight of air required for 5 kg of the coal, if it contains C = 91%, H = 4%, S = 0.5%, ash = 3%, N_2 = 1.5%.

   Ans. 70.58 kg air.

3. Calculate the quantity of air for complete combustion of a vegetable oil (1 lit.). If it's density is 0.91 kg/lit and its composition is, C = 80%, H = 8%, O = 12%.

    Ans. 10.495 kg air.

4. A gas has the following composition by volume: H_2 = 20%, CH_4 = 6%, CO = 18%, O_2 = 5%, N_2 = 43%. If 25% excess air is used, find the volume of air actually supplied per m^3 of the gas.

    Ans. Actual volume of air supplied with 25% excess air for combusting 1 m^3 of the gaseous fuel is **1.548 m^3**.

5. A gaseous fuel has the composition by volume, CH_4 = 40%, C_2H_2 = 6%, C_2H_6 = 24%, C_3H_8 = 16%, O_2 = 3%, CO = 5% and N_2 = 6%. If 20% excess air is used for combustion, calculate air-fuel ratio and analysis of dry flue gas.

    Ans. % CO_2 = **13.38%**,   % N_2 = **82.27%**, % O_2 = **4.48%**.

6. A petrol sample contains 14% H and 86% C. Calculate the volume of oxygen and air required for complete combustion of 1 kg of the petrol at STP conditions.

    Ans. Volume of air at STP = **11377.8 litres air.**

7. Calculate the volume and weight of air required for complete combustion of 2 kg of carbon.

    Ans. Weight of air = **23.18 kg air.**

    Volume of air = **17948 litres air.**

8. A gaseous fuel contains H_2 = 50%, CH_4 = 30%, N_2 = 2%, CO = 7%, C_2H_4 = 3%, C_2H_6 = 5% and H_2O vapour = 3%.

    Calculate the volume of air required for complete combustion of 1 m^3 of the gas.

    Ans. Volume of air = **5476 litres air**.

9. A sample of coal requires 20% excess air for complete combustion. Calculate the weight of air for 250 gm of the coal, if it's composition is, C = 81%, H = 4%, N = 1.5%, S = 1.2%, O = 3%, ash = 9.3%.

    Ans. Weight of air for 250 gm of coal requires **3.211 kg air**.

10. A LNG has the following composition: propane = 30%, butane = 35%, pentane = 15%, hexane = 16%, CO = 3% and H_2O = 1%.

    Find the 5% excess air volume required for combustion of 2 m^3 of the gas.

    Ans. 5% excess air = **65.1 m^3 air.**

11. A petrol sample contains 85% C, 14% H and 1% S. Calculate the minimum air required for complete combustion of 1 kg petrol and its calorific values.

    Ans. Weight of air = **14.768 kg air**

    HCV   = **48.956 × 10^6 J/kg**

    NCV   = **10972 cal/gm**.

12. A producer gas has the following composition: CH_4 = 4%, CO = 26%, H_2 = 10%, N_2 = 50%, CO_2 = 10%. Calculate

    (a) Minimum air for complete combustion of 1 m^3 of the gas.

    (b) % of dry products of combustion by volume than 20% excess air used.

    Ans. (a) Volume of air = **1.2381 m^3**

    (b) % CO_2 = **18.82%**, % N_2 = **78.75%**, % O_2 in dry product = **2.446%**.

13. Volumetric analysis of producer gas is, H_2 = 20%, CO = 22%, N_2 = 50%, CH_4 = 2%, CO_2 = 6%. Find the volume of air required for complete combustion of 1 m^3 of the gas.

    Ans. Volume of air required = **1.19 m^3**.

14. A coal containing 62.4% C, 4.1% H, 6.9% O, 1.2% N, 0.8% S, 15.1% moisture and 9.7% ash was burnt in such a way that dry flue gas contained 12.9% CO_2, 0.2% CO, 6.1% O_2 and 80.8% N_2. Calculate:

    (a) Weight of air theoretically required per kg of coal.

    (b) Weight of air actually used.

    Ans. Weight of air actually supplied per kg of the coal = **12.902 kg air**.

15. A petrol sample contains 84% carbon and 16% hydrogen by weight. Its fuel gas compositional data by volume is as under:

    CO_2 = 12.1%, CO = 1.1%, O_2 = 1.3% and N_2 = 85.5%. Calculate:

    (a) Theoretical air for combustion of 1 kg petrol.

    Ans. (a) 14.61 kg air.

UNIVERSITY QUESTIONS

DECEMBER 2012

1. What is biodiesel? Explain the reaction with conditions involved. Give advantages and disadvantages. **(6 Marks)**

   Ans. Refer to Article 4.9 on Page No. 4.38.

2. Explain proximate analysis of coal. **(6 Marks)**

   Ans. Refer to Article 4.5.2 (A) on Page No. 4.17.

MAY 2013

1. A gas used in internal combustion engine contain, H_2 = 45%; CH_4 = 35%; CO=15% and N_2=5% by volume. Find the minimum quantity (volume) of air required per m^3 gas for its complete combustion. **(3 Marks)**

   Ans. Refer to Example No. 4.13 on Page No 4.49.

2. Define - Gross/higher calorific valve and justify the relationship between GCV and NCV of the fuel, if fuel contains H% hydrogen. **(3 Marks)**
   Ans. Refer to Article No 4.3.1 on Page No. 4.4.

3. Explain knocking in petrol engine. Define octane number and explain effect of chemical structure of hydrocarbons present in petrol on knocking. **(3 Marks)**
   Ans. Refer to Article No 4.8.1 on Page Nos. 4.38 and 4.39.

NOVEMBER 2013

1. Give the reaction involved in biodiesel formation and state any three advantages of biodiesel. **(3 Marks)**
   Ans. Refer to Article 4.9 on Page No. 4.41.

2. Calculate the amount of air (20% excess) required for complete combustion of 1 kg wood if it contains 55% carbon, 8% hydrogen, 5% oxygen and remaining non combustible part. **(3 Marks)**
   Ans. Refer to Example No. 4.6 on Page No. 4.23. [Problem is same only values are different.]

3. Give construction, working and calculation for finding gross calorific value of a solid fuel by Comb calorimeter. **(6 Marks)**
   Ans. Refer to Article 4.4.1 on Page Nos. 4.6, 4.7 and 4.8.

MAY 2014

1. What is power alcohol? Give its preparation with reactions and any two disadvantages. **(3 Marks)**
   Ans. Refer to Article 4.10 manufacturing and 2 disadvantages only on Page No. 4.39.

2. A coal sample contains C: 80%, H: 10%, S: 2.5%, N: 4% and remaining is ash. Calculate the theoretical quantity of oxygen and air required for complete combustion of 1 Kg of given coal sample. **(3 Marks)**
   Ans. Refer to example 4.5 (2) on Page No. 4.22.

3. What is proximate analysis? Explain the procedure for determination of each constituent with its formula. **(6 Marks)**
   Ans. Refer to Article 4.5.2(A) on Page No. 4.16.

DECEMBER 2014

1. What is biodiesel ? Give its synthesis and advantages. **(3 Marks)**
   Ans. Refer to Article 4.9 on Page No. 4.38.

2. A gaseous fuel used in internal combustion engine contain CH_4 = 45%, H_2 = 30%, CO = 20%, N_2 = 5% by volume. Find the minimum quantity (volume) of air required for complete combustion of 1 M^3 of gaseous fuel. **(3 Marks)**
   Ans. Similar to Example 4.13 on Page No. 4.56.

3. Draw neat labelled diagram and give the construction, working of bomb calorimeter to determine GCV of a fuel. **(6 Marks)**
   Ans. Refer to Article 4.4.1 on Page No. 4.6.

MAY 2015

1. Define: **(3 Marks)**
   (i)   Cetane No.   **Ans.** Refer to Article 4.8.2 on Page No. 4.37.
   (ii) Power alcohol   **Ans.** Refer to Article 4.10 on Page No. 4.39.
   (iii) N.C.V.   **Ans.** Refer to Article 4.3.1 on Page No. 4.4.

2. Calculate carbon, hydrogen and sulphur percentage present in the coal sample from the following data: **(3 Marks)**
   (i)   0.15 gm coal sample on burning in combustion chamber in current of pure O_2 was found to increase weight of $CaCl_2$ U-tube by 0.08 gm. and KOH U-Tube by 0.49 gm.

   Ans. Refer to Example 4.11 on Page No. 4.27. (Same method).

   (ii) 0.65 gm coal was combusted in Bomb calorimeter. Solution from bomb on treatment with $BaCl_2$ solution, forms 0.031 gm $BaSO_4$ dry ppt.

   Ans. Refer to Example 4.11 on Page No. 4.27. (Same method).

3. What are fuel cells ? Explain working of Phosphoric Acid Fuel Cell (PAFC) with figure and cell reactions. State its advantages. **(6 Marks)**

   Ans. Refer to Articles 4.15 and 4.15.1 on Page No. 4.51 and 4.52.

NOVEMBER 2015

1. Define GCV and NCV. Give the justification of how they are related. **(3 Marks)**
   Ans. Refer to Article 4.3.1 on Page No. 4.4.

2. A coal sample has the following composition: **(3 Marks)**
   C = 70%, H = 10%, N = 3%, S = 3%, O = 2% and ash = 12%. If 20% excess air is required for complete combustion, then calculate the amount of air required for complete combustion of 1 kg of coal.

   Ans. Refer to Example 4.13 on Page No. 4.49.

3. Explain in brief the process of fractional distillation of petroleum with diagram. Give the composition and boiling range of petrol and diesel obtained. **(6 Marks)**
   Ans. Refer to Article 4.7 on Page No. 4.30.

MAY 2016

1. What is power alcohol ? Give preparation with reaction and advantages of power alcohol. **(3 Marks)**
   Ans. Refer to Article 4.10 on Page No. 4.39.

2. Draw neat labelled diagram and give the construction working of Bomb calorimeter to determine GCV of a fuel. State formula with corrections to calculate GCV. **(6 Marks)**
   Ans. Refer to Article 4.4.1 on Page No. 4.6.

✠ ✠ ✠

CHEMISTRY OF HYDROGEN AND CARBON

5.1 INTRODUCTION

Air, water, food, clothier, fuel, lubricants, jewellary all contain hydrogen as a significant constituent, infact hydrogen forms highest number of compounds. Its chemical element with symbol H and atomic number 1. With an average atomic weight of 1.00794 u (1.007825 u for hydrogen-1), hydrogen is the lightest element and its monoatomic form (H_1) is the most abundant chemical substance, constituting roughly 75% of the Universe's baryonic mass.

At standard temperature and pressure, hydrogen is a colourless, odourless, tasteless, toxic nonmetallic, highly combustible gas with the molecular formula H_2. Naturally occurring atomic hydrogen is rare on Earth because hydrogen readily forms covalent compounds with most elements and is present in the water molecule and in most organic compounds. Hydrogen plays a particularly important role in acid-base chemistry with many reactions exchanging protons between the combining molecules.

- In ionic compounds, it can take a negative charge (an anion known as a hydride and written as H^-) or as a positively charged species H^+. The cation is written as though composed of a bare proton, but in reality, hydrogen cations in ionic compounds always occur as more complex species.

- The most common isotope of hydrogen is protium (name rarely used, symbol ^{1}H) with a single proton and no neutrons. As the simplest atom known, the hydrogen atom has been of theoretical use. For example, as the only neutral atom with an analytical solution to the Schroedinger equation, the study of the energetics and bonding of the hydrogen atom played a key role in the development of quantum mechanics.

- Hydrogen gas was first artificially produced in the early 16th century, by mixing of metals with strong acids. In 1766-81, Henry Cavendish was the first to recognize that hydrogen gas was a discrete   substance and that it produces water when burned, a property which later gave it its name in Greek, hydrogen means "water-former".

- Industrial production is mainly from the steam reforming of natural gas, and less often from more energy-intensive hydrogen production methods like the electrolysis of water. Most hydrogen is employed near its production site, with the two largest uses being fossil fuel processing (e.g. hydrocracking) and ammonia production, mostly for the fertilizer market.

- Hydrogen is a concern in metallurgy as it can embrittle many metals, complicating the design of pipelines and storage tanks.

- The IUPAC states that while this use is common it is not preferred. The ordinary isotope of hydrogen, with no neutrons, is sometimes called "*protium*". (During the early study of radioactivity, some other heavy radioactive isotopes were given *names* but such names are rarely used today).

5.2 ISOTOPES AND THEIR SIGNIFICANCE   [Dec. 12, 14]

Hydrogen-1 (Protium):

^1H is the most common hydrogen isotope with an abundance of more than 99.98%. Because the nucleus of this isotope consists of only a single *proton*, it is given the descriptive but rarely used formal name *protium*.

Hydrogen-2 (Deuterium):

^2H, the other stable hydrogen isotope, is known as *deuterium* and contains one proton and one *neutron* in its nucleus. Deuterium comprises 0.0026–0.0184% (by population, not by mass) of hydrogen samples on Earth, with the lower number tending to be found in samples of hydrogen gas and the higher enrichments (0.015% or 150 ppm) typical of ocean water. Deuterium is not radioactive and does not represent a significant toxicity hazard. Water enriched in molecules that include deuterium instead of normal hydrogen is called *heavy water*. Deuterium and its compounds are used as a non-radioactive label in chemical experiments and in solvents for ^1H-NMR *spectroscopy*. Heavy water is used as a *neutron moderator* and coolant for nuclear reactors. Deuterium is also a potential fuel for commercial *nuclear fusion*.

Hydrogen-3 (Tritium):

^3H is known as *tritium* and contains one proton and two neutrons in its nucleus. It is radioactive, decaying into *helium-3* through *β-decay* with a *half-life* of 12.32 years. Small amounts of tritium occur naturally because of the interaction of cosmic rays with atmospheric gases. Tritium has also been released during *nuclear weapons tests*. It is used in thermonuclear fusion weapons, as a tracer in *isotope geochemistry*, and specialized in *self-powered lighting devices*.

The most common method of producing tritium is by bombarding a natural isotope of lithium, *lithium-6*, with neutrons in a *nuclear reactor*.

Tritium was once used routinely in chemical and biological labelling experiments as a *radiolabel* (this has become less common). D-T *nuclear fusion* uses tritium as its main reactant, along with *deuterium*, liberating energy through the loss of mass when the two nuclei collide and fuse under massive temperatures.

Hydrogen-4

^4H contains one proton and three neutrons in its nucleus. It is a highly *unstable isotope* of *hydrogen*. It has been synthesized in the laboratory by bombarding *tritium* with fast-moving *deuterium* nuclei. In this experiment, the tritium nuclei captured neutrons from the fast-moving deuterium nucleus. The presence of the hydrogen-4 was deduced by detecting the emitted protons. Its *atomic mass* is 4.02781 ± 0.00011. It decays through *neutron emission* with a half-life of $(1.39 \pm 0.10) \times 10^{-22}$ seconds.

Hydrogen-5:

^5H is a highly *unstable isotope* of *hydrogen*. The nucleus consists of a proton and four neutrons. It has been synthesized in the laboratory by bombarding *tritium* with fast-moving tritium nuclei. In this experiment, one tritium nucleus captures two neutrons from the other, becoming a nucleus with one proton and four neutrons. The remaining proton may be detected, and the existence of hydrogen-5 deduced. It decays through double *neutron emission* and has a half-life of at least 9.1×10^{-22} seconds.

Hydrogen-6:

^6H decays through triple *neutron emission* and has a *half-life* of 2.90×10^{-22} seconds. It consists of 1 proton and 5 neutrons.

Hydrogen-7:

^7H consists of a *proton* and six *neutrons*. It was first synthesized in 2003 by a group of Russian, Japanese and French scientists at *RIKEN's* RI Beam Science Laboratory by bombarding *hydrogen* with *helium-8* atoms. In the resulting reaction, the helium-8's neutrons were donated to the hydrogen nucleus. The two remaining protons were detected by the "RIKEN Telescope", a device composed of several layers of sensors, positioned behind the target of the RI Beam cyclotron.

Preparation:

The preparation of hydrogen gas is usually from a reduction of a compound containing hydrogen that is in the +1 oxidation state. This reduction is accomplished either electrically or chemically.

5.3 METHODS OF PREPARATION
[Dec. 06, 09, May 09, 10, 11, 14, 15]

5.3.1 Preparation by Action of Acids

Hydrogen is prepared in the laboratory by the action of acids on metals. Dilute sulphuric acid containing 1 volume of concentrated acid to 5 volumes of water, or dilute hydrochloric acid containing 1 volume of concentrated acid to 4 volumes of water, is added to granulated zinc. Zinc sulphate or zinc chloride is formed in solution and the hydrogen that is evolved is collected over water in a trough.

$$Zn + H_2SO_4 \rightarrow ZnSO_4 + H_2$$
$$Zn + 2HCl \rightarrow ZnCl_2 + H_2$$

Since hydrogen is very much lighter than air, it may also be collected by upward displacement.

Warning:

Before collecting hydrogen great care must be taken to ensure that all the air has been displaced from the apparatus since a mixture of hydrogen with air is highly explosive.

5.3.2 Preparation by Steam Reforming

Pure hydrogen is manufactured industrially by the steam reforming of natural gas, and by the electrolysis of water.

The manufacture of hydrogen on an industrial scale involves the reaction between steam and iron. Spongy iron from the reduction of spathic iron ore (ferrous carbonate) is heated to redness and steam passed over it.

$$3Fe + 4H_2O \rightarrow Fe_3O_4 + 4H_2$$

The hot ferrosoferric oxide, Fe_3O_4, is then reduced with water gas:

$$Fe_2O_4 + 4H_2 \rightarrow 3Fe + 4H_2O$$

$$Fe_2O_4 + 4CO \rightarrow 3Fe + 4CO_2$$

Water gas is made by passing steam over red hot carbon and it consists of a mixture of carbon monoxide and hydrogen, with a smaller amount of carbon dioxide.

$$C + H_2O \xrightarrow{\text{Bright-red heat}} CO + H_2$$

$$C + 2H_2O \xrightarrow{\text{Dull-red heat}} CO_2 + 2H_2$$

5.3.3 Preparation by Electrolysis

Electrolytic hydrogen is the purest commercially available grade of hydrogen and is made by the electrolysis of water.

$$2H_2O_{(l)} \rightarrow 2H_{2\,(g)} + O_{2\,(g)}$$

Pure hydrogen is best prepared by electrolysis with nickel electrodes of a warm saturated barium hydroxide solution. The gas is passed over hot platinum gauze which oxidises any residual oxygen in the gas, and it is then dried by passing the gas over potassium hydroxide pellets and pure redistilled powdered phosphorus pentoxide. 'Electrolytic Hydrogen' is relatively expensive because of the cost of the electrical energy necessary to make it.

5.3.4 Preparation by Action of Metals

The alkali metals lithium, sodium, and potassium react violently with water at the ordinary temperature, yielding hydrogen.

$$2Li + 2H_2O \rightarrow H_2 + 2LiOH$$

Calcium reacts with water more slowly unless the water is hot, when the action is more vigorous.

$$Ca + 2H_2O \rightarrow H_2 + Ca(OH)_2$$

5.3.5 Preparation by Decomposition of Water

Cold water is decomposed by amalgamated aluminium (i.e. an alloy of aluminium and mercury which is made by rubbing aluminium foil with damp mercuric chloride).

$$2Al + 6H_2O \rightarrow 2Al(OH)_3 + 3H_2$$

Hot water is decomposed by zinc-copper couple (i.e. solid granules of zinc covered by a surface layer of copper which is made by pouring a solution of copper sulphate over granulated zinc).

$$Zn + 2H_2O \rightarrow Zn(OH)_2$$

Boiling water is slowly decomposed by magnesium powder.

$$Mg + 2H_2O \rightarrow Mg(OH)_2 + H_2$$

Steam is decomposed when passed over heated magnesium, zinc and iron.

$$Mg + H_2O \rightarrow MgO + H_2$$

$$Zn + H_2O \rightarrow ZnO + H_2$$

$$3Fe + H_2O \rightarrow Fe_3O_4 + 4H_2$$

The last reaction (i.e. the action of iron on steam) is reversible, depending on the experimental conditions.

5.4 HYDROGEN STORAGE   [Dec. 13, May 13, 15]

- Hydrogen storage describes the methods for storing H_2 for subsequent use. The methods span many approaches, including high pressures, cryogenics, and chemical compounds that reversibly release H_2 upon heating.

- *Underground hydrogen storage* is useful to provide *grid energy storage* for *intermittent energy sources*, like *wind power*, as well as providing fuel for transportation, particularly for ships and airplanes. Most research into hydrogen storage is focused on storing hydrogen as a lightweight, compact *energy carrier* for *mobile applications*.

- *Liquid hydrogen* or *slush hydrogen* may be used, as in the *Space Shuttle*. However, liquid hydrogen requires *cryogenic* storage and boils around 20.268 K (−252.882°C or −423.188°F). Hence, its liquefaction imposes a large energy loss (as energy is needed to cool it down to that temperature).

- The tanks must also be well insulated to prevent *boil off*. Insulation by design for liquid hydrogen tanks is adding costs for this method. Liquid hydrogen has *less energy density* by volume than *hydrocarbon* fuels such as *gasoline* by approximately a factor of four. This highlights the density problem for pure hydrogen: there is actually about 64% more hydrogen in a litre of gasoline (116 grams hydrogen) than there is in a litre of pure liquid hydrogen (71 grams hydrogen). The carbon in the gasoline also contributes to the energy of combustion.

- *Compressed hydrogen*, in comparison, is quite different to store. Hydrogen gas has good *energy density by weight*, but poor energy density by volume versus hydrocarbons, hence it requires a larger tank to store. A large *hydrogen tank* will be heavier than the small hydrocarbon tank used to store the same amount of energy, all other factors remaining equal.

- Increasing gas pressure would improve the energy density by volume, making for smaller, but not lighter container tanks (see *hydrogen tank*). Compressed hydrogen will require 2.1% of the energy content to power the compressor. Higher compression without *energy recovery* will mean more energy lost to the compression step. Compressed hydrogen storage can exhibit very low permeation.

Established Technologies: The established technologies are as given below.

5.4.1 Compressed Hydrogen

- Compressed hydrogen is the gaseous state of the element hydrogen which is kept under pressure. Compressed hydrogen in hydrogen tanks at 350 bar (5,000 psi) and 700 bar (10,000 psi) is used for in hydrogen vehicles. Car manufacturers have been developing this solution, such as Honda or Nissan.

5.4.2 Liquid Hydrogen

- BMW has been working on liquid tank for cars, producing for example the BMW Hydrogen 7.

5.4.3 Metal Hydride Hydrogen Storage

- Metal hydrides, such as MgH_2, $NaAlH_4$, $LiAlH_4$, LiH, $LaNi_5H_6$, $TiFeH_2$ and palladium hydride, with varying degrees of efficiency, can be used as a storage medium for hydrogen, often reversibly. Some are easy-to-fuel liquids at ambient temperature and pressure, others are solids which could be turned into pellets. These materials have good energy density by volume, although their energy density by weight is often worse than the leading hydrocarbon fuels.

- Most metal hydrides bind with hydrogen very strongly. As a result high temperatures around 120°C (248°F) – 200°C (392°F) are required to release their hydrogen content. This energy cost can be reduced by using alloys which consist of a strong hydride former and a weak one such as in $LiNH_2$, $NaBH_4$ and $LiBH_4$.

- These are able to form weaker bonds, thereby requiring less input to release stored hydrogen. However, if the interaction is too weak, the pressure needed for rehydriding is high, thereby eliminating any energy savings. The target for onboard hydrogen fuel systems is roughly <100°C for release and <700 bar for recharge (20-60 kJ/mol H_2).

- Currently the only hydrides which are capable of achieving the 9 weight % gravimetric goal for 2015 are limited to lithium, boron and aluminium based compounds; at least one of the first-row elements or Al must be added. Research is being done to determine new compounds which can be used to meet these requirements.

- Proposed hydrides for use in a hydrogen economy include simple hydrides of magnesium or transition metals and complex metal hydrides, typically containing sodium, lithium or calcium and aluminium or boron.

- Hydrides chosen for storage applications provide low reactivity (high safety) and high hydrogen storage densities. Leading candidates are lithium hydride, sodium borohydride, lithium aluminium hydride and ammonia borane. Arizona State University is investigating using a borohydride solution to store hydrogen, which is released when the solution flows over a catalyst made of ruthenium.

5.5 PROPERTIES   [May 16]

5.5.1 Physical Properties

The physical properties of hydrogen are as given below:

- It is a colourless, odourless, gaseous element.

- It is sparingly soluble in water and the solubility is not much affected by change of temperature.

- It does not support respiration although it is not poisonous. When hydrogen is breathed and mixed with some air for a short time, it weakens the voice and raises its pitch.

- It is a better conductor of heat than other gases, its conductivity being about five times that of air.

5.5.2 Chemical Properties

- It forms compounds with a large number of elements. In many cases, these compounds are formed by direct combination of the elements.

- Chemically, hydrogen reacts with most elements.

Combustion of Hydrogen:

Hydrogen burns in oxygen or air to form water.

$$2H_2 + O_2 \rightarrow 2H_2O$$

Oxygen will also burn in hydrogen.

Hydrogen does not itself support combustion, as may be shown by passing a lighted taper into an inverted jar of hydrogen, when the taper is extinguished.

A mixture of hydrogen with oxygen or air explodes violently when kindled, provided either gas is not present in too large excess.

Reaction with Non-Metals:

Hydrogen readily combines with fluorine and chlorine, less readily with bromine, iodine, sulphur, phosphorus, nitrogen, and carbon.

$$H_2 + F_2 \rightarrow 2HF$$

Hydrogen burns in chlorine gas and a mixture of hydrogen and chlorine explodes violently when kindled or exposed to bright sunlight.

$$H_2 + Cl_2 \rightarrow 2HCl$$

Hydrogen combines with nitrogen on sparking or in presence of a catalyst, forming ammonia.

$$N_2 + 3H_2 \rightarrow 2NH_3$$

Reducing Properties:

When hydrogen is passed over many heated metallic oxides (e.g. copper oxide, iron oxide, or lead oxide), they are reduced to metals.

$$CuO + H_2 \rightarrow Cu + H_2O$$

5.6 COMPOUNDS OF HYDROGEN

Hydrogen is widely distributed in industrially important compounds and is present

- in a wide range of inorganic compounds, including

  Ammonia   Hydrogen sulphide   Water

- in strong acids, including

  Sulphuric acid   Nitric acid   Hydrochloric acid

  Hydrobromic acid   Hydrofluoric acid   and

- in almost all organic compounds:

  Alkanes   Alkenes   Alkynes

  Alcohols

5.6.1 Hydrides

- Hydrogen forms hydrides (e.g. NaH) with a number of metals, including lithium, sodium and calcium.

$$H_2 + 2Na \rightarrow 2NaH$$

These hydrides when pure are white salt-like compounds rapidly decomposed by water.

$$NaH + H_2O \rightarrow NaOH + H_2$$

- The hydrogen atom in these hydrides behaves to some extent like a halogen or electronegative element. For example, on electrolysis of fused lithium hydride, the hydrogen is liberated at the positive electrode (i.e. a negatively charged hydrogen ion is discharged), and not the negative electrode as is the case when water is electrolysed.

- Hydrogen is also evolved at the anode in the electrolysis of a solution of calcium hydride, in fused mixture of potassium chloride and lithium chloride. This indicates that the ionic structure of lithium hydride is Li(+)H(−).

- Dihydrogen, under certain reaction conditions, combines with almost all elements, except noble gas to form binary compounds, called hydrides. If 'E' is the symbol of an element then hydride can be expressed as EH_x (e.g. MgH_2) or E_mH_n (e.g. B_2H_6).

The hydrides are classified into three categories

1. Ionic or saline or salt-like hydrides.

2. Covalent or molecular hydrides

3. Metallic or non-stoichiometric hydrides

1. Saline Hydrides (Ionic Hydrides):

- These are compounds of hydrogen with most of s-block elements. They are non-volatile, non-conducting, crystalline solids. They are also referred to as 'salt-like' hydrides. However, BeH_2 and MgH_2 have covalent polymeric structures.

- The binary hydrides of alkali metals (LiH, NaH, KH , RbH, CsH) have rock salt structures. The thermal stability of alkali metal hydrides decreases from LiH to CsH. The order of stability in the alkaline earth metal hydrides is:

$$CaH_2 > SrH_2 > BaH_2$$

- Electrolysis of solutions of saline hydrides in molten alkali halides produces hydrogen at the anode which confirms the existence of the hydride ion H^- ion. Saline hydrides react explosively with water The fires so produced cannot be extinguished by carbon dioxide as it gets reduced by hot metal hydride. Only sand is useful as it is a solid. Alkali metal hydrides are used as reagents for preparing other hydride compounds, e.g. $LiAlH_4$ and $LiBH_4$. While the hydrides of heavier members of each group are supposed to have ionic bonds ; there seems to be significant covalent character in the lighter metal hydrides (LiH, MgH_2 and BeH_2).

2. Molecular Hydrides (Covalent Hydrides):

- Dihydrogen forms molecular compounds with most of p-block elements. Most of the familiar examples are CH_4, NH_3, H_2O and HF. For convenience hydrogen compounds of non-metals have also been considered as hydrides. Being covalent, they are volatile compounds.

- The systematic names for molecular hydrides are usually formed from the name of the element and the suffix-ane. *Phosphane* for PH_3, *oxidane* for H_2O and *azane* for NH_3. Molecular hydrides are further classified according to the relative numbers of electrons and bonds in their Lewis structures.

  ➢ Electron deficient molecular hydride.

  ➢ Electron precise molecular hydride .

  ➢ Electron rich molecular hydride.

- An electron deficient molecular hydride has too few electrons for writing its conventional Lewis structure. Diborane B_2H_6 is an example. *Electron-precise compounds* are formed by elements of group 14. The molecules are tetrahedral, for example CH_4. The bond distance increases on going down the group.

- Ammonia and water are electron-rich hydrides. The excess electrons being present as lone pairs of electrons (ammonia: one lone pair, water: 2 lone pairs and hydrogen fluoride: 3 lone pairs). The presence of lone pairs and highly electronegative atoms like nitrogen, oxygen and fluorine in electron-rich hydrides result in hydrogen bond formation between the molecules. This leads to association of molecules.

3. **Metallic Hydride or Non-Stoichiometric (Interstitial) Hydrides:**

- These hydrides are formed by d-block (Groups 3, 4 and 5) and f-block elements. In Group 6 chromium alone forms the hydride CrH. The metals of group 7, 8 and 9 do not form hydrides. The region of the periodic table from group 7 to 9 is referred to as the Hydride Gap.

- These hydrides conduct heat and electricity though not as efficiently as their parent metals do. Unlike saline hydrides, they are almost always non-stoichiometric, being deficient in hydrogen. For example, $LaH_{2.87}$, $YbH_{2.55}$, $TiH_{1.5 - 1.8}$, $ZrH_{1.3 - 1.75}$, $VH_{0.56}$, $NiH_{0.6 - 0.7}$, $PdH_{0.6 - 0.8}$ etc. In such hydrides, law of constant composition does not hold good.

- Earlier it was thought that in these hydrides, hydrogen occupies interstices in metal lattice producing distortion without any change in its type. Consequently, they were termed as interstitial hydrides. However, recent studies have shown that except for hydrides of Ni, Pd, Ce and Ac, other hydrides of this class have lattice different from that of the parent metal.

- The property of absorption of hydrogen on transition metals is widely used in catalytic reduction/hydrogenation reactions for the preparation of large number of compounds. Some of the metals (e.g. Pd, Pt) can accommodate a very large volume of hydrogen and therefore, can be used as storage media. This property has high potential for hydrogen storage and as source of energy.

5.6.2 Carbohydrates

- Carbohydrates (polymeric $C_6H_{10}O_5$) releases H_2 in an bioreformer mediated by the enzyme cocktail - cell-free synthetic pathway biotransformation. Carbohydrate provides high hydrogen storage densities as a liquid with mild pressurization and cryogenic constraints. It can also be stored as a solid power. Carbohydrate is the most abundant renewable bioresource in the world.

- In May 2007 biochemical engineers from the Virginia Polytechnic Institute and State University and biologists and chemists from the Oak Ridge National Laboratory announced a method of producing high-yield pure hydrogen from starch and water.

- In 2009, they demonstrated to produce nearly 12 moles of hydrogen per glucose unit from cellulosic materials and water. Thanks to complete conversion and modest reaction conditions, they propose to use carbohydrate as a high energy density hydrogen carrier with a density of 14.8 wt%.

5.6.3 Synthesized Hydrocarbons

- An alternative to hydrides is to use regular hydrocarbon fuels as the hydrogen carrier. Then a small hydrogen reformer would extract the hydrogen as needed by the fuel cell. However, these reformers are slow to react to changes in demand and add a large incremental cost to the vehicle power train.

- Direct methanol fuel cells do not require a reformer, but provide a lower energy density compared to conventional fuel cells, although this could be counterbalanced with the much better energy densities of ethanol and methanol over hydrogen. Alcohol fuel is a renewable resource.

- Solid-oxide fuel cells can operate on light hydrocarbons such as propane and methane without a reformer, or can run on higher hydrocarbons with only partial reforming, but the high temperature and slow startup time of these fuel cells are problematic for automotive applications.

5.6.4 Ammonia

- Ammonia (NH_3) releases H_2 in an appropriate catalytic reformer. Ammonia provides high hydrogen storage densities as a liquid with mild pressurization and cryogenic constraints. It can also be stored as a liquid at room temperature and pressure when mixed with water. Ammonia is the second most commonly produced chemical in the world and a large infrastructure for making, transporting, and distributing ammonia exists.

- Ammonia can be reformed to produce hydrogen with no harmful waste, or can mix with existing fuels and under the right conditions burn efficiently.

- Pure ammonia burns poorly at the atmospheric pressures found in natural gas fired water heaters and stoves. Under compression in an automobile engine it is a suitable fuel for slightly modified gasoline engines. Ammonia is a toxic gas at normal temperature and pressure and has a potent odour.

- In September 2005 chemists from the Technical University of Denmark announced a method of storing hydrogen in the form of ammonia saturated into a salt tablet. They claim it will be an inexpensive and safe storage method.

5.7 USES OF HYDROGEN   [May 13, 14]

Following are the uses of hydrogen:

- In reduction of oxide ores,
- In refining of petroleum,
- In production of hydrocarbons from coal,
- To fill balloons and airships, as it is the least dense gas known (i.e. it is lighter than air). Previously, coal gas was often used for the same purpose, as it contains a high

percentage of hydrogen. However, because the flammable nature of hydrogen makes it dangerous for such use, this use of hydrogen has been to be replaced by helium,

- In the synthesis of ammonia,

- As a fuel in oxy-hydrogen blowpipes,

- For the hardening of vegetable or animal oils (i.e. to convert them into saturated fats which are solids), and

- For hydrogenating petroleum fractions, coal and other organic compounds.

5.7.1 Hydrogen as a Future Fuel

- Hydrogen is seen as one of the important energy vectors of this century. Hydrogen as an energy carrier, provides the potential for a sustainable development particularly in the transportation sector.

- A hydrogen fueled engine has the potential for substantially cleaner emissions than other internal combustion engines. Other benefits arise from the wide flammability limits and the high flame propagation speed, both allowing better efficiency.

- Hydrogen is the most plentiful and ubiquitous substance in the universe, representing about half of all matter, and it is everywhere - in the rocks and soil, in the air and especially in the water that covers three quarters of the globe. Hydrogen is a gas at normal temperatures. It is highly reactive, combining readily with a number of elements and compounds, the most familiar example being oxygen to form water (H_2O). The $2H + O = H_2O$. (hydrogen plus oxygen equals water) combustion reaction is highly charged, explosive, producing a great deal of heat as a byproduct, thus making hydrogen a true competitor with fossil fuels as a source of power.

- The same reactive quality that makes hydrogen a good fuel source, however, also makes free hydrogen rare in nature - it is almost always found bound to other chemicals. One of the challenges, then, of moving to a hydrogen energy regime is to develop economical ways of freeing hydrogen from the chemicals to which it is bonded so it can be used as a fuel, then returned to nature.

- While there are many compounds containing hydrogen and, thus, many methods for its extraction - too many to go into here - the ideal, and certainly most universally available source is water itself. Extracting hydrogen from water is simple enough, in principle, through a technique known as electrolysis in which an electrical current is passed through water breaking down its molecules into their component hydrogen and oxygen ions, both of which can be put to various uses.

- The only problem with the water-to-water scenario is that electrolysis, at present, is expensive-hydrogen currently costs about three times as much as it's fossil fuel competitors.

- This is mostly a problem of scale, however. As more and more hydrogen fuel applications come on line and the demand increases, mass produced hydrogen costs will drop. Another aspect of the problem, though, is that the cost of electricity for electrolysis is increasing and most electricity, as discussed above, is produced by environmentally degrading technologies such as coal fired and nuclear power plants or hydroelectric dams.

5.8 CARBON: THE ELEMENT

5.8.1 Introduction

The element carbon is essential to all living organisms on the surface of the Earth. This is because it is a key component of a large group of chemical compounds called organic compounds which forms the basis of life. Read on to know more.

Fig. 5.1

The element carbon is a nonmetallic chemical substance. It has derived its name from the Latin word "carbo". Carbon is one of the most abundant chemical element in the universe, and it comes fourth after hydrogen, helium and oxygen. In the human body, it is the second most abundant element behind oxygen.

In the periodic table, carbon is positioned in the group 14. Chemically, it is represented by the symbol C. Its atomic number is 6. This means its outermost orbit carries four electrons which can form covalent type of chemical bonds during chemical reactions. Carbon is found in nature in three isotopic forms. Carbon-12 and carbon-13 are stable but carbon-14 is radioactive in nature.

5.9 ALLOTROPES OF CARBON   [Dec. 12, 13, 14, May 12, 13, 14, 15, 16]

Diamond, graphite (crystalline) and carbon black (amorphous) are well-known allotropic forms of carbon, they are known from a long time but recently other less abundant and newly added members of the family include (c) Lonsdaleite, (d) C_{60} (Buckminsterfullerene or buckyball), (e) C_{540}, (f) C_{70}, (g) Amorphous carbon, and (h) single-walled carbon nanotube or buckytube. Structure of all forms are as given below.

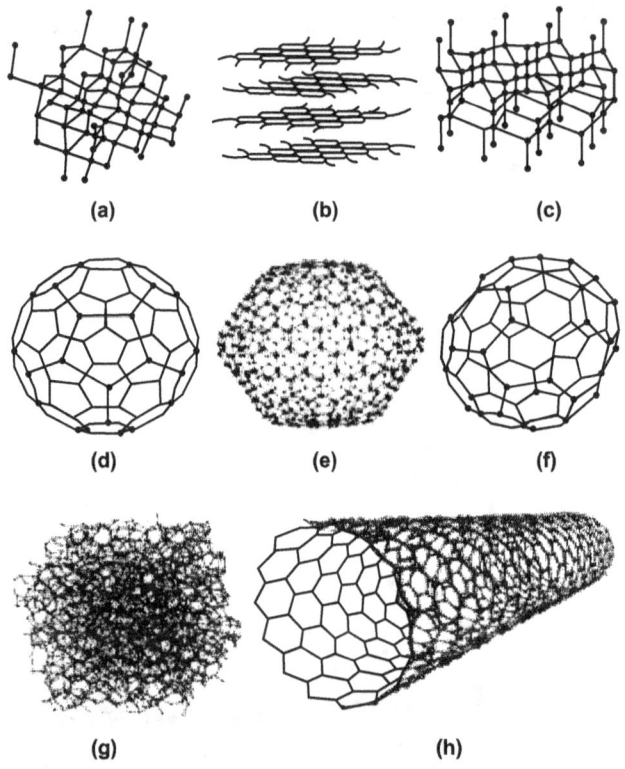

(a)   (b)   (c)

(d)   (e)   (f)

(g)   (h)

Fig. 5.2: Allotropes of carbon

5.9.1 Diamond

- Diamond is one well-known allotrope of carbon. The hardness and high dispersion of light of diamond make it useful for both industrial applications and jewellery.

- Diamond is the hardest known natural mineral. This makes it an excellent abrasive and makes it hold polish and luster extremely well. No known naturally occurring substance can cut (or even scratch) a diamond, except another diamond. [See Fig. 5.2 (a)]

- In industry, Diamond is used because of properties like hardness and heat conductivity, whereas gemological value of diamond is because of clarity and colour. This helps explain why 80% of mined diamonds (equal to about 100 million carats or 20 tonnes annually) are unsuitable for use as gemstones and known as *bort*, are destined for industrial use.

Applications:

- The dominant industrial use of diamond is in cutting, drilling (drill bits), grinding (diamond edged cutters), and polishing. Most uses of diamonds in these technologies do not require large diamonds; in fact, most diamonds that are gem-quality can find an industrial use.

- Diamonds are embedded in drill tips or saw blades, or ground into a powder for use in grinding and polishing applications. Specialized applications include use in laboratories as containment for high pressure experiments, high-performance bearings, and limited use in specialized windows.

- With the continuing advances being made in the production of synthetic diamond, future applications are beginning to become feasible. Garnering much excitement is the possible use of diamond as a semiconductor suitable to build microchips from, or the use of diamond as a heat sink in electronics.

- Significant research efforts in Japan, Europe, and the United States are underway to capitalize on the potential offered by diamond's unique material properties, combined with increased quality and quantity of supply starting to become available from synthetic diamond manufacturers.

Bonding (sp^3 Hybridization): Each carbon atom in a diamond is covalently bonded to four other carbons in a tetrahedron. These tetrahedrons together form a 3-dimensional network of six-membered carbon rings (similar to cyclohexane).

5.9.2 Graphite

Graphite is the most common allotrope of carbon. Unlike diamond, graphite is an electrical conductor. [See Fig. 5.2 (b)]

Applications:

- It can be used in electrical arc lamp electrodes. As it is the most stable form of carbon, therefore, it is used in thermochemistry as the standard state for defining the heat of formation of carbon compounds.

- Graphite (sp^2 hybridization) conducts electricity, due to delocalization of one pi bond per carbon atom are free to move, so are able to conduct electricity. However, the electricity is only conducted along the plane of the layers. In diamond, all four outer electrons of each carbon atom are 'localised' between the atoms in covalent bonding. The movement of electrons is restricted and diamond does not conduct an electric current. In graphite, each carbon atom uses only 3 of its 4 outer energy level electrons in covalently bonding to three other carbon atoms in a plane. Each carbon atom contributes one electron to a delocalised system of electrons that is also a part of the chemical bonding. The delocalised electrons are free to move throughout the plane. For this reason, graphite conducts electricity along the planes of carbon atoms, but does not conduct in a direction at right angles to the plane.

- Graphite powder is used as a dry lubricant. Although it might be thought that this industrially important property is due entirely to the loose interlamellar coupling between sheets in the structure, infact in a vacuum environment (such as in technologies for use in space), graphite was found to be a very poor lubricant. This fact led to the discovery that graphite's lubricity is due to adsorbed air and water between the layers, unlike other layered dry lubricants such as molybdenum disulfide. Recent studies suggest that an effect called superlubricity can also account for this effect.

- When a large number of crystallographic defects bind these planes together, graphite loses its lubrication properties and becomes what is known as pyrolytic carbon, a useful material in blood-contacting implants such as prosthetic heart valves.

- Natural and crystalline graphites are not often used in pure form as structural materials due to their shear-planes, brittleness and inconsistent mechanical properties.

- In its pure glassy (isotropic) synthetic forms, pyrolytic graphite and carbon fiber graphite are extremely strong, heat-resistant (to 3000 °C) materials, used in reentry shields for missile nose cones, solid rocket engines, high temperature reactors, brake shoes and electric motor brushes.

Properties:

Chemical Activity: It is slightly more reactive than diamond. This is because the reactants are able to penetrate between the hexagonal layers of carbon atoms in graphite. It is unaffected by ordinary solvents, dilute acids, or fused alkalies. However, chromic acid oxidises it to carbon dioxide.

5.9.3 Graphene

- A single layer of graphite is called graphene and has extraordinary electrical, thermal, and physical properties. It can be produced by epitaxy on an insulating or conducting substrate or by mechanical exfoliation (repeated peeling) from graphite. Its applications may include replacing silicon in high-performance electronic devices. [See Fig. 5.2 (c)]

Amorphous Carbon

- Amorphous carbon is the name used for carbon that does not have any crystalline structure. As with all glassy materials, some short-range order can be observed, but there is no long-range pattern of atomic positions. While entirely amorphous carbon can be produced, most amorphous carbon actually contains microscopic crystals of graphite-like or even diamond-like carbon.

- Coal and soot or carbon black are informally called amorphous carbon. However, they are products of pyrolysis (the process of decomposing a substance by the action of heat), which does not produce true amorphous carbon under normal conditions. The coal industry divides coal into various grades depending on the amount of carbon present in the sample compared to the amount of impurities. The highest grade, anthracite, is about 90% carbon and 10% other elements. Bituminous coal is about 75-90% carbon, and lignite is the name for coal that is around 55% carbon.

5.9.4 Buckminster Fullerenes

- The **buckminster fullerenes** or usually just fullerenes or buckyballs for short, were discovered in 1985 by a team of scientists from Rice University and the University of Sussex, three of whom were awarded the 1996 Nobel Prize in Chemistry. They are named for the resemblance of their allotropic structure to the geodesic structures devised by the scientist and architect Richard Buckminster "Bucky" Fuller. Fullerenes are molecules of varying sizes composed entirely of carbon, which take the form of a hollow sphere, ellipsoid, or tube.

- As of the early twenty-first century, the chemical and physical properties of fullerenes are still under heavy study, in both pure and applied research labs. In April 2003, fullerenes were under study for potential medicinal use – binding specific antibiotics to the structure to target resistant bacteria and even target certain cancer cells such as melanoma.

5.9.5 Carbon Nanotubes

- Carbon nanotubes, also called buckytubes, are cylindrical carbon molecules with novel properties that make them potentially useful in a wide variety of applications (e.g. nano-electronics, optics, material applications, etc.).

- They exhibit extraordinary strength, unique electrical properties, and are efficient conductors of heat. Inorganic nanotubes have also been synthesized.

- A nanotube is a member of the fullerene structural family, which also includes buckyballs. Whereas buckyballs are spherical in shape, a nanotube is cylindrical, with at least one end typically capped with a hemisphere of the buckyball structure.

- Their name is derived from their size, since the diameter of a nanotube is on the order of a few nanometers (1×10^{-9} m) while they can be upto several centimeters in length. There are two main types of nanotubes, single-walled nanotubes (SWNTs) and multi-walled nanotubes (MWNTs).

5.9.6 Carbon Nanobuds

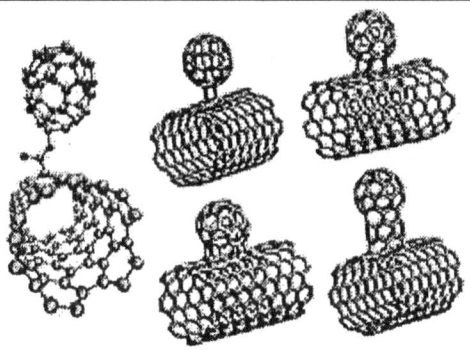

Fig. 5.3: Carbon nanobuds

- **Computer Models of Stable Nanobud Structures**

  Carbon nanobuds are a newly discovered allotrope of carbon in which fullerene like "buds" are covalently attached to the outer sidewalls of the carbon nanotubes. This hybrid material has useful properties of both fullerenes and carbon nanotubes. For instance, they have been found to be exceptionally good field emitters.

5.9.7 Glassy Carbon

- Glassy carbon or vitreous carbon is a class of non-graphitizing carbon widely used as an electrode material in electrochemistry, as well as for high temperature crucibles and as a component of some prosthetic devices.

Preparation:

- It was first produced by Bernard Redfern in the mid 1950s at the laboratories of The Carborundum Company, Manchester, UK. He had set out to develop a polymer matrix to mirror a diamond structure and discovered a resole (phenolic) resin that would, with special preparation, set without a catalyst. Using this resin the first glassy carbon was produced.

- The preparation of glassy carbon involves subjecting the organic precursors to a series of heat treatments at temperatures upto 3000°C. Unlike many non-graphitizing carbons, they are impermeable to gases and are chemically extremely inert, especially those prepared at very high temperatures. It has been demonstrated that the rates of oxidation of certain glassy carbons in oxygen, carbon dioxide or water vapour are lower than those of any other carbon.

- They are also highly resistant to attack by acids. Thus, while normal graphite is reduced to a powder by a mixture of concentrated sulfuric and nitric acids at room temperature, glassy carbon is unaffected by such treatment, even after several months.

5.9.8 Atomic and Diatomic Carbon

- Under certain conditions, carbon can be found in its atomic form. It is formed by passing large electric currents through carbon under very low pressures. It is extremely unstable, but it is an intermittent product used in the creation of carbenes.

- Diatomic carbon can also be found under certain conditions. It is often detected via spectroscopy in extraterrestrial bodies, including comets and certain stars.

5.9.9 Carbon Nanofoam

- Carbon nanofoam is the fifth known allotrope of carbon discovered in 1997 by Andrei V. Rode and co-workers at the Australian National University in Canberra. It consists of a low-density cluster-assembly of carbon atoms strung together in a loose three-dimensional web.

- Each cluster is about 6 nanometers wide and consists of about 4000 carbon atoms linked in graphite-like sheets that are given negative curvature by the inclusion of heptagons among the regular hexagonal pattern. This is the opposite of what happens in the case of buckminster fullerenes, in which carbon sheets are given positive curvature by the inclusion of pentagons.

• The large-scale structure of carbon nanofoam is similar to that of an aerogel, but with 1% of the density of previously produced carbon aerogels – only a few times the density of air at sea level. Unlike carbon aerogels, carbon nanofoam is a poor electrical conductor.

5.9.10 Lonsdaleite (Hexagonal Diamond)

Lonsdaleite is a hexagonal allotrope of the carbon allotrope diamond, believed to form from graphite present in meteorites upon their impact to Earth. The great heat and stress of the impact transforms the graphite into diamond, but retains graphite's hexagonal crystal lattice. Hexagonal diamond has also been synthesized in the laboratory, by compressing and heating graphite either in a static press or using explosives. It can also be produced by the thermal decomposition of a polymer, poly (hydridocarbyne), at atmospheric pressure, under inert gas atmosphere (e.g. argon, nitrogen), starting at temperature 110°C (230°F).

All the forms discussed are very rare and much less known.

Linear Acetylenic Carbon (LAC)

A one-dimensional carbon polymer with the structure $-(C \!:\!:\!: C)_n^-$.

Crystal structure of C_8 cubic carbon

• **Chaoite** is a mineral believed to have been formed in meteorite impacts. It has been described as slightly harder than graphite with a reflection colour of grey to white. However, the existence of carbyne phases is disputed – see the entry on chaoite for details.

• **Metallic Carbon:** Theoretical studies have shown that there are regions in the phase diagram, at extremely high pressures, where carbon has metallic character.

• **bcc-carbon:** At ultrahigh pressures of above 1000 GPa, diamond is predicted to transform into the so-called C_8 structure, a body-centered cubic structure with 8 atoms in the unit cell. This cubic carbon phase might have importance in astrophysics. Its structure is known in one of the metastable phases of silicon and is similar to cubane. Superdense and superhard material resembling this phase has been synthesized and published in 2008.

• **bct-carbon:** Body-centered tetragonal carbon proposed by theorists in 2010.

• **M-carbon:** Monoclinic C-centered carbon was first thought to have been created in 1963 by compressing graphite at room temperature. Its structure was theorized in 2006, then in 2009 it was related to those experimental observations. Many structural candidates, including bct-carbon, were proposed to be equally compatible with experimental data available at the time, until in 2012 it was theoretically proven that this structure is kinetically likeliest to form from graphite. High-resolution data appeared shortly after, demonstrating that among all structure candidates only M-carbon is compatible with experiment.

- There is an evidence that white dwarf stars have a core of crystallized carbon and oxygen nuclei. The largest of these found in the universe so far, BPM 37093, is located 50 light-years (4.7×10^{14} km) away in the constellation Centaurus. A news release from the Harvard-Smithsonian Center for Astrophysics described the 2,500 mile (4,000 km) wide stellar core as a **diamond** and it was named as **Lucy**, after the Beatles' song "Lucy in the Sky With Diamonds", however, it is more likely an exotic form of carbon.

- **Prismane C_8** is a theoretically-predicted metastable carbon allotrope comprising an atomic cluster of eight carbon atoms, with the shape of an elongated triangular bipyramid – a six-atom triangular prism with two more atoms above and below its bases.

5.9.11 Variability of Carbon: Comparison between Diamond and Graphite

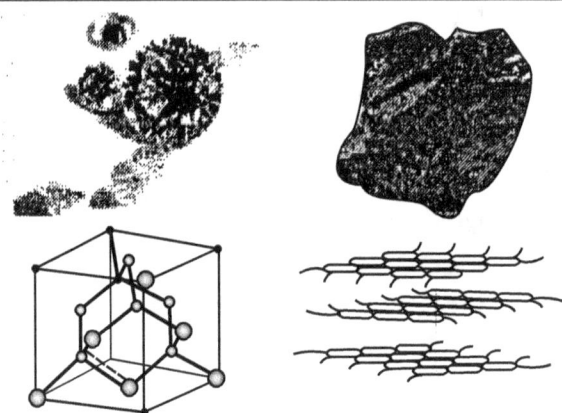

Fig. 5.4: Variability of carbon

Diamond and graphite are two allotropes of carbon: pure forms of the same element that differ in structure.

The system of carbon allotropes spans an astounding range of extremes, considering that they are all merely structural formations of the same element.

Comparison between Diamond and Graphite

- Diamond crystallizes in the cubic system but graphite crystallizes in the hexagonal system.

- Diamond is clear and transparent, but graphite is black and opaque.

- Diamond is the hardest mineral known (10 on the Mohs scale), but graphite is one of the softest (1-2 on Mohs scale).

- Diamond is the ultimate abrasive, but graphite is soft and is a very good lubricant.

- Diamond is an excellent electrical insulator, but graphite is a conductor of electricity.

- Diamond is an excellent thermal conductor, but some forms of graphite are used for thermal insulation (for example, heat shields and firebreaks).

- At standard temperature and pressure, graphite is the thermodynamically stable form. Thus diamonds are not forever. The conversion from diamond to graphite, however, has a very high activation energy and is therefore extremely slow.

Despite the hardness of diamonds, the chemical bonds that hold the carbon atoms in diamonds together are actually weaker than those that hold together graphite. The difference is that in diamond, the bonds form an inflexible three-dimensional lattice. In graphite, the atoms are tightly bonded into sheets, but the sheets can slide easily over each other, making graphite soft.

Physical Properties of Diamond and Graphite

- Carbon in its atomic form is in a very transient state. Hence, in order to make it stable in multi-atomic structures, it is arranged in a wide variety of molecular configuration called allotrope. Diamond, graphite and amorphous carbon are the most common allotropic forms of carbon.
- The physical properties of these allotropic forms are very different from each other. While diamond is the hardest of all substances, graphite is a very soft substance.
- Diamond is transparent but graphite is opaque. Graphite is a good conductor of electricity but diamond is a poor conductor of electricity. Graphite has lubricant properties but diamond is an abrasive.
- Carbon is one of the most important elements on Earth and forms the chemical basis of life. It is the fifteenth most abundant element in the Earth's crust and the fourth most abundant element in the entire universe, in terms of mass.

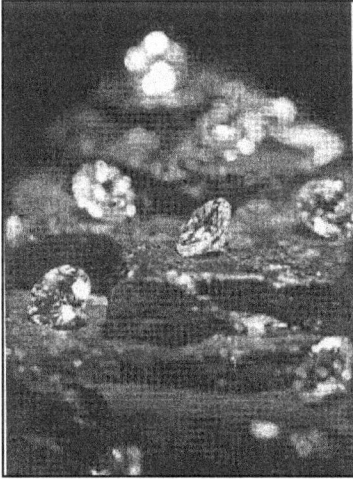

Fig. 5.5

5.10 CARBON ISOTOPES   [Dec. 12, May 14, 15]

The identity of a distinct chemical element is established by its unique atomic number. Atomic number is the number of protons in an atomic nucleus. Another property is the atomic mass of the element, which is the sum of protons and neutrons in the nucleus or the mass of the atomic nucleus. The nuclei of same chemical element may have the same atomic number but different atomic mass numbers. Such nuclei are called the isotopes of the element. Since, the chemical properties depend on the atomic number, these isotopes are chemically similar, but differ in certain physical properties.

5.10.1 How Many Isotopes of Carbon Exist?

- Just how many carbon isotopes are there? Carbon has as many as 15 isotopes! They all have an atomic number of 6, but differ in their atomic masses. Though they all have the same number of protons (6), each one differs in the number of neutrons in the nucleus. Most of them are radioactive. Radioactivity indicates that these nuclei are unstable and decay by emitting ionizing radiation. Here is a list of all the isotopes, along with some of their most important properties.

Carbon Isotope	Neutron Number	Atomic Weight (in amu)	Half Life
C^{12}	6	12	Stable (non-radioactive)
C^{13}	7	13.0033548378	Stable (non-radioactive)
C^{14}	8	14.003241989	5.70×10^3 years

5.10.2 Which are the Most Stable Isotopes?

- As you can see in the table above, three of the carbon isotopes are unstable and exist for very short periods of time, before they decay. Out of the 15, 13 are radioactive isotopes. The three most stable are C^{12}, C^{13} and C^{14}. These are also the naturally occurring isotopes, while others are created through artificial transmutation of elements. Of these three, C^{14} is radioactive, while the other two are not. C^{12} is the most abundant on Earth, constituting about 98.93% of the atoms in one mole of carbon, C^{13} is about 1.07% and C^{14} is the rarest (1 part in trillion).

5.11 COMPOUNDS OF CARBON

- The element carbon is capable of forming long chains of carbon-carbon bonds which are strong and stable in nature. This property is known as catenation. Due to this property, compounds of carbon are found in infinite numbers.

- It is a fact that the number of compounds of carbon are much higher than the compounds of any other element, except hydrogen.

- Any organic molecule is made up of hydrocarbons, which can be described as a class of compounds in which hydrogen atoms are bonded with a chain of carbon atoms. The characteristics of an organic molecule depend upon the length of the carbon chain, its side chains and the functional group with which it is associated.

- When carbon is bonded with oxygen and hydrogen, a large variety of important biological compounds are formed. They are compounds like carbohydrates, alcohols, fats, esters, carotenoids, etc. Bonding between carbon and nitrogen leads to the formation of alkaloids.

- Addition of sulfur to carbon bonds give amino acids, antibiotics and rubber products. When phosphorus is added to these other elements they form essential molecules like DNA, RNA (key components of living cells) and ATP (adenosine triphosphate, responsible for transferring of energy in all living cells), which are critical for life.

- Those compounds of carbon which are found in minerals and do not have any hydrogen or fluorine content, usually are not formulated as typical organic compounds. Carbon reacts with oxygen to form carbon dioxide. When dissolved in water, it forms a weak acid known as carbonic acid which is unstable in nature. Some other such bonds are carbides, carbonates, cyanides, calcites, etc.

5.12 USES OF CARBON

- Carbon is a major component of various foods that we eat. Another very important form of carbon is the fossil fuels - coal, petroleum, etc. The uses of element carbon are innumerable. It is used with iron in the manufacturing of various types of alloys. Graphite is used to make the lead that is used in pencils.

- It is also used as electrodes of dry batteries. It acts as moderators in nuclear reactors.

- Diamonds are used in making jewellery. It is also used in industries for the purpose of cutting.

Fig. 5.6: The space shuttle main engine

The Space Shuttle Main Engine burnt hydrogen with oxygen, producing a nearly invisible flame at full thrust.

- Hydrogen gas (dihydrogen or molecular hydrogen) is highly flammable and will burn in air at a very wide range of concentrations between 4% and 75% by volume. The enthalpy of combustion for hydrogen is –286 kJ/mol.

$$2H_{2\ (g)} + O_{2\ (g)} \rightarrow 2H_2O_{(l)} + 572\ kJ\ (286\ kJ/mol)$$

- Hydrogen gas forms explosive mixtures with air if it is 4-74% concentrated and with chlorine if it is 5-95% concentrated. The mixtures spontaneously explode by spark, heat or sunlight. The hydrogen autoignition temperature, the temperature of spontaneous ignition in air is 500°C (932°F).

- Pure hydrogen-oxygen flames emit ultraviolet light and are nearly invisible to the naked eye, as illustrated by the faint plume of the Space Shuttle Main Engine compared to the highly visible plume of a Space Shuttle Solid Rocket Booster. The detection of a burning hydrogen leak may require a flame detector; such leaks can be very dangerous.

- The destruction of the Hindenburg airship was an infamous example of hydrogen combustion, the cause is debated, but the visible flames were the result of combustible materials in the ship's skin. Because hydrogen is buoyant in air, hydrogen flames tend to ascend rapidly and cause less damage than hydrocarbon fires. Two-thirds of the Hindenburg passengers survived the fire, and many deaths were instead the result of falls or burning diesel fuel.

- H_2 reacts with every oxidizing element. Hydrogen can react spontaneously and violently at room temperature with chlorine and fluorine to form the corresponding hydrogen halides, hydrogen chloride and hydrogen fluoride, which are also potentially dangerous acids.

5.13 BONDING IN CARBON

As carbon gives numerous compounds by covalent as well as ionic bonding, let us classify the compounds based on covalent and ionic bonding.

Covalent bonding in Organic Compounds:

- A carbon-carbon bond is a *covalent bond* between two *carbon atoms*. The most common form is the *single bond*: a bond composed of two *electrons*, one from each of the two atoms. The carbon-carbon single bond is a *sigma bond* and is said to be formed between one *hybridized* orbital from each of the carbon atoms.

- In ethane, the orbitals are sp^3 *hybridized* orbitals, but single bonds formed between carbon atoms with other hybridisations do occur (e.g. sp^2 to sp^2). Infact, the carbon atoms in the single bond need not be of the same hybridisation. Carbon atoms can also form double bonds called alkenes or triple bonds called alkynes. A double bond is formed with an sp^2 hybridized orbital and a p-orbital that is not involved in the hybridization. A triple bond is formed with an sp hybridized orbital and two p-orbitals from each atom. The use of the p-orbitals forms a pi bond.

- Carbon has the unique characteristic among all elements to form long chains of its own atoms, a property called catenation. This coupled with the strength of the carbon-carbon bond gives rise to an enormous number of molecular forms, many of which are important structural elements of life, so carbon compounds have their own field of study: organic chemistry.

- Branching is also common in C-C skeletons. Different carbon atoms can be identified with respect to the number of carbon neighbours:
  - ➤ Primary carbon atom: one carbon neighbour
  - ➤ Secondary carbon atom: two carbon neighbours

➢ Tertiary carbon atom: three carbon neighbours

➢ Quaternary carbon atom: four carbon neighbours

5.14 CARBON COMPOUNDS

• *Carbon-carbon bond-forming reactions* are *organic reactions* in which a new carbon-carbon bond is formed. They are important in the production of many man-made chemicals such as *pharmaceuticals* and *plastics*.

• Some examples of reactions which form carbon-carbon bonds are *Aldol reactions, Diels-Alder reaction*, the addition of a *Grignard reagent* to a *carbonyl group*, a *Heck reaction*, a *Michael reaction* and a *Wittig reaction*.

Carbon Bonding in Inorganic Compounds:

There is a rich variety of *carbon chemistry* that does not fall within the realm of *organic chemistry* and is thus called inorganic carbon chemistry.

5.14.1 Carbon-Oxygen Compounds

• There are many *oxides* of carbon (*oxocarbons*), of which the most common are *carbon dioxide* (CO_2) and *carbon monoxide* (CO). Other less known oxides include *carbon suboxide* (C_3O_2) and *mellitic anhydride* ($C_{12}O_9$). There are also numerous unstable or elusive oxides, such as *dicarbon monoxide* (C_2O), *oxalic anhydride* (C_2O_4), and *carbon trioxide* (CO_3).

• There are several *oxocarbon anions*, negative ions that consist solely of oxygen and carbon.

• The most common are the *carbonate* (CO_3^{2-}) and *oxalate* ($C_2O_4^{2-}$) . The corresponding acids are the highly unstable *carbonic acid* (H_2CO_3) and the quite stable *oxalic acid* ($H_2C_2O_4$), respectively. These anions can be partially deprotonated to give the *bicarbonate* (HCO_3^-) and *hydrogen oxalate* ($HC_2O_4^-$). Other more exotic carbon-oxygen anions exist, such as *acetylene dicarboxylate* ($O_2C - C \equiv C - CO_2^{2-}$), *mellitate* ($C_{12}O_9^{6-}$), *squarate* ($C_4O_4^{2-}$) and *rhodizonate* ($C_6O_6^{2-}$). The anhydrides of some of these acids are oxides of carbon; carbon dioxide, for instance, can be seen as the anhydride of carbonic acid.

• Some important carbonates are Ag_2CO_3, $BaCO_3$, $CaCO_3$, $CdCO_3$, $Ce_2(CO_3)_3$, $CoCO_3$, Cs_2CO_3, $CuCO_3$, $FeCO_3$, K_2CO_3, $La_2(CO_3)_3$, Li_2CO_3, $MgCO_3$, $MnCO_3$, $(NH_4)_2CO_3$, Na_2CO_3, $NiCO_3$, $PbCO_3$, $SrCO_3$ and $ZnCO_3$.

- The most important bicarbonates include NH_4HCO_3, $Ca(HCO_3)_3$, $KHCO_3$ and $NaHCO_3$.
- The most important oxalates include $Ag_2C_2O_4$, BaC_2O_4, CaC_2O_4, $Ce_2(C_2O_4)_3$, $K_2C_2O_4$ and $Na_2C_2O_4$.
- *Carbonyls* are coordination complexes between transition metals and *carbonyl* ligands. *Metal carbonyls* are complexes that are formed with the neutral ligand CO. These complexes are covalent. Here is a list of some carbonyls: $Cr(CO)_6$, $Co_2(CO)_8$, $Fe(CO)_5$, $Mn_2(CO)_{10}$, $Mo(CO)_6$, $Ni(CO)_4$, $W(CO)_6$.

5.14.2 Carbon-Sulfur Compounds

- Important inorganic *carbon-sulfur* compounds are the carbon sulfides: *carbon disulfide* (CS_2) and carbonyl sulfide (COS). *Carbon monosulfide* (CS) unlike *carbon monoxide* is very unstable. Important compound classes are *thiocarbonates*, *thiocarbamates*, *dithiocarbamates* and *trithiocarbonates*.

$$:C \equiv S: \qquad S = C = S \qquad O = C = S$$

| Carbon monosulfide | Carbon disulfide | Carbonyl sulfide |
| 1.5349 A | 155.26 pm | 156.01 pm / 115.78 pm |

5.14.3 Carbon-Nitrogen Compounds

- Small inorganic carbon-nitrogen compounds are *cyanogen, hydrogen cyanide, cyanamide, isocyanic acid* and *cyanogen chloride*.

Table 5.1: Carbon Nitrogen Compounds

Composition			Molar Mass (g/mol)	Boiling Point, °C	Melting Point, °C
Cyanogen	$(CN)_2$	$N \equiv C - C \equiv N$	52.03	−21	−28
Hydrogen cyanide	HCN	$H - C \equiv N$	27.03	25-26	−12 – 14
Cyanamide	CN_2H_2		42.04	260 (decomp.)	44
Isocyanic acid	HNCO		43.03	23.5	−86
Cyanogen chloride	CNCl	$N \equiv C - Cl$	61.47	13	−6
Chlorosulfonyl isocyanate	$CNClO_3S$		141.53	107	−44
Cyanuric chloride	$(NCCl)_3$		184.41	192	154

5.14.4 Inorganic Carbon-Nitrogen Compounds

• *Paracyanogen* is the polymerization product of cyanogen. *Cyanuric chloride* is the trimer of cyanogen chloride and *2-cyanoguanidine* is the dimer of cyanamide.

• Other types of inorganic compounds include the inorganic *salts* and *complexes* of the carbon-containing cyanide, *cyanate, fulminate, thiocyanate and cyanamide* ions. Examples of cyanides are *copper cyanide* ($CuCN$) and *potassium cyanide* (KCN), examples of cyanates are *potassium cyanate* ($KNCO$) and *silver cyanate* ($AgNCO$), examples of fulminates are *silver fulminate* ($AgOCN$) *and mercury fulminate* ($HgOCN$) and an example of an thiocyanate is *potassium thiocyanate* ($KSCN$).

5.14.5 Carbon Halides

• Carbon halides are *carbon tetrafluoride* (CF_4), *carbon tetrachloride* (CCl_4), *carbon tetrabromide* (CBr_4), *carbon tetraiodide* (CI_4), and a large number of other carbon-*halogen* compounds.

5.14.6 Carboranes

• A *carborane* is a cluster composed of boron and carbon atoms such as $H_2C_2B_{10}H_{10}$.

Alloys

There are *several alloys* that contain carbon of which the best known *alloy* is *carbon steel* (see *Category: Steels*). Besides *steel*, other alloys based on *iron* and *carbon* are: *anthracite iron, cast iron, pig iron, wrought iron*, but also *spiegeleisen* (which contains also *manganese*). *Stellite* is an alloy of carbon with *cobalt, chromium* and *tungsten*. To some degree, these alloys could be considered as *carbides*.

5.15 APPLICATIONS OF CARBON

Considering that the applications are to be meant to engineering industry, all organic compounds and their applications are not discussed.

• Carbon is an in indipensable element in industry. By far, the greatest single use of carbon is in the form of coke for the *iron* and steel industry. The major portion of this coke is used in the reduction of *iron* ore in blast furnaces.

• As in the rubber industry, the major applications for carbon blacks are in the printing ink, paint, paper and plastic industries. Minor amounts are used in the manufacture of dry cells and carbon brushes, and as insulation.

• The largest single application for gas phase activated carbons is in the recovery of volatile organic solvents from air or vapour mixtures. Another large application is in the purification and separation of natural and industrial gases.

• Main applications for pyrographite and the fibre forms of manufactured graphite are found as components for *rockets*, missile and other aerospace vehicles.

- Carbon is unique among the elements because it forms a vast number of compounds, more than the total of all other elements combined with the exception of *hydrogen*. It exists in three allotropic forms, namely, *diamond, graphite* and *amorphous carbon*. Recently new carbon molecules such as C-60 were discovered. The C-60 shape is an example of a new class of substances called fullerenes.

- Diamond and graphite are naturally occurring crystalline solids with widely divergent properties, whereas amorphous carbon is a term applied to a comparatively large variety of carbonaceous substances not classified as either diamond or graphite.

Table 5.2: Applications of Carbon

Gasoline Vapour Recovery	Gasoline Fuel Recovery, ELCD		
		Solvent recovery	MEK, Cyclohexanone, CS2, Furon, Trichloroethane
	Other removal	Room odour removal	Taboacco, CO, Room filters, Toilet odour, Pet odour
		Refrigerator	Deodorizer
		Automobile	Cabin air filters
		Tobacco	Cigarette filter
		Hospital	Anaesthetic gas removal
		Ozone removal	Copiers, Laser printers
	Harmful gas	Closed environment	Dioxin removal, Space ships, Underground CO_2
	Gas separation	Nitrogen PSA	Nitrogen gas separation
		Other PSA	Radio active gas
Liquid phase	Water treatment	Factory waste water	Cleaning waste water
		Drinking water treatment	Trihalomethane, Chlorine, VOCs, Lead, Arsenate removal
	Decolourization of industrial chemicals	Industrial use	Sugar refinement, Pharmaceutical use, Whisky distillment
	Medical applications	Medical and Nursing	Kidney machine, Nursing supplies, Respirators
	Electronics	Electrodes	Double layer capacitors, Harddisks
	Mineral recovery	Gold recovery	Gold recovery

The development of carbon and graphite to produce grades suitable for the very highest demands of high temperature, lubrication, chemical inertness, dimensional stability and impermeability together with machining techniques and impregnation processes puts Erodex in a strong position for supplying.

Applications in Mechanical Industry:

- Radial Bearings
- Thrust Bearings
- Mechanical Seals
- Piston Rings
- Packings
- Vanes

EXERCISE

1. What are the three isotopes of hydrogen called ? What are their approximate natural abundances ? Which one is radioactive ?

2. What is the chief large-scale use for D_2O ?

3. What is one thing that helps to explain the relatively low reactivity of elemental hydrogen ?

4. What are the three principal electronic processes that lead to formation of compounds by the hydrogen atom ?

5. When a hydrogen bond is symbolized by H–X...Y, what do the solid and dotted lines represent ? Which distance is shorter ?

6. How does hydrogen-bond formation affect the properties of HF, H_2O, and NH_4 ? Compared with what ?

7. What is the usual range of enthalpies of a hydrogen bond ?

8. Describe the main features of the structure of ice. How is the structure of water believed to differ from that ?

9. In what two principal ways is water bound in salt hydrates ?

10. Can it safely be assumed that whenever a salt hydrate is heated at 100-120°C the responding anhydrous salt will remains ?

11. What is the true nature of so-called chlorine hydrate ($Cl_2 \cdot 7.3H_2O$) ?

12. What is a saline hydride ? What elements form them ? Why are they believed to contain cations and H^- ions ?

13. Define and cite examples of different types of hydrogen-containing compounds that are discussed in this chapter, listing the distinguishing electronic, structural and reactive characteristics of each class.

14. Which are the types of metals that react directly with hydrogen to form (a) ionic and (b) interstitial hydrides ?

15. Give an explanation of the structural role of water in each of the following types of compounds, together with an example of a specific chemical substance for each type:

    (a) A hydrated compound.   (b) A hydrous compound.

    (c) A gas hydrate.   (d) A liquid hydrate.

    (e) A salt hydrate.

16. How could a nonstoichiometric hydride be made ? What metal might one use ? How could the hydratic character of the product be demonstrated ?

ADDITIONAL EXERCISE

1. Suggest a means of preparing pure HD.

2. It is believed that the shortest H bonds becomes symmetrical. How must he conventional description (X–H...Y) be modified to cover this situation ?

3. Which H bond would you expect to be stronger and why ?

    S–H...O or O–H...S

4. Prepare a qualitative Born-Haber cycle to explain why only the most electropositive.

5. Complete and balance the following reactions featuring hydrides:

    (a) $CaH_2 + H_2O \rightarrow$

    (b) $B_2H_6 + NaH \rightarrow$

    (c) $SiCl_4 + LiAlH_4$ to give silane, SiH_4

    (d) $Al_2Cl_6 + LiH$ to give $LiAlH_4$

6. The boiling points of the hydrogen halides follow the trend:

    HF (20°C) > HCl (–85°C) < HBr (–67°C) < HI (–36°C). Explain.

7. The three different aspects of the chemistry of hydrogen can be illustrated by the reactivity of water with NaH, CH_4 and HCl. Explain.

8. Compare the bonding in BH_3 and BCl_3. Why is BCl_3 monomeric and BH_3 dimeric ?

9. Suggest a synthesis of H_2Se and H_2S, of $NaBH_4$ and $LiAlH_4$, of HCl and HI, of NaH and CaH_2.

10. Prepare an MO description of the linear and symmetrical hydrogen bond in [F–H–F]⁻ using the 1s atomic orbital on the central hydrogen atom and ligand group orbitals (formed from appropriately oriented 2p atomic orbitals) on the two fluorine atoms. Prepare the MO energy-level diagram that accompanies these three MO's and add the proper number of electrons to it. What is the bond order in each F–H half ?

11. Finish and balance the following equations:

   (a) $CaH_2 + H_2O$ (b) $K + C_2H_5OH$

   (c) $KH + C_2H_5OH$ (d) $UH_3 + H_2O$

   (e) $UH_3 + H_2S$ (f) $UH_3 + HCl$

   [**Hint:** Dihydrogen is a product of all of these reactions.)

12. Suggest a two-step synthesis of lithium aluminium hydride ($LiAlH_4$), using only elements and Al_2Cl_6. Repeat this for $NaBH_4$, using B_2H_6.

13. Write balanced equations for the reaction of dihydrogen with sodium, B_2H_6, calcium, lithium, nitrogen, oxygen and uranium.

14. Write balanced equations representing the steam reforming of ethane, reduction of Fe_2O_3 hydrogen, reaction of CaH_2 with water and the water-gas shift reaction.

15. Draw the unit cell for NaH. What is the coordination number of Na^+ in this structure ?

16. Draw a Born-Haber cycle for NaH. After considering each step of the cycle, explain what two steps in the cycle give sodium (and the other alkali metal hydrides) an advantage over other metals in the formation of an ionic hydride as opposed to a covalent hybride.

17. The gallium analog of $LiAlH_4$, namely, $LiGaH_4$, is thermally unstable, decomposing to LiH and elements. Write a balanced equation to represent this. Why do you expect that the same reaction for $LiAlH_4$ is not observed.

18. Fill in the blanks with appropriate terms.

   (a) _____ element gives highest number of compounds)

   (Oxygen, Carbon, Hydrogen)

   (b) Most abundant isotope of hydrogen is

   (H^1, H^2, H^3)

   (c) Most abundant isotope of carbon is

   (C^{12}, C^{13}, C^{14})

   (d) Compounds of hydrogen with s-block metals are called as

   (Covalent hydrides, saline hydrides, borderline hydrides

   (e) _____ shows highest hydrogen storage capacity.

   (LiH, $LiAlH_4$, AlH_3

   (f) The chief large scale use of D_2O is _____

   (moderator in nuclear reactor, to make high density water, to make radioactive water)

(g) Industrially hydrogen is manufactured by

(action of metal on acids, steam reforming, splitting of water)

(h) Tritium exists in _____

(troposphere, stratosphere, thermosphere)

(i) Classic example of hydrogen bridge bonds is in

(diborane, electron deficient compounds, saline hydrides)

(j) Saline hydrides have

(covalent character, ionic character, bridge bonds)

UNIVERSITY QUESTIONS

DECEMBER 2012

1. Explain the structure of fullerene. How does it influence its properties and applications?   **(5 Marks)**

    Ans. Refer to Article 5.9.4 on page 5.17.

2. Describe the use of sodium alanate for hydrogen storage.   **(4 Marks)**

    Ans. Refer to Article 5.4 on page 5.5.

3. Explain the storage of hydrogen in compressed and liquified form. Explain difficulties in the said storage systems.   **(4 Marks)**

    Ans. Refer to Articles 5.4.1, 5.4.2 and 5.4.3 on page 5.6.

4. Explain the isotopes of carbon and hydrogen.   **(5 Marks)**

    Ans. Refer to Article 5.2 on page 5.2 and Article 5.10 on page 5.21.

5. Explain the steam reforming of methane to obtain hydrogen gas.   **(4 Marks)**

    Ans. Refer to Article 5.3.2 on page 5.4.

6. Discuss the types of CNT with respect to their structure. Give their applications.

    (4 Marks)

    Ans. Refer to Article 5.9.5 on page 5.17.

MAY 2013

1. Explain chemical storage of hydrogen in the form of metal hydrides. How sodium alanates can be used In hydrogen storage.   **(5 Marks)**

    Ans. Please Refer to Article No 5.4.3 on Page No 5.6

2. Explain preparation and structure of activated carbon and carbon black.   **(4 Marks)**

    Ans. Please Refer to Article No 5.9.7 on Page No 5.18

3. What are carbon nanotubes. Explain their types in detail   **(4 Marks)**

   Ans. Please Refer to Article No 5.9.5 on Page No.5.17.

4. Explain production of hydrogen by water splitting using solar energy.   **(4 Marks)**

   Ans. Please Refer to Article No 5.3.5 on Page No 5.5

5. Explain how saline hydrides are formed. Give preparation and application of any one saline hydride.   **(4 Marks)**

   Ans. Please Refer to Article No 5.6.1 on Page No.5.8.

6. Explain the structure and applications of graphene.   **(5 Marks)**

   Ans. Please Refer to Article No 5.9.3 on Page No.5.16.

NOVEMBER 2013

1. Give industrial methods of manufacturing of hydrogen gas.   **(5 Marks)**

   Ans. Refer to Article 5.3.2 on Page No. 5.4.

2. Explain structure of diamond, give its properties and applications.   **(5 Marks)**

   Ans. Refer to Article 5.9.11 on Page No. 5.20 and 5.21.

3. Give preparation, reactions of saline hydrides.   **(3 Marks)**

   Ans. Refer to Article 5.6.1 on Page No. 5.8.

4. State the difficulties in storage of hydrogen gas. Give its chemical storage in alanates and metal hydrides.   **(5 Marks)**

   Ans. Refer to Article 5.4 on Page No. 5.5 and 5.6.

5. Give preparation, reactions of silance.   **(4 Marks)**

   Ans. Refer to Article 5.6 on Page No. 5.8, 5.9 and 5.10.

6. Give any one method of preparing carbon nanotubes. State applications of carbon nanotubes.   **(4 Marks)**

   Ans. Refer to Article 5.9.5 on Page No. 5.17.

MAY 2014

1. Explain manufacturing of hydrogen gas by steam reforming of

   (i)   methane and   (ii) coke   **(5 Marks)**

   Ans. Refer to Article 5.3.2 on Page No. 5.4.

2. Explain the structural features of fullerene with diagram and give its applications.   **(4 Marks)**

   Ans. Refer to Article 5.9.4 Fig. 5.2 on Page No. 5.17.

3. Explain the isotopes of carbon with their applications.   **(4 Marks)**

    Ans. Refer to Article 5.10.1 on Page No. 5.22.

4. Explain structural features and applications of diamond and graphite.   **(4 Marks)**

    Ans. Refer to Article 5.9.1 and 5.9.2 and Page No. 5.14 and 5.15.

5. Explain difficulties in storage and transportation of hydrogen.   **(4 Marks)**

    Ans. Refer to Article 5.4 Pg. 5.5 and 5.6 on Page no. 5.5 and 5.6.

6. What are different types of hydrides? Give preparation reaction of germane, silane and lithium hydride.   **(4 Marks)**

    Ans. Refer to Article 5.6.1 on Page No. 5.8

DECEMBER 2014

1. Explain structure, properties and applications of fullerene.   **(5 Marks)**

    Ans. Refer to Article 5.9.4 on Page No. 5.17.

2. Explain industrial production of hydrogen by steam reforming of methane and coke.

    Ans. Refer to Article 5.4 on Page No. 5.5.   **(4 Marks)**

3. Explain the structure and properties of graphite.   **(4 Marks)**

    Ans. Refer to Article 5.9.2 on Page No. 5.15.

4. Give the isotopes of hydrogen with their applications and write the properties of hydrogen which makes it more difficult to store and transport.   **(5 Marks)**

    Ans. Refer to Article 5.4 and 5.5 on Page No. 5.5 and 5.7.

5. What are the types of CNTs with respect to their structure ? Give the applications of CNTs.   **(4 Marks)**

    Ans. Refer to Article 5.9.5 on Page No. 5.17.

6. Explain chemical storage method of hydrogen gas in the form of alanates and metal hydrides.   **(4 Marks)**

    Ans. Refer to Article 5.6.1 on Page No. 5.18.

MAY 2015

1. What are carbon nanotubes ? Give types with respect to their structure. Give applications of CNTs.   **(5 Marks)**

    Ans. Refer to Article 5.9.5 on Page no. 5.17.

2. What are alanates ? Explain how hydrogen gas is released from sodium alanates when used for hydrogen storage.   **(4 Marks)**

    Ans. Refer to Article 5.6.1 on Page no. 5.18.

3. Give structure, one method of preparation and applications of silane. **(4 Marks)**

   Ans. Refer to Article 5.6.1 on Page no. 5.8.

4. Explain industrial production of hydrogen by steam reforming of methane and coke. **(5 Marks)**

   Ans. Refer to Article 5.3.2 on Page no. 5.4.

5. Explain the isotopes of carbon with their applications. **(4 Marks)**

   Ans. Refer to Article 5.10 on Page no. 5.21.

6. Explain structure of diamond based on bonding. Give its applications. **(4 Marks)**

   Ans. Refer to Article 5.9.1 on Page no. 5.14.

NOVEMBER 2015

1. Explain the structure of fullerene. Give any two properties and two applications of fullerene. **(5 Marks)**

   Ans. Refer to Article 5.9.4 on Page no. 5.17.

2. Give the preparation reaction and applications of germane and lithium hydride. **(4 Marks)**

   Ans. Refer to Article 5.6.1 on Page no. 5.18.

3. Discuss the properties of hydrogen which make it difficult for storage. **(4 Marks)**

   Ans. Refer to Article 5.4.3 on Page no. 5.6.

4. Explain the production of hydrogen by water splitting using solar energy. **(5 Marks)**

   Ans. Refer to Article 5.3.5 on Page no. 5.5.

5. Discuss the different types of carbon nano tubes with respect to their structure. Give any two applications of it. **(4 Marks)**

   Ans. Refer to Article 5.9.5 on Page no. 5.17.

6. Explain the structure of graphite. Give its properties and applications. **(4 Marks)**

   Ans. Refer to Article 5.9.2 on Page no. 5.15.

MAY 2016

1. Explain industrial production of hydrogen by steam reforming of methane and coke. **(5 Marks)**

   Ans. Refer to Article 5.3.2 on Page No. 5.4.

2. Give structure, one method of preparation and application of silane. **(4 Marks)**

   Ans. Refer to Article 5.6.1 on Page No. 5.8.

3. Explain the structure and properties of graphite. **(4 Marks)**

   Ans. Refer to Article 5.9.2 on Page No. 5.15.

4. What are carbon 'nanotubes'? Give types with respect to their structure and its applications. **(5 Marks)**

    Ans. Refer to Article 5.9.5 on Page No. 5.17.

5. Discuss the properties of hydrogen which make it difficult for storage. **(4 Marks)**

    Ans. Refer to Article 5.5 on Page No. 5.7.

6. Explain the structure of Diamond, give its properties and applications. **(4 Marks)**

    Ans. Refer to Article 5.9.1 on Page No. 5.14.

✠ ✠ ✠

CORROSION SCIENCE

6.1 INTRODUCTION [May 06, 07, 09, 10, 12, 16, Dec. 07, 08, 09]

- Naturally almost all elements occur in their combined states such as oxides, sulphates, nitrates, sulphides, etc. This combined form of the metals is called as its ore or mineral. In order to obtain the pure metals from the ores, one needs to carry out many chemical/physical processes. The science of obtaining pure element from its ore is called as metallurgy.
- Thermodynamically, the compounds of metals are more stable (hence less energetic) as compared to the pure metals. i.e. if a pure metal is obtained after metallurgy, then slowly they get converted to their combined form (or compounds) naturally.

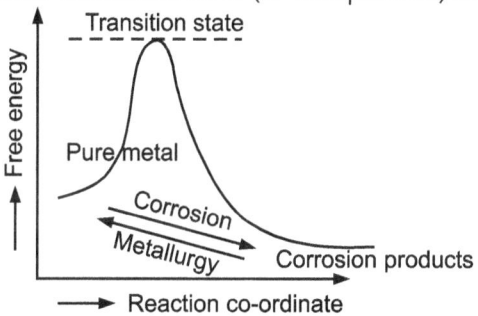

Fig. 6.1: Free energy change during corrosion

Corrosion (Definition):

- The unintentional and undesired destruction of metals by chemical or electrochemical reactions starting at the surface of the metal is called as its corrosion.
- The corrosion products formed due to corrosion are oxides (most common), sulphates, nitrates, sulphides, etc.
- It can be seen from Fig. 6.1 that, there is lowering of Gibb's free energy during corrosion, hence it is a spontaneous process (ΔG is negative).

6.2 TYPES OF CORROSION [May 10, 11, 12, 13, 14, Dec. 09, 10, 11, 12]

The corrosion of metals is a result of chemical reaction between metal surface and the environment. Depending on the nature of attack of environment on metal, corrosion is classified as

(A) Direct Chemical or Dry Corrosion:

The corrosion caused by chemical reaction of gases such as oxygen, halogens, hydrogen, nitrogen and sulphur dioxide with metal or alloy surface is called as dry corrosion.

(B) Electrochemical or Wet Corrosion:

- Corrosion due to the presence of an electrolyte in contact with a metal is called as wet corrosion. In wet corrosion, there is a transfer of electron i.e. the process is electrochemical in nature. Hence, this type of corrosion is sometimes called as electrochemical corrosion.

- Electrolyte is an aqueous solution of salt, acid or alkali. This type of corrosion of metals occurs as a result of electrochemical reaction between metal surface and electrolyte.

Dry or Atmospheric or Direct Chemical Corrosion:

The extent of corrosion due to attack of atmospheric gases depends on the chemical affinity between gas and metal as well as on the ability of a metal to form a protective film.

(i) Corrosion Due to Oxygen or Oxidative Corrosion:

Surfaces of many metals, oxidise very rapidly when they are exposed to air. These oxides form a film on the metal surface.

$$M + O_2 \rightarrow MO_2$$

Formation of oxide film and their growth is a stepwise process. At the initial stage, oxygen gas is adsorbed on the metal surface. Van der Waal's forces are responsible for this adsorption. After adsorption, oxygen molecules dissociate into atoms or ions. These oxygen ions combine with metal by electron transfer or electron sharing between oxygen and metal atoms.

$$M \rightarrow M^{n+} + ne^- \text{ (oxidation)}$$
$$O_2 + ne^- \rightarrow 2O^{n-} \text{ (reduction)}$$

i.e $\qquad M^{n+} + 2O^{n-} \rightarrow MO_2$

where, n is an oxidation state of metal and it can be +1, +2, +3 ......

6.3 MECHANISM OF CORROSION DUE TO OXYGEN
[May 09, 10, 11, 12, 13, 15, Dec. 10, 11, 12]

- Corrosion of a metal starts at its surface and a film of corrosion product is formed. The mechanism of dry corrosion can be explained using three important steps as:

  (i) Adsorption: When clean and uncorroded surface of a metal is exposed to oxygen, it gets adsorbed on the surface. Initially, there is no chemical bond between the metal surface and oxygen but they are held together by secondary forces of attraction such as weak van der Waal's forces. This is shown in Fig. 6.2 (b).

  (ii) Chemisorption: After adsorption, actual process of corrosion starts. Oxygen is an electronegative element and metals are electropositive in nature. So slowly electrons from metal get transferred to oxygen. Due to such electron transfer oxygen acquires negative charge and the metal surface becomes positively charged. Hence, there is a chemical bond formation between the metal atom and oxygen.

This type of adsorption is called chemisorption, it continues till unimolecular oxide layer covers the metal surface.

(iii) Film Formation: When chemisorption complete, a strong adhering film of metal oxide is formed on the surface and the metal is corroded. [Fig. 6.2 (d)]

Fig. 6.2 depicts all these three steps in dry corrosion.

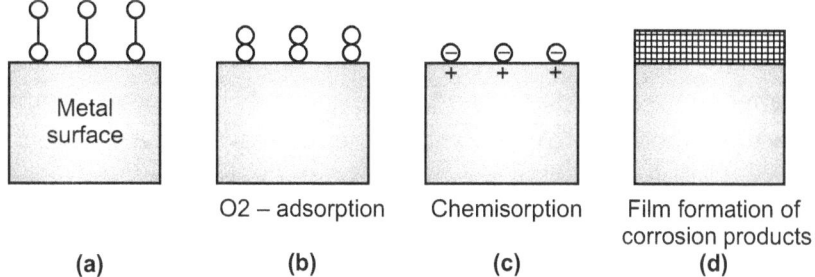

(a)   (b)   (c)   (d)

Fig. 6.2: Mechanism of dry corrosion due to oxygen

6.3.1 Nature of Oxide Film Formed

*   Stable oxide film.

*   Porous oxide film.

*   Unstable film.

*   Volatile oxide film.

Stable Oxide Film: This film is made up of fine particles of oxide and has a compact packing. Such a type of film is tightly adhered to the metal surface. It is observed that the volume of metal oxide film formed is greater than that of metal surface. Such type of film protects the metal from further corrosion and acts as a protective layer.

Example: Oxide films on **Al, Sn, Cr, Cu** etc.

Unstable Oxide Film: Generally, such types of films are observed on the nobel metal surfaces. In this case, the oxidation reaction is reversible i.e. as soon as the oxide of the metal is formed, the reversible reaction i.e. conversion of oxide into metal and oxygen takes place spontaneously as

Corrosion

$$M + O_2 \rightleftharpoons MO_2$$

Reverse corrosion

It can be seen that although the corrosion of the metals takes place, they do not get affected because of the reverse reaction.

Example: Au, Ag, Pt etc.

Porous Oxide Film: This type of film is observed on the alkali and alkaline earth metals. Some of the transition group elements such as iron also show this type of film. The film formed is porous, so that oxygen from air can diffuse the film and again come in contact with the metal surface. This process continues till the metal is corroded completely. It is observed that for such films, the volume of film is less than that of metal surface.

Example: **Na, K, Li, Ca, Fe** etc.

Volatile Oxide Film: As soon as the oxide layer is formed on the metal surface, it evaporates. So after some time of corrosion, the oxide layer disappears completely and the new metal surface is exposed to oxygen and further corrosion takes place so if such oxide layer forming metal is placed in the atmosphere, after some time the metal completely disappeares.

Example: **molybdenum**.

6.4 PILLING-BEDWORTH RATIO   [Dec. 10, May 11, 14]

Protective value or protectivity of films can be decided from Pilling-Bedworth ratio.

$$\text{Pilling-Bedworth ratio} = \frac{\text{Volume of oxide formed}}{\text{Volume of equivalent amount of metal consumed to form oxide}}$$
$$(\text{P.B. ratio})$$

If P.B. ratio > 1, coating will be non-porous and protective. e.g. Cr, Ni, W, Al, etc.

If P.B. ratio < 1, coating will be porous and non-protective. e.g. Alkali and alkaline earth metals.

6.5 CORROSION DUE TO OTHER GASES   [May 09]

- Gases like carbon dioxide, sulphur dioxide, nitrogen oxides, chlorine, fluorine under dry conditions corrode metals. The degree of corrosion due to these gases depends on chemical affinity of metal and the gases, as well as the protective nature of the films formed on the surface of metal.

- In the case of silver, due to action of chlorine, silver chloride film is formed. It protects the metal from further corrosion.

$$2\,Ag + Cl_2 \rightarrow 2\,AgCl \text{ (Protective film)}$$

- But chlorine when it attacks tin, stannic chloride being volatile, easily escapes as soon as it is formed leaving metal for further exposure. Thus, more and more tin metal gets corroded due to chlorine attack.

$$Sn + 2\,Cl_2 \rightarrow SnCl_4 \text{ (Volatile film)}$$

- In an industrial atmosphere, all types of contaminants of sulphur in the form of sulphur dioxide and hydrogen sulphide are corrosive. In petroleum industry, hydrogen sulphide at high temperature corrodes steel.

$$H_2S + Fe \rightarrow FeS + H_2^-$$

Scale

- The burning of fossil fuels generate a large amount of sulphur dioxide. Primary cause of atmospheric corrosion is the dry deposition of sulphur dioxide on metallic surface.

$$S + O_2 \rightarrow SO_2 ;$$

$$SO_2 + H_2O \rightarrow H_2SO_3$$

(Sulfurous acid)

$$SO_2 + H_2O + \frac{1}{2}O_2 \rightarrow H_2SO_4$$

- In the presence of oxygen and moisture, sulphur dioxide is oxidised to sulphuric and sulphurous acid, which are highly corrosive to metallic equipments. Oxides of nitrogen emitted in combustion process cause atmospheric corrosion.

The basic reaction is

$$N_2 + O_2 \xrightarrow{\frac{1210 \text{ to}}{1700^\circ C}} 2\,NO \uparrow$$

Nitric oxide

$$2\,NO + O_2 \xrightarrow{1100^\circ C} 2\,NO_2 \uparrow$$

Nitrogen dioxide

They react with ozone from atmosphere.

$$NO_2 + O_3 \rightarrow NO_3 + O_2 \uparrow$$

$$NO_2 + NO_3 \rightarrow N_2O_5$$

$$N_2O_5 + H_2O \rightarrow 2\,HNO_3$$

Sulfuric acid and nitric acid are extremely corrosive.

6.6 CORROSION DUE TO HYDROGEN   [May 16]

6.6.1 Hydrogen Embrittlement or Hydrogen Blistering

- Action of hydrogen on metals at low temperature is called hydrogen embrittlement. Under specific environment, as a result of chemical or electrochemical action of metal surface, atomic hydrogen is formed. For example, aqueous solution of hydrogen sulphide reacts with iron surface and evolves atomic hydrogen. This atomic hydrogen diffuses into a metal and collects in voids. There it combines to form molecular hydrogen.

- If this process continues, large amount of molecular hydrogen gets accumulated in voids. Some amount tries to escape over the surface which causes blistering in metal fissure formation. Penetration of hydrogen into metal decreases ductility and tensile strength in metals which is called hydrogen embrittlement.

$$Fe + H_2S \rightarrow FeS + 2H$$

Atomic or Nascent hydrogen

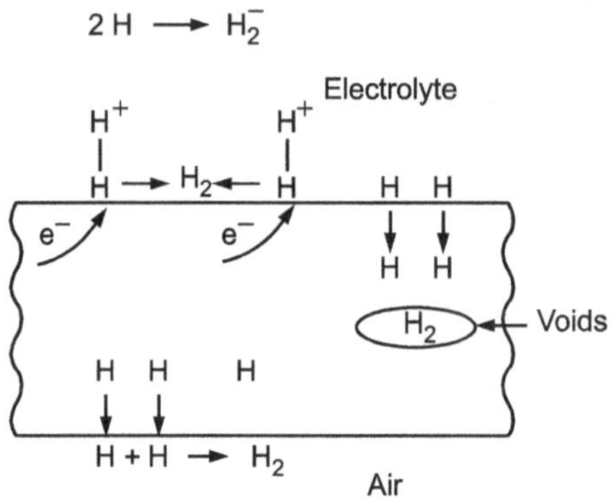

$$2H \longrightarrow H_2^-$$

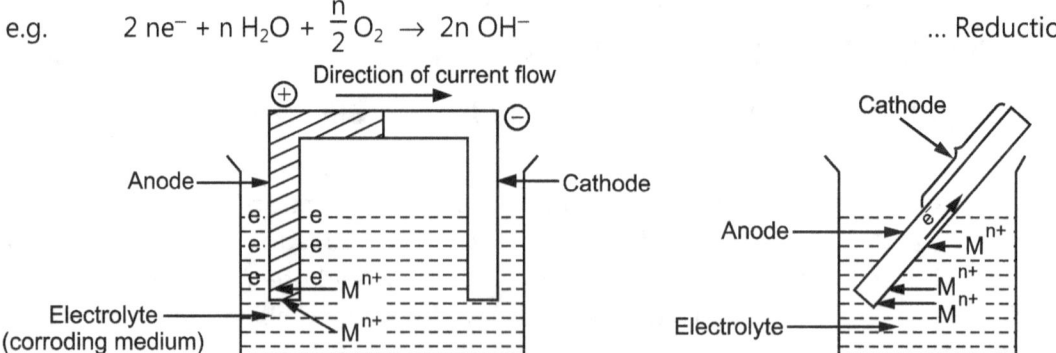

Fig. 6.3: Hydrogen blistering

6.7 WET OR ELECTROCHEMICAL OR IMMERSION CORROSION
[May 08, 11, Dec. 08, 11, 12]

Definition:

Electrochemical corrosion can be defined as the corrosion caused by exposure of metal or two dissimilar metals in contact with an electrolytic solution (acid, base or salt) leading to the formation of an electrochemical or galvanic cell.

- Anodic area dissolves, corrodes or oxidizes leading to the formation of metallic ions or cations and the electrons are set free by the reaction

$$M \rightarrow M^{n+} + n\,e^- \qquad \qquad \text{... Oxidation}$$

- At cathodic area, on the other hand, reduction reaction takes place to discharge anions (e.g. O^{2-}, OH^- etc.) depending upon the nature of conducting or corroding medium (electrolyte).

e.g. $\qquad 2\,ne^- + n\,H_2O + \dfrac{n}{2}O_2 \rightarrow 2n\,OH^- \qquad \qquad \text{... Reduction}$

Fig. 6.4: Electrochemical corrosion

Mechanism of Wet Corrosion:

Wet corrosion of metal is associated with flow of electric current between anodic and cathodic areas. At anode, metal dissolves forming corresponding positive ions and electrons.

$$M \rightarrow M^{n+} + n\,e^-$$

While depending upon the nature of the corrosive environment, cathodic reactions will be of two types:

(1) Hydrogen evolution mechanism

(2) Oxygen absorption mechanism

(1) Hydrogen Evolution Mechanism:

- Hydrogen evolution from metals occurs when they are exposed to acidic environment. It is nothing but displacement of hydrogen ions from the solution by metal ions which can be written as

At anode: $M \rightleftharpoons M^{2+} + 2\,e^-$

At cathode: $Acid \rightleftharpoons H^+$

$$2\,H^+ + 2\,e^- \rightarrow H_2^-$$

- The cathodic reaction consists of evolution of hydrogen gas.

  All metals above hydrogen in the electrochemical series will dissolve in acid solution with the evolution of hydrogen gas.

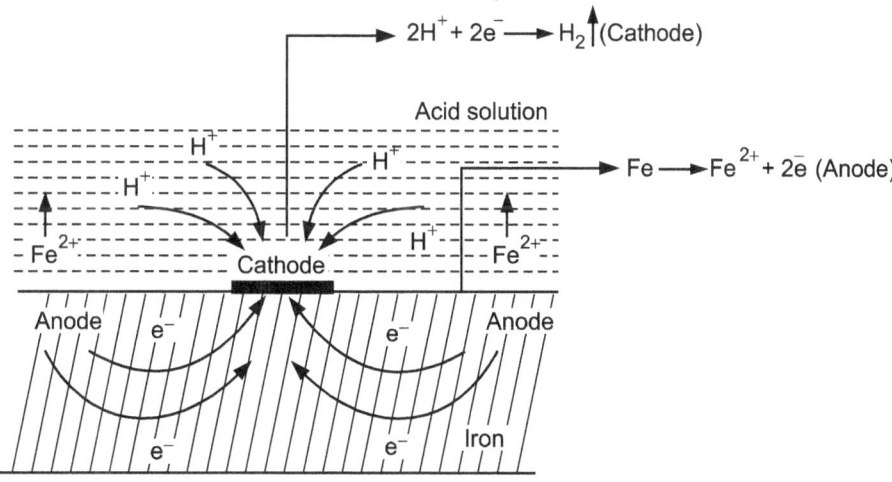

Fig. 6.5: Mechanism of corrosion - Hydrogen evolution

- Consider a metal surface exposed to acidic medium.

- Impurity in the metal can either acts as a cathode or anode depending on its position in the electrochemical/galvanic series.

- In the above diagram, the metal surface acts as a anode and impurity acts as a cathode.
- Oxidation reaction takes place at anode releasing electrons.
- These electrons flow towards cathode (impurity) where reduction reaction takes place.

(2) Oxygen Absorption Mechanism:

- Rusting of iron in water containing dissolved oxygen occurs by oxygen absorption mechanism.
- At anodic area, iron will dissolve by oxidation.

$$Fe \rightleftharpoons Fe^{2+} + 2e^-$$

- The electrons will flow to cathodic area through iron and will be accepted by oxygen.

$$2e^- + H_2O + \frac{1}{2}O_2 \rightleftharpoons 2OH^-$$

$$Fe^{2+} + 2OH^- \rightarrow Fe(OH)_2 \downarrow$$

$$2Fe(OH)_2 + \frac{1}{2}O_2 + H_2O \rightarrow 2Fe(OH)_3 \downarrow$$

rust

- In this case, anodic areas on the surface of iron are due to the presence of cracks in the oxide coating of the metal. The cathodic areas will be at the surface of coated metal i.e. cathode will be large while anode will be small area. This results in localised corrosion attack on the exposed iron surface.

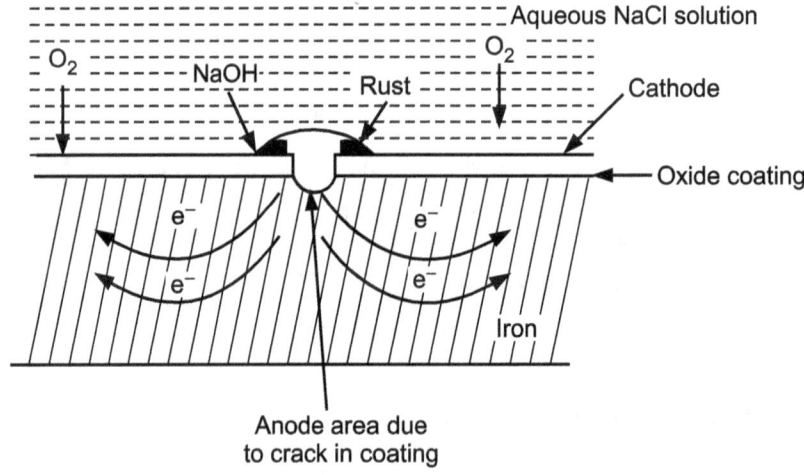

Fig. 6.6: Mechanism of corrosion - Oxygen absorption

- If environment is neutral aqueous solution of an electrolyte (NaCl) containing dissolved oxygen

As $$NaCl \xrightarrow{H_2O} Na^+ + Cl^-$$

At cathode ....　$Na^+ + OH^- \rightarrow NaOH$, sodium hydroxide is formed.

At anode ....　$Fe^{2+} + 2\,Cl^- \rightarrow FeCl_2$, ferrous chloride is formed.

- As cathodic product NaOH and anodic product $FeCl_2$ are soluble in water, when they meet, ferrous hydroxide precipitates and in enough oxygen it oxidises to ferric hydroxide.

$$Na^+ + OH^- + Fe^{2+} + Cl^- \rightarrow Fe(OH)_2$$

$$2\,Fe(OH)_2 + \tfrac{1}{2}\,O_2 + H_2O \rightarrow Fe(OH)_3 \downarrow$$

Ferric hydroxide

- Thus, ferrous iron formed is removed as a precipitate of ferric hydroxide, the corrosion proceeds till fresh oxygen is available. Oxygen absorption type corrosion is more in strongly aerated solutions. Here corrosion product is formed in the vicinity of cathode although corrosion takes place at anode.

6.8 GALVANIC CORROSION   [May 11, 15, Dec. 10]

- It is a wet corrosion. When two dissimilar metals are in electrical contact with each other and are exposed to an electrolyte, a potential difference is created between them.

- This potential difference produces electron flow between them.

- The less noble metal will dissolve and act as anode while more noble metal will act as the cathode. This type of corrosion of metal is called as galvanic corrosion.

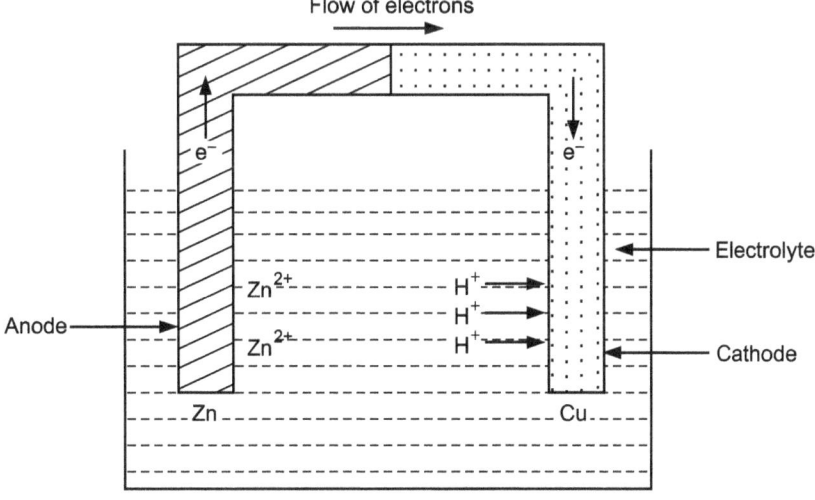

Fig. 6.7: Galvanic corrosion

- In Fig. 6.7, zinc and copper plates are in electrical contact with each other and are immersed into a solution of an electrolyte.

- As zinc has more negative potential than copper, it acts as a anode while copper acts as a cathode.

  The reaction at the anode will be,

$$Zn \rightarrow Zn^{2+} + 2\,e^-$$

- The electrons flow from anode to cathode through the metal and also corrosion current flows from anode to cathode with the dissolution of anode metal.
- In the galvanic corrosion, cathodic metal is always protected from the corrosion attack.
- The extent of corrosion depends on corrosive environment as well as the difference in the electrode potential of the two contacting metals i.e. their position in the galvanic series. (Refer article 6.10).
- If the separation between two metals in galvanic series is large, the extent and rate of corrosion is more.
- Galvanic corrosion also depends upon relative areas of anode and cathode.
  - e.g. (1) Steel screws corrode when in contact with brass in marine environment.
  - (2) Steel pipes corrode preferentially when connected to copper plumbing.

6.9 CONCENTRATION CELL CORROSION   [May 07, 11, 15]

- The corrosion of metals due to electrochemical attack on metal surface exposed to electrolytes of varying concentration or of varying aeration is called as concentration cell corrosion.
- It is a wet corrosion. The difference in concentration of metal ions may be due to difference in temperature or inadequate agitation of solution of metal ions.

Forms of Concentration Cell Corrosion:

(a) Differential Aeration:

- When one part of metal is exposed to air and other part is immersed in an electrolyte, it causes a difference in potential between differently aerated areas. The part exposed to less air undergoes corrosion.

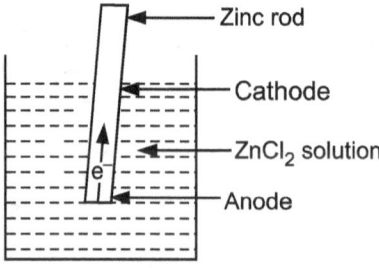

Fig. 6.8: Differential aeration

- The areas on the metal surface where oxygen concentration is low are anodic and the areas where the oxygen concentration is high are cathodic.

- This creates a small difference of potential thus setting up differential aeration or oxygen concentration cell and causes flow of current between them.

- Metal dissolves at the anodic area. (Refer Fig. 6.8)

Example 1:

- If a piece of zinc metal is partially immersed in a solution of its salt, the parts above the water line are strongly aerated, thus become cathodic.

- The part immersed in water see small concentration of oxygen and becomes anodic.

- This creates a difference of potential and causes a flow of current between two differentially aerated areas of zinc.

- As an anodic reaction, zinc will dissolve by forming electrons, which will be taken by oxygen at cathodic area to form hydroxyl ions.

- Circuit gets completed by the flow of OH^- ions through electrolyte and flow of electrons from anode to cathode through the metal.

$$Zn \rightarrow Zn^{2+} + 2\,e^- \qquad\qquad \text{... Anodic reaction}$$

$$\frac{1}{2}O_2 + 2\,e^- + H_2O \rightarrow 2\,OH^- \qquad\qquad \cdots \text{Cathodic reaction}$$

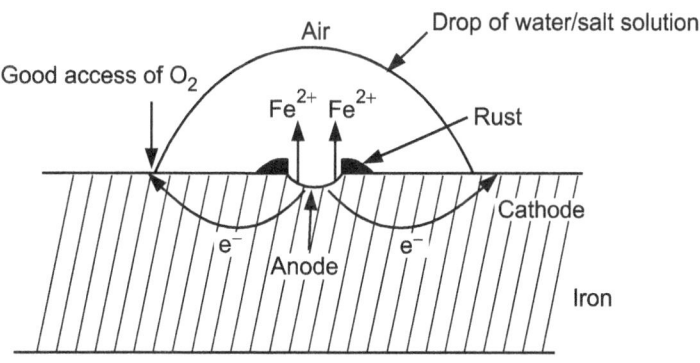

Fig. 6.9: Differential aeration

Example 2:

Iron corrodes under drop of water or drop of salt solution in the similar way. Area of metal covered by droplet, have less access of oxygen, so it becomes anodic with respect to other areas exposed to air. (See Fig. 6.9)

Thus, a difference of potential is created which causes a current to flow between differentially aerated areas of the metal.

Crevice Corrosion:

- Corrosion occurring within crevices and other shielded areas on metal surfaces exposed to corrosives like dirt, sand particles and other solids is called crevice corrosion.

e.g. A riverted plate section of metal - iron or steel - immersed in aerated sea water. Mechanism of crevice corrosion is oxygen absorption type.

$$M \rightarrow M^{2+} + 2\,e^- \qquad \text{... Oxidation}$$
$$2\,H_2O + O_2 + 4\,e^- \rightarrow 4\,OH^- \qquad \text{... Reduction}$$
$$M^{2+} + 2\,OH^- \rightarrow M(OH)_2 \downarrow$$
$$\text{Insoluble hydroxide}$$

Crevice corrosion is intense in a medium containing chloride ions. When oxygen is depleted, no further oxygen reduction occurs.

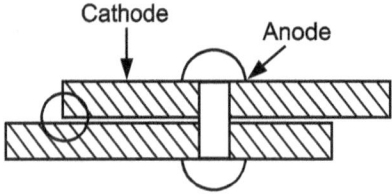

Fig. 6.10: Crevice corrosion

Pitting:

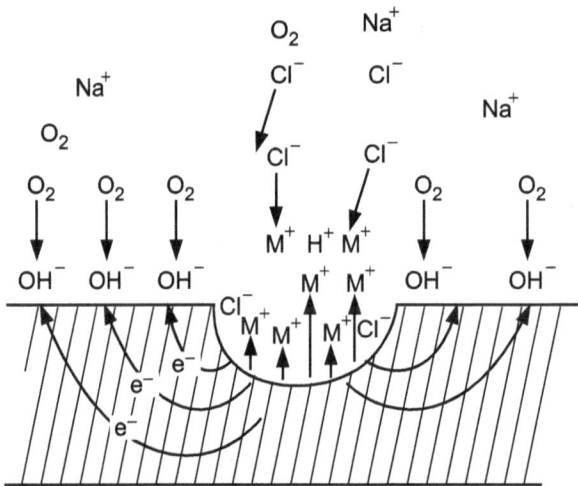

Fig. 6.11: Autocatalytic processes occurring in corrosion pits

- Pitting corrosion is extremely localised attack resulting in the formation of cavities or holes in the metal around which the metal is relatively unattacked.
- Pitting may penetrate deep into the metal, is very destructive and can ruin the metal.
- Pits usually grow in the direction of gravity i.e. they grow downward from horizontal surfaces.

Pitting is the result of the breakdown or cracking of the protective film on a metal at specific points. Breakdown of films may be because of mechanical factors like surface roughness, scratches, cut edges, sliding under load or because of particular type of chemical attack. Cracking of protective films form small anodic and big cathodic areas which in corrosive environment give rise to corrosion current.

e.g. Corrosion of stainless steel by sulphuric acid containing ferric chloride.

6.10 FACTORS INFLUENCING CORROSION RATE

Corrosion is destruction of a metal through electrochemical action with its environment. So it depends on nature of metal, nature of environment and the nature of corrosion product formed.

(A) Factors Related to Nature of Metal:

(a) Position of Metal in Galvanic Series:

- The rate of corrosion of metals depend upon its position in the electrochemical series and galvanic series.
- More the negative value of the standard electrode potential, more the metal corrodes. e.g. If zinc, sodium and copper electrodes are dipped in the solution of electrolyte, having the same concentration, for some period, it is found that sodium corrodes more as compared to zinc.
- It is clear that metals/alloys with higher position in galvanic series corrode rapidly as compared to lower ones.

(b) Hydrogen Overvoltage or Overpotential:

- Overpotential of hydrogen is the difference between the potential of the electrode at which evolution of hydrogen gas is observed and the theoretical value of potential at which hydrogen gas evolution takes place.
- The hydrogen overvoltage is inversely related to the corrosive tendency of metals.
- All the metals above hydrogen in the electrochemical series (refer article 6.9) liberate hydrogen when they are immersed in an acid solution and corrode easily.
- But some metals above hydrogen in the electrochemical series, do not liberate hydrogen from dilute hydrochloric acid solution.
- For example, pure tin and lead in absence of air do not get attacked by dilute hydrochloric acid solution. Pure zinc with high negative value is attacked by acid very slowly first. These observations are because of hydrogen overpotentials of metals.

Table 6.1 : Hydrogen Overvoltage or Overpotential

Metal	Electrode Potential (Volts)	Hydrogen Overvoltage (Volts)
Platinum	1.20	0.12
Silver	0.797	0.29
Copper	0.337	0.25
Hydrogen	0.00	–
Lead	– 0.13	0.60
Tin	– 0.14	0.50
Nickel	– 0.23	0.25
Iron	– 0.44	0.27
Zinc	– 0.761	0.70

- The overpotential of tin and lead are 0.5 and 0.6 volts respectively, while their electrode potentials are -0.14 and -0.13 volts respectively.

- So evolution of hydrogen in normal acid solution will not take place as net potential of tin and lead has become $0.5 - 0.14 = 0.36$ volts and $0.6 - 0.13 = 0.47$ volts.

- In case of zinc, electrode potential is slightly higher than its hydrogen overvoltage, so evolution of hydrogen is slow at the beginning.

- More the hydrogen overvoltage, less the corrosion tendency of metals and less the hydrogen overvoltage, more the corrosion tendency of metals.

(c) Relative Areas of Cathode and Anode:

- The important factor in galvanic corrosion is the area effect i.e. ratio of cathodic to anodic areas.

- When cathode and anode areas are equal, cathodic and anodic current densities are equal and corrosion phenomenon will not get accelerated.

- If cathode area is much larger than anode area, anodic current density will be greater, as a result corrosion of anode metal will be more.

- One can say that if the areas of cathode and anode are different, the intensity of corrosion of anode is directly proportional to the area of cathode.

- Corrosion is more if the area of cathode is larger than the area of anode. This is because if cathode area is larger than anode, the demand of electrons is more for reduction reaction to take place and thus more dissolution of metal at anode takes place.

  e.g. Steel rivets in copper plate get completely corroded in corrosive environment because of unfavourable area ratio. (Copper is noble which acts as a cathode).

(d) Nature of Protective Films:

- Many metals are susceptible to oxidation when exposed to air and they get covered with oxide films.

- Depending upon the protective nature of film, corrosion continues or stops. If films are porous, metal or oxygen will diffuse, thus further corrosion. If films are non-porous, they protect the metal from further attack.

- Lead forms lead sulphate surface coatings with strong sulphuric acid which protects lead for a long time in sulphuric acid environment.

- Titanium is a reactive metal but is resistant to erosion corrosion in many environments because of stability of the TiO_2 film formed.

(e) Purity of Metals:

- The corrosion resistance of pure metal is usually better than that of one containing small amounts of impurities.

- Presence of impurities accumulated on certain areas of metal are the sources of the potential difference on the metal.

- In corrosive environment, minute galvanic cell will form and anodic metal will corrode.

e.g. Pure aluminium (99.5 % plus) has good corrosion resistance. But minute amount of impurities even 0.02 % iron and 0.05 % nickel present in aluminium will decrease its corrosion resistance.

(B) Factors Related to Nature of Environment:

(a) Temperature:

- As rates of all chemical reactions increase with temperature, corrosion increases with temperature.

- Increase in temperature increases ionisation and mobility of all reacting ions and molecules. It also increases diffusion rate. e.g. Intergranular corrosion like caustic embrittlement takes place at high temperature in high pressure boilers.

- The rate of corrosion of copper and *monel metal* is less in boiling sulphuric acid while steel corrodes more in boiling sulphuric acid.

(b) Presence of Moisture:

- Atmospheric corrosion of few metals is slow in dry air but it increases rapidly in the presence of moisture.

- Moisture provides solvent for oxygen or other gases and furnishes electrolyte for setting corrosion cell. In some cases, moisture reacts with metal and oxides.

- Corrosion of iron is more in moisture than that in presence of dry air. In moisture primary product of rusting is ferrous hydroxide which oxidises to ferric hydroxide.

(c) Effect of pH:

- Acidic environment is more corrosive than alkaline or neutral environments. Zinc rapidly corrodes in weakly acidic solution but suffers less corrosion in a solution having pH 10 to 11.

- Many metals are readily attacked by acid but are resistant to alkali. By altering the chemical character of corroding medium i.e. pH, corrosion rate of a given metal can be controlled.

(d) Conductance of Medium:

- Many times stray current is leaked from an electric power circuit and flows through the metallic structures in earth.

- The points at which stray current leaves the metallic structure, become anode where metal dissolves.

- In stray current corrosion, cathodes and anodes are remote from each other. If soil contains moisture and soluble salts, it will increase conductivity of soil. Increase in conductivity will increase stray current corrosion. Moisture present in soil also increases conductance of medium, which increases underground soil corrosion of metals.

(e) Nature of Electrolyte:

The electrolyte itself is a source of potential difference. The solution potential of metal depends on the type of ions and their concentration in the solution. So change in concentration of an electrolyte will change the electrode potential and in turn will affect corrosion of metal. Crevice corrosion is intense in a medium containing chloride ions. Stray current corrosion is more in a soil containing soluble salts.

(C) Factors Related to Nature of Corrosion Products:

Solubility of Corrosion Product: Corrosion products (metal oxides) are formed by cations generated at anodic area and anions are generated at cathodic area. This process takes place due to diffusion of ions through the wet medium. If the corrosion product is soluble in the corroding medium, rate of corrosion at anode is comparatively faster.

(i)   Either in the vicinity of the anode or cathode then the corrosion product forms a protective barrier either around the anode or cathode and thus corrosion rate is affected substantially.

(ii) In between the anode and cathode or away from either of them, corrosion rate is not much affected.

6.11 PASSIVITY OR PASSIVATION

Definition

- It is defined as a phenomenon in which a metal or an alloy exhibits outstanding higher corrosion resistance than its position in the electrochemical or galvanic series. Passivity is the result of the formation of highly protective but very thin invisible film on the surface of metal or an alloy, which makes the metal more noble.

- Metals become passive because of this unimolecular adsorbed film of oxide which is self repairing on the metal surface.

- Titanium, aluminium, chromium and stainless-steel alloys containing chromium are passive in oxidising environment. But they become chemically active in reducing environment.

- By physical isolation of the metal from the corroding environment, pseudopassivity can be achieved which is useful in reducing corrosion. This is due to the deposition of thick protective reaction product films on metal. e.g. Film of lead sulphate on lead in sulphuric acid. Use of inhibitors, anodic polarisation, etc. are different ways of achieving pseudopassivity in metals.

- Active metals like Al, Fe when treated with concentrated nitric acid produce a protective oxide film. This reduces anodic corrosion making metal passive, but in dilute nitric acid rapid corrosion of metal (i.e. iron) occurs without evolution of hydrogen, as dilute nitric acid stimulates cathodic reaction.

6.12 POURBAIX DIAGRAM   [May 07, Dec. 09]

Pourbaix Diagram

- Pourbaix diagrams show the effect of pH on electrode potential of the electrode.
- Redox potentials are useful in predicting corrosion behaviour of metals. Corrosion will not occur till spontaneous direction of the reaction indicates metal oxidation.
- The applications of thermodynamics or more specifically, half cell potential to corrosion phenomena can be understood by means of these potential-pH plots. These plots are known as Pourbaix diagrams, after the scientist M. Pourbaix. He first suggested the use of the above plots. The diagram for iron is given in Fig. 6.12.

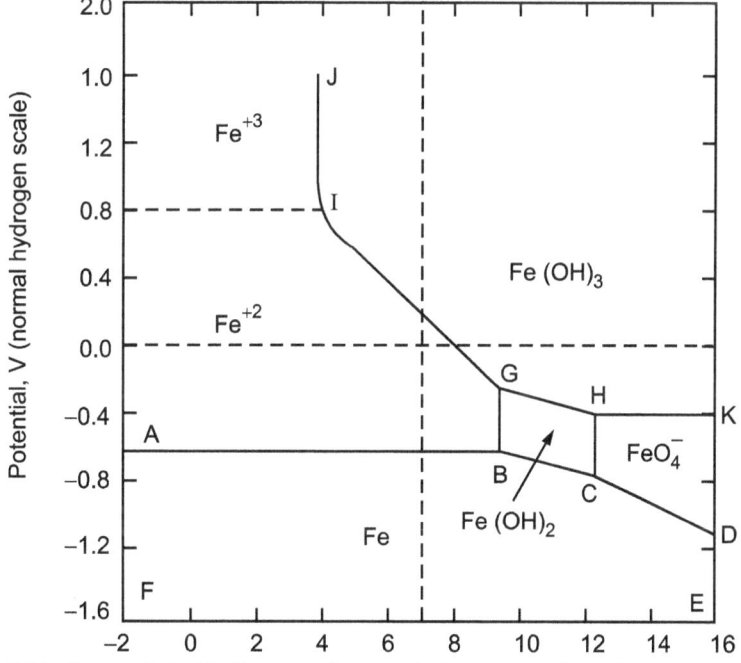

Fig. 6.12: Potential-pH diagram for Fe-H$_2$O system given by M. Pourbaix

The electrode potential of a system in which the reactants are not at unit activity, can be calculated using the Nernst equation

$$E = E^o + 2.303 \frac{RT}{nF} \log \frac{[\text{Oxidised species}]}{[\text{Reduced species}]}$$

where   E - half cell potential of an electrode
           E^o - the standard half cell potential of an electrode
           F - Faraday's constant
           n - number of electrons transferred.

Pourbaix diagrams can be constructed using the above calculations. In the above diagram, iron, iron hydroxide, ferrous ions etc. are thermodynamically stable in particular areas. They are in their states of lowest free energies.

Uses of these diagrams are:

- We can predict spontaneous direction of a reaction.

- Composition of corrosion products can be estimated.

- The environmental changes which will prevent or reduce corrosion attack also can be predicted.

  - Fig. 6.12 shows the potential-pH diagram for Fe-H_2O system.

  - Let us consider a dotted vertical line at pH = 7. During the upward movement upto potential of –0.6 V, the region of pure Fe exists since the metal is in its purest form and no corrosion takes place.

  - Above potential of –0.6 V, the region of Fe^{2+} starts indicating that, at pH = 7, if potential is increased, the metal undergoes rapid corrosion.

  - If the potential is increased further, ferric hydroxide is formed as the corrosion product.

  - At lower pH region < 4, Ferric oxide (Fe^{3+}) is formed and at high pH region > 4 ferric hydroxide is formed at higher electrode potential.

  - In the region ABCDEF, pure Fe exists, hence it is called as region of stability.

  - In the region BCHG, ferrous hydroxide $Fe(OH)_2$ is formed that forms a dense protective film on the metal surface. Hence this region is also called as region of stability.

  - In highly basic medium, there is a formation of FeO_4^- (ferrite). In this region, caustic embrittlement takes place.

6.13 CORROSION AND CONTROL

After learning about the ill effects of dry, electrochemical and atmospheric corrosion, it is appropriate to study corrosion prevention and corrosion control. As you have already learnt that corrosion, its extent and rate depends upon:

- Nature of metal,

- Nature of environment and

- Design of the specimen under study.

It is practically impossible to avoid corrosion entirely but it can be controlled by

- Retarding either the anodic or cathodic reactions known as cathodic and anodic protection.

- Conditioning of metal which is done by either coating of metal or by alloy formation.

- Conditioning of corrosive environment which mainly includes removal of oxygen from the electrolyte, modification in pH, use of inhibitors, modification in temperature which is more relevant for wet corrosion.

- Application of various types of organic coatings which include use of paints, polymer films.

- 'Prevention is better than cure' it is best to prevent corrosion rather than controlling the rate of corrosion. Given below are some methods of corrosion prevention.

Prevention of Bimetallic Corrosion:

- By isolating the metals electrically using insulators.

- By isolating the metals from the environment using a coating.

- By choosing metals that are close together in galvanic series or coating one of them to achieve this.

6.14 METHODS OF CONTROLLING CORROSION
[May 09, 10, 11, 12, 14, Dec. 11, 12, 14]

(A) Proper Selection and Design of Material:

The selection of the proper metal or alloy for a particular corrosive environment and sound engineering design are the best means of controlling and preventing corrosion.

The criteria in the design selection are:

- Noble metals should be used in surgical instruments, ornaments as they are most immune to corrosion.

- The use of two dissimilar metal contacts should be avoided.

- If two dissimilar metals have to be used, they should be as close as possible in the galvanic series.

- Weld rather than rivet tanks and other containers.

- The anodic metal should have as large area as possible while cathodic material should have much smaller area (nuts, bolts, etc.).

- An insulating material should be applied to prevent access of an electrolyte to the junction, but it should not be porous, as porous materials absorb and hold liquids.

- Avoid electrical contact between two dissimilar metals to prevent galvanic corrosion.

- Design tanks and other containers such that it provides for easy draining and easy cleaning.

- Sharp corners and recesses should be avoided because they favour accumulation of solids.

- During designing, presence of crevices between adjacent parts of structure should be avoided.

- The corrosion resistance of a pure metal is usually better than that of one containing small amounts of other elements. So pure metals should be used. But pure metals are expensive and are soft and weak, so it can be used in few cases. Exception is aluminium metal, it is not expensive and it can be used in a fairly pure state, 99.5 % plus purity.

(B) Modifying the Environment:

Altering the environment helps in reducing corrosion. The environment can be made less corrosive either by adding some chemicals which will neutralize the effect of corrosive material or by removing harmful constituent.

Deaeration:

Lowering temperature decreases corrosion rate. But under some conditions, increasing temperature decreases corrosion attack. Boiling sea water or boiling fresh water is less corrosive than hot sea water because of decrease in oxygen content of boiling sea or fresh water. Thus, by decreasing oxygen content of aqueous solutions, corrosion of metals can be reduced. This can be done by deaeration. Carbon dioxide content is also reduced by deaeration.

Deactivation:

Sodium sulphite (Na_2SO_3) or hydrazine hydrate ($N_2H_4 \cdot H_2O$) are used to remove oxygen from corrosive environment.

Alkali Neutralisation:

Alkaline neutralisers like ammonia, sodium hydroxide, lime, sodium salts of petroleum, phenols reduce corrosive rates of an acidic environment.

(C) Use of Inhibitors:

A corrosion inhibitor is a substance which when added in a small concentration to a corrosive environment, decreases the corrosion rate. They are divided into cathodic and anodic inhibitors on the basis of whether they inhibit anodic or cathodic reaction.

(a) Anodic and Cathodic Inhibitors:

- As corrosion is electrochemical in nature, the inhibitive action of any substance is the result of control of anodic and cathodic reactions.

- Anodic inhibitors form soluble compounds with dissolved metal ions, which deposit on metal surface to form a protective film, which reduces corrosion of anode. They are oxidising agents like chromates, nitrates and ferric salts.

- In an acidic environment, evolution of hydrogen gas takes place at the cathode. Corrosion can be reduced by slowing diffusion of hydrated hydrogen ions to the cathode or by increasing the overpotential of hydrogen evolution. Antimony and arsenic ions deposit metallic film on the cathode and retard hydrogen-evolution reaction.

- In a neutral environment, cathodic reaction is the result of oxygen absorption and formation of hydroxyl ions. Sodium sulphite or hydrazine are used to remove oxygen from the solution.

$$2\ Na_2S_2O_3\ +\ O_2\ \rightarrow\ 2\ Na_2SO_4$$

$$N_2H_4\ +\ O_2\ \rightarrow\ N_2 \uparrow +\ 2\ H_2O$$

- Cathodic inorganic inhibitors like magnesium, zinc or nickel salts are effective in neutral and alkaline environment. They react with hydroxyl ions at cathode and form insoluble hydroxides. These get deposited on the cathode. Above inhibitors can also be classified as:

(b) Inorganic Inhibitors and Organic Inhibitors:

- In neutral and alkaline solutions, chromates and nitrites act as anodic inhibitors. They are the most efficient inhibitors for controlling the corrosion of iron and steel in neutral and alkaline waters. Alkali inhibitors like sodium hydroxide, sodium carbonates and bicarbonates form metal hydroxides which serve as protective deposits. They are anodic inhibitors.

- Inorganic inhibitors do not give any protection in presence of acids and reducing conditions. For such conditions, polar organic compounds and colloidal organic materials are used as inhibitors. Their inhibitive action is because of physical and chemical adsorption of molecules on metal surface.

- They act as anodic, cathodic or mixed inhibitors. Due to physical adsorption of inhibitor, resistance to current flow at cathodic area increases. Due to chemisorption, co-ordinate covalent bond is formed between inhibitor and metal, so anodic polarisation takes place. Amines, heterocyclic nitrogen compounds, substituted urea and thiourea and metal soaps are used as organic inhibitors.

- Vapour-phase inhibitors are used to inhibit atmospheric corrosion of metals without placing it in direct contact of metal's surface. They possess high vapour pressure and are effective if used in close spaces like inside of packages. Some heterocyclic nitro-compounds, esters of carboxylic acid can be used as vapour-phase inhibitors.

(D) Use of Pure Metals:

- Pure metals exhibit higher corrosion resistance than the impure ones.

- Even minute impurities form galvanic cells and corrosion of metal takes place. But in many cases, it is practically not possible to produce metal of high purity.

- Very pure metals have inadequate mechanical properties as they are weak and soft. Further getting metals in pure form is expensive and the purpose of obtaining it in a pure form is served provided we know the nature of environment.

Use of Metal Alloys:

- Corrosion resistance and strength of most commercial metal is best secured by alloying them with suitable constituents.

- Homogeneous alloys have maximum corrosion resistance. Aluminium, magnesium and lead have more corrosion resistance than their alloys have because they form heterogeneous alloys with other elements.

6.15 CATHODIC AND ANODIC PROTECTION
[May 09, 11, 12, 14, Dec. 11, 12, 14]

6.15.1 Cathodic Protection

The science of cathodic protection was born in 1824, when Sir Humphry Davy made a presentation to the Royal Society of London about the rapid decay of the copper sheeting on ships of war, and Davy succeeded in protecting copper against corrosion from sea water by the use of iron anodes.

6.15.2 Principle

"The metal or an alloy that is to be protected is forced to act as cathode either by electrically connecting it to a metal whose position in the galvanic series is higher or by connecting it to the negative terminal of DC power supply".

There are two ways to protect a structure cathodically:

(1) By an external power supply and

(2) By appropriate galvanic coupling.

(1) Cathodic Protection by External Power Supply (Cathodic Protection by Impressed Current):

- Underground metallic structure can be protected by this method. Here external dc power supply is connected to underground metallic tank or pipe line to be protected.

- Negative terminal of the current source is connected to the tank and positive end to an inert anode like graphite, immersed in corroding medium.

- Anode is surrounded by backfill consisting of gypsum or bentonite to improve contact between anode and surrounding soil.

- Current from the anode passes to metallic structure through an electrolyte and corrosion of cathode is suppressed.

- This cathodic protection by impressed current is economical where electric power supply is cheap.

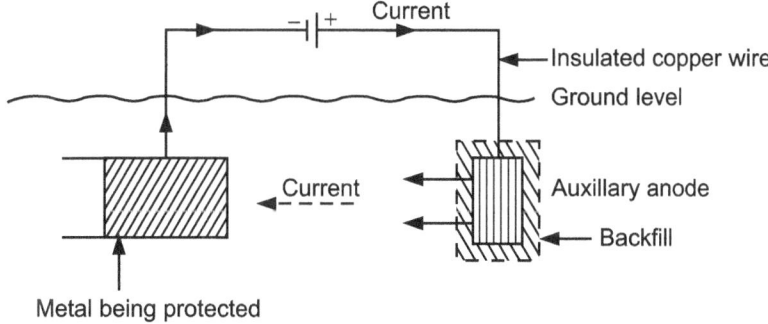

Fig. 6.13: Impressed current protection of underground tank

(2) Cathodic Protection by Galvanic Coupling or Sacrificial Anode Method or Galvanic Protection:

- In this method, the metallic structure to be protected is connected by wire to metal which has more negative potential i.e. anodic with respect to the metal to be protected.

- The anodic metal gets corroded while cathodic metal is protected. The anodic metal should have higher position in galvanic series as compared to metallurgy to be protected.

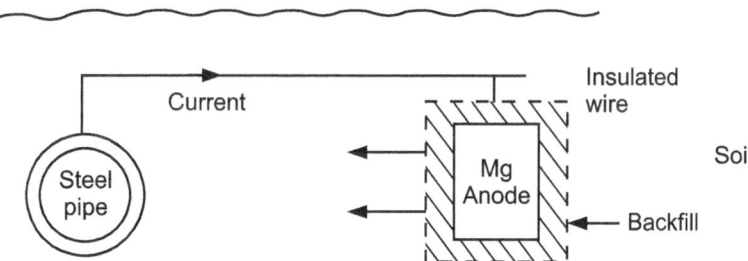

Fig. 6.14: Cathodic protection by galvanic coupling/Sacrificial anode method

- Magnesium is anodic with respect to steel and corrodes preferentially when galvanically coupled with steel. The anode in this case is called sacrificial anode, since it is consumed during protection of steel structure.

- Cathodic protection using sacrificial anodes can be used to protect buried pipelines as shown in Fig. 6.15.

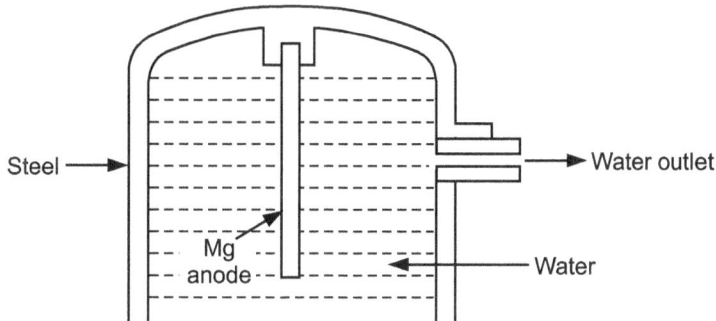

Fig. 6.15: Cathodic protection of domestic hot water tank using sacrificial anode

- Anode selection for cathodic protection is based on engineering and economic considerations. Among several sacrificial anodes (steels, graphite, silicon, iron, magnesium), magnesium is widely used.

6.15.3 Anodic Protection

- Anodic protection is based on the formation of a protective film on metals by externally applied anodic currents. i.e. by passivating the metal. Actually the application of anodic current to a structure increases the dissolution rate of a metal.

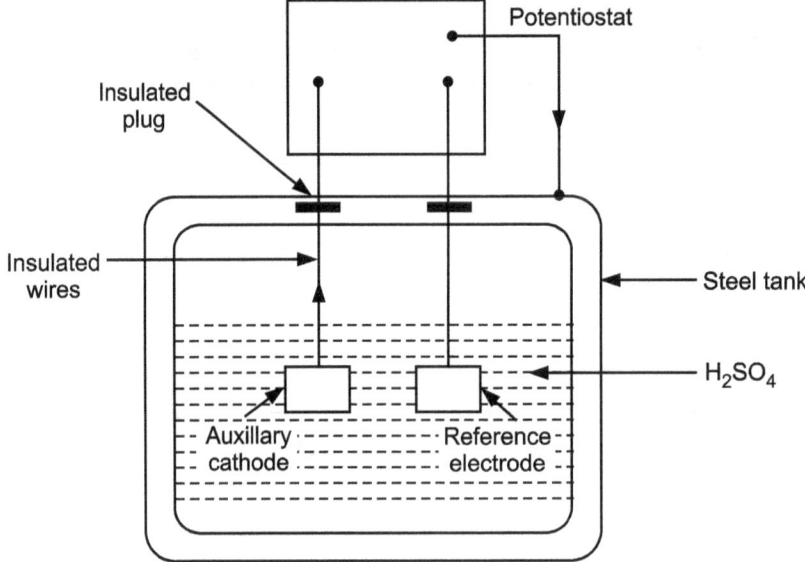

Fig. 6.16: Anodic protection of steel storage tank

- This type of behaviour occurs except for metals exhibiting active-passive transitions. Anodic protection can be applied for metals like nickel, chromium, titanium and their alloys as they exhibit active - passive transitions.
- If carefully controlled anodic currents are applied to the above metals, they are passivated and the rate of metal dissolution is decreased.
- To protect the structure anodically, an electronic device potentiostat is used. Potentiostat maintains a metal at a constant potential with respect to reference electrode.
- Out of the three terminals of potentiostat, one is connected to the metal i.e. tank to be protected, another to an auxiliary cathode (platinum) and third to reference electrode. (Calomel electrode). Potentiostat maintains a constant potential between tank and reference electrode.
- Anodic protection is limited to passive metals and alloys, it requires low current and is applicable in extremely corrosive environment. Cathodic protection is applicable in moderately corrosive conditions and current requirement for this is high. Installation cost for cathodic protection is less while for that of anodic protection is high.

6.16 PROTECTIVE COATINGS

The surface of engineering material can be protected from corrosion by covering it with metallic, inorganic or organic materials.

Properties of Good Protective Coatings:

- They provide satisfactory barrier between metal and its environment.

- These coatings impart mechanical properties, thermal insulating properties, electrical properties and oxidation resistance to the protected surface. Coatings are used for decoration also.

- The effectiveness of these coatings depend on their thickness, type of environment and required degree of protection.

Surface Preparation or Surface Treatment Methods:

To obtain excellent surface adhesion and service behaviour, surface treatment is a must.

For application of any type of coating, the surface to be coated must be free from dirt and other corrosion products and it must be properly prepared. Cleaning and preparation of metal surface for coating is done in steps.

(a) Removal of Greases and other Impurities:

Oils, greases and fatty substances present on metal surface are removed by using organic solvents like naphtha, xylene, toluene, acetone, etc. Then surface is cleaned with steam and hot water containing wetting agents like alkalies. After alkali cleaning, the surface is washed with water followed by water containing 1 % chromic acid to remove last traces of alkali.

(b) Removal of Oxides, Scales and Corrosion Product:

Mechanical cleaning is done by bristle brush and detergent, knife scrapers, grinder and cutters followed by hot water. This removes dirt and scales. Loose scale is removed by flame heating and mechanical brushing while oxide scale is removed by sand blasting. Sand blasting consists of introducing sand into an air stream under pressure. The blast impacts on the surface to be cleaned and removes scales present on the surface.

For complete removal of scales, metals are immersed in various pickling solutions. Acid pickling is a more convenient method of scale removal than mechanical cleaning and sand blasting. Temperature of bath, time of immersion and composition of pickling solution depend on the type of scale to be removed.

Plane carbon steels are pickled in dilute warm sulphuric acid, then cold hydrochloric acid with inhibitor and finally with alkaline solution of soda ash or lime.

6.16.1 Metallic Coatings

Metal coatings are applied by electrodeposition, flame spraying, cladding, hot dipping or vapour deposition. Inorganic coatings are formed by spraying, diffusion or chemical conversion. Spraying is followed by baking or firing at an elevated temperature. In both cases, a complete barrier must be provided. Porosity or defect in coating results in an accelerated localized attack on metal. Metal to be protected is called base metal while the metal used for protection is called coating metal.

Methods of Applying Metallic Coatings on Base Metal:

(1) Electroplating:

- It is one of the most important methods for the application of metallic coatings on the metals. In this method, coating metal is deposited on the base metal by immersing base metal in a solution of coating metal and passing direct current between base metal and another electrode.

- Electroplating consists of immersing a part to be coated in a solution of salt of coating metal and passing a direct current between the part and another electrode. The base metal is made a cathode of an electrolytic cell and anode is of coating metal.

- The metal to be plated electrolytically is cleaned and surface is made proper. Then it is made cathode of an electrolytic cell. The electrolytic solution is of soluble salt of metal to be coated. Direct current is passed after immersing cathode and anode in electroplating tank. Metal at anode dissolves and ions migrates to cathode and gets deposited on base metal. Thus, a thin coating layer is formed on a base metal. Properties of coating depend on the concentration of plating solution, agitation, temperature of solution and its pH.

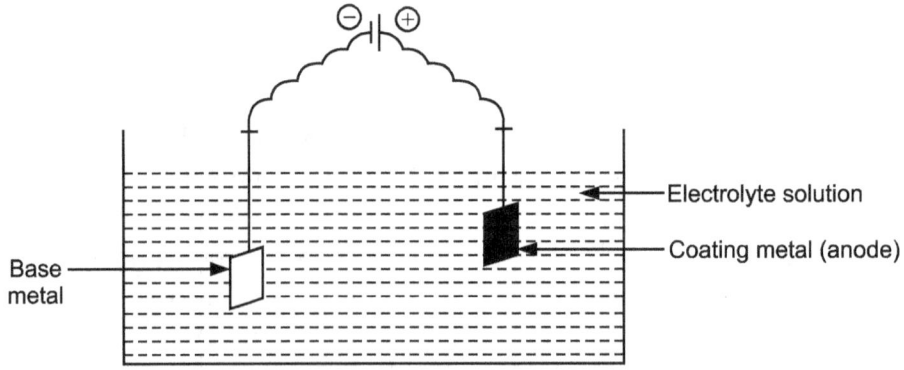

Fig. 6.17: Electroplating bath

- Electroplating is one of the most important methods for commercial production of metallic coatings. Zinc, lead, nickel, iron, tin, chromium and copper are frequently used for metallic coating. Precious metals like gold, silver, platinum are used for plating to a smaller extent. Recently certain alloys like lead - tin, tin - copper, tin - zinc are used in electroplating.

6.16.1.1 Types of Metallic Coating

Depending upon the position of coating metal in the electrochemical series with respect to the base metal, the coatings are called cathodic coatings or anodic coatings.

(a) Anodic Coating:

In anodic coating, coatings are produced from metals which are anodic to base metal. Aluminium, zinc, cadmium have their solution potentials greater than that of steel. So they are used to coat steel anodically. If any scratch is developed on zinc coated steel, a galvanic cell is formed between zinc and exposed iron. Zinc being anodic to steel, it will dissolve protecting steel or iron. Thus, iron is protected cathodically by sacrificial zinc. No attack on iron or steel occurs till all zinc gets corroded almost practically.

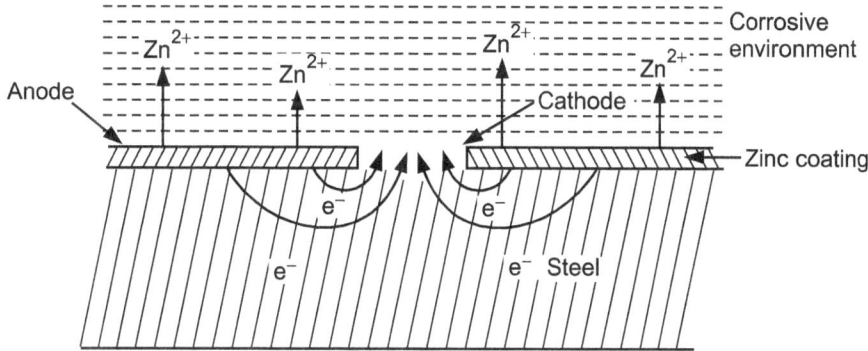

Fig. 6.18: Anodic coating

(b) Cathodic Coating:

Cathodic coatings can be obtained by application of more noble metal than base metal, for coating of base metal. They protect base metal because they have more corrosion resistance than base metal. Gold, copper, platinum, nickel, silver and chromium are the metals which can be used for cathodic coatings. Only continuous and pore-free coating gives protection to the base metal. If pores are present on the cathodically coated iron, iron being anodic to coating, intensive localized attack at the pores will take place. This will result in severe pitting.

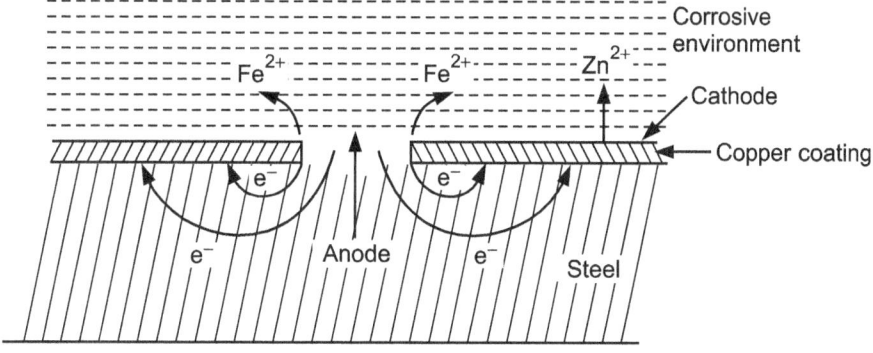

Fig. 6.19: Cathodic coating

Table 6.2 : Differences between Anodic Coating and Cathodic Coating

Anodic Coating	Cathodic Coating
1. If a metal that is to be protected (base metal) is selected then the metal whose coat is to be provided on base metal is chosen in such a way that, its position in galvanic series is higher as compared to the base metal.	1. The metal whose coat is to be provided on the base metal lies lower in the galvanic series as compared to the base metal.
2. The coat metal undergoes corrosion if galvanic cell formation takes place due to scratch or stress and base metal is protected.	2. If there is formation of galvanic cell due to scratch or stress then base metal undergoes corrosion rapidly.
3. The coat metal acts as an anode (oxidation) whereas base metal acts as a cathode.	3. The coat metal acts as a cathode and the base metal acts as an anode.
4. This type of coating is preferred as even if there is galvanic cell formation, the base metal is protected.	4. This type of coating is not preferred because if galvanic cell formation takes place, base metal gets corroded rapidly.
5. e.g. Zinc coating on steel.	5. Cr, Pt or Au coating on iron.

(2) Immersion:

- In this process, coating is produced by immersing base metal in an electrolyte solution containing a salt of coating metal. For this process, current is not required, the deposition occurs by simple displacement. The base metal should be anodic to coating metal. Ions of nobler metal are displaced from salt solution by ions of active metal.

- Immersion coatings are uniform but thin. By controlling composition of bath, temperature of bath and pH, uniform coatings can be produced by this method. These coatings are used as a base for other metallic coatings. Coating of zinc on aluminium and magnesium is used as a base for nickel plating on aluminium and magnesium. Nickel, gold, silver and tin platings can be produced by this method.

(3) Hot Dipping:

- Hot dip coatings are applied on base metal by immersing them in molten metal bath covered by molten flux layer of $ZnCl_2 \cdot 3\ NH_4Cl$. This method is useful for producing coatings of metals having low melting points, on the metals having high melting points. Zinc, tin and lead are used to coat steel, iron and copper. Hot dipping coatings are of two layers, first layer is alloying layer adhering directly to metal while second layer is of pure coating metal. For proper adhesion, base metal surface must be cleaned properly.

- For coating lead on iron, first iron is coated with thin coating of tin by immersion method and then by hot dipping lead is applied on it to form a second layer.

- Galvanized steel is a popular example of steel sheets having thin coat of zinc. Zinc prevents steel from corrosion due to atmosphere. But galvanized iron has poor acid resistance. Galvanized wares cannot be used for preserving food-stuffs as zinc will form toxic compounds with food preservatives.

- Tin is applied on iron in a similar way as zinc is applied on iron. But tin cannot protect iron like galvanized iron, as tin coating cannot cover the iron surface completely. When coated surface is exposed to air, iron being anodic to tin, rapid corrosion of iron takes place (See Fig. 6.20). Tin can be used for coating over mild steel. Tin-coated containers can be used for storing and preserving food-stuffs because tin has corrosion resistance to dilute acids and water and it is non-toxic.

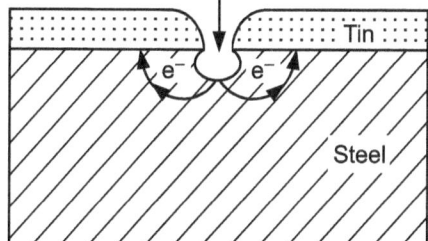 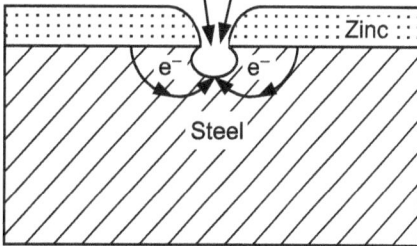

Fig. 6.20: Galvanic corrosion in tin and zinc coated steel
arrows indicate corrosive attack

- By hot dipping method, thickness of the coating produced on base metal is more. Afterwards the coated part is heat treated to form an alloy bond between coating and base metal.

(4) Metal Spraying or Flame Spraying:

- Metallized coatings are obtained by spraying heated metal particles on the roughened surface of base metal. This can be achieved by using spraying guns or by powder method. When the molten metal particles strike the metal surface, they flatten and fill up the surface irregularities. Finely divided molten metal particles are obtained by feeding metal wire through a melting flame.

- Oxyacetylene flame is commonly used for melting the metal. The atomized metal is then blown out into a fine spray with the help of compressed air. Thus, the sprayed metal adheres to the surface of base metal.

- This method is limited to low melting metals like zinc, lead, tin as coating metals. Coatings produced by spraying are uniform but porous, so they are less protective under severe corrosion attack. Sprayed metal provides a good base for paint.

(5) Power Coating:

- It is a process of applying a free flowing powder on the substrate to avoid its corrosion. It is a type of dry coating as no solvent is involved.
- The powder is generally applied electrostatically.
- The powder coating for corrosion resistance is generally applied on metals, household appliances, aluminium materials, automobile and bicycle parts.
- Powder being applied as coating is generally a thermosetting or thermosoft polymer.
- Depending on the type of polymer used for coating, two types of powder coatings are possible i.e. thermoset polymer powder coating and thermoplast polymer powder coating.

Process:

(1) Pretreatment Step:

- This step consists of removal of foreign materials from the metal surface such as oil, soil, gases, lubricants, metal oxides etc. Pretreatment is done either chemically or physically.

(2) Power Application Process:

- The polymer powder on the metal surface is sprayed with the help of a gun. The process is electrostatic in nature.
- Powder in the gun is made negative with respect to metal and powder is pushed on the metal surface with the help of air pressure.
- The schematic diagram for powder coating is shown in Fig. 6.21.

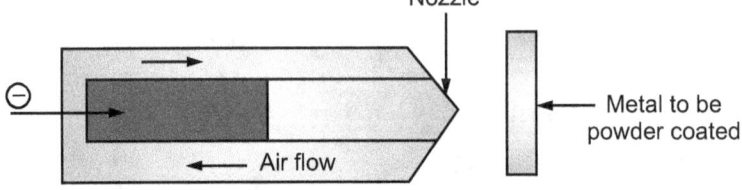

Fig. 6.21 : Power coating

Advantages:

- No chemical environmental pollution.
- Thick coating of metal is possible.
- Recycling of excessive powder is possible.
- Low cost.

Disadvantages:

- Powder coating of thin metal sheets is difficult.
- Smaller subject cannot be powder coated.
- Polymer powder coated object cannot be used at extremely high temperatures.

(6) Cladding:

- Cladding is bonding of two dissimilar metals.
- The cladding of two metals is achieved by pressing or rolling two metals together.
- Now-a-days metallic cladding is generally done with the help of lasers.
- A powder metal is melted and deposited on the surface of other metal with the help of laser beam.
- Metallic cladding is used to improve mechanical strength of metal or to make it corrosion resistant.

Advantages:

- Any metallic shape can be coated.
- Deposition on repairing parts of machine is possible after disconnecting.
- No reformation of substrate takes place.
- Good microstructures lead to better life of coated material.
- Low cost technology.

(7) Electroless Coating:

- It is an autocatalytic chemical process of application of nickel-phosphorus or nickel boron on metal or plastic.
- The process takes place in the presence of strong reducing agent such as sodium hypophosphite ($NaPO_2H_2 \cdot H_2O$). The reducing agent reacts with metal surface ions for deposition.
- Depending on the percentage of phosphorus during coating, the coating can be classified as low phosphorus, medium phosphorus (3 to 9%) and high phosphorus coating (9 to 13%).

Advantages:

- It does not use electrical power.
- Even coating is possible as the process is chemical.
- Thickness and volume of coating can be controlled.
- Bright coatings can be obtained.

Disadvantages:

- Life span of chemical is limited.
- Generation of waste chemicals and their disposal is difficult.

(8) Cementation:

- Cementation is a process in which wrought ion is converted into steel by heating it with charcoal.
- In cementation, wrought iron in the form of metallic bars is thoroughly mixed with powdered charcoal and placed in a furnace.

- As the temperature of the furnace increases, the carbon enters in the iron leading to the formation of steel.

- Generally, heating is confined for a week followed by cooling for 15 days.

6.17 CHEMICAL CONVERSION COATINGS   [Dec. 09, May 08, 11]

Inorganic Coatings:

They are produced by 'corroding' the metal surface to form an adherent and protective corrosion product. They are also called chemical conversion coatings because metallic surface is converted into some other chemical form by a chemical reaction. They are used as primary coatings.

(a) Anodizing:

- Anodizing consists of anodic oxidation in an acid bath to build up an oxide layer. Anodized coatings can be produced on aluminium, magnesium and their alloys by electrolysis in acid like sulphuric acid, chromic acid or phosphoric acid at moderate temperature and current densities. Initially, the oxide film formed as a result of anodic oxidation is thin, it grows in thickness as oxidation proceeds. The surface layers - coatings - are porous, so are used as adherent layer for paints. Minute pores can be sealed by exposing the coat to boiling water or sealed with oils, waxes, chromates and various resins.

(b) Phosphate Coatings:

- A process of producing phosphate coatings on a base metal by a reaction between aqueous solution of phosphate and phosphoric acid with the base metal is called phosphatizing.

- Automobile bodies are examples of phosphatizing, it provides good base for paints. Phosphate coatings are applied on iron, steel, zinc by using phosphates of iron, manganese and zinc and various accelerators. These coatings can be produced by spraying, brushing or by immersion.

(c) Chromate Coatings:

- These conversion coatings are applied by immersion of base metal into a solution of hexavalent chromium ion and mineral acid. They are used for protection of zinc, aluminium and magnesium. Chromate coatings have more corrosion resistance than that of phosphate coating. They can be applied in various colours and shades.

(d) Oxide Coatings:

- These are produced by treating base metal with alkaline oxidising solution. This increases thickness of original oxide film. They have less protective value and are mostly used for decorative purpose.

6.18 BLACODIZING OR BLACK OXIDIZING

- Blacodizing is an industrial process during which heat and chemical treatment is done on the metal surface so that a uniform film of corresponding metal oxide is produced. Since generally these coatings are produced on iron alloys, which produces black iron oxide i.e. magnetite (Fe_2O_3), hence it is also called as black oxidizing.

- The metals and alloys that can be blacodized are steel, stainless steel, cast iron, copper, brass, cadmium, zinc, nickel and electroless nickel etc.

  There are two commonly used methods for blacodizing: (i) Room temperature or Cold blacodizing and (ii) High temperature blacodizing.

(i) Room Temperature or Cold Blacodizing:

  ➤ This process is carried out at room temperature. Usually at this temperature, oxide film is not produced on the metal surface but copper selenite or selenate layer is uniformly produced.

  ➤ This type of blacodizing is done on the surface of steel, stainless steel, aluminium, cadmium etc. The metal is cleaned and rinsed thoroughly and it is blackened for   1-2 minutes at relatively lower temperatures of 25 to 30°C. Once the film formation takes place, the metal is rinsed again to ensure proper fixation of the film.

  ➤ The films are not strongly adhered and become unstable at higher proper temperature and are not abrasion and friction resistant.

  ➤ The blackened methods are further treated with oils and waxes so that a well finished object is obtained.

Advantages and Disadvantages of Cold Blacodizing:

- The method is simple and rapid.

- No hazardous chemicals are used during the process and hence there is no chemical effluent pollution.

- The process is economical as it consumes less energy.

- The film formed is not strong and not resistant to friction and abrasion and may undergo further corrosion.

- It is not stable at high temperature.

(ii) Hot Blacodizing:

  ➤ This process is carried out at elevated temperatures in the range of 125 to 150°C and in presence of certain oxidizing chemicals. At this temperature the metal gets converted to their corresponding oxides and a uniform thickness film of black colour is formed on the surface.

> ➤ The commonly used metals and alloys for hot blacodizing are steel, stainless steel, copper, cadmium, alloys of copper such as bronze etc.

> ➤ The oxidizing chemicals used are (1) Concentrated NaOH, (2) Sodium nitrite, (3) Stabilizers, (4) Wetting reagents and (5) Activators.

> ➤ Initially a bath is prepared which contain the predetermined volumes of the oxidizing chemicals. A metal surface that is to be blacodized is cleaned, degreased and rinsed thoroughly. Then it is put in the chemical bath and heated at the temperature of 125-150°C.

> ➤ The films formed in this process are strongly adherent and have excellent corrosion resistance. The blackened metals are further treated with oils and waxes so that a well finished object is obtained.

Advantages and Disadvantages of Hot Blacodizing:

- The film formed is strongly adherent, corrosion resistant, stable towards heat, friction and abrasion.
- The method is costly as it consumes more electricity.
- It is not ecofriendly as many hazardous chemicals are discharged in the biosphere.

SUMMARY

- Corrosion is destruction of metal on subjecting it to chemical or electrochemical attack.
- Corrosion can be dry or wet based on conditions in which it takes place.
- Oxidative corrosion involves metal destruction due to metal oxide formation. Kind of film decides its further corrosion.
- Corrosion due to other gases like oxygen is governed by the chemical affinity between metal and the attacking agent and nature of film formed.
- Hydrogen embrittlement is corrosion due to diffusion of hydrogen (atomic) through metal bringing about fissures and reducing its strength.
- Electrochemical corrosion is accompanied by either evolution of hydrogen or absorption of oxygen depending upon exposure to acidic or aerated salt solution of metals.
- Galvanic corrosion takes place due to formation of galvanic cell/s (due to difference in electrode potentials between two metals/alloys).
- Differential aeration or oxygen concentration cell corrosion takes place due to exposure of metal to varying air or concentration. e.g. pitting, waterline crevice etc. are all examples of concentration cell corrosion.
- Passivation is the phenomenon due to which a given metal shows an outstanding corrosion resistance than expected from its position in the electrochemical/galvanic series.

- Rate of corrosion is mainly influenced by the nature of metal and nature of environment and the factors falling within purview of it.
- Pourbaix diagram is a pH v/s potential plot which represents corrosion behaviour of metals with change in chemical character of solution.
- Corrosion can be controlled and not prevented by using suitable methods like proper design selection, modifying environment, use of pure metals/alloys, etc.
- Inhibitors are substances which check either anodic or cathodic reaction and thus reduce corrosion.
- Cathodic and anodic protection methods involve forcing the metal to behave as either cathode or anode to control corrosion respectively.
- Protective coatings of various kinds like metallic, inorganic, organic are used to check corrosion.
- Metallic coatings are either anodic or cathodic. These can be applied by methods like hot dipping, electroplating, cladding, etc.
- To get an excellent service behaviour of a protective coating, the metal to be protected should be treated for unwanted materials.

EXERCISE

1. What is corrosion ? Discuss the corrosion caused due to the combination of metals of different electrode potentials.
2. What is corrosion ? How do metals undergo corrosion ?
3. Define corrosion. Explain with suitable example dry corrosion theory.
4. Why does the steel pipe connected to the copper plumbing get corroded ? Name and explain the type of corrosion.
5. Explain galvanic corrosion with the help of galvanic series.
6. Define the term corrosion. Explain electrochemical theory of corrosion.
7. Explain rusting of iron with a suitable diagram and chemical reaction.
8. Explain hydrogen evolution and oxygen absorption mechanism of electrochemical corrosion.
9. What happens when metals like gold, aluminium and iron are exposed to moist atmosphere ?
10. Discuss atmospheric corrosion in case of silver, molybdenum, sodium and aluminium.
11. Define the term corrosion. What are the consequences of corrosion ?
12. Define the terms uniform corrosion and localised corrosion. Explain with a suitable example why is latter more severe than the former ?
13. What is the principle underlying differential aeration corrosion ? Explain the various forms of corrosion coming within the purview of it ?

14. What is the relation between hydrogen overvoltage and corrosion rate ? Explain.
15. "Passivity is not a static but a dynamic phenomenon." Comment.
16. "Anodic metallic coatings provide better protection to metals than cathodic ones". Comment.
17. What are the preventive measures for corrosion ? Explain.
18. Distinguish between hydrogen evolution and oxygen absorption mechanisms for corrosion.
19. Distinguish between cathodic and anodic protection methods for controlling corrosion.
20. Distinguish between anodic and cathodic metallic coatings. Which is the more preferred one ? Why ?
21. What are the merits and demerits of organic and inorganic coatings ?
22. Give an account of non-metallic coatings for protection against corrosion.
23. How do inhibitors inhibit corrosion ? Explain.
24. What are the precautions to be taken in the choice of suitable metal and proper design selection in checking corrosion ?
25. What are the merits and limitations in the use of a pure metal and metal alloys methods ?
26. Which method would you choose under the following circumstances for controlling corrosion:
    (a) Modification of the environment is not possible.
    (b) Chances of electrochemical corrosion to occur are more.
    (c) The metal surface is to be coated with a primer coat.
    (d) When the metal is to be made to behave as passive.
    (e) When modification in the corrosive environment is possible.
27. Explain chemisorption.
28. Explain the mechanism of corrosion due to oxygen.
29. What is oxidative corrosion ?
30. Enlist the types of oxide film formed due to corrosion and explain any two in brief.
31. Why do the metal not get affected by unstable oxide film ?
32. Explain the corrosion due to sulphur.
33. How nitrogen and its compounds are responsible for atmospheric corrosion.
34. What is electrochemical cell ? What are the types of electrochemical cells ?
35. Explain galvanic cell with it's cell reaction and cell diagram.
36. Explain concentration cell with cell reaction and cell diagram.
37. What is electrode potential ? How it is expressed ? Write the meaning of each term involved in the expression.

38. Give the reason for formation of Helmholtz double layer.
39. Write Nernst equation and explain the terms involved in it.
40. What is electrochemical series ? What are the applications of electrochemical series ?
41. What are the disadvantages of electrochemical series ?
42. Explain galvanic series. What are the advantages of galvanic series over electrochemical series ?
43. What is hydrogen over potential? How it is related to corrosion tendency of metal ?
44. Explain the attack of hydrogen on metal at high temperature.
45. Explain with diagram immersion corrosion.
46. What is galvanic corrosion ? Explain in brief.
47. Give the cell reaction taking place during galvanic corrosion.
48. Define concentration cell corrosion. What are the different forms of concentration cell corrosion ?
49. What is differential aeration ?
50. What is crevice cross ion ? Give the mechanism.
51. Write a short note on pitting emission.
52. Give the relation between galvanic corrosion and areas of cathode and anode.
53. Enlist the factors affecting corrosion related to nature of metal and explain each in brief.
54. Explain with respect to corrosion
    (a) temperature of environment   (b) pressure of moisture
    (c) effect of pH   (d) conductance of medium
    (e) nature of electrolyte
55. How the stability factor of corrosion product affects rate o corrosion ?
56. What is Pourbaix diagram ? For what it is used ?
57. How can the corrosion be avoided ?
58. Briefly explain the difference between oxidation and reduction electrochemical reaction. Which reaction occurs at the anode and which at cathode.
59. List five metals that are cathodic to hydrogen and give their standard reduction potential.
60. List five metals that are anodic to 'H' and give their standard reduction potential.
61. A standard galvanic cell has electrodes of zinc and tin. Which electrode is the anode ? Which electrode corrodes ?
62. What is the e.m.f. of cell ? Define passivation of metal or alloy ? Give examples of some metals and alloys that shows passivity.
63. Why metals are not found in their free state ?
64. Differentiate between electrochemical and galvanic series.

65. What are differences between galvanization and tinning ?
66. What is cathodic protection ?
67. Rusting of water is quicker in saline water than in ordinary water, why ?
68. Explain in detail how the finish is applied ?
69. Describe how cathodic protection works. Which of the following metals can cathodically protect iron ? Mg, Zn, Cu, Pb.
70. Explain sea water as an electrolyte.
71. A steel can is protected by coating it with zinc. Explain in detail how zinc prevents corrosion.
72. A buried iron pipeline is protected by magnesium bars which are connected by a copper wire. Answer the following:
    (a) the cathode is   (b) the anode is
    (c) give anode reaction   (d) give cathode reaction
73. Indicate the principle of anodic protection.
74. What is cathodic protection ? Under what conditions is this protection more useful ?
75. Mention the theories of corrosion and explain one of them.
76. What are differences between e.m.f. and galvanic series ?
77. What is the mechanism by which rusting occurs ?
78. How does corrosion product influence further corrosion.
79. Explain why magnesium corrodes faster when it is in contact with copper than when it is in contact with iron.
80. Describe briefly the important parameters involved in electroplating.
81. What are the conditions of electrochemical corrosion ?
82. How pilling – bedworth ratio is related to the protective capacity of an oxide layer ?
83. What are the limitations of electroplating ?
84. What are the drawbacks of cathodic protection ?
85. Why does any impure metal corrode faster than pure metal under identical condition ?
86. Enlist the types of metallic coating and explain in detail hot dipping.
87. What is metal spraying or flame spraying ?
88. How are nickel, gold being plated ?
89. What is inorganic coating ? What are the types ?
90. Explain anodizing ?
91. Write a short note on phosphate coating.
92. Explain in detain chromate coatings ?
93. What is meant by black oxidizing ? What are the methods used for black oxidising ?
94. Explain the blackodizing done on the surface of aluminium.

95. What are the advantages of cold blacodizing ?

96. What are the advantages and disadvantages of hot blacodizing ?

97. Distinguish between cold blacodizing and hot blacodizing.

98. What is sacrificial anode method ?

99. Differentiate between anodic and cathodic inhibitors.

100. Write a note on: organic and inorganic inhibitor.

101. Write some of the criterias for proper selection of design of material.

102. How will you prevent bimetallic corrosion ?

103. A solution with 0.2 m Ag^+ and 0.2 m H^+ is electrolysed between Pt electrodes. What is the concentration of Ag^+ when H_2 just begins to be liberated at the cathode.

UNIVERSITY QUESTIONS

DECEMBER 2012

1. Explain cathodic protection of underground structure. Give the principle involved.

   (5 Marks)

   Ans. Refer to Articles 6.15.1 and 6.15.2 on Page No. 6.22.

2. How does the nature of environment influence the rate of corrosion? Explain any four factors with examples. **(4 Marks)**

   Ans. Refer to Article 6.10 (B) on Page No. 6.15.

3. Discuss various steps involved in powder coating. **(4 Marks)**

   Ans. Refer to Article 6.16.1 (5) on Page No. 6.30.

4. Explain the Mechanism of Dry corrosion. Discuss the oxidation corrosion in case of Mg, Cr, Mo. **(5 Marks)**

   Ans. Refer to Articles 6.3 and 6.3.1 on Page No. 6.2 and 6.3.

5. How is steel galvanized? Explain the process with the help of a flow diagram.

   (4 Marks)

   Ans. Refer to Article 6.8 on Page No. 6.9.

6. Give conditions under which the wet corrosion occurs. Explain the mechanism of wet corrosion by hydrogen evolution with suitable example. **(4 Marks)**

   Ans. Refer to Article 6.7 on Page No. 6.7.

MAY 2013

1. Explain various factors affecting corrosion on the basis of nature of metal **(5 Marks)**

   Ans. Refer to Article No 6.10 on Page Nos. 6.13 and 6.15.

2. Describe Anodic protection of metal for corrosion control **(4 Marks)**

   Ans. Refer to Article No 6.15.3, on Page No. 6.25 and 6.26.

3. Compare : Galvanizing and Tinning **(4 Marks)**

   Ans. Refer to Article No 6.16.1(3) on Page No. 6.30.

4. What is Powder coating? Explain any one method   **(4 Marks)**

    Ans. Refer to Articles No6.16.1 (5) on Page No. 6.30

5. Explain corrosion control using proper designing and material selection method.   **(4 Marks)**

    Ans. Refer to Articles No 6.14 [A] on Page No. 6.19.

6. Define oxidation corrosion. Explain general mechanism of oxidation corrosion. Compare oxidation corrosion which occurs in Na metal Cu metal and Molybdenum (Mo) metal.   **(3 Marks)**

    Ans. Refer to Article No 6.3 on Page No. 6.2 and 6.3.

NOVEMBER 2013

1. Give the mechanism of electrochemical corrosion.   **(5 Marks)**

    Ans. Refer to Article 6.7 on Page No. 6.6, 6.7 and 6.8.

2. Explain nature of metal factors affecting rate of corrosion.   **(5 Marks)**

    Ans. Refer to Article 6.10 on Page No. 6.13, 6.14 and 6.15.

3. What are types of metallic coatings ? Which is preferred ? Why ?   **(3 Marks)**

    Ans. Refer to Article 6.16.1 on Page No. 6.27, 6.28 and 6.29.

4. Give principle construction and applications of cathodic protection.   **(5 Marks)**

    Ans. Refer to Article 6.15.1 on Page No. 6.22.

5. Explain 'power coating' method for corrosion control.   **(4 Marks)**

    Ans. Refer to Article 6.16.1 on Page No. 6.26.

6. Account on 'nature of oxide film' on metal surface and its effect on further corrosion.   **(4 Marks)**

    Ans. Refer to Article 6.3.1 on Page No. 6.3 and 6.4.

MAY 2014

1. What is Pilling-Bedworth ratio? Give four types of oxide films formed on surface of metal with suitable example.   **(5 Marks)**

    Ans. Refer to Article 6.4 and 6.3.1 on Page No. 6.3 and 6.4.

2. Explain galvanization with neat labeled diagram to protect Iron from corrosion.   **(6 Marks)**

    Ans. Refer to Article 6.16.1.1 (3) hot dipping Fig 6.20 on Page No. 6.28.

3. What the principle of Cathodic protection? Explain it with any one method.   **(4 Marks)**

    Ans. Refer to Article 6.15.1, 2 Fig. 6.13, 14 on Page No. 6.22

4. Explain wet corrosion with H_2 evolution and O_2 absorption mechanism.   **(5 Marks)**

    Ans. Refer to Article 6.7 Fig. 6.5 and 6.6 on Page No. 6.7 and 6.8.

5. Distinguish between anodic and cathodic coatings.   **(4 Marks)**

    Ans. Refer to Article 6.16.1.1 Pg 6.27.

6. Discuss factors affecting rate of corrosion, two each, for nature of metal and nature of environment. **(4 Marks)**

Ans. Refer to Article 6.10 A (a) or (d) any two B (a) to e any two on Page No. 6.13.

DECEMBER 2014

1. Define corrosion and explain effect of following factors on rate of corrosion
   (i) Purity of metal
   (ii) Relative area of anode and cathode. **(5 Marks)**

Ans. Refer to Article 6.1 and 6.10 on Page No. 6.1 and 6.13.

2. State the types of oxide film formed on the surface of following metals with reactions. **(4 Marks)**
   (1) Na (2) Al
   (3) Au (4) Mo

Ans. Refer to Article 6.2 and 6.7 on Page No. 6.2 and 6.8.

3. What is cathodic coating ? Explain timing with neat labelled diagram to protect metal from corrosion. **(4 Marks)**

Ans. Refer to Article 6.16.1.1 (b) on Page No. 6.27.

4. Explain electrochemical corrosion by H_2 evolution and O_2 absorption mechanism.

Ans. Refer to Article 6.7 on Page No. 6.6. **(5 Marks)**

5. What is principle of cathodic protection and explain it with any one suitable method?

Ans. Refer to Article 6.15.1 and 6.15.2 on Page No. 6.22. **(4 Marks)**

6. Define electroplating. Explain electroplating process with neat labeled diagram and applications. **(4 Marks)**

Ans. Refer to Article 6.16.1 (1) on Page No. 6.26.

MAY 2015

1. What is dry corrosion ? Explain mechanism of oxidation corrosion with suitable figure and reactions. **(5 Marks)**

Ans. Refer to Articles 6.1 and 6.3 on Page No. 6.1 and 6.3.

2. Explain how nature of metal affects the rate of corrosion. **(4 Marks)**

Ans. Refer to Article 6.10(A) on Page No. 6.15.

3. What are electroless coatings? Explain with suitable example. Give its application. **(4 Marks)**

Ans. Refer to Article 6.16.1 on Page No. 6.31.

4. Define corrosion. State the conditions under which wet corrosion occurs. Explain oxygen absorption mechanism of wet corrosion. **(5 Marks)**

Ans. Refer to Article 6.1 and 6.7 on Page Nos. 6.1 and 6.8.

5. Explain cementation and cladding methods of applying metallic coatings on base metal. **(4 Marks)**

Ans. Refer to Articles 6.16.1 on Page No. 6.26.

6. Compare: Cathodic protection and Anodic protection.   **(4 Marks)**
   Ans. Refer to Article 6.16.1.1 on Page No. 6.33.

NOVEMBER 2015

1. Give the Pilling-Bedworth ration and its significance. Give the oxidation reaction involved and state the type of film formed on the surface in the case of Mg, Cr and Mo.   **(5 Marks)**
   Ans. Refer to Articles 6.4 and 6.3.1 on Page Nos. 6.4 and 6.3.

2. Explain the process of galvanizing with labeled diagram. Give the applications and limitations of this technique.   **(4 Marks)**
   Ans. Refer to Article 6.16.1.1 (3) on Page No. 6.34.

3. State the different types of corrosion inhibitors with their examples. Discuss in brief their role in corrosion prevention.   **(4 Marks)**
   Ans. Refer to Article 6.14 on Page No. 6.19.

4. Discuss any five factors affecting corrosion.   **(5 Marks)**
   Ans. Refer to Article 6.10 on Page No. 6.13.

5. Define corrosion. Explain the hydrogen evolution mechanism of wet corrosion.   **(4 Marks)**
   Ans. Refer to Articles 6.1 and 6.7 on Page Nos. 6.1 and 6.5.

6. What is the principle of cathodic protection ? Discuss any one technique of cathodic protection and give its applications.   **(4 Marks)**
   Ans. Refer to Article 6.15.1 on Page Nos. 6.22.

MAY 2016

1. Discuss any five factors affecting corrosion.   **(5 Marks)**
   Ans. Refer to Article 6.10 on Page No. 6.13.

2. What is cathodic protection? Explain any one method in detail.   **(4 Marks)**
   Ans. Refer to Article 6.15.1 on Page No. 6.26.

3. Define electroplating? Explain process with neat labelled diagram and its applications.   **(4 Marks)**
   Ans. Refer to Article 6.16.1 on Page No. 6.26.

4. Define Net corrosion. Explain corrosion by hydrogen evolution mechanism.   **(5 Marks)**
   Ans. Refer to Article 6.6 on Page No. 6.5.

5. What is anodic and cathodic coating ? Which is more protective and why?   **(4 Marks)**
   Ans. Refer to Article 6.15 on Page No. 6.22.

6. What is Galvanising ? Explain process with neat labelled diagram to protect iron from corrosion.   **(4 Marks)**
   Ans. Refer to Article 6.15 on Page No. 6.22.

✠ ✠ ✠

Sample Question Paper

End-Sem. (Theory) Examination

Time : 2 Hours   **Max. Marks : 50**

Instructions to the Students :

1. Answer Q.1 or Q.2, Q.3 or Q.4, Q.5 or Q.6 and Q.7 or Q.8.

2. Neat diagrams must be drawn wherever necessary.

3. Figures to the right side indicate full marks.

4. Use of algorithmic table or electronic pocket calculator is allowed.

5. Assume suitable data if necessary.

---

1. (a) Discuss the traditional pathway and greener pathway for the synthesis of adipic acid. **(6)**

    (b) Explain principle and construction of calomel electrode. **(3)**

    (c) What do you understand by λ_{max}? Explain the terms chromophore and auxochrome. **(3)**

OR

2. (a) State and explain the Beer-Lambert's law. Discuss the basic components of spectrophotometer **(6)**

    (b) What do you understand by atom economy? Discuss it with respect to a multi stage reaction. **(3)**

    (c) 20 ml of standard hard water containing 5 g $CaCO_3$ per lit required 25 ml of EDTA solution for endpoint. 100 ml of water sample required 16.9 ml of EDTA solution, while same water after boiling required 12 ml EDTA solution. Calculate permanent and temporary hardness of water. **(3)**

3. (a) What is vulcanization of rubber? Give the structural changes taking place during vulcanization. State the effects on properties of rubber. **(6)**

    (b) Give a brief description of the design of a PEMFC. **(3)**

    (c) Discuss the importance of ultimate analysis of coal. **(3)**

OR

4. (a) Explain with neat diagram, determination of calorific value of solid fuel by bomb calorimeter. **(6)**

    (b) Write a note on: Biodegradable polymer – PHBV **(3)**

    (c) Give synthesis, properties and related applications of Epoxy resins. **(3)**

---

5. (a) Explain thermal splitting of water with the help of Fe_3O_4/FeO cycle. **(5)**

   (b) Explain the structure of graphite and related properties. **(4)**

   (c) What are the amorphous carbon materials? Give its applications. **(4)**

OR

6. (a) Discuss the structure of carbon nano tubes. Give their applications. **(5)**

   (b) How is hydrogen prepared by steam reforming of coke? **(4)**

   (c) Compare the properties of diamond and graphite. **(4)**

7. (a) What are different types of conversion coatings? Explain. **(5)**

   (b) Define and explain the terms, 'Decomposition potential', 'Over voltage' with respect to metal corrosion. **(4)**

   (c) Describe the mechanism of wet corrosion on the basis of oxygen absorption. **(4)**

OR

8. (a) Give the various factors affecting rate of corrosion. **(5)**

   (b) Describe the cementation method of applying metallic coating. Give its advantages and limitations. **(4)**

   (c) What are corrosion inhibitors? Name two anodic and cathodic inhibitors. **(4)**

✠ ✠ ✠

UNIVERSITY QUESTION PAPERS
DECEMBER 2012

Time : 2 Hours   Max. Marks : 50

Instructions to the Students

1. Answer Q.1 or Q.2, Q.3 or Q.4, Q.5 or Q.6, Q.7 or Q.8.
2. Neat diagrams must be drawn wherever necessary.
3. Figures to the right side indicate full marks.
4. Use of algorithmic table slide rule, Mollier charts, electronic pocket calculator and steam tables is allowed.
5. Assume suitable data if necessary.

---

1. (a) Explain the method of internal treatment of Boiler Feed water. **(6)**

(b) Explain different types of electronic transitions that occur in an organic molecule after absorbing UV radiations. **(6)**

OR

2. (a) Explain any six principles of Green Chemistry. **(6)**

(b) Explain the pH metric titration of mixture of weak acid-strong acid against standard alkali, giving chemical reactions, procedure, titration curve and calculations.

(6)

3. (a) Explain bulk and emulsion polymerization techniques. **(6)**

(b) What is biodiesel? Explain the reaction with conditions involved. Give advantages and disadvantages. **(6)**

OR

4. (a) Explain Kevlar and FRP with respect to their properties and applications. **(6)**

(b) Explain proximate analysis of coal. **(6)**

5. (a) Explain the structure of fullerene. How does it influence its properties and applications? **(5)**

(b) Describe the use of sodium alanate for hydrogen storage. **(4)**

(c) Explain the storage of hydrogen in compressed and liquified form. Explain difficulties in the said storage systems. **(4)**

OR

6. (a) Explain the isotopes of carbon and hydrogen. **(5)**

(b) Explain the steam reforming of methane to obtain hydrogen gas. **(4)**

(c) Discuss the types of CNT with respect to their structure. Give their applications.

(4)

---

7. (a) Explain cathodic protection of underground structure. Give the principle involved.

(5)

(b) How does the nature of environment influence the rate of corrosion? Explain any four factors with examples. **(4)**

(c) Discuss various steps involved in powder coating. **(4)**

OR

8. (a) Explain the Mechanism of Dry corrosion. Discuss the oxidation corrosion in case of Mg, Cr, Mo. **(5)**

(b) How is steel galvanized? Explain the process with the help of a flow diagram.

(4)

(c) Give conditions under which the wet corrosion occurs. Explain the mechanism of wet corrosion by hydrogen evolution with suitable example. **(4)**

MAY 2013

Time : 2 Hours **Max. Marks : 50**

1. (a) Explain boiler corrosion and caustic embrittlement as ill effects of using hard water in boilers. state their causes and preventive measures. **(6)**

(b) Which are possible transitions, that occur when molecule absorbs uv-visible radiation? which type of electronic transitions will be possible in following molecules.

(3)

i) $CH_2 = CH - CH_2 - CH_3$ ii) $CH_3 - CH_2 - OH$

iii) $CH_3 - \overset{\overset{\displaystyle O}{\|}}{C} - CH_3$ iv) $CH_3 - CH_2 - CH_2 - CH_2 - CH_3$

(c) State the reference electrode and standard electrode used in pH metery, potentiometry and conductometry. **(3)**

OR

2. (a) 50 ml std. hard water containing 1.2 gm $CaCO_3$ per lit. required 15 ml EDTA solution for the end point. Where as 50 ml sample water required 19 ml of EDTA solution and 50 ml boiled sample water required 11 ml of EDTA solution for the end point. Calculate, total, temporary and permanent hardness of sample water in ppm.

(3)

(b) What are the drawbacks of traditional synthesis of Indigo dye? Which is the starting substance in its green route synthesis? What are the advantages of green route synthesis over traditional? **(3)**

(c) (i)   Explain effect of dilution on specific conductance and equivalent conductance.

(3)

   (ii) Explain the titration curve for conduct metric titration in case of strong acid weak base titration. **(3)**

3. (a) Define vulcanization. Explain vulcanization of natural rubber along with Chemical reaction involved. Compare natural rubber with vulcanized rubber w.r.t their properties. **(6)**

   (b) A gas used in internal combustion engine contain, H_2 = 45%; CH_4 = 35%; CO=15% and N_2=5% by volume. Find the minimum quantity (volume) of air required per m^3 gas for its complete combustion. **(3)**

   (c) Define - Gross/higher calorific valve and justify the relationship between GCV and NCV of the fuel, if fuel contains $H^%$ hydrogen. **(3)**

OR

4. (a) Explain free-radical reaction mechanism for addition polymerization w.r.t monomer as vinyl chloride and initiator as acetyl peroxide. **(3)**

   (b) What are intrinsic and extrinsic polymers? Explain with their examples **(3)**

   (c) Explain knocking in petrol engine. Define octane number and explain effect of chemical structure of hydrocarbons present in petrol on knocking. **(3)**

5. (a) Explain chemical storage of hydrogen in the form of metal hydrides. How sodium alanates can be used In hydrogen storage. **(5)**

   (b) Explain preparation and structure of activated carbon and carbon black. **(4)**

   (c) What are carbon nanotubes. Explain their types in detail **(4)**

OR

6. (a) Explain production of hydrogen by water splitting using solar energy. **(4)**

   (b) Explain how saline hydrides are formed. Give preparation and application of any one saline hydride. **(4)**

   (c) Explain the structure and applications of graphene. **(5)**

7. (a) Explain various factors affecting corrosion on the basis of nature of metal **(5)**

   (b) Describe Anodic protection of metal for corrosion control **(4)**

   (c) Compare : Galvanizing and Tinning **(4)**

OR

8. (a) What is Powder coating? Explain any one method **(4)**

   (b) Explain corrosion control using proper designing and material selection method. **(4)**

   (c) Define oxidation corrosion. Explain general mechanism of oxidation corrosion. Compare oxidation corrosion which occurs in Na metal Cu metal and Molybdenum (Mo) metal. **(3)**

NOVEMBER 2013

Time : 2 Hours   **Max. Marks : 50**

1. (a) Explain formation of scales in boiler, give their disadvantages and methods of removal. **(6)**

    (b) Calculate potential or redox electrode dipped in titration mixture, when 20 m l of 0.1 N Ce^{4+} soluition from the burette is added in 100 ml 0.1 N Fe^{2+} solution. Standard reduction potentials for $Fe^{3+} \rightarrow Fe^{2+}$ and $Ce^{4+} \rightarrow Ce^{3+}$ are 0.75 V and 1.45 respectively. **(3)**

    (c) Explain the conductometric titration of KCl against $AgNO_3$ solution from burette. **(3)**

OR

2. (a) Explain the principle, instrumentation and applications of UV-visible spectrophotometer. **(6)**

    (b) State the problems in traditional synthesis route and advantages of green route in manufacture of adipic acid. **(3)**

    (c) A zeolite softner gets exhausted on softening 4000 litres of hard water. Calculate hardness of the water if the exhausted zeolite requires 10 litres of 10% NaCl solution for regeneration. **(3)**

3. (a) (i) Give structural change on vulcanization of natural rubber molecules with sulphur. How does it affect the strength? **(3)**

      (ii) State the purpose of compounding polymers with plasticizers and filters. **(3)**

    (b) (i) Give the reaction involved in biodiesel formation and state any three advantages of biodiesel. **(3)**

      (ii) Calculate the amount of air (20% excess) required for complete combustion of 1 kg wood if it contains 55% carbon, 8% hydrogen, 5% oxygen and remaining non combustible part. **(3)**

OR

4. (a) (i) Define biodegradation of polymers. State favourable structure of polymer for biodegradation. Write structure of biopol (PHBV). **(3)**

      (ii) Give any six differences in thermosoftening and thermosetting polymers. **(3)**

    (b) Give construction, working and calculation for finding gross calorific value of a solid fuel by Comb calorimeter. **(6)**

5. (a) Give industrial methods of manufacturing of hydrogen gas.   **(5)**

(b) Explain structure of diamond, give its properties and applications.   **(5)**

(c) Give preparation, reactions of saline hydrides.   **(3)**

OR

6. (a) State the difficulties in storage of hydrogen gas. Give its chemical storage in alanates and metal hydrides.   **(5)**

(b) Give preparation, reactions of silance.   **(4)**

(c) Give any one method of preparing carbon nanotubes. State applications of carbon nanotubes.   **(4)**

7. (a) Give the mechanism of electrochemical corrosion.   **(5)**

(b) Explain nature of metal factors affecting rate of corrosion.   **(5)**

(c) What are types of metallic coatings ? Which is preferred ? Why ?   **(3)**

OR

8. (a) Give principle construction and applications of cathodic protection.   **(5)**

(b) Explain 'power coating' method for corrosion control.   **(4)**

(c) Account on 'nature of oxide film' on metal surface and its effect on further corrosion.

(4)

MAY 2014

Time : 2 Hours   **Max. Marks : 50**

1. (a) Describe Ion exchange method for softening of hard water.   **(6)**

(b) What is reference electrode? Draw neat labeled diagram of Glass electrode and give its representation.   **(3)**

(c) Explain condutometric titration curve for reaction between weak acid and strong base.   **(3)**

OR

2. (a) Explain different types of electronic transitions occurring in organic molecules on absorption of UV-visible radiations.   **(6)**

(b) Define caustic embrittlement. Give causes and prevention of caustic embrittlement in boiler.   **(3)**

(c) A water sample is not alkaline to phenolphthalein. However 100 ml of water sample on titration with N/50 HCl required 16.9 ml of acid to get methyl orange end point. Identity the type and determine the extent of alkalinity.   **(3)**

3. (a) Define addition polymerization. Explain free radical reaction mechanism with suitable example. **(6)**

   (b) What is power alcohol? Give its preparation with reactions and any two disadvantages. **(3)**

   (c) A coal sample contains C : 80%, H : 10%, S : 2.5%, N : 4% and remaining is ash. Calculate the theoretical quantity of oxygen and air required for complete combustion of 1 Kg of given coal sample. **(3)**

OR

4. (a) What is proximate analysis? Explain the procedure for determination of each constituent with its formula. **(6)**

   (b) Distinguish between LDPE and HDPE (any four Points). **(3)**

   (c) Give preparation reaction, properties and uses of SBR. **(3)**

5. (a) Explain manufacturing of hydrogen gas by steam reforming of

   (i)   methane and   (ii) coke **(5)**

   (b) Explain the structural features of fullerene with diagram and give its applications. **(4)**

   (c) Explain the isotopes of carbon with their applications. **(4)**

OR

6. (a) Explain structural features and applications of diamond and graphite. **(4)**

   (b) Explain difficulties in storage and transportation of hydrogen. **(4)**

   (c) What are different types of hydrides? Give preparation reaction of germane, silane and lithium hydride. **(4)**

7. (a) What is Pilling-Bedworth ratio? Give four types of oxide films formed on surface of metal with suitable example. **(5)**

   (b) Explain galvanization with neat labeled diagram to protect Iron from corrosion. **(6)**

   (c) What the principle of Cathodic protection? Explain it with any one method. **(4)**

OR

8. (a) Explain wet corrosion with H_2 evolution and O_2 absorption mechanism. **(5)**

   (b) Distinguish between anodic and cathodic coatings. **(4)**

   (c) Discuss factors affecting rate of corrosion, two each, for nature of metal and nature of environment. **(4)**

DECEMBER 2014

Time : 2 Hours   **Max. Marks : 50**

1. (a) Define scale and sludge. Give the causes, disadvantages and removal of scale and sludge formation in boiler. **(6)**

    (b) State and derive Beer Lamberts law. **(3)**

    (c) Define specific conductance, equivalent conductance and molar conductance.

                                                         (3)

OR

2. (a) Explain the pH metric titration of – mixture of weak acid – strong acid against std. Alkali giving chemical reaction procedure with titration curve. **(6)**

    (b) What are the merits of green synthesis and demerits of traditional synthesis of indigo dye ? **(3)**

    (c) A water sample is non alkaline to phenolphthalein indicator. However, 100 ml of the same sample on titration with 0.02 N H_2SO_4 requires 14.5 ml of acid to obtain end point using methyl orange indicator. Identify type of alkalinity and determine its extent. **(3)**

3. (a) Give preparation reaction, properties and uses of following polymers. **(3)**

        (a) LDPE   (b) Styrene-butadiene rubber

    (b) What is biodiesel ? Give its synthesis and advantages. **(3)**

    (c) A gaseous fuel used in internal combustion engine contain CH_4 = 45%, H_2 = 30%, CO = 20%, N_2 = 5% by volume. Find the minimum quantity (volume) of air required for complete combustion of 1 M^3 of gaseous fuel. **(3)**

OR

4. (a) Draw neat labelled diagram and give the construction, working of bomb calorimeter to determine GCV of a fuel. **(6)**

    (b) Distinguish thermoplastic and thermosetting, polymer with suitable example.

    (c) What is biodegradable polymer ? Give the structure of PHBV and its applications ?

5. (a) Explain structure, properties and applications of fullerene. **(5)**

    (b) Explain industrial production of hydrogen by steam reforming of methane and coke.

    (c) Explain the structure and properties of graphite. **(4)**

OR

6. (a) Give the isotopes of hydrogen with their applications and write the properties of hydrogen which makes it more difficult to store and transport. **(5)**

   (b) What are the types of CNTs with respect to their structure ? Give the applications of CNTs. **(4)**

   (c) Explain chemical storage method of hydrogen gas in the form of alanates and metal hydrides. **(4)**

7. (a) Define corrosion and explain effect of following factors on rate of corrosion

   (i) Purity of metal

   (ii) Relative area of anode and cathode. **(5)**

   (b) State the types of oxide film formed on the surface of following metals with reactions. **(4)**

   (1) Na   (2) Al

   (3) Au   (4) Mo

   (c) What is cathodic coating ? Explain timing with neat labelled diagram to protect metal from corrosion. **(4)**

OR

8. (a) Explain electrochemical corrosion by H_2 evolution and O_2 absorption mechanism.

   (b) What is principle of cathodic protection and explain it with any one suitable method?

   (c) Define electroplating. Explain electroplating process with neat labeled diagram and applications. **(4)**

MAY 2015

Time : 2 Hours   Max. Marks : 50

1. (a) What are 'zeolites' ? Explain zeolite process of softening of water. Give regeneration reactions, advantages and disadvantages of the process. **(6)**

   (b) Explain titration curve of conductometric titration in case of strong acid and weak base. **(3)**

   (c) Explain the following terms with suitable example : **(3)**

   (i) Chromophore   (ii) Auxochrome.

OR

2. (a) Explain the pH metric titration of mixture of H_3PO_4 (phosphoric acid) and HCl (hydrochloric acid) against std. NaOH, giving chemical reactions, procedure, titration curve and calculations. **(6)**

(b) Explain any three principles of Green Chemistry. **(3)**

(c) 50 ml of water sample requires 18 ml of 0.5 MEDTA during titration. Whereas 50 ml of boiled water sample requires 12.5 ml of same EDTA in the titration. Calculate total, temporary and permanent hardness of water sample. **(3)**

3. (a) What is vulcanization of rubber ? Explain chemical reaction involved in vulcanization process. Compare natural rubber with vulcanized rubber. **(3)**

(b) Define : **(3)**

   (i) Cetane No.

   (ii) Power alcohol

   (iii) N.C.V.

(c) Calculate carbon, hydrogen and sulphur percentage present in the coal sample from the following data : **(3)**

   (i) 0.15 gm coal sample on burning in combustion chamber in current of pure O_2 was found to increase weight of $CaCl_2$ U-tube by 0.08 gm. and KOH U-Tube by 0.49 gm.

   (ii) 0.65 gm coal was combusted in Bomb calorimeter. Solution from bomb on treatment with $BaCl_2$ solution, forms 0.031 gm $BaSO_4$ dry ppt.

OR

4. (a) What are fuel cells ? Explain working of Phosphoric Acid Fuel Cell (PAFC) with figure and cell reactions. State its advantages. **(6)**

(b) Explain with suitable diagram bulk polymerization technique to bring about addition polymerization. **(3)**

(c) Give structure, properties and applications of polyphenylenevinylene (PPV). **(3)**

5. (a) What are carbon nanotubes ? Give types with respect to their structure. Give applications of CNTs. **(5)**

(b) What are alanates ? Explain how hydrogen gas is released from sodium alanates when used for hydrogen storage. **(4)**

(c) Give structure, one method of preparation and applications of silane. **(4)**

OR

6. (a) Explain industrial production of hydrogen by steam reforming of methane and coke. **(5)**

(b) Explain the isotopes of carbon with their applications. **(4)**

(c) Explain structure of diamond based on bonding. Give its applications. **(4)**

7. (a) What is dry corrosion ? Explain mechanism of oxidation corrosion with suitable figure and reactions. **(5)**

(b) Explain how nature of metal affects the rate of corrosion. **(4)**

(c) What are electroless coatings? Explain with suitable example. Give its application. **(4)**

OR

8. (a) Define corrosion. State the conditions under which wet corrosion occurs. Explain oxygen absorption mechanism of wet corrosion. **(5)**

   (b) Explain cementation and cladding methods of applying metallic coatings on base metal. **(4)**

   (c) Compare : Cathodic protection and Anodic protection. **(4)**

NOVEMBER 2015

Time : 2 Hours   **Max. Marks : 50**

1. (a) Discuss the Ion-Exchange method for softening of hard water with the help of reactions involved in removal of ions and regeneration of the exchangers. Draw a neat labelled diagram and give limitations of the process. **(6)**

   (b) Define the following terms : **(3)**
      (i) Bathochromic shift   (ii) Hypochromic shift
      (ii) Chromophore.

   (c) Explain the conductometric titration curve for the reaction between KCl and $AgNO_3$. **(3)**

OR

2. (a) Explain the potentiometric titration of Fe^{2+} against Ce^{4+} giving reactions. Draw the titration curve and give the formulae for calculating emf of the cell at various stages of the titration. **(6)**

   (b) Give the demerits of the traditional route and merits of the green route of synthesis of polycarbonate. **(3)**

   (c) 50 ml of water sample required 12.1 ml of N/50 HCl to reach the phenolphthalein end-point and 18.5 ml of the same acid for the methyl orange end-point. Calculate types and amount of alkalinities present. **(3)**

3. (a) Define glass transition temperature. Give its significance and discuss any four factors affecting it. **(6)**

   (b) Define GCV and NCV. Give the justification of how they are related. **(3)**

   (c) A coal sample has the following composition : **(3)**
      C = 70%, H = 10%, N = 3%, S = 3%, O = 2% and ash = 12%. If 20% excess air is required for complete combustion, then calculate the amount of air required for complete combustion of 1 kg of coal.

OR

4. (a) Explain in brief the process of fractional distillation of petroleum with diagram. Give the composition and boiling range of petrol and diesel obtained. **(6)**

   (b) Give the purpose and examples of the following constituents used during the compounding of plastics : **(3)**
      (i) Fillers   (ii) Lubricants   (iii) Plasticizers.

(c) Explain solution polymerization technique. Draw the figure and state the disadvantages of this technique. **(3)**

5. (a) Explain the structure of fullerene. Give any two properties and two applications of fullerene. **(5)**

(b) Give the preparation reaction and applications of germane and lithium hydride. **(4)**

(c) Discuss the properties of hydrogen which make it difficult for storage. **(4)**

OR

6. (a) Explain the production of hydrogen by water splitting using solar energy. **(5)**

(b) Discuss the different types of carbon nano tubes with respect to their structure. Give any two applications of it. **(4)**

(c) Explain the structure of graphite. Give its properties and applications. **(4)**

7. (a) Give the Pilling-Bedworth ration and its significance. Give the oxidation reaction involved and state the type of film formed on the surface in the case of Mg, Cr and Mo. **(5)**

(b) Explain the process of galvanizing with labeled diagram. Give the applications and limitations of this technique. **(4)**

(c) State the different types of corrosion inhibitors with their examples. Discuss in brief their role in corrosion prevention. **(4)**

OR

8. (a) Discuss any five factors affecting corrosion. **(5)**

(b) Define corrosion. Explain the hydrogen evolution mechanism of wet corrosion. **(4)**

(c) What is the principle of cathodic protection ? Discuss any one technique of cathodic protection and give its applications. **(4)**

MAY 2016

Time : 2 Hours   **Max. Marks : 50**

1. (a) Describe Demineralisation/Deionization method with figure, process, ion exchange and regeneration reactions for softening of hard water. **(6)**

(b) What is reference electrode ? Draw neat labelled diagram of glass electrode and give its representation. **(3)**

(c) Define the terms : **(3)**
   (i) Resistance
   (ii) Cell constant
   (iii) Equivalent conductance.

OR

2. (a) Explain principle, instrumentation and applications of UV visible spectrophotometer. **(6)**

(b) Explain any three principles of green chemistry. **(3)**

(c) An exhausted zeolite softener was regenerated by passing 150 litres of NaCl solution having strength 150 gms./lit. of NaCl. How many litres of hard water sample having hardness 400 ppm can be soften by using softener. **(3)**

3. (a) Give preparation, reaction, properties and applications of following : **(6)**

    (i) Styrene-butadiene rubber   (ii) HDPE.

4. (b) What is power alcohol ? Give preparation with reaction and advantages of power alcohol. **(3)**

(c) Calculate carbon and hydrogen in coal sample from the following data 0.25 gm of coal sample on burning in combustion chamber in current of pure O_2, was found to increase weight of $CaCl_2$ U tube by 0.12 pta and KOH U tube by 0.57 gm. **(3)**

OR

4. (a) Draw neat labelled diagram and give the construction working of Bomb calorimeter to determine GCV of a fuel. State formula with corrections to calculate GCV. **(6)**

(b) Explain bulk polymerisation technique. Draw the figure and state its disadvantages. **(3)**

(c) Distinguish between thermosoftening and thermosetting polymer with example. **(3)**

5. (a) Explain industrial production of hydrogen by steam reforming of methane and coke. **(5)**

(b) Give structure, one method of preparation and application of silane. **(4)**

(c) Explain the structure and properties of graphite. **(4)**

OR

6. (a) What are carbon 'nanotubes'? Give types with respect to their structure and its applications. **(5)**

(b) Discuss the properties of hydrogen which make it difficult for storage. **(4)**

(c) Explain the structure of Diamond, give its properties and applications. **(4)**

7. (a) Discuss any five factors affecting corrosion. **(5)**

(b) What is cathodic protection? Explain any one method in detail. **(4)**

(c) Define electroplating? Explain process with neat labelled diagram and its applications. **(4)**

OR

8. (a) Define Net corrosion. Explain corrosion by hydrogen evolution mechanism. **(5)**

(b) What is anodic and cathodic coating ? Which is more protective and why? **(4)**

(c) What is Galvanising ? Explain process with neat labelled diagram to protect iron from corrosion. **(4)**

NOVEMBER 2016

Time : 2 Hours   **Max. Marks : 50**

N.B. : -

(1) Neat diagram must be drawn wherever necessary.

(2) Figures to the right indicate full marks.

(3) Use of logarithmic tables, slide rule, Mollier charts, electronic pocket calculator and steam table is allowed.

(4) Assume suitable data if necessary.

1. **(a)** Explain zeolite process of softening of water with figure, process, ion exchange and regeneration reactions along with advantages.   **(6)**

   (b) Explain the titration curve for conductometric titration in case of strong acid-strong base titration.   **(3)**

   (c) What is reference electrode? Draw neat labelled diagram of glass electrode and give its representation.   **(3)**

OR

2. **(a)** Explain different types of electronic transitions that occur in an organic molecule after absorbing uv radiations.   **(6)**

   (b) State the problems in traditional synthesis route and advantages of green route in manufacture of polycarbonate.   **(3)**

   (c) 100 ml of an alkaline water sample requires 5.2 ml of N/50 HCl upto phenolphthalein end point and 15.8 ml for methyl orange end point. Find the type and amount of alkalinity in water sample.   **(3)**

3. **(a)** Define vulcanization. Explain vulcanization of natural rubber along with chemical reaction involved. Compare natural rubber with vulcanized rubber with respect to any 3 properties.   **(6)**

   (b) What is power alcohol? Give merits and demerits of power alcohol.   **(3)**

   (c) A gaseous fuel contains : CH_4 = 55% and H_2 = 25% by volume. Calculate volume of air required for complete combustion of $1m^3$ of the gas.   **(3)**

OR

4. **(a)** Explain determination of calorific value of a fuel by Bomb calorimeter with figure, construction, working and formula for calculation of GCV. Give formula with corrections for determination of GCV by Bomb calorimeter.   **(6)**

(b) Explain bulk polymerisation technique. Give its advantages. **(3)**

(c) Give synthesis, properties and applications of LDPE. **(3)**

5. **(a)** Explain manufacturing of H_2 gas by steam reforming of : **(5)**

    (i)   Methane and

    (ii) Coke.

(b) Discuss types of carbon nanotubes with respect to their structure. Give any two applications of CNT. **(4)**

(c) Explain isotopes of carbon and hydrogen. Give two applications of each. **(4)**

OR

6. **(a)** Explain structure of fullerene with diagram and give its applications. **(5)**

(b) Explain how H_2 gas is released from sodium alanates when used for H_2 storage. **(4)**

(c) Explain how saline hydrides are formed. Give preparation and application of any one saline hydride. **(4)**

7. **(a)** Explain mechanism of wet corrosion by hydrogen evolution and oxygen absorption mechanism of electrochemical corrosion with suitable examples. **(5)**

(b) What is galvanizing of iron ? Explain process of galvanization of iron with neat labelled diagram. **(4)**

(c) Explain 'nature of oxide films' on metal surface and its effect on further corrosion. **(4)**

OR

8. **(a)** Explain any five factors affecting rate of corrosion. **(5)**

(b) Give principle of cathodic protection of metal. Explain sacrificial anodic protection of metal. **(4)**

(c) What is anodic coating and cathodic coating ? Which is preferred ? Why ? **(4)**

✠ ✠ ✠

MAY 2017

Time : 3 Hours   **Max. Marks : 50**

N.B. : -

(1) Neat diagram must be drawn wherever necessary.

(2) Figures to the right indicate full marks.

(3) Use of logarithmic tables, slide rule, Mollier charts, electronic pocket calculator and steam table is allowed.

(4) Assume suitable data if necessary.

1. **(a)** What are zeolites? Explain zeolite process for softening of water. Give regeneration reactions, advantages and disadvantages of the process. **(6)**

   (b) What is reference electrode? Draw neat labelled diagram of calomel electrode and give its representation. **(3)**

   (c) Explain conductometric titration curve for the reaction between KCl and $AgNO_3$. **(3)**

                                    OR

2. **(a)** Explain the pH metric titration of mixture of weak acid-strong acid against standard alkali, giving chemical reactions, procedure, titration curve and calculations. **(6)**

   (b) 50 ml of water sample requires 15 ml of 0.02 M EDTA during titration. Whereas 50 ml of boiled water sample requires 11 ml of same EDTA in the titration. Calculate total, temporary and permanent hardness of water sample. **(3)**

   (c) What are the merits of green synthesis and demerits of traditional synthesis of polycarbonate. **(3)**

3. **(a)** What is vulcanisation of rubber ? Explain chemical reaction involved in vulcanisation process. Compare natural rubber with vulcanised rubber. **(6)**

   (b) Define : **(3)**

   (i) Octane number

   (ii) Power alcohol

   (iii) Gross calorific value

   (c) A fuel has the following composition by mass :

   e = 83%, H_2 = 12%, S = 1%, O_2 = 3.2% and remaining being ash. Calculate quantity of air. **(3)**

OR

4. **(a)** What is proximate analysis of coal? Explain the procedure for determination of each constituent with its formula. **(6)**

    (b) Distinguish between LDPE and HDPE. **(3)**

    (c) What is biodegradable polymer ? Give the structure of PHBV and its applications. **(3)**

5. **(a)** State the difficulties in storage of hydrogen gas. Give its chemical storage in analates and metal hydrides. **(5)**

    (b) Give the preparation reaction and applications of germane and lithium hydride. **(4)**

    (c) Explain the structure and properties of graphite. **(4)**

OR

6. **(a)** Explain the structure of fullerene. Give any two properties and two applications of fullerene. **(5)**

    (b) Explain the production of hydrogen by water splitting using solar energy. **(4)**

    (c) Explain the isotopes of carbon with their applications. **(4)**

7. **(a)** Explain the mechanism of dry corrosion. Discuss the oxidation corrosion in case of Mg, Cr, Mo. **(5)**

    (b) What is the principle of cathodic protection. Explain it with any one suitable method. **(4)**

    (c) Explain cementation and cladding methods for applying metallic coatings on base metal. **(4)**

OR

8. **(a)** Define wet corrosion. Explain corrosion by oxygen absorption mechanism. **(5)**

    (b) What are the factors affecting corrosion ? (Explain nature of metal only) **(4)**

    (c) Discuss various steps involved in powder coating. **(4)**

✠ ✠ ✠

---

www.ingramcontent.com/pod-product-compliance
Lightning Source LLC
Chambersburg PA
CBHW081145020726
47504CB00009B/2011